Praise for the novels of Brenda Novak

"*Summer on the Island* is a big, tantalizing read!"
—Susan Elizabeth Phillips,
New York Times bestselling author

"*Summer on the Island* will resonate with many readers who, in the midst of a global pandemic, may be rethinking what is truly important in life.". —*Booklist*

"*The Bookstore on the Beach* is a page-turner with a deep heart."
—Nancy Thayer, *New York Times* bestselling author
of *Girls of Summer*

"The prose is fast-paced and exciting, making this a breathless page-turner." —*New York Journal of Books* on *The Bookstore on the Beach*

"An abundance of heart and humor. *The Bookstore on the Beach* is an escapist treat with emotional heft."
—*Apple Books*, Best Book of the Month selection

"This heartwarming story of sisters who bond as adults is sure to please the many fans of Novak as well as those who enjoy books by Susan Mallery and Debbie Macomber."
—*Library Journal* on *One Perfect Summer*

"I adore everything Brenda Novak writes. Her books are compelling, emotional, tender stories about people I would love to know in real life."
—RaeAnne Thayne, *New York Times* bestselling author

"Brenda Novak is always a joy to read."
—Debbie Macomber, #1 *New York Times* bestselling author

"Brenda Novak doesn't just write fabulous stories, she writes keepers."
—Susan Mallery, #1 *New York Times* bestselling author

Also by Brenda Novak

For a full list of Brenda's books,
visit www.brendanovak.com.

Look for Brenda Novak's next novel
TOURIST SEASON
available soon from MIRA.

Brenda Novak

The Messy Life of Jane Tanner

mira

mira™

Recycling programs
for this product may
not exist in your area.

ISBN-13: 978-0-7783-6952-3

The Messy Life of Jane Tanner

Copyright © 2024 by Brenda Novak, Inc.

For questions and comments about the quality of this book, please contact us
at CustomerService@Harlequin.com.

Mira
22 Adelaide St. West, 41st Floor
Toronto, Ontario M5H 4E3, Canada
www.Harlequin.com

Printed in U.S.A.

To Vinny. I'm so glad you are who you are—a kind, wonderful human being. There is no greater joy for a mother than to know her child's heart is in good hands. Welcome to the family, and thank you for showing you care about me, too. I'm so touched by the support you have offered me in reading my books, participating in Brenda Novak's Book Group on Facebook, helping with the monthly Brenda Novak's Book Boxes (and sometimes the meetings, too!), coming to my book signings, searching each store you visit to see if they carry my books and contributing in so many ways to our family gatherings.

One

Jane Tanner felt like a dragonfly in amber—something that was meant to be free and swift, to change direction at a whim and evolve, but was forever caught and held in place.

Alone in her little vintage thrift shop on Lincoln Street, the main drag of Coyote Canyon, she gazed out the front window and saw the same sleepy scene she saw almost every morning around ten o'clock. She'd often considered moving to the big city, like her best friend, Talulah, did when she went to Seattle and started a dessert diner. But even Talulah hadn't escaped Coyote Canyon in the end. She'd come back nearly two years ago and married Brant Elway, a local rancher—and, wow, did *that* cause a stir. There were still aftershocks. Those aftershocks affected Jane's life, too. But at least Talulah was happy. She and Brant were living in the Victorian house Talulah had purchased from her great aunt's estate, and she claimed she no longer wanted to leave.

Jane wondered if *she* could ever be content here and quit imagining a better life somewhere else...

She could leave her hometown if she really wanted

to, she reminded herself. No one would stop her or even blame her. Her lease on the store ended in thirty days. Although the owner had been nagging her to renew, she hadn't signed the document LaVeryle White had dropped off. Even the possibility of starting over someplace else where she felt she'd find people whose interests better matched her own was exciting. The Haight-Ashbury district in San Francisco was one idea. From what she'd seen online, she'd fit right in—with her love of vintage clothing and furniture. She knew she would thrive in that iconic city with its cultural diversity, its museums, theater, concerts, sports, parks and beaches. The cute coffee shops, bookshops and delicious restaurants also appealed to her, as did living by the ocean and being treated to such incredible views of the Bay.

She ached with longing when she imagined it, but she couldn't leave Montana right now. Moving would require putting her grandfather in a care facility, and she didn't have the heart to do that. But his memory was getting worse. That was why, almost a year ago, she'd given up the small apartment above her store, which still sat empty, and moved in with him. Now she lived in his white brick rambler several blocks away, on the very edge of town.

Given all the things he was starting to forget, some would argue it was time she put him in the care of professionals. But she knew how much happier he'd be if he could remain in his own home, where he'd lived since marrying Grandma Ruby—or Nana, as Jane had called her. Nana had died ten years ago on the operating table while having a stent put in her heart, but her pictures still hung on the walls, her sewing kit still rested next to the couch and her beloved piano still filled the dining room, leaving no space for a table and chairs. Those items and all the others surrounding Papa kept the love of his life present. How could Jane move him to an assisted-living facility? It would mean taking him to Bozeman or Billings, where he wouldn't get many visitors—only those who were willing to make the drive. He'd no longer be able to chat with his longtime neighbor, Herbert Hensley, as they stood watering their lawns or wave to Martha Grimmy when she delivered his mail or tinker in his large workshop the way he liked to. And if he went into a care center, he'd have to give up his beloved dog, Otis, which would probably kill him.

Jane couldn't allow to that happen, let alone *make* it happen. If their roles were reversed, he'd never do such a thing to her. Besides, he still managed okay on his own while she was at work. If that ever changed, she might have to reconsider. But for now…

Her phone lit up with a message from her mom.

How's he doing?

Jane's mother checked in two or three times a week asking about Papa, which was nice and showed she cared. But she wasn't any real help. She and her husband, Jane's stepfather, Richard, had moved to Wyoming so they could be closer to Richard's son, who'd always lived with his mother. That meant they were out of the picture, except when they came back for visits.

Papa was Jane's father's father, anyway, so her mother didn't feel much obligation to him. Her half sister was still in the area and helped out when she could. But Kate was Richard's daughter, and wasn't close with Papa the way she was. Papa and Nana had helped raise her. She'd lived with them for three years after her parents' divorce, while her mother went back to school and her father rambled on—sponging off one woman after another as he moved through life.

Seemed to be a little better this morning, she wrote back.

You still feel like you can leave him while you're at the store?

He manages pretty well.

You're so good to be there for him.

What choice did she have? There was no one else, which meant she'd have to sign the extension on the store's lease, stay another year and see what developed—not that she was wishing for Papa to pass so she could leave. Just the thought of losing him brought a lump to her throat. But she also didn't want his quality of life to continue to deteriorate and hoped he'd go before that could happen. In his right mind, he'd hate to suffer the many indignities that were in store for him otherwise.

It's okay. I love him.

Timing was the only problem. He'd started going downhill right when she'd begun to think seriously about moving on with her life.

I know. But it's a lot for you to contend with. You're young. You should be free to live your life.

How? She couldn't let him down. He and Nana had

been there for her when she'd needed them most. She was going to be there for him, especially since she couldn't depend on her father to step in and help. He hadn't changed over the years. These days, he was living in Oregon, anyway.

Her mother sent another text before Jane could respond. Want me to help you find the best home for him?

Not yet. I'll know when the time is right. And that time isn't now.

She wasn't sure that was true. She only knew what her heart would allow, and it would not allow her to leave him quite yet.

With a frown, she navigated away from her mother's texts to the message she'd received from her landlady first thing this morning.

Can I swing by and pick up that lease?

She could see why LaVeryle would be getting impatient. She needed to know whether she was going to have to find another tenant and would like as much notice as possible. It was ridiculous to continue putting her off. Why inconvenience her for no reason?

A ding signaled another text from her mother: Honey, if he's losing his mind, he won't know the difference.

Jane rolled her eyes. Papa would know. He'd be lost, wondering where she'd gone and why he no longer had Otis at his side. She couldn't even bear the thought of it.

He's not ready. Neither am I.

Feeling more conviction, she returned to the desk where she kept the cash register and pulled the lease from the drawer. But as she held her pen poised above the signature line, her thoughts reverted to what she'd been daydreaming about lately—a plan B that made staying in Coyote Canyon not only palatable but somewhat appealing.

It wasn't a solution most women would ever consider, but she was thirty-five, didn't have a boyfriend—not since she'd broken up with Devon, who lived forty minutes away—and there weren't any new romantic prospects on the horizon. If she was going to stay in Coyote Canyon, she felt she should be able to move forward in *some* regard and build the sort of life that would make her happy. Why not?

Before signing, she set the pen down and brought up Kurt Elway's last text.

Were you serious about what you said to me on Saturday night? Because that was a little nuts...

He'd sent that two days ago, but she hadn't yet responded. In her mind, the question wasn't whether *she'd* been serious; it was whether *he'd* been serious. His reaction to what she'd shared with him had taken her completely by surprise. She hadn't been able to stop thinking about it.

She could say she'd been tipsy when they were playing pool at Hank's Bar & Grill on Saturday. He'd been drinking, too. He could use the same excuse. That way they could laugh about the conversation in question, then forget they'd ever had it.

That was probably what he expected. But...she hadn't been able to bring herself to kill the possibility. She was too excited to think he might be open to helping.

What would you say if I was serious? Would you back out?

She typed that but didn't send it. She stared at the words instead, letting them roll around in her mind the way a wine connoisseur might let a sip of fine merlot roll around in his mouth. Would it be too risky—too unconventional?

Most likely. They lived in such a small, conservative town. Comparing it to how everyone else around here did things would make it seem even more outlandish. But the longer she thought about the idea, the more she began to believe she could overcome the obstacles and barriers that stood in the way—as long as she was willing to be brave and a little different.

Nibbling anxiously on her bottom lip, she pictured the people closest to her who were in the same stage of life. Talulah and Brant were married. Ellen Truesdale, Talulah's neighbor, who'd become a good friend, was engaged to be married. Even Kate, her *younger* sister, was getting ready to settle down. Averil was a notable exception. Like Jane, she wasn't in a serious relationship. But she had a son, at least.

Jane was the only one who'd reached her thirties without any prospects for marriage or starting a family. She could change that if she really wanted to—the family part, at least—and if Kurt was willing to help her, she probably would.

So…should she take the risk of letting him know she'd meant what she'd said at Hank's?

He'd probably run for the hills. But she'd never know unless she gave him the opportunity…

Holding her breath, she hit Send. She could feel the beat of her heart in her throat afterward. But there was no immediate answer.

He was probably out on the ranch, knee-deep in mud, patching a fence or riding a horse and didn't have his phone with him. It was sometimes three or four in the afternoon before she heard from him, and that was generally after he'd returned to the house to shower, when he was finished for the day and wanted to get together and have some fun. With most of her friends now in committed relationships, and the same thing happening to him, the people they used to hang out with were less available. Over the past six months or so, they'd become good friends and spent a fair amount of time together, even though he was five years her junior and had occasionally dated her younger sister.

He'd get back to her eventually, she told herself. Or… maybe not. She wouldn't blame him if he ignored her latest text. Everyone she knew would be shocked if she actually went through with what she wanted to do. If he participated, and anyone found out, his friends and family would be stunned, too. There'd also be all kinds of logistical questions and concerns—how and when they'd proceed, and what she and Kurt would do in certain scenarios. They'd have to think through it all and prepare well in advance.

But it was possible to work it out. That was the thing.

Grabbing the lease, she signed it so she couldn't let Papa down, regardless of Kurt's response. Then she sent a text to LaVeryle, letting her know the paperwork was ready.

For better or worse, she was sticking around Coyote Canyon for at least another year. But depending on what Kurt said, and what she decided after receiving his reply, it could be a year like no other.

Much to his parents' chagrin, Kurt Elway had always been a risk-taker. When he was at a rodeo ten years ago, he'd made a bet with a friend that he could ride a bull, even though he'd never been on one, and had been thrown and nearly trampled. Five years ago, he'd jumped into a bar fight simply because it was four on three and he felt bad for some dude who was getting his ass kicked, and a chick with the group pulled out a knife and buried it in his thigh. And just a year ago last winter, he'd landed in the hospital with hypothermia when he skied out of bounds, searching for better powder, and fell into a deep crevasse from which he had to be rescued.

His mother said she'd known he was going to be trouble when he jumped off the barn and broke his leg and his collarbone at six years old, attempting to fly. She also said that danger was irresistible to him, and she was mostly right. So he felt he'd done fairly well up to this point. He would soon turn thirty, and he was still alive and fully functional.

As he grew older, he tried to be more cautious and conservative, like his brother Brant, but as far as he was concerned, taking chances was what kept life interesting.

Still, what Jane wanted was *way* out there.

He whistled as he gazed down at the text she'd sent.

"What is it?" Brant asked.

Kurt was taking a break from wiring a large diesel-fueled generator to the pump of the new well so they could water more of their two-thousand-acre cattle ranch. When he'd sat beneath a black cottonwood tree, seeking shade while he ate lunch, he'd thought he'd have a few minutes alone. Since that wasn't the case, he quickly hid the shock he'd been feeling behind a more neutral expression. "Nothing, why?"

Brant dropped down beside him. "You just whistled

at something on your phone as if you couldn't quite believe it."

He wasn't sure he *could* believe it. During the past several months he'd wanted Jane to show more interest in him. Because he was younger than she was and had dated her sister, he knew he was at a disadvantage where she was concerned. That was probably why he'd responded positively on Saturday night. He'd been hoping to prove he was willing to do more for her than the next guy.

But they'd been drinking and playing pool. He'd thought they were just *talking…*

He had to say no, right? He couldn't do what he'd said he'd do. That would be one hell of a risk, even for a guy like him.

"Well?" Brant prompted.

Lifting himself off the ground so he could shove his phone back in his pocket, Kurt cleared his throat. Brant was married to Talulah, one of Jane's best friends. No way was he going to tell him what Jane wanted. "I told you. It's nothing."

Brant gave him a skeptical look but let it go. "You about finished wiring this up?" he asked, gesturing at the electrical box.

"Shouldn't take much longer," Kurt replied.

"Good, because it's time to move the cattle."

"Already?" he grumbled. "It's got to be your turn by now."

Brant scowled at him. "You know it's not."

"What about Ranson? Or Miles?" Their other two brothers worked on the ranch they'd inherited from their parents, too. "It doesn't seem like they ever have to do it."

"Because you had them cover for you while you went to Snowbowl in February, remember?" Brant leaned over and stole the apple out of his lunch. "You have to pay them back sometime. Might as well even things up."

Kurt wiped the sweat from his forehead. He felt like he'd been paying for that ski trip for weeks. "I'll give you fifty bucks to do it for me."

A crisp snap sounded as Brant took a big bite of the apple and then had to talk around it. "Sorry, bro. I've got a full day, and I told Talulah I'd help at the diner tonight."

Kurt couldn't imagine Brant wanted to spend several hours at the diner after he finished at the ranch. They were all exhausted by the end of the day. But his brother never complained about the heavy load he'd taken on since getting married. The diner meant a lot to Talulah, so he supported her.

"Talulah's business seems to be doing well…"

"You've tasted my wife's cooking. Of course it's doing well." His brother shot him a cocky grin as he got up to walk off, but Kurt called him back.

"When you were dating Talulah…"

Brant raised his eyebrows. "Yes?"

"If she needed you to do something sort of…unconventional, would you have done it?"

"That would depend on what it was, right?"

"I mean…something you're not quite comfortable with…"

"There isn't much I wouldn't have done for her. And now there's nothing. But you have me intrigued. Why do you ask?"

Because Brant always did the right thing, and Kurt was hoping to use him as a guide. He didn't want to screw up his life, and what he was considering could easily do that. He was standing at a fork in the road. One path was safe, while the other could bring him what he really wanted—or turn out to be the biggest mistake he'd ever made. "Just trying to figure something out."

"I'm completely in the dark here. Do you mind explaining what we're talking about so I can give you an informed answer?"

Kurt wished he could say more. If ever he'd needed advice from someone as stable and dependable as Brant, it was now. But he couldn't explain. "Never mind. Don't worry about it."

Brant came back toward him. "You're acting weird. Is this about Jane?"

"No." Kurt scrambled to his feet. "Of course not. What made you think that?"

A funny look crossed Brant's face. "Um, it could be that she's beautiful. And available. And you two have been spending a lot of time together lately…"

"That doesn't mean anything. We're just friends."

"That's what everyone says when they don't want other people to know they feel more," Brant said with a laugh.

"I *don't* feel more," Kurt lied. "She'd never give me a chance, anyway."

"Can you blame her? Dude, you slept with her sister."

"Only once or twice. Kate's my age, so she was a more natural choice at the time."

Brant gestured toward him with the now-half-eaten apple. "That brings up another good point. The age difference hasn't changed. You're too young for Jane."

"Five years might've been a big deal a decade ago. But it doesn't matter now."

"It sort of does," Brant insisted. "You were in junior high when she was graduating high school. I don't think she's likely to forget that. And as I've already said, you've been with her younger sister."

If only he'd known he might have the chance to date Jane later, Kurt would've left Kate alone. But he'd always considered her too far out of his league. "Is that what Talulah says? Has she mentioned how Jane feels about me?"

Finished with the apple, Brant threw the core as far as he could. "I thought you two were just friends."

"We are, but…"

Brant rolled his eyes. "It's obvious you like her."

"Fine. Fuck you. I like her. So tell me…what's Talulah got to say about it?"

After studying him for a few seconds, Brant said, "Nothing so far. I think she'd be surprised if you two got together. But Talulah's a romantic. She thinks love can overcome anything."

"You're more skeptical."

"I'm more skeptical," he admitted. "Most women would steer clear of a man who's been with her sister."

"Kate and I were never a real couple," Kurt pointed out.

"That might make a difference."

Kurt scratched his neck. "But I shouldn't bet on it?"

"*I* wouldn't. Then again, who would've thought Talulah and I would ever get together with all we had going against us. So…what do I know?"

"Yeah, what *do* you know?" Kurt said, teasing to cover for his disappointment, and waved as his brother left. Brant's last statement offered him a *little* hope, but just because Brant had been able to get Talulah didn't mean he'd be able to get Jane.

Although…he did have the opportunity she was offering him. Maybe giving her what she wanted would change the dynamic between them and *finally* start her thinking of him in an entirely new light.

Two

Jane put a sign on the door to alert any potential customers that she was out to lunch, even though she'd already eaten—it was almost three—and hurried down the sidewalk to Talulah's Dessert Diner. She didn't usually visit the diner until she'd closed her own store, Vintage by Jane. Then about once a week she'd stop by and help Talulah clean up the café. Or if it'd been a particularly slow night and Talulah was already done, they'd sit down and have a glass of wine together, outside if the weather allowed it.

They'd been able to rebuild a lot of the comradery that'd been lost when Talulah jilted Averil Gerhart's brother seventeen years ago and put Jane in the middle of a tug-of-war between her two best friends. When Talulah left town, Jane had grown closer to Averil. But thanks to Talulah coming back and Averil's recent behavior, which Jane couldn't condone, that dynamic had changed. Now she was closer to Talulah than to Averil. Since they were both businesswomen and had stores on Lincoln Street, only two blocks apart, they saw each other more often, which helped.

On weekdays, Talulah didn't open until two. When Jane burst in, there was no one other than her friend in the restaurant, which didn't surprise her. The fancy desserts Talulah created were for the dinner crowd, so afternoons could be slow at first. "Well?" she demanded, breathless from walking so fast. "Are you?"

Talulah looked up in surprise. "What are you talking about? Am I what?"

Jane thought Talulah knew. That was why she hadn't simply called or sent a text. She needed to see her friend's face and read her body language. "You told me last night you thought you might be expecting. You were going to grab a test on your way home. I was wondering if you'd done that—and taken it."

Talulah glanced at the large front window that had her logo on it as if to make sure no one else was about to walk in and overhear them. "Well—" a smile curved her lips as though she couldn't suppress the excitement any longer "—I picked up a test and I took it, but nothing will be for sure until I visit a doctor and a blood test confirms the results."

Jane stepped up to the register. "Those home pregnancy tests have become pretty accurate, Lu. Thousands of women rely on them every day. So…are you pregnant? I hate to pry, and of course you don't have to tell me if you don't want to, but it's all I've been able to think about."

Talulah flushed. They'd talked about how hard it would be for her to manage her current workload if she were to have a baby. But since she and Brant really wanted a family, and were only getting older, Talulah had admitted they needed to get started sooner rather than later. Last night she'd said she'd just have to figure out how to juggle motherhood with maintaining a business, like so many other women. "Of course I'll tell you," she said but lowered her voice. "I was just holding off until I had some official word from the doctor, so please don't share the news with anyone else. I haven't even told Brant."

Jane stiffened in surprise. She would've thought he'd be the first to know. "Why not?"

Talulah closed the display case she'd been getting into when Jane arrived. "I'll tell him as soon as I see a doctor. There's no need to get his hopes up before then. But I might not tell anyone else for a while."

"Because…"

"I'm afraid to announce it too soon. My sister had a miscarriage last year—after eleven weeks—and it was hard on her to explain to everybody that she wouldn't be having another child, after all. It made the pain of losing the baby that much worse, for her and her husband. I don't want to set myself up for a similar experience, but, according to the faint pink line, I am," Talulah admitted.

"You're not going to lose the baby," Jane said. "But I won't tell a soul. I'm just…delighted for you." It wasn't quite *that* simple. She also wanted a baby, despite not having a partner. True love had proved so elusive for her that she'd all but given up searching for the right man. Maybe she'd find someone later in life, when it was too late to have a child, but every relationship she'd had so far had ended before it had ever really gotten off the ground—and the strange part was that she was always glad when it was over. Never had she been as invested as she should be, certainly not enough to promise any of the men she'd known "till death do us part."

Maybe she was too much of a free spirit to be tied down.

Or the lack of options here in Coyote Canyon had left her feeling hopeless and jaded. She'd tried online dating. The past few years, that was the only way for her to meet someone new. But even when a relationship seemed to be working, she wrestled with a great deal of doubt and fear that continuing with whomever she was seeing would turn out to be a mistake. She didn't want to get to the altar and back out the way Talulah had. So she'd break things off, wondering if she'd regret it and possibly reunite.

Instead, she'd be relieved and move on to the next guy, only to have a similar experience.

No doubt she had her parents' divorce to thank for some of her issues. Her father had made her distrustful, somewhat cynical and overly cautious when it came to men. But for good reason. Without Nana and Papa, where would she be? Her mother could not have coped on her own. And it wasn't as if her father had straightened up over the years. He was more of a con man now than he'd ever been. He'd just married again, for the *fifth* time, and still didn't have a job.

"Provided a blood test confirms it, I'll be due in early November," Talulah said.

Due. That word. If Jane had any doubt she was also ready for a baby, the thrill that ran through her in that moment eliminated it. She'd always wanted to be a mother, and she was tired of waiting. What if marriage never happened for her? Why not take her destiny into her own hands and share her life with a child? And since she was putting herself in control, why not do it now, when it would be so much more enjoyable to go through the process with Talulah? "I'm *really* happy for you."

Talulah put a hand to her belly, which was flat now but wouldn't be for long. "I can't wait to let Brant in on the secret. I do want to visit the doctor first. But after that…how do you think I should tell him? I'd like to do something special."

"Why don't we look on the internet for ideas? I'll come by at closing tonight, so we can plan."

Talulah's smile widened. "Sounds like fun."

"He's going to be thrilled," Jane predicted. He was two years older than they were, thirty-seven, and she'd heard him joke on more than one occasion that he didn't want to be old and gray before they started a family. She had no doubt he'd be over the moon.

"Averil won't be pleased to hear the news," Talulah said with a grimace. "She's already mad that Brant and I are married. I can only imagine how she's going to feel when she hears we're having a baby."

"She has to expect it to happen at some point. But you're right. She won't be happy, and neither will her brother." Jane believed Charlie was still in love with Talulah, even though it'd been an eternity since she'd broken off their relationship. He was the man she'd left standing at the altar when they were just eighteen. Jane would never forget that day. It'd meant the friendship between her, Averil and Talulah, which they'd enjoyed since kindergarten, would fall apart.

Even after so many years, Jane felt the loss. Life had been so different when it was all three of them against the world. Once Talulah had come back to town to take care of her great-aunt's funeral and handle the estate, Jane had hoped Averil could forgive her for what she'd done to Charlie. But then Talulah had gotten involved with Brant, who was not only Charlie's best friend—former best friend—but the man Averil had set her heart on since her divorce, and that had destroyed all chance of a reconciliation.

Although it'd been a significant disappointment, Jane had to accept the current dynamic. So much had come between Averil and Talulah, she doubted their relationship would ever improve.

At least Ellen had moved to town a few years ago. She lived in the house next to Talulah's, was a good friend of hers, and Jane was quickly growing fond of Ellen, too. So she was part of a strong friendship between three women again. The relationships just didn't go back as far, and they no longer included Averil. She'd been replaced with Ellen, which only added fuel to Averil's anger.

"I don't care what Charlie thinks," Talulah said. "But I will always care about Averil."

When Jane went over to the water cooler to get a drink, Talulah offered her a coffee or another beverage, but she refused. "This is fine," she said, helping herself to one of the small glasses stacked nearby before returning to their conversation. "I guess we shouldn't be too hard on Averil. She hasn't had an easy life since she married Chase. That ex of hers is a piece of work."

"It would be hard to raise a child on your own," Talulah said. "And yet Averil seems to be doing a great job with Mitch."

Jane put her empty cup in the tub Talulah would eventually take to the kitchen to wash. Her friend's comment was the perfect lead-in to talk about what she was thinking. Dare she say something?

Talulah reached back into the display case to slide the seven-layer chocolate fudge cake farther from the three-tiered red velvet cake. "Averil's living with her parents. I don't think she's perfectly happy. Judging by her behavior the past few years, and all the trash she's talked about everyone else, I'd say she's miserable but can't move out because she needs her folks."

"They help her a great deal."

"They also take over and tell her how to care for her own child. She's admitted that much." Talulah closed the case again. "They make her feel like she's still a kid herself. That would be frustrating."

"It's a trade-off. I know because I was raised with the help of my grandparents, right? Papa and Nana had to help my mom a lot, and my mom probably resented their involvement and advice. But not every single mother has to move in with her parents."

Talulah had started to straighten the area around the register. At this, she looked up. "You're advocating for single parenthood?"

"I'm just saying it doesn't have to be a bad thing. That would depend on whether you could afford a child. Whether you have a place to live. Whether you have the time and mental wherewithal. Someone who's been through a painful divorce and works for an employer eight to ten hours a day may not want to take on the challenge. But someone who has some savings, a comfortable home and has her own business—so she can set her hours or bring the child to work—might feel differently."

Talulah cocked her head. "You're not talking about yourself…"

Jane had never broached the subject with Talulah or anyone else—other than Kurt when she'd had a bit too much to drink on Saturday night—but the desire to have a baby was getting stronger and stronger, and she was feeling ready to fight for what she wanted. "What if I am?"

Talulah's eyes widened. "You want to have a baby—
on your own?"

"In a perfect world, no. I'd love to be as happily married as you are. But that hasn't happened for me. Why
should I let what I don't have deny me the privilege of
motherhood?"

Talulah's lips parted but she didn't say anything.

"Quit looking at me that way," Jane snapped, uncomfortable because she knew almost everyone else in their
hometown would be even more shocked. "I'm thirty-five,
Lu. That's plenty old enough to know what I'm doing. I
don't want to wait another five or ten years. I want to experience what most of my friends are experiencing—go
through it with them rather than watch enviously from
the sidelines."

"I didn't know you felt that way," Talulah said. "You've
talked more about heading to Portland or San Francisco
or New York City than having a child."

Because she was embarrassed. It was easier to act as
though she didn't want what so many of her friends and
acquaintances were getting. "If I had the opportunity to
move and do this somewhere else, I would. But I can't
leave Coyote Canyon."

"I wouldn't rush into anything you might regret, Jane.
You'll meet someone eventually."

That was what she'd been told for years. She no longer believed it. The compassion on her friend's face also
bothered her. She didn't want anyone feeling sorry for
her. It wasn't as if she had a *bad* life. "There's no guarantee that I will. And even if I do, *when* will it happen?
When I'm in my forties? My fifties? By then, it'll be
too late."

Talulah came around the counter and motioned to

an empty table, indicating they should both sit down. "Okay. If you want a child right away, how would you go about it?"

Jane hated knowing others might not approve, especially when she thought she'd be a good mother. She was devoted to Papa, took great care of him. Didn't that say something about her commitment to those she loved? "There are options, especially these days."

"Are you talking about artificial insemination?"

She scooted closer to the edge of her chair. She'd been thinking, if Kurt was amenable it wouldn't *have* to be artificial. But if he gave her a baby the traditional way, it would probably be weird to run into him afterward… "Yes."

"That's expensive. And health insurance won't cover it."

"You're thinking of infertility treatments. As far as I know, I won't need in vitro or anything like that. A vial of sperm is about a thousand dollars. And it'll only be four hundred or so for the insemination process."

"You know that?"

"I've looked into it."

"But that's still almost fifteen hundred bucks."

Simply sleeping with Kurt would certainly save some money. But even if they decided to avoid that kind of close contact, and Kurt provided the vial, he wouldn't charge her so it would only be four hundred. "I've been able to set some money aside, more since I moved in with Papa and haven't been paying rent. I also have the Mustang." Her vintage car was something her grandfather had restored and had kept covered in his garage for years—until he'd insisted on giving it to her when she moved in with him. Because of him, she hadn't had a car payment, either, not since she'd sold the truck she'd been driving before. "I could sell it and get something cheaper, if I had to," she told Talulah. "It's worth a fortune these days."

"You also own your own business," Talulah mused. "Giving you maximum flexibility."

"And my business is doing well." She managed to sell quite a lot of clothing, household items and furniture in Coyote Canyon, which was kind of surprising. Vintage by Jane had started out as a run-of-the-mill thrift shop, where she sold mostly secondhand leftovers, but it had grown into something more akin to a gift and furnishings shop. She still took some donations, but only what fit her style, and she'd become highly selective. Even then, she often refinished, recovered or repainted whatever it was. She also purchased her stock from estate sales in Montana and surrounding states—which meant she had to pull it back to town in her horse trailer—and she had a talent for staging what she sold. She believed presenting what she had in its best possible light was the secret to her success. Because of that, the store had become something she was very proud of.

"You're just lacking half the DNA."

"And for that there are sperm banks."

Talulah smoothed the branded apron she wore. "How does that work exactly? You just…go to a certain location, look at genetic profiles, purchase what you want and they give you a vial?"

Jane winced. Even to her ears that sounded so transactional. But at least that avenue was open to her. Otherwise, what would women like her do? "It's handled online at cryobanks. You can choose the ancestry, the hair and eye color, even the height and sometimes the educational level of the donor, and it brings up matches—kind of like a dating site."

Talulah began to dig at her cuticles. "You seem serious about this…"

Jane gestured to what she was doing with her hands. "And you seem worried."

"I am. I'm sorry if this upsets you, but…wouldn't it be difficult to have a stranger's baby?"

It would. No matter how much information the cryobank provided, Jane wasn't sure she'd ever be able to trust it, which was why she was so excited that Kurt had said he'd help her out. She knew the Elway brothers. Admired them. If he was serious, at least she could be certain of the DNA she'd be getting—that there'd be no trickery involved, like being told she was getting a vial of sperm from a particular donor when it was really the genetic material of the director of the facility or something.

After all, such things had been in the news. She preferred a known entity. People could argue that cryobanks were the safest bet if she didn't want the donor to have a relationship with her child. That was probably true. But if everything lined up the way she thought it might, she'd only be in Coyote Canyon another year, which meant she'd be moving away shortly after the baby was born. As far as Kurt was concerned, unless he wanted to be part of the baby's life, they could make it as if nothing had ever happened. "It wouldn't be easy," she allowed. "But…what are my other options?"

"I don't know." Talulah tucked her hair behind her ears. "I'm not sure I can encourage you to do this, though."

Jane tried not to feel stung by her friend's response. "You don't trust me to know what I want?"

"I trust you. I'm just…protective. And this plan is fraught with potential pitfalls."

Talulah didn't even know that Kurt, her brother-in-law, might be involved, which would make their babies first cousins. Then she'd only worry more, because she'd feel as if she also had to protect him. "There are potential pitfalls along any path. Besides, I've been thinking about this for a long time. It's not something I just came up with."

"Why haven't you said anything about it before?"

"It's not an easy subject, Lu. Think about where we live—what a difficult concept this will be to everyone."

Talulah blew out a puff of air. "Exactly. I can't see it *not* making a stir, and that means there'll be people who say stuff you may not like, or snub you, or…whatever."

"The people who would do something like that are not my friends to begin with. Besides, no one has to know the details. Plenty of women get pregnant by a boyfriend or from some other encounter that doesn't lead to marriage. It's not like I'd be the first in Coyote Canyon."

Talulah tightened the neck on her apron. "What about Papa? What will you tell him about…about how you came to be 'with child'?"

"I don't have to explain too much to him. He's no longer in his right mind most of the time."

"He still has lucid moments…"

"Some. But I'm not worried about it. He's just glad I'm there to take care of him. And he'll love having a baby around. I actually think it'll be good for him, make what's left of his life better."

"And your sister? How will you explain what you're planning to her?"

"Just like I'm explaining it to you."

"You don't think she'll have a problem with it?"

"She may not like it, but it's my choice. She's probably going to get married this year, anyway, so she'll be preoccupied with her own life. Chances are she'll be having a baby soon, too."

Talulah tapped her fingernails on the table. "I see."

Jane leaned forward. "Why would I passively accept what life gives me when I have the power to change things?"

"You've made some good points…"

"I'd like you to be supportive," Jane said. "I feel as if…as if that will make a huge difference."

"Of course I'll be supportive. I'll always stand by you. I just want to be convinced you know what you're doing."

"I can't make any guarantees," she said. "But getting what you want sometimes means taking a chance."

"True. I guess there could be problems no matter how you have a baby. We all face risks."

"Yes!"

"Fine. If it's really what you want to do, I'll keep my mouth shut about the potential problems."

Jane reached over to squeeze her hand. "Thank you, Lu. Having a baby this way is not ideal, not the way I really want it. But not everyone can have what you have."

Talulah smiled sadly. "I know. I've been wishing Averil could find a good guy, too. That might finally fix what's broken between us, make it possible for her to forgive me—not just for Charlie but for Brant."

The bell jingled over the door, and Jane pulled her hand back. It probably looked as though they'd been caught scheming about something. But she forgot all about that when she saw who it was.

Brant had just walked in—and Kurt was with him.

Three

Kurt hadn't anticipated running into Jane—not here. He knew she owned the shop down the street, of course, and had been thinking he might stop by later. They needed to talk. But first, he had to decide what he was going to do. After he finished wiring the pump for the new well and moved the cattle to the appropriate paddock, he'd headed straight to the house for a shower. He didn't normally cut out of work early, but it was only by an hour, and he figured he'd just stay late tomorrow to make up for it. His mind wasn't on what he was doing; it was on Jane and the mess he'd gotten himself into.

Then Brant had seen that he was done for the day and asked him to come to the diner, and he'd figured he could pick up a slice of Talulah's lemon cream cheese pound cake—his favorite of her desserts—and, if he had the opportunity, talk to her about Jane. He should at least try to get a feel for what Jane had said about him, shouldn't he? Did he have *any* chance with her? Or was it only a baby she was after? And when had she started thinking about becoming a mother?

"Brant!" Talulah got up the second she saw her husband. "You're earlier than I expected. And look who you brought with you. My favorite brother-in-law."

Kurt liked Talulah, was glad she and Brant had ended up together. They were perfect for each other. "You don't fool me," he said with a mock scowl. "You say the same thing to whatever brother you're with."

Her smile turned into more of a devilish grin as Brant said, "You told me you ordered a lot of supplies. I figured this beast could carry a few sacks of flour and sugar into the pantry in exchange for bumming a piece of lemon cake off you."

Kurt shot a glance in Jane's direction, hoping she might be glad to see him, but she kept her eyes averted.

"He knows he's welcome to anything he wants. He doesn't have to work for it," Talulah said. "But in the interest of full disclosure, we should warn him that we're doing more than carrying a few supplies this afternoon. I'm running out of room in the pantry. You were going to build me some more shelves, remember?"

"Shelves? We're building shelves?" Kurt glowered at his brother. "You didn't tell me you were signing me up for hard labor."

Brant chuckled. "Did I forget to mention that? Well, no worries. It won't take us long."

Talulah turned to Jane. "Before these guys get started on the pantry, would you like to have a piece of cake and a cup of coffee with us?"

Jane stood and edged around the table as though she was purposely giving Kurt a wide berth. "No, I'd better get back to the store. I don't want any customers to come and be disappointed that they can't get in."

"Okay, well, don't forget about tonight," Talulah said.

Jane made a dismissive gesture. "If Brant's going to

be here, I won't bother you. I'll let the two of you work on the shelves and then enjoy your evening together."

"You're welcome to come back whether I'm here or not," Brant reassured her, but Talulah spoke at the same time.

"He won't be around more than a few hours. He's been up since before dawn and needs to get some rest. The shelves should go fast. Then, if it's not too busy in here, I'll order dinner, and we'll eat together before he heads home. If I let him stay too late, tomorrow will be a long, difficult day on the ranch."

"Oh, come on," Kurt said. "Stop babying him. He can take it."

Brant cocked an eyebrow at him. "You're here so the shelf building goes even faster. And since Jane's leaving, I vote we wait for cake until after we're done. Otherwise, what will we use to motivate you?"

"Fine," Kurt grumbled. "As long as you give me a piece of the chocolate cake, too."

"You can have whatever you want," Talulah said. "But I have no idea where you put all the calories I feed you. It's not fair that you Elway brothers can eat anything and never gain a pound."

Jane cleared her throat, presumably to get their attention. "Just text me if anything changes, Lu. Otherwise, I'll see you later." Ducking her head, she kept her eyes on the black-and-white-checkered flooring as she started to leave.

Kurt got the impression she was eager to escape him. But when he held the door for her, she glanced up.

"Thanks. And—" She looked over her shoulder, where Talulah and Brant were already heading to the kitchen. "I'm sorry if…if I've put you in an awkward position.

You can just forget about what I said. I don't know what I was thinking."

He felt a flicker of disappointment, which surprised him. He wanted to help her. He just wasn't sure if he could figure out an arrangement he could feel good about. "Are you sure?" he said. "Because I'm willing to consider it."

Her jaw dropped. "Are you serious? You're sober now," she said jokingly.

"I'm still thinking about it," he admitted. "That's why I haven't responded yet. This isn't a decision that can be made lightly."

"No…"

"And we'd need to agree on a few things first."

"True."

The first thing was how they would do it. For him, the possible method was part of the temptation…

They stared at each other for several seconds—until Kurt couldn't help lowering his gaze to her mouth. He wanted to kiss her. He'd wanted to kiss her for ages. But he didn't know how she'd react.

Still, he knew better than to do it at the diner.

"You coming, bro?" Brant yelled from the kitchen. "These shelves aren't going to build themselves."

"I'm coming!" Kurt called back. Then to Jane he murmured, "I'll stop by the store when we're done here, so we can talk about it."

Mrs. Biloxi, who'd been Jane's English teacher in high school, came in around five thirty and bought an antique dresser Jane had painstakingly restored in Papa's workshop. Her grandfather, who'd always been good with his hands, had helped her. They'd taken it from the mahogany finish that'd been so popular for Duncan Phyfe furniture, painted it white and made it look distressed, so it had a "farm chic" vibe, and her former teacher had fallen in love with it. "This is going to be perfect for my guest bedroom," she'd gushed.

Jane had offered to have it delivered. She provided that service for heavier items and paid two high school kids, who used her grandfather's old horse trailer, to make the deliveries. Mrs. Biloxi declined, however, saying her husband and brother would pick it up for her the following morning.

Jane had worked so hard to make the dresser fit her vision of what it could be that she was excited to know it was going to a good home. By the time she finished some of her favorite projects, she wanted to keep them, but she currently had nowhere to put anything. Her store's back room was already bursting with inventory she was hoping to bring into the front as items sold and she made space, and she'd filled Papa's garage with the overflow and was reluctant to take anything else into his workshop or house. In her opinion, she needed to keep everything the same for him, so it would all be familiar. That meant she wound up selling everything she really wanted to keep. While she was eager to furnish her own place again one day, she told herself there would be plenty of great finds then, too. The hunt—and making something appealing out of an object that was dated, worn or out of style—was half the fun.

Still, it could be hard to part with certain acquisitions, and this dresser was one of them. It might be the last piece Papa was able to help her with. He'd gone downhill quite a bit, just in the past month. She'd never known him to use bad language, but as dementia took a firmer hold, he lost his filter and said exactly what was going through his mind, peppered liberally with swear words.

Most of the time Jane found his bad language funny— she didn't mind it when they were alone—but taking him out in public could be embarrassing. The shock on people's faces when he dropped a string of f-bombs always made her squirm. "I said I wanted a fucking burrito. Where's my fucking burrito?" he'd yelled at the taco stand last night.

After covering the dresser in plastic, she wrote "Sold" on a big red ticket and was just taping it to the plastic when Averil breezed in. "Hey."

Jane blinked. These days, Averil didn't seek her out very often. The chasm between Averil and Talulah had gotten too great, finally forcing Jane to choose sides. She hadn't liked doing it. She sympathized with Averil and what she'd been through, could see why she might be hurt and angry. But Averil was holding Talulah responsible for too much. Charlie wasn't meant for Talulah. The marriage would've been a disaster. And Brant wouldn't have been interested in Averil even if he hadn't fallen in love with Talulah. He'd had plenty of opportunities to make a move on her before Talulah returned to town. He'd been giving horseback riding lessons to her son, trying to help out since the boy didn't have a father who played an active role in his life, but she'd taken it to mean too much. He'd never even asked her to dinner.

"What's going on?" Jane smiled as though she was happy to see her lifelong friend, but she wasn't eager to have a personal visitor right now, didn't want Averil to be around when Kurt showed up. She'd been looking forward to the opportunity to hear what he had to say.

"I'm considering moving out of my parents' house

and was wondering if the apartment above this place was still available," Averil said. "Do you know the status?"

Jane froze. Living with Papa was much easier knowing she could lease the apartment above the store again if, for some reason, he *had* to go into a home before her lease expired—or the worst happened and he passed away. She'd known if she didn't keep it under contract, there was a possibility someone else could lease it. But there hadn't been much interest so far. She could tell because LaVeryle rarely showed it to anyone. Jane had begun to think it would continue to sit empty, and that had given her a sense of security that made the challenges in her life easier to bear.

The last thing she'd expected was for *Averil* to move in.

"I…I think it's available," she said, struggling to keep her voice neutral. "But…why pay rent when you can live with your folks for free?"

"Because I can't take it anymore. I've got to have my own place." She huffed dramatically as she plopped her large purse on the register desk. "I don't have any privacy, can't invite any of the guys I date to the house. My parents are wonderful with Mitch. He loves having them around all the time, which is why I've stayed as long as I have. But it's hell for me."

Jane picked up the pen she'd just used and returned it to its holder, which she kept by the pink tissue paper and brown sacks. She wrapped almost everything she sold—the small items, anyway—in fancy packaging, tied with a ribbon and decorated with a cute sticker bearing her logo. "It's a great option, but it's not furnished. You know that, right? I emptied it when I moved out and sold all my stuff here in the store."

"Furnishing it won't be a problem. I could get basic

castoffs—a couch, a TV, a bedroom set and maybe a bunk bed for Mitch's room from my older siblings. It won't look like much at first, not until I can replace the furniture, which I'll do as quickly as I can afford to. But at least I'd have my own space and can get back to living my life. I feel like it's been on hold forever."

Although it was for different reasons, Jane could certainly relate to that "stuck" feeling. "I could help you find inexpensive stuff secondhand, too, of course. But you won't have a babysitter close by," she pointed out. "Every time you want to go somewhere that isn't kid friendly, you'll have to take Mitch over to your folks'."

"That's what other young mothers face," she said. "I guess I can deal with childcare, too. Do you have the owner's contact information?"

A heavy weight settled on Jane's heart. That apartment had been so convenient for her. But even if Papa passed away, she'd have his home and belongings to dispose of. She couldn't even try to save the apartment for herself. And once Papa was gone, and her lease expired again, she was leaving for San Francisco. "Her name's LaVeryle White. Do you know her?"

"No. But I bet my brother does."

Charlie was in real estate. He handled most of the house and land sales in the area, but LaVeryle owned the building and managed it herself, and that was true for the apartment, too. "I can give you her number. She just picked up the lease I signed on the store half an hour ago. I'm sure she'll be happy to hear from you."

Although she hated having to do it, Jane sent Averil the contact information via her phone. "There you go."

Averil dug her phone out to check that it'd come

through. "I'm excited. Just think—if I rent the apartment, I'll be right above you. We'll see each other all the time."

Was that what Averil wanted? Because she'd completely withdrawn from their friendship, acted as though Jane couldn't be friends with her if she was also friends with Talulah.

Jane hoped this wouldn't cause more friction. There'd been enough of that in the past. "That would be great," she lied.

"We'll have a blast!"

"You must be making good money," Jane commented. "Or is Chase finally paying his child support every month?"

"He's doing better."

"You still working at the gas station?"

"No, I quit that job last week. The hours were terrible."

Since her divorce, when she'd moved back to Coyote Canyon after living in California with Chase, Averil had held various jobs around town—all of them menial. Some were only part-time work. She'd never been interested in school and had dropped out of college to marry Chase. So she didn't have a degree or much job experience to rely on. But, so far, she hadn't needed a lot. Her parents covered food, rent and babysitting. "What are you doing now?"

"I'll be a checker at the feedstore."

"With Peggy Nett?" Although she'd been taking care of Otis since she was afraid Papa would forget to feed him, Jane didn't have farm animals to worry about. Papa had sold the horses when Nana died. So there was no reason for her to visit the feedstore. But Peggy was one of her customers.

"No. She's going on maternity leave. That's why I'm taking over."

Peggy was someone else Jane knew who would be having a baby. It seemed to be happening for every woman but her. "Oh, that's right. I haven't seen her recently, didn't realize she was that far along. So…the job's only temporary?"

"Yeah, but I'll find something else when it comes to an end. And since I'll be living so close to you, I can watch the store for you—for free—when you need to run an errand or whatever."

"I wouldn't expect you to do that—"

"It won't be any trouble," she broke in. "You'll just have to show me how to ring up customers on your system and that sort of thing."

"That's really nice of you. And I'll be happy to help with Mitch here and there when I'm available."

"It'll be like old times," Averil said with a nostalgic grin.

Jane couldn't help missing those days. But she wasn't convinced she could trust Averil to be the kind of friend she used to be—the kind of friend who wouldn't constantly get jealous of Talulah or Ellen and cause problems. "You still seeing Jordan?"

"Every now and then," she said as she started to look around the store.

Jordan was someone Ellen had met via an online dating site. He lived and worked in Libby, five hours away, but once when he'd come to Coyote Canyon to see Ellen, who wasn't interested in him, he'd met Averil, and they'd been dating ever since. At least, Jane had assumed they were still dating. Although she never saw Jordan in town, she knew Averil drove to Libby every once in a while.

Jane guessed Averil had realized he wasn't a great guy, because the relationship never seemed to advance, and she rarely mentioned him these days. She was probably too embarrassed to admit that Ellen had been right about him. "Do you think it'll go anywhere?"

She shook her head. "It's never been serious between us."

That was good to hear. What Ellen had to say about the way Jordan had treated her was a red flag. But Jane didn't dare mention that. "Are you seeing anyone else?"

"Not right now. You?"

"No. I've been too busy with the store and taking care of Papa. I'm afraid I'm going to be single for the rest of my life."

"Welcome to the party." She picked up a scented candle, removed the lid and sniffed it. "How's your grandfather doing?"

"Some days he seems like the man I used to know. Other days, he's different—almost a stranger. Lately, he's started swearing—I mean *a lot*—and there's nothing I can do about it."

Averil's expression registered sympathy. "I'm sorry. Is it like…Tourette's or what?"

"Sort of. It just comes out. I don't mind when we're at home. But it's not fun to be in the grocery store or a restaurant when he goes off."

Averil put down the candle. "I still can't believe he told Rhonda Covington that she needs to lose weight."

The mere memory of that made Jane cringe. "I felt terrible. She was serving us breakfast at the Golden Biscuit when he noticed she had a brace on her knee and said it probably wouldn't hurt if she wasn't so fat. Poor thing."

"I'm sure she understands that he doesn't know what he's saying."

"I pulled her aside and explained that to her when I apologized, but it would still hurt to hear it."

"True."

The bell went off over the door and Kurt stepped in. "Hey."

Averil's smile brightened. "Hi, Kurt. How are things at the ranch?"

"Busy," he replied. "How's Mitch?"

Jane wondered if it was awkward for the two of them to see each other, given what'd happened with Brant. But she decided it'd been long enough since Talulah had come back that everyone had figured out a way to ignore the past and move on. It was a small town. Stuff like that occurred once in a while and people had to get beyond it.

"Doing great," Averil replied.

Kurt looked around as though he expected to see her son. "He's not here?"

"No. He's over at the school with a group of kids who stayed to color a big St. Patrick's Day poster for the assembly on Friday." She checked her watch. "Speaking of which, I'd better go. I have to pick him up in five minutes."

Jane breathed a silent sigh of relief. Maybe she'd have the opportunity to speak to Kurt alone, after all…

"What grade's he in now?" Kurt asked as Averil gathered her purse. "Second?"

"Yeah. He's growing up fast."

"Hard to believe you have a kid that old."

"At least I have something," she said as though his comment had struck a nerve. She walked out.

Kurt raised his eyebrows at Jane. "Do you think she was suggesting people like us aren't going anywhere?"

Jane laughed. "Basically. I think it's been hard on her to have the responsibility of motherhood while we're all still free to do whatever we want. She hates being a single mom, constantly fighting with her ex for child support, having to rely on her folks. It wouldn't be easy."

"And yet you think that's what you want…"

"I'm in a completely different situation."

"Why not wait until…until you can have a child in the conventional way? Wouldn't you rather do that?"

"If I haven't met a man I'd be willing to marry in thirty-five years, I doubt I ever will."

He seemed taken aback. "Well, you never know. Prince Charming could be right around the corner," he said, his lips curving into an endearing grin.

She used to think so, too. Problem was, she'd given up on that fantasy. "There's no one in Coyote Canyon," she said firmly. "And I'm done with online dating. I never liked it to begin with."

He opened his mouth to respond, then closed it again.

"I know contributing the, er, DNA I need is a lot to ask," she said. "I won't blame you if you tell me to get lost. But I admit I'd rather use your DNA than some stranger's from a cryobank. At least I'd have some frame of reference for my child's father, be able to describe him to my child."

"What if the child wants to meet his or her father?"

She'd anticipated this question. "That would be up to you," she assured him. "And if the answer is no, that's okay. It's not like I'm planning to raise the kid around here, where you'd have to see him or her all the time and be reminded. As soon as the situation changes with Papa, I'm out of here—and that could be as early as next year. That's when my new lease ends. If I have to put him in a home, I'll just have to come back regularly to see him. So…depending on when we scheduled the insemination, I might not even have had the baby yet."

He looked down for a several seconds before raising his eyes again. "I see."

She got the feeling she'd said something wrong, but

she couldn't imagine what. She'd been trying to reassure him that there'd be no strings attached to his donation and that she'd protect him from the more difficult ramifications—all the responsibility, even being faced with his decision later down the line. That was a good thing, wasn't it? "Kurt?"

His chest lifted as he drew a deep breath. "What?"

"Is something wrong?"

"No, nothing."

She peered at him more closely. Was he trying to figure out a way to tell her no? "If you've thought twice about saying what you did on Saturday, it's okay. I'll understand if you've changed your mind."

"It's not that I've changed my mind, exactly. It's just…" He let his words fall off as he combed his fingers through his short brown hair. "Is there any rush to make this happen?" he asked. "I mean, could we take a few weeks to think about it? Because I feel like it would be a mistake to rush into anything."

"Of course," she said. "Take all the time you need. I wouldn't want you to do something you might later regret."

"Okay," he said. "I'll think about it."

He shoved his hands in his pockets as he turned to go, but she called him back. "Kurt?"

He seemed distracted when he faced her. "Hmm?"

"Are you upset with me? It's a lot to ask, which is why I was so surprised you seemed somewhat open to the idea on Saturday. But I know we were both drinking—"

"I'm not upset," he broke in.

It certainly seemed that way. She tried to think of other things she could say to reassure him. "I also meant to tell you—we could keep it a total secret. At a certain point, the pregnancy would be obvious, of course, but no one—not a single soul—would have to know that *you* contributed the DNA."

"What about Talulah?"

"What about her?"

"She's your best friend. You wouldn't tell her?"

"Not if we decided to keep it a secret." She was firmly committed to that. Her commitment to her child—and to Kurt if he gave her a child—would come first.

"And if the child looks just like me?"

"That sort of thing is never conclusive," she said with a shake of her head. "Some people may see a resemblance, others won't. And if people wonder, they wonder. It won't be anything unless we confirm it."

He rubbed the beard growth on his chin as though he was deep in thought and wasn't processing her words as quickly as he usually did. She knew he'd heard her, however, when he finally mumbled, "Keeping it to ourselves might be the way to go."

She followed him to the door as he walked out and watched through the window as he made his way down the street to where he'd parked in front of the diner. Unfortunately, after waiting all afternoon for the chance to speak to him, the past few minutes hadn't gone nearly as well as she'd hoped.

"Shoot." She couldn't help being disappointed. But what she was asking wouldn't be an easy thing for a man, even a man who was her friend. She needed to allow Kurt the time he'd requested to think things through and adapt to the idea. If she was patient, and lucky, maybe there was still a chance he'd agree.

Otherwise, she'd have no choice except to use a cryobank even though she'd much rather have Kurt Elway's baby.

Four

"Where've you been all day?" Papa demanded, yelling above the TV, which was loud enough to rattle the walls, when Jane walked through the door.

Jane gathered her patience. Usually, her grandfather was in bed by now. Their neighbor Herbert came over each weeknight when the store was open to take Otis out and to look in on Papa and make sure he hadn't had any trouble heating up what she'd made him for dinner.

Tonight, she'd talked to Herbert just as she was closing the store, before she went back to the diner to help Talulah plan her pregnancy reveal, and he'd indicated Papa was set for the night. Why hadn't her grandfather gone to bed?

Or maybe he *had* gone to bed and gotten up again. He was sitting in his recliner wearing nothing but his underwear, and what little remained of his hair was sticking up on both sides of his head like a devil's horns.

"What do you mean?" she asked, keeping her voice calm and level as she dropped her keys on the small table in the entryway. "I was at the store."

He turned off the TV—a blessed relief as far as Jane

was concerned—and dropped the remote on the floor while trying to escape the grip of his recliner, which, like everything else, seemed to be getting harder for him. "What grocery store?" he asked skeptically.

"Vintage by Jane, Papa. It's not a grocery store. It's the store I own."

His scraggly gray eyebrows slammed together as he came tottering toward her. "Since when do you own a goddamn *store*?"

Here he went with the language again… Jane could already tell this was going to be a rough night. They seemed to be having more of those lately. "Since I opened it more than ten years ago, remember?" she said gently. "You were the one who gave me the seed money."

"No store is open this late," he said.

"Some are, but you're right—mine is not. I stopped by Talulah's after closing. She's going to have a baby. We were trying to figure out a clever way to tell her husband and decided on a bottle of wine with a label that reads, 'I can't drink this, but you can.'"

He stared at her blankly, giving her the impression she was talking about things that didn't relate directly to his own life so he couldn't quite absorb the information.

"Anyway, it's going to be cute," she added lamely, remembering all the other ideas they'd considered—scratch-off lottery cards that looked authentic but had "I'm pregnant" under the film, "Mom" and "Dad" T-shirts bearing "established" dates, a cake with an "I'm having a baby" plastic topper. Talulah had said she baked enough cakes and didn't want to go with the last option. Because she was so busy, the wine seemed easiest and would be something he could either drink or keep as a memento. "Brant will be excited."

Papa followed her into the kitchen, where she put the small take-home bag she'd brought from the diner in the fridge. "Talulah sent you a slice of her triple fudge cake. She knows how much you like it."

"Who the fuck is Talulah?" he asked. "And Brant?"

When he said stuff like that, Jane could either laugh or cry. Tonight, she felt more like crying. "Talulah Elway, Papa. My best friend. She's married to Brant. You know his parents."

"Derrick and Jeanie?"

She looked up in surprise. "Yes! There you go."

"I'd like to see them again," he said. "It's been ages."

He used to buy fresh beef from the Elway Ranch once a year, and Nana would take the wrapped meat and stack it in the Deepfreeze. Jane remembered going out to the garage to get certain cuts for her when she was ready to defrost and cook them. But he'd never done anything socially with the Elways, at least not that Jane knew of. She was certain what he missed was his old self and the world he'd been familiar with. It made her heart ache to think of how lost and bewildered he had to feel most of the time, especially during moments like this. "It's getting late," she said. "Aren't you tired?"

"Not too tired to eat cake."

"Are you sure you should have so much sugar right before bed?"

"I'm not a child!" he snapped.

His occasional belligerence was the most difficult aspect of the dementia—worse than the unfiltered language. "I'm afraid you won't sleep well if you do."

"Then I'll just sleep in."

"So far, you haven't been able to do that." Even dementia hadn't been able to overcome a lifelong habit of getting up early. He rose at four thirty, regardless of how much rest he'd had the night before. Usually, he went out to work in the yard or putter around in his workshop. Sometimes he sat at his desk in the house, where a stack of mail awaited his attention. He spent hours reading every solicitation he received—insisted she not throw any of his mail away, even the junk mail, until he'd seen it—and loved sending small amounts of money to various charities and political candidates. She guessed it made him feel as though he was getting something done, still working and making a difference in the world, which was important.

When he wasn't reading mail, he was paying bills. It took him an inordinate amount of time to write out the checks. His hand shook terribly. But he wouldn't allow her to set up automatic bill payment online. He used a myriad of sticky notes fastened to the metal filing cabinet beside the desk to remind him when he was supposed to pay the hazard insurance or property taxes on the house, life insurance or other obligations—or order new medication, including Ambien, since he was having more and more trouble sleeping. He couldn't seem to get even a solid four hours anymore, which was why she'd been worried about feeding him Talulah's chocolate cake right before bed.

"We need to make sure you get enough rest," she added.

"Who gives a fuck about rest?" he said. "I'm going to die anyway—and with the mess I'm in, the sooner the better."

Sometimes he made comments like that—comments that indicated he was more self-aware than she realized. "Don't talk like that," she murmured.

"I can take care of myself, you know," he said. "You don't have to be here."

"I *want* to be here. I love you," she said and that seemed to drain all the bluster out of him.

"You're such a good girl." He reached out to pat her shoulder with an oversize hand, scarred and calloused from thirty years of working for the federal government at the Bureau of Reclamation before he retired fifteen years ago, at sixty-five. "You've more than made up for all the heartache your father has caused—and I know your nana felt the same."

Jane turned away so he wouldn't see the tears gathering in her eyes. "You know what?" she said. "I think you're right. What the hell—let's eat the cake."

"Have you heard?" Ranson asked, the door slamming behind him as he came into the house.

Kurt had his legs propped up on the coffee table while trying to find something on TV that might distract him so he wouldn't call Jane. He wanted to see her. The weekend lay ahead, and they'd been spending more and more time together the past several months, so it seemed natural.

But after what she'd said at her store two days ago—that there was no one in Coyote Canyon she was interested in—he felt it was futile to continue to hope she might suddenly give him a chance. Apparently, she wasn't as attracted to him as he was to her, which made it especially hard for him to decide what to do about the genetic contribution she wanted.

At first, he'd been excited to hear her talk about having his baby—that she'd be interested in that—and thought the issue might, with time, resolve itself naturally if they got together. That was why he'd been open to the discussion. He'd seen it as a potential lever he could pull to get closer to her—or make her see him through fresh eyes.

But now… Could he follow through with what he'd said and help her have a baby the way *she* wanted to?

He'd been wrestling with that question for the past two days. Would it bother him to know he had a child out in the world he had no relationship with?

He thought it might. What made it worse was that he couldn't see how he and Jane could continue to be friends afterward. If they kept in contact, he'd be part of the child's life, too, wouldn't he? And that meant taking on *way* more responsibility than donating a vial of sperm, even though he wouldn't truly be part of the family or have any say in how the child was raised.

"Heard what?" he asked his brother. Ranson was younger than he was by eighteen months, but none of them were kids anymore. Brant and Miles were in their thirties, and he and Ranson were right on the cusp. But only Brant was married. Kurt lived with Miles and Ranson in the ranch house where they'd been raised. Their parents had retired and moved to town several years ago, but their mother still came over once a week or every ten days to cook and clean. He knew it was probably more than she should be doing for them now that they were all adults, but she seemed to enjoy it. She wouldn't stop, regardless, and he wasn't sad about that. He loved her cooking.

"Brant and Talulah are having a baby," Ranson announced.

Kurt sat up straight. "How do you know?"

"I just had dinner in town with my buddy Baker, and we stopped by the diner afterward for a piece of cake.

Brant was there, and he and Talulah were laughing because he'd just opened a box and found a bottle of wine inside with a label that said, 'I can't drink this, but you can.'"

"He randomly opened a box?" Kurt said in confusion. "Or she gave it to him to open?"

"Neither. He thought it was a regular delivery. Supplies or something. She *didn't* want him to see it—not yet—which was why she had it shipped to the store. She was going to hide it in the pantry until she was ready for the big reveal, but…"

No wonder Jane had been thinking about babies. Talulah was her best friend. They talked all the time. It was probably hard for her to be stuck taking care of her grandfather while everyone else seemed to be settling down and starting a family. She'd never said so, but he'd bet she was feeling left behind.

Kurt turned off the TV, which hadn't been holding his interest anyway. "Brant's wanted a baby ever since they got married."

"And now he's getting one," Ranson said, "which means we'll soon have a little niece or nephew running around."

"Does she know what it is yet?"

"You mean whether it's a boy or girl?" Ranson shook his head. "It's way too soon for that. She said she's only about six weeks along."

"Interesting…" he said.

Ranson gave him a funny look. "*Interesting?* I tell you there's going to be a baby born in the family for the first time in nearly thirty years, and that's what you've got to say?"

He could see why Ranson might not find his response

entirely appropriate. But he'd been thinking about how this revelation played into the situation with Jane. "I meant to say, 'That's cool.' It'll be fun to have a little one around."

"Hell, yeah," he said. "I can't wait. I hope it's a girl. We've got enough testosterone in this family already."

Kurt checked his phone to see if he'd missed any texts, even though he knew he hadn't—he'd been looking all night—as his brother walked into the kitchen. He heard the fridge open, the clink of one bottle against another and the pop of a cap. Then his brother sauntered back into the living room with a cold beer.

"What are you doing tonight?" Ranson asked.

Kurt had nothing planned. But it wasn't helping his frame of mind to just sit around. He figured he might as well contact Jane and tell her how he was feeling. Although it wouldn't be easy to disappoint her, he couldn't give her what she wanted and then continue to hang out with her occasionally, or even just see her around town, with her belly getting bigger each month with his baby. It'd be too weird.

"I was thinking about going out for a drink," he said. "Want to go with me?" Maybe Jane would walk down to Hank's after she closed the store. She often met him there. Then, after they played some pool with his brother, he could sort of ease into the conversation they needed to have while he walked her to her car.

"Sure. Why not?" Ranson said.

Averil hoped she wouldn't have to see Brant or Talulah tonight. Running into them wasn't only awkward; it evoked so many difficult emotions—pain, disappointment, regret, envy, even embarrassment at how she'd behaved. She couldn't seem to reach a place in her life where the past didn't cut her, so she was nervous about going to Hank's. It was the most popular bar in town; Brant's brothers came here quite often. She didn't need them to make her self-conscious and remind her that she was now an outsider with most of the people she'd once loved and admired. That was why, lately, when she wanted to go out, she went to the bar at the other end of Lincoln Street. Or she drove all the way to Bozeman. There, she didn't run the risk of seeing anyone she'd grown up with.

Fortunately, on both Friday and Saturday nights, Talulah was at the dessert diner until ten, when she closed, or later if she had a lot of cleanup to do. Since it was only nine, there was nothing to worry about quite yet. If Talulah and Brant stopped by, it wouldn't be for a while—unless Brant came in with one of his brothers.

"Band's good tonight," Jane commented, sitting across from her holding a Moscow mule by the handle.

Hank's hosted a live band on weekends. It made the place so much livelier than the smaller club Averil had relegated herself to recently. That bar, called Alley Cats, appealed to an older crowd, so she missed hanging out with people her own age. But her life had changed a great deal since she'd blown up so many of her personal relationships. Most days, she felt like an ocean liner steaming across a vast sea with no other ship in sight. She'd been isolated by motherhood and divorce and losing the man she truly loved to her former best friend.

Her response to all that certainly hadn't helped...

Occasionally, she considered moving away and starting over. She felt beleaguered. But where would she go? Her entire family lived here. And right now she needed them. Sometimes it felt like they were the only friends she had left.

"They *are* good," she agreed. So far, the conversation had been stilted. She wasn't sure why she'd asked Jane to come out for a drink. Jane had grown so close to Talulah that Averil couldn't help assuming they'd both decided she wasn't worthy of them—and, in a way, she didn't blame them. She *had* been angry and jealous and resentful. She *had* said and done things she shouldn't have. But they hadn't lived her life, didn't know how difficult the last ten years had been. She'd never dreamed she'd be divorced, with such limited resources, raising a child on her own because her ex was such a selfish, deadbeat dad.

She wouldn't even have seen Jane tonight if she hadn't gone to tour the apartment with LaVeryle just as Jane was closing the store. She'd come down the back stairway—the entrance to the apartment was off the alley, where there was also a back entrance to the store—*so* excited about the possibility of getting her own place that she'd wanted to head to Hank's and celebrate, and she'd hoped if Jane went with her, it'd be like old times.

But too many things had changed. Jane's loyalty was one of them. Averil could sense how firmly anchored Jane had become in her friendship with Talulah.

Even that didn't seem fair. Talulah already had Brant. She didn't need Jane. Not as much as Averil did.

Averil watched Jane check her phone, something she did often in case her grandfather tried to reach her. "Everything okay?" she asked.

"So far," Jane replied, setting her cell back on the table. "He should be asleep by now, but the last time I thought he'd be in bed I found him sitting in his recliner in his underwear. So I texted our neighbor to see if he could check."

"It's so nice of you to take care of your grandfather. I'd like to think I'd do the same for mine, but the truth is…I'm not sure I could."

"It's not easy. Sometimes he acts like a total stranger—an *angry* stranger. But I don't see how I can do anything different. Not right now."

"I remember when he gave you the money so you could open the store…"

Jane smiled fondly. "That's not all he's done. He came to everything I did in school, remember? Every time the cheer squad performed for an assembly or a game, or I was nominated for Homecoming royalty, or…or I performed in a flipping spelling bee, he'd be there to support and encourage me. He'd help me with my math homework, since I hated math and Nana wasn't any good at it. He bought me my first telescope and would spend hours with me outside at night, searching for various stars and teaching me about black holes and the formation of the universe. He paid my college tuition. He restored the Mustang I'm driving." She threw up her hands. "The list goes on and on. He's been so integral to my life—the one constant I could count on like the sun coming up each morning. I can't turn my back on him. I won't. My father gave me a peek at what my life would've been like without Papa."

Averil cradled her blackberry margarita in her hands. She had a fairly large family and wasn't likely to face the same challenge. She figured she could be grateful for that, at least. "I hate to sound callous, but…does he even know the difference?"

"Most of the time, yes. Even if it gets to the point

where he doesn't, at least I know I'm doing my best to take care of him. I wouldn't be able to live with myself if I felt I was letting him down." She took another sip of her drink. "But enough about me and my situation. What did you think of the apartment?"

"I love it."

"Even though it's small and you won't have a yard? Where will Mitch play?"

"I'll take him to the park. And he'll be at my folks' a lot. We just won't be living with them anymore, you know?"

"Can you really afford the rent? You won't enjoy the apartment if you're scraping to get by each month."

"I have to get out on my own again. Having some privacy and peace of mind, and finally feeling as though I'm building my life instead of barely hanging on will make any sacrifice worth it."

"Then if it means that much, I'd do it, too, if I were you," Jane said.

Because the apartment was too small for a family and wouldn't work for an older couple, thanks to the stairs, it was probably the cheapest housing in town. But Averil wanted to feel welcome. When she'd first thought of living above Jane's store, she'd hoped it would bring the two of them back together, to help her fix what'd gone wrong between them. Now, she wasn't so sure anything could do that. "You won't mind if I'm there?"

"Not at all," Jane said, but she was treating Averil with such careful niceness. That wasn't how things used to be between them. They'd always been perfectly comfortable and confident with each other.

It was hard not to blame Talulah for this, too. Talulah had become the bane of Averil's existence.

Locking eyes with Jane, Averil lowered her voice. "I'll behave," she said. "If that's what you're worried about. I'm...I'm sorry for what I've done."

Jane seemed startled, probably because Averil had never attempted to apologize before. She'd been too angry to put into words the remorse she felt more and more often these days.

"What's in the past is in the past, Av," she said. "Let's just...move forward in a more positive direction."

Averil nodded, hoping Jane was as sincere as she sounded. Now that she'd finally broached the subject, she might've said more. But the door opened, and she saw Kurt and Ranson stride in.

Of course she couldn't come here even once without running into a reminder of Brant, she thought bitterly.

"What is it?" Jane asked, obviously reacting to the expression on Averil's face. She twisted around to see for herself. "Kurt," she said as if Ranson wasn't even with him.

The Elway brothers noticed them almost immediately, and Kurt drew his brother to their booth. "Hey."

Jane finished her drink almost in one gulp, as if she needed a little something to bolster her for the next several minutes. "Hi," she said as she put down the mug.

Averil realized that although Brant's brothers had to know all about what had transpired between her and Brant, they didn't seem to care. Certainly, they never said anything to her about their brother. Maybe she was making a bigger deal out of it than she needed to.

Either way, she'd had enough to drink that she was beginning to feel less concerned about all the things she normally worried about.

"Mind if we join you?" Ranson asked.

"Of course not," Averil said, actually pleased that he'd asked. She was tired of being a pariah. If she was going to move into the apartment above Jane's store, she should also reconnect with the other single adults in town, stop avoiding so many of them. Coming back to Hank's was part of that effort. If she let go of her own resentment and embarrassment, maybe others would forget how various situations had developed, and she could get a fresh start without having to leave town.

Kurt glanced at Jane as if he wanted her approval, too. "Maybe we should grab a drink first..."

"No, sit." Jane slid over. "The waitress will be around in a minute."

Averil slid over, too, and Kurt, who was closest to her side, sat next to her. "You two interested in playing some pool?" he asked.

"Sure, as soon as you get your drinks," Averil replied.

Slouching comfortably in the booth, Ranson crossed his legs under the table. "Have you heard the good news?"

"Good news?" Averil echoed.

Jane didn't seem to know what he was talking about, either. Averil could tell she was perplexed when she looked over at him.

"Talulah's pregnant," he announced. "She and Brant are going to have a baby."

Averil's good mood evaporated instantly. Brant and Talulah were starting a family?

She'd been secretly hoping they'd separate. Why did everything seem to work out so well for Talulah when *she* couldn't catch a single break? Brant would've made such a great dad for Mitch.

And it wasn't just Mitch who'd missed out. She still dreamed about him...

Jane shot her a worried glance before focusing on Ranson. "How do *you* know?"

Ranson seemed confused by the emphasis Jane had placed on "you."

"I was at the diner tonight. Brant was so excited he was offering everyone who came in a free slice of cake. So…I don't think it's a secret anymore."

"Oh." Jane sagged in apparent relief. "She told me she wasn't going to tell Brant until she visited a doctor and took a blood test. Sounds like she went ahead and told him early."

"Not on purpose," Ranson explained. "He opened a box that arrived at the diner—thought it was supplies—and found a bottle of wine with a label that read, 'I can't drink this, but you can.'" He grinned. "Clever, huh?"

Jane agreed. But Averil struggled to find the words. She felt as though he'd kicked her in the stomach. It wasn't just the baby. It was that Jane already knew Talulah was pregnant and hadn't said anything. Which indicated—pretty clearly—that Talulah meant more to her than she did.

First, Talulah had hurt her brother terribly—and didn't become the sister-in-law Averil had expected. Then she'd returned to town and married the one man Averil had always admired. And after that, she'd stolen Jane.

Averil felt as though she'd lost so much, and all she'd been trying to do was protect what she had. "That's… nice," she managed to say, even though her mouth had gone so dry she could barely speak.

Lines creased Ranson's forehead. He could tell something was wrong, but it was obvious he had no idea what. "She's due in November," he added as if that piece of information might smooth over whatever gaffe he'd made.

"I'm happy for her." Averil knew she didn't sound happy at all, but she couldn't help it. She'd just been feeling better, just been starting to crawl out of the safe place inside her heart and mind where she'd withdrawn the past year.

"Averil…" Jane started to say.

But Averil had to get out of the bar before she broke down. She could already feel the sting of tears. Looking at her watch, she said, "Is it nearly nine thirty already? I'd better get going. It's past Mitch's bedtime, and my mom sometimes has trouble getting him to sleep."

That was entirely untrue. Dinah was better at putting him to bed than she was, because Dinah was a better disciplinarian. That was another thing Averil was struggling with—the fact that she had to compete with her own mom when it came to taking care of her son and always seemed to fall short.

"You're leaving?" Kurt said in surprise. "I thought… I thought we were going to play pool."

"The three of you can play." She slid from the booth as soon as he got out of her way. "Jane, I'll…call you," she said and threw twenty bucks on the table to cover her portion of the bill.

Five

Jane didn't go after Averil. She would have if she thought it'd do some good. But she didn't know how to reach her childhood friend these days. The chasm between them seemed too wide.

"That didn't go over very well," Kurt said.

"Why not?" Ranson seemed shocked. "I know Averil had a thing for Brant. But it's been a few *years*. And they never even dated. Surely, that's not the problem—is it?"

Jane had known Averil would be upset by the news. She'd never expected to have to deal with it tonight, though. "I think…it's a lot of things," she said, but she didn't go into detail because she didn't want to share Averil's problems with the Elway brothers. Or anyone else, for that matter.

Ranson gave her a sheepish look. "I'm sorry. I didn't mean to upset her."

"It's okay." Jane nudged him playfully with her shoulder. He hadn't done anything wrong. He was just excited about the baby. "She would've heard eventually."

The waitress came by to take their order. Kurt got a draft beer and Ranson a Guinness.

"I can't believe Brant stumbled onto that box at the diner," she said, imagining how things must've gone down. "What were the chances?"

"Right?" Kurt said. "I know Talulah's probably sad that what she had planned for the surprise didn't work out. But the real story is even better. He'll be telling that for years."

Turning her empty mug in a circle, Jane toyed with the condensation on the table. "Now the whole town will find out. And Talulah planned to keep the pregnancy quiet until after the first trimester."

"Why?" Ranson asked.

Jane didn't want to say. It seemed like it'd be bad luck. "Just to make sure a doctor has confirmed it and given her a solid due date and all of that."

Ranson made a clicking sound with his tongue. "A lot of people are settling down."

"We're getting to that age," Kurt pointed out. "Has Ellen set a date for *her* wedding?"

"She's talking about having it this summer," Jane told him.

The waitress reappeared with their drinks. "She'll probably be having a kid soon, too," Ranson said as Kurt sucked the foam off his beer. "That makes me feel old."

Given what Jane was hoping to get from Kurt, it was hard for her not to look up and catch his eye. But the fact that he immediately pulled his gaze away let her know it might be something else that wouldn't go the way she wanted.

After Averil left the bar, she drove slowly past the dessert diner. It was thriving, just like Talulah and Brant. Everything they touched turned to gold. So what was going on with her? She'd done all she could to be happy. But she couldn't seem to recover from the wrong turn she took when she got involved with Chase. Her life simply hadn't been the same since she met him. It'd been like having a giant asteroid strike her and now she was barely hanging on, hoping it wouldn't cause the complete extinction of the person she'd been before.

Her phone signaled a text message. She didn't have Bluetooth in the old rattletrap car that was the only thing she'd gotten in her divorce—because she'd bought it with her own money, and they hadn't been together long enough to accumulate much else—so she had to wait until she got home to see who was trying to reach her.

Then she saw that the message was from her mother.

Don't forget to lock the front door when you come in.

What the hell? Did her mother think she was still in high school?

Averil couldn't take it anymore. She was going in, signing the lease on the apartment, scanning and emailing it back to LaVeryle immediately, so she could move out as soon as possible—at the first of the month, which was only three weeks away.

After parking in her designated spot on the grass so her parents could get their vehicles in and out of the garage—after all, she was a guest in their home—she collected her purse and trudged to the door.

"You're back already?" her mother said when she came in, turning from the kitchen sink, where she was running water for dishes.

The house smelled of beef and garlic. Her mother was always cooking casseroles and putting them in the fridge so food was readily available to whoever wanted to eat. That she could simply warm up a delicious meal whenever she wanted was one of the advantages of living with her folks. But she couldn't lean on them forever. "Yeah, I'm back. Where's Mitch?"

On the way home, she'd planned to play Hungry Hippos, Operation, Husker Du or some other board game with him before bed. She was suddenly feeling like a bad mother on top of everything else, simply because she'd let her own mother take over and do so much for her son.

"I put him to bed at eight thirty, as usual," Dinah said.

Averil tossed her keys in the drawer where the scissors, tape and other utility items were kept. "And he went to sleep?"

Her mother turned off the water and looked over at her. "Why wouldn't he?"

Because he wouldn't do that for her. When *she* tried to get him to bed that early, especially when he didn't have school the following morning, he kept creeping into the hallway, trying to slip into the living room so he could watch more TV with his grandpa. Or he'd quietly close the door, turn on the light and get out his toys.

"No reason," she muttered and crossed the living room, where her father was glued to an old Western and didn't even look up.

"Is something wrong?" Dinah called. "You seem upset."

"I'm not upset," she yelled back and went into her room, closing the door behind her. Talulah was pregnant. Brant would never leave her now, and Averil would have to witness her former best friend growing big with his child—a child she'd always wanted to have.

He would never have left Talulah, anyway, she realized. She'd been hoping and dreaming for something that would never happen.

On the brink of tears, she dropped onto the bed and stared up at the ceiling, listening to the drone of the TV down the hall.

She didn't want to hear that blaring in the background, didn't want her mother putting her son to bed and then acting as though it was easy, didn't want her mother telling her to lock the front door when she came home as if she was still sixteen.

With a sigh, she got up and took the lease from the envelope she'd put in her purse. She'd just sat down at the small desk where she used to do her homework and was about to sign it when the door opened.

"Averil? What's going on?"

She was thirty five, and her mother couldn't remember to knock before coming in. "Nothing," she said. "I'm fine."

Dinah jerked her head to indicate the document she was about to sign. "What's that?"

Averil leaned back so she could see for herself.

"You're signing a lease?"

"For the apartment above Jane's store."

"Why would you do that when you can live here for free?"

"I'm feeling smothered, Mom. I have to get out, live my own life."

"Smothered! Your father and I have been good to you!"

Squeezing her eyes closed, Averil lifted her hand and took a deep breath before looking at her mother again. "Please don't start." She'd heard this lecture more times than she could count. "I realize I'm lucky to have you. And I'm grateful for all you've done, but…I have to be on my own."

"What about Mitch?"

"What about him?"

"Are you going to leave him here with us?"

"Of course not!" she cried. "He's my son."

"But you just got that new job at the feedstore. How will you work?"

"I'll bring him over so you can watch him—if…if that's still okay. Otherwise, I'll have to pay for childcare." To do that, she'd probably have to go on government assistance or something. But she didn't care. She was going to move out.

"He's used to being with me."

"And we can keep things that way. That's no problem."

Her mother glared at her. "I would like to know why you're doing this."

"Because I feel as though it's important. For my sake. For Mitch's. And it'll probably be good for you and Dad, too."

"We don't mind having you here," she said.

"I'm glad of that. I can't tell you how much I appreciate it. I just don't want to be living with my parents anymore at this age."

Her mother's lips compressed into a thin line.

"Can you let me go? Please?"

Dinah's rigid body language finally softened. "It's just…scary," she said. "We love you and Mitch so much."

"I know. You want to protect me, and you have. I'm only moving five minutes away, Mom."

Her mother finally nodded. "Okay. I understand."

The few games of pool they played turned out to be fun. Jane always enjoyed Kurt. Ranson, too—just not as much. In her opinion, he had some growing up to do.

But Kurt, who used to be far too much of a daredevil for her, had turned into the kind of man who had a calm, understated manner. He drew people to him without even trying. He also noticed certain nuances she felt escaped most other guys, which impressed her. And he had such a healthy ego he didn't mind losing. He'd go easy on his opponents at pool just to keep it competitive, wouldn't actually start trying until the end, which meant he risked being unable to pull off the win. Or he'd go ahead and let her win and pretend he hadn't.

He was such a good player, she knew what he was doing, even though he protested every time she accused him. He probably could've made a fortune as a pool hustler. But then, she got the impression he was good at most things. She admired how hard he worked at the ranch, too.

In short, the more she was around him, the more she believed she'd never find a more perfect sperm donor. She felt he would oblige her, too, if only she could leave town with the sample he gave her—or leave shortly after she was inseminated—so he'd never have to see her visibly pregnant or face the reality of the baby.

But she couldn't leave right away, couldn't even promise when that might be possible. Papa—and the unknown where he was concerned—stood in the way.

Jane texted Talulah and Ellen, hoping they'd both come to Hank's. Ellen and Hendrix, her fiancé, were backpacking in Colorado—she'd forgotten about that—but Talulah and Brant came down after closing the diner to have a drink. Talulah ordered a glass of cranberry juice, since she could no longer have alcohol, and they laughed and talked as they shot pool.

Since Ellen wasn't there, Brant was the only one who

had a chance of beating Kurt. But in three games, he only managed to do it once. Then Talulah said that after a long day at the diner she was too tired to continue standing, so they found a booth and listened to the band while talking about the baby—what sex it might be, what they might name it, if they'd be excited to learn they were having twins.

Twins didn't run in either family, so it was a long shot, but it was fun to consider.

Midnight came before Jane realized it, and everyone was ready to go home. She smiled and waved as Brant took his wife's hand and they left the bar. She thought Kurt and Ranson would leave together, too. But as they were walking to the parking lot, Kurt asked if she'd give him a ride home.

"Sure," she said.

When Ranson swayed while holding out a hand to get the keys from his brother, she worried that he might need a ride, too, and insisted they both go with her— even though it would mean they would have to return to get the truck tomorrow and cram Ranson, who was over six feet tall, into the back of her Mustang. She wanted the chance to talk to Kurt. She guessed that was why he'd suggested she drive him home. But it wasn't until they arrived at the ranch, and Ranson got out and went in, that they had some privacy.

"Tonight was a good time," she said when he looked over at her.

"I enjoyed it, too, which is why I feel so bad about what I have to tell you."

"It's okay," she said. "I've already guessed."

"I'm sorry, Jane. I wish I could do it. But knowing you were out there somewhere with my baby would be too hard. I'm afraid it's all I'd think about. I'd be so curious as to whether the baby was a girl or a boy, what he or she was like, whether you had what you needed... It just wouldn't work for me."

She felt an acute stab of disappointment in spite of expecting his refusal. After tonight, she'd wanted him to be the donor more than ever. She really liked him. But she couldn't say she didn't understand, because she did. In his place, she'd probably make the same decision.

"Well...you wouldn't want to be part of the baby's life, would you?"

The way he'd framed his response made her curious.

He sighed as he glanced away. "That route is just not how I envision... I mean, the whole concept is foreign to me."

She nodded and forced a smile, trying to be a good sport. "No worries. I knew it was a lot to ask."

"I feel doubly bad because you *didn't* ask. Not really. You just opened up to me about what you'd like to do, and I sort of volunteered—"

"We'd been drinking," she broke in, waving off his regret. "You weren't making a commitment."

"Still. I feel like I'm backing out on you."

"No. It was nice of you to even consider it."

He stared at her for several seconds, as if he wanted to say more.

"Really," she insisted. "Don't think about it again. There are other...*avenues* available to me."

"A cryobank—and what else?"

"Well, basically a cryobank," she said with a laugh. "So I have *one* avenue. But it's an avenue that should work—and it's not that expensive."

"After you get inseminated you're going to move away?"

"As soon as I can. But that depends on my grandpa, of course."

"What you're doing for him is so admirable." He rubbed his forehead. "It says a lot about who you are."

She shrugged off the compliment. "I wouldn't be who I am without him, so he did his part first."

"How do you feel about Talulah's pregnancy?" he asked. "It must be hard to be excited for her when you want a baby, too."

"Not really," she insisted.

"I don't think Averil has the same attitude."

She managed a lopsided smile. "Fortunately, I'm not in love with Brant."

"I'm glad to hear that," he said with a laugh.

She had to chuckle, too.

"What don't you like about Coyote Canyon?" he asked.

"It isn't that I don't like it," she replied. "It's a great town. But don't you ever want to get out and see more of the world?"

"Not necessarily. I'm happy here. And if I want to travel, I can do that later."

"What about meeting someone? Don't you want to get married?"

He toyed with his phone, which he had in his hand. "Eventually."

"Well, this is such a small town, it's hard to meet someone."

"What about you?" he asked. "Do you see yourself married with kids? Or just…with kids?"

"If I meet the right man, I'd love to get married," she

said. "But I don't want to hang all my hopes on that and then have it not happen."

"Got it." He reached for the door handle. "I'd better go in. Thanks for the ride. Again, I'm sorry I'm not the right man," he said and got out.

Jane stared after him. Something about his final words had given her pause. They'd seemed…loaded somehow. He meant he wasn't the right man to donate sperm, didn't he?

She shook her head as if that would rid her mind of the idea that he could've meant anything else. "Of course that was what he meant," she said aloud. "He's five years younger than me. And he went out with Kate!"

Six

When Jane got out of bed on Saturday, Papa was already up, as she'd come to expect. She found him sitting on the front porch, gazing at the mountains and enjoying an unseasonably warm morning, Otis by his side.

She was still tired from being out so late and stewing after she got home about whether she should move forward with the pregnancy—and, if so, when. It would be smart to wait another year, at least. That was the thought that kept creeping into her head, and as impatient as she'd become, she couldn't deny the wisdom of it. Then she might know more about Papa and his mental state—and whether she'd be forced to put him in a home.

One more year wouldn't matter, would it?

Yes. It felt like it would. She'd miss the experience of having a child at the same time Talulah did. And she'd rather spend the next year pregnant than get pregnant in her new city, right when she wanted to explore. Since she had at least a year to wait in Coyote Canyon, anyway, it seemed like a good use of time.

"Hey, how'd you sleep?" she asked as she carried two mugs of coffee outside with her.

"Slept great," Papa said, but the words were automatic. He'd say he slept well even if he'd been up all night. He'd never been a complainer. That was one of the characteristics of her grandfather she loved the most, and fortunately, that part of him hadn't changed as his mind deteriorated.

Not yet, anyway.

He looked up as she put his coffee in his hand. Whenever he could remember how to work the coffee maker, he'd brew a pot himself in the morning, since he got up much earlier than she did. But she'd noticed there was no coffee today.

"I'm glad," she said with a smile.

"What about you?" he asked as he brought the mug to his lips.

She felt as though she'd barely shut her eyes before her alarm went off and she wished she could go back to bed. But she had to get going. She sold more on Saturdays than any other day of the week, and she still had to prepare Papa's meals before she opened the store.

Fortunately, she wouldn't be gone as long as she was during the week. The store was open ten to six on Saturdays, instead of ten to eight. Sundays were even shorter, since she was only open from noon to five. And she was closed on Mondays.

She was already looking forward to her day off. That was when she did the majority of the cleaning, grocery shopping and meal preparation they needed to get them through the week, so she worked hard that day, too, but at least she had a break from her regular routine and could spend more time with Papa. Even though their neighbor was good to check in on him often, she was always less anxious if she was around herself. "I slept well, too."

"Don't you have to work today?"

"I do." It was only eight. She never left this early, but she didn't point that out. She sat next to him and studied the mountains as he'd been doing.

Would she miss them when she moved to San Francisco?

She supposed she would. She loved the rugged Montana countryside. She wouldn't be surprised if she wound up back in Coyote Canyon when she got older. There was just so much of the world to experience and discover before then.

"I'll leave in an hour and a half," she told him. "Aren't you hungry? Wouldn't you like me to make some breakfast before I go?"

She was mostly teasing. She cooked him breakfast every morning, even if he said he wasn't hungry.

"If you've got the time." He held up his cup. "Coffee tastes good."

He liked the way she made it, but all she did differently was grind the beans of her favorite brand instead of using the canned stuff he relied on. "Glad you're enjoying it."

"When's your grandma coming home?" he asked.

She froze. He was starting to talk about Nana a lot more lately, and most of the time he acted as though she was still alive. It always put Jane in a difficult position. She didn't know whether to remind him of the painful fact that Nana was gone for good or play along.

This morning she chose not to ruin the peace and tranquility they were enjoying. "Hopefully soon."

"I sure miss her," he said. "Seems like she's been gone a long time."

She cleared her throat so she could speak around the lump that'd formed there. "It does indeed."

They sat in silence, the obedient Otis unleashed at their feet, for the next few minutes, enjoying the beauty around them as well as their coffee. These were the moments Jane cherished, because she felt they were some of the last good moments she'd have with her grandfather.

"I thought I'd make potato tacos for dinner tonight," she commented. "What do you think?"

"I think that's a good idea."

"And Nana's salsa to go with them."

He didn't ask why Nana wouldn't be making the salsa herself. If he was expecting Ruby back, that would be a logical question. But he wove in and out of reality, probably knew even as he'd asked when she'd be coming home that there was something futile about it—that it was more hope and longing on his part than anything else. "That sounds even better," he said with a nostalgic smile.

They talked about getting some more horses. He said he missed having them, so Jane told him she'd look into it, even though she had no plans to do so. Then he pointed out the antics of a prairie dog burrowing to one side of the driveway, and they chuckled.

When the prairie dog disappeared from view, she told him she'd sold the dresser they'd refinished together. He asked when they'd be working on something else, and she assured him she was always on the lookout for their next project.

After they'd both finished their coffee, she took his cup, but before she got up, she said, "Papa?"

He turned his head to look at her.

"How would you feel if I were to have a baby?"

A baffled look came over his face. "I thought it was Kate who had a man."

She set both cups on the small table between them,

scooted forward in her chair and reached out to take his hand. "It is. But I'm getting older, and I don't have any prospects for marriage—not in the near future. What would you think if I were to have a baby anyway?"

"On purpose?" he said with a scowl.

She smiled as she nodded. "Have you ever heard of a sperm bank?"

"I've heard of it…"

But to him it was probably like asking if he'd heard that Elon Musk was planning to start a colony on Mars— it was that "out there."

"If I use one, I could have a baby. I wouldn't have to wait anymore. I wouldn't have to wonder if I was ever going to become a mother. I wouldn't have to risk missing out."

She thought he might find what she was saying so radical he'd start swearing about how crazy the world was getting and that the younger generations didn't know what they were doing. He went off like that occasionally, when he encountered something that was completely out of his comfort zone—like a girl wearing big gauges or tattooing or piercing her face.

But he remained peaceful as he stared down at their clasped hands. She felt like it was the comfort of that physical contact that grounded him, calmed him. "I'd help you in whatever way I could, sweetie," he said. "You know that, don't you?"

She lifted his hand to kiss his knuckles. "Yes, I know," she said, but would he even remember having this conversation?

Thanks to the warm weather, the first breath of spring, the store was as busy as Jane hoped it would be. She sold a couple of lamps she'd found at an estate sale, a leather side chair she'd moved in from the storage room just last week, two scented candles, an entire collection of arty pink French dishware and several other gift items—all before noon. She hoped her luck would hold out. The more successful she was, the more money she could save and the more she'd be able to offer a child.

She was just eyeing the clock, trying to figure out when there might be a lull in foot traffic so she could close for a few minutes and run down the street to get lunch when her sister walked into the store with a bag smelling like that problem had been solved.

"Brought you a sandwich," Kate announced as she set it on the register desk.

Jane opened the top of the sack and peered inside. Kate had brought her a Philly cheesesteak sandwich— her favorite offering from the small deli inside Vidlar's, the five-and-dime-type store where Kate worked as a pharmacy technician—and some chips. "You must've read my mind," she said. "I was in too big a hurry to eat with Papa this morning, and I was beginning to sorely regret it."

Kate had her long blond hair in a loose bun on top of her head and was dressed in her work smock with "Vidlar's" stitched on the pocket over her left breast. She'd worn glasses for years but always chose an especially stylish frame. When they were together, Jane heard comments about how much they looked alike, but she couldn't see it. They each resembled their fathers.

Her sister jerked her head toward two women who were in the corner of the store bent over a glass case containing vintage jewelry. "Has it been busy?"

Jane nodded. "So busy that I was hesitant to close for lunch."

"Well, I was grateful to have an excuse to get out of the pharmacy, so this works for both of us."

There was a lot of drama where Kate worked. The pharmacist she helped was in his fifties, and he was married, but he stayed fit and seemed interested in attracting younger women. At any rate, he kept saying inappropriate things to her. She'd finally complained about it to the store owners—Mauve and Bing Vidlar, some of the wealthiest citizens in Coyote Canyon—but they hadn't done much about it. In such a small community, it would be difficult to find another licensed pharmacist to take over for Leon Johnson. They couldn't lose him. From what Kate had told Jane, they'd said they'd speak to him about his behavior, but nothing had changed, and she was reluctant to press them too hard. She had a job with hours she liked and decent pay, and there weren't a lot of better alternatives for her in town. She was afraid they'd solve the problem by finding an excuse to fire *her* and hire a dude instead, so the same thing couldn't happen again, right when she was saving for her wedding.

"What's going on at Vidlar's today?" Jane asked.

Kate lowered her voice so the women who were browsing the store couldn't hear. "Leon's been driving me nuts."

Jane shoved up the sleeves on her sweater before taking out her sandwich and unwrapping the paper. "What's he doing now? Don't tell me he's been trying to get you to go to another pharmaceutical seminar with him."

"No. Now that I'm with Will, he's given up on that. But he's still says stuff that makes me uncomfortable."

"Like…"

"Mostly innuendos. He thinks he's being clever because if I ever complain about him again and tell the Vidlars what he said, he could claim he meant something entirely different than the way I interpreted his words. Lately, he's been coming in with a new blonde joke every day, too."

Jane's hair was also long and blond. "Trying to establish what he considers his mental superiority?"

"I guess," Kate replied. "It's not like he gropes me or anything—or drives past my house at all hours of the night. Nothing I can really point to if someone were to ask me what he does wrong. It's more subtle than that. He just gives me too much attention—or requires too much of *my* attention."

"I'm surprised Will hasn't asked you to quit." Jane liked her sister's boyfriend. A horse trainer and farrier, he used to ride in the rodeo and seemed to be a good man. He was certainly protective of her.

"He *would* be bugging me to quit if I told him all the things I've told you. But I haven't, because I don't want to be looking for a job before the wedding."

Jane opened the bag of chips. "Maybe it'd be worth it."

"On days like today I might agree. But, fortunately, Leon's usually too busy to get on my nerves *this* much."

"Not many prescriptions being filled today—even though it's Saturday?"

"Not that we didn't anticipate and get ready for during the week."

"I see." Jane typically closed for lunch. But the two customers she had weren't paying her any attention, so she felt it would be okay to go ahead and eat. Settling on the stool behind the register, she took a bite of her sandwich. "God, this is good. I'll Venmo you."

"Don't worry about it. The Vidlars cover one meal per shift if we get it at the deli."

"I don't want to eat *your* lunch—"

"It's okay. I had a burrito. I needed a change. As good as their sandwiches are, you get tired of them if that's all you ever eat."

"That's a nice problem to have," she commented as she chewed. "Thanks for thinking of me."

One of the women asked to see a necklace. Jane stood, but Kate waved for her to continue eating, took the key and opened the case.

"I love black onyx," Jane heard the woman say to her friend right before she brought the necklace to the register and bought it.

The bell rang over the door as the woman and her friend left, and Kate checked her watch. "I only have a few more minutes. But I wanted to see which days you needed me to watch Papa next week."

Since Jane worked later on weekdays, Kate came over to sit with him when she could. Otherwise, he'd be alone for too many long stretches, even with the neighbor looking in on him regularly. "Can you do Tuesday and Thursday again? That seems to break up the week nicely."

"I think so. I forgot to tell you I brought a puzzle with me last time, thinking he'd really enjoy it. We used to do a new puzzle at Nana and Papa's every Christmas, remember? But once I spread it out on the table, he just sat there, looking at all the pieces. I don't think he could figure out how to do it anymore," she said sadly. "And it wasn't any fun for me to do it alone."

Jane swallowed what was in her mouth. "I didn't see it when I got home…"

"I packed it up and put it in the games cupboard before I left. I didn't think it would make him feel good to have it sitting there, staring at him."

"I can barely get him to play cards with me these days," Jane confessed. "Not even canasta. And he used to love that game. I think he's struggling to remember the rules but doesn't want to say so."

Kate sighed. "What are we going to do?"

"I'm afraid there's nothing we can do." Jane took another bite of her sandwich. "I signed the extension on the lease for this place, so…we'll just keep doing our best to make him comfortable and happy."

"For how long?" her sister asked.

"I don't know."

Kate gave her a remonstrative look. "Jane, as nice as it is of you to make the sacrifices you're making, Mom and Dad really want you to be free to move on with your life."

"I appreciate that." She plucked a chip from the bag. "But do you think Mom would feel the same if we were talking about one of her parents?"

Luckily, their grandparents on that side were alive and well, playing pickleball, traveling and enjoying their retirement.

"Maybe not," Kate admitted. "Heaven forbid it was her—or Dad—who needed the help. But I have to be honest. It's enraging that your father doesn't do *anything* for Papa—that the entire responsibility of looking after him falls on you."

"*You* help me out."

"Four to six hours a week is nothing compared to what you do."

"It's enough to get me by."

"I'm happy to hear that, but it should still be your dad's place to make the decisions you're making."

"I learned a long time ago not to expect anything from him."

A man and a woman eating ice cream cones while sauntering down the sidewalk outside looked like they were about to come in. The woman put a hand on the door, but the man said something and drew her away.

While Jane wanted as much business as she could get, she was glad of the respite. It provided her with more time to finish her lunch and visit with her sister. "Any plans for tonight?" she asked Kate.

"Will's grilling steaks."

It seemed like Kate was never available. If she wasn't working, she was with her boyfriend, whom she lived with these days. Will even joined her on the evenings she spent with Papa—some of the time, anyway.

It'd been lonely since her sister had fallen in love; it made what Jane was going through worse. But her sister was so happy she couldn't complain.

"What about you?" Kate asked. "What are you doing tonight?"

Jane's social life had dwindled to almost nothing. Talulah was busy with her business and her marriage. Ellen was in a similar situation. Averil was probably available more than Ellen or Talulah, but she'd become so sullen and angry. That was why Jane had been hanging out with Kurt. He had two single brothers, so he had more options than she did, but he worked with them all day and seemed eager enough to spend time with her instead. At least, that was the routine they'd fallen into. "I'll probably watch a movie with Papa," she said. "I was out last night, and I don't like to leave him alone all weekend."

She also didn't have any invitations...

"What'd you do when you went out last night?" Kate asked.

"Averil and I went to Hank's for a bit."

"Averil!" her sister exclaimed. "I thought you two had drifted apart."

"We have, but she's moving into the apartment above the store, so she was here looking at the place and asked if I'd like to get a drink. We went to Hank's, but she left after only an hour—as soon as Kurt and Ranson showed up and announced that Talulah's pregnant."

Kate's eyebrows shot up. *"Talulah's pregnant?"*

"You haven't heard?"

"No. When did she find out she was expecting?"

"A few days ago."

"Then that *is* strange. The rumor mill around here usually works a lot faster," she said jokingly as she stole one of Jane's chips. "Brant must be excited."

"He is."

"How do *you* feel about it?"

Startled by the question, Jane swallowed. "I'm happy for her. Why wouldn't I be?"

"It's not easy seeing your friends enter a new stage of life when you feel as though you're stuck where you'd rather not be, especially when it's due to circumstances beyond your control."

Jane hadn't realized her pathetic situation was quite that apparent. She did have a thriving business, after all. In her view, that put her ahead of Averil and Kate, at least in one category. They both had jobs she wouldn't want. "Maybe I'll *take* control," she said.

Uncomprehending, her sister blinked at her. "We've tried and tried to get you to move Papa into a facility so you can head to San Francisco or wherever you want to go. You won't do it."

"That's not what I mean."

"Then what *do* you mean?"

Jane took a drink from her water bottle. "Nothing."

Her sister gave her a funny look, as if she wanted to press her on the subject, but she was out of time. "We'll have to talk about it later," she said as she moved to the door. "I can't be late, can't give the asshole I work with a legitimate excuse to complain to the Vidlars about *me*."

"Okay." Jane wadded up the paper that'd been used to wrap her sandwich and tossed it in the wastebasket. "Thanks for bringing me lunch."

Kate had her hand on the door when Jane called her name.

"What?" she said, turning.

"You've always liked Kurt, right?"

"Elway? For the most part. I mean, we've had our frustrations with each other over the years, but…we're friends now. Why?"

Jane tightened her grip on her water bottle. "Did you two ever…you know…sleep together?"

Her sister's face flushed. "What makes you ask me *that*? Has he said something to you about it?"

"No. Not a word. I just…don't remember you talking about it."

"Because we could never get on the same page. I'd be into him when he was interested in someone else. Then he'd be into me when I was interested in someone else."

Jane couldn't help feeling some disappointment. "But you *did* sleep with him." Somehow, it suddenly seemed important to clarify that.

"Once or twice, if you must know, but the first time

was when I was on the rebound after David Polk cheated on me. I was so heartbroken I slept with Kurt *and* Eugene Dreyfus in about a two-week span." She chuckled self-consciously. "That's embarrassing to admit, but I was hurting so badly I would've done anything to numb the pain."

"So you and Kurt were mostly…friends?"

"We were friends and then we weren't. We were more and then we weren't. It's complicated, because it went back and forth so much, which even made us enemies at times. But ultimately, it wasn't meant to be. Why?"

Jane couldn't help remembering Kurt's comment right before he got out of her car last night: *I'm sorry I'm not the right man.* "Just curious."

Her sister looked perplexed. "You're not interested in Kurt…"

"Of course not!" she said, so Kate wouldn't think she was desperate enough to go after one of her old boyfriends.

Kate's expression immediately cleared. "Good, because we have enough history I'd feel so uncomfortable."

That was what Jane had been wondering: if—hypothetically and thinking *way* outside the box—she ever allowed the line between her and Kurt to blur, would a more intimate relationship make things awkward between her and her sister?

Now she had her answer.

"And you know you'd never be able to leave Coyote Canyon if you got with him," Kate continued. "That ranch is his whole life—all he's ever done and all he knows. He'd never leave it, so you could kiss all your dreams of adventure goodbye."

"I wasn't asking for that reason," Jane said. "We've

become friends, and since I see him quite a bit, I was curious how you felt about him. That's all."

"Got it." She opened the door. "Text me next time you can't get out of the store for lunch. Don't go hungry—I'm happy to bring you a sandwich anytime."

"Thanks." The door swung shut after her sister left, and Jane had a moment alone, before another customer came in. She walked to the front window and stared out at the street beyond, which was far busier than usual. Too bad circumstances weren't slightly different where Kurt Elway was concerned, she thought. She knew how nice he was. And he was certainly attractive. Regardless of his age and prior affiliation with her sister, she had to admit that.

Seven

It was nearly dinnertime on Monday. Kurt was cleaning his horse's hooves, eager to finish up for the day so he could go in and eat—his mother had been over this morning and made lasagna—when Brant entered the barn.

"So what'd you decide?" his brother asked.

Kurt continued to hold Poseidon's hoof while using the metal pick. "'Bout what?"

"That question you were asking me the other day when you were wiring up the generator—if I'd do something sort of unconventional for Talulah if she asked me to, something that made me uncomfortable."

Grateful he had a good excuse for not looking his brother in the eye, Kurt moved to his horse's second hoof and pulled the hairs of Poseidon's fetlock to let him know what he wanted. "Forget about that," he said as he removed the dirt and grass, being careful to clean the sole and collateral groove without digging into the triangular part of the foot called the frog. "It was nothing."

"It was a strange question—that's what it was," Brant said. "And it has me a little worried."

"Come on. You know I wouldn't do anything you wouldn't do," Kurt said jokingly.

Brant leaned against the stall, resting his arms along the top rail. "The last time I relied on the idea that you knew how to take care of yourself, you ignored the Out of Bounds signs that were clearly posted on the ski slope, fell down a deep crevasse and nearly froze to death."

"Don't be so dramatic," he grumbled.

"I'm not being dramatic," Brant said. "You could've died!"

"But I didn't. I made it out."

When Kurt started to move to the other side of his horse, Brant reached out and grabbed his shoulder. "Smart is always better than lucky—at least in the long run. So what's going on now? Who were you talking about that day? Jane, right? What could she possibly want you to do that would make you uncomfortable?"

Kurt had planned to keep it to himself. He knew Brant would probably tell Talulah. But he was so torn about having refused Jane when he really wanted to get close to her, that he needed Brant to tell him he'd done the right thing. "She wants me to give her a baby."

Brant let go of him and stepped back in surprise. "*What?* You two aren't even a couple. Are you?"

"No. That's the thing. She's not asking for a relationship—only a genetic donation."

"In other words, she wants to have your baby, but she doesn't want to sleep with you…"

"Thanks for putting it so delicately. You wouldn't want to damage my ego."

Brant ignored the sarcasm. "I just want to be sure I have this straight. You're talking about artificial insemination?"

"Yeah."

"Why would she do something like that?"

Kurt sighed. "She wants a baby. She's staring her grandfather's death in the face, watching him go downhill, and it's frightening. It makes her more motivated to be sure she's getting everything she can out of her own life."

"And that includes a child."

"Apparently."

"Which beats a sperm bank."

"For her it does. And I can see why she'd want someone she knows."

Brant began to pace at the end of the stall. "Wow…"

"It didn't sound so shocking when I'd had several drinks in me," Kurt admitted. "She'd been drinking, too, when she told me about it. That was when the subject first came up."

Brant shook his head disbelievingly. "Why not wait for it to happen the usual way?"

"Because she's worried it won't happen, not while she's stuck in a small town where almost everyone else our age has already paired off."

"*Our* age?" he echoed.

Kurt shot him a dirty look. "*Her* age, okay?"

"Although…" Brant kicked a tuft of hay from one side to the other with his boots. "In this case, you being so much younger is a good thing."

"*So* much younger?" Brant was trying to needle him, and Kurt knew it.

"Five years is five years."

Kurt didn't bother arguing about that. He was too interested in where his brother was going with this. "Why's it good?"

"Better sperm."

"Thanks." He smiled broadly. "I knew I had you beat in *something*. If you and Talulah need a donation for your next kid, be sure to let me know."

Brant rolled his eyes. "That was a general statement."

Kurt curved his lips into a cocky grin. "Doesn't make it untrue in this specific circumstance."

"Just tell me you refused," his brother said. "I mean, that could create so many freaking problems…"

"I refused, but…"

"What?"

"I can't quit thinking about her," he admitted. "The more I'm around her, the more I want to be around her."

"I'm not sure I've ever seen you crush on a woman quite this hard…"

"If that's what you want to call it. I've always liked her, but it hasn't been until recently that she's shown any interest in even hanging out with me."

Brant rubbed his chin.

"What are you thinking?" Kurt asked.

"I'm thinking Talulah will know what to do."

Kurt circled Poseidon to finish cleaning his feet but was too intent on getting the answer he needed from his brother to actually do anything. "No. You can't tell her. I don't want her saying anything to Jane, and you know she would."

"Fine. I won't tell her about the baby request—"

"Swear it," Kurt insisted, looking at his brother over his horse's back. "Swear it or I'll never trust you with anything again as long as I live."

"Relax!" Brant snapped with an impatient scowl. "I'll just tell her you're interested in Jane. I want to see if she thinks you two would ever have a chance as a couple. Maybe that'll make a difference."

Relieved, Kurt picked up Poseidon's foot so he could finish what he'd started. "How?"

"Well, I know Jane's a good person. And I know you're a good person. I guess there's no absolute reason a relationship between you couldn't work. Except…I've heard a lot about her wanting to move away from here. What will you do if you get together, and she doesn't change her mind about going?"

"I'd probably regret getting involved with her," Kurt admitted.

His brother frowned at him. "You really want to take that chance?"

No, he told himself. He didn't. It would be smarter to stay away, avoid the potential heartbreak of losing a relationship he wanted. Or having a child he rarely—if ever—saw. Avoiding that risk was what most guys would do. He wasn't holding a good hand.

But since when had he ever been afraid of risk?

"She's here now," he said with a shrug.

"You want me to talk to Talulah? See if she might be able to set up a double date or something? We could have you both over for dinner."

Would something like a date make a difference? Maybe if Jane felt she had Talulah and Brant's support and approval where he was concerned, it would make her more open to the idea of dating him…

"You'd do that?" Kurt asked. "Without telling her about the baby?"

A devilish expression appeared on his brother's face. "If you'll go move the cattle for me."

Kurt groaned. "I just took the saddle off Poseidon."

Brant jerked his head toward the door. "Lady's tied up outside."

"Really? You're going to make me do this?"

"How much do you like Jane?" he asked as he laughed.

"You're an ass. I never should've told you."

His brother's grin only widened. "But you did, and now I have the chance to get out of here. I'd like to surprise Talulah when she gets home from the diner—have a nice dinner made, lots of flowers, chocolates. I'm so bad at all that stuff it's going to take me an eternity."

How could Kurt say no? Brant was so excited he and Talulah were going to have a child. Double date aside, they deserved some time to have a little celebration.

"Damn it," he grumbled by way of acquiescing and Brant followed him out of the barn, chuckling.

"You'd better deliver big time," Kurt told him as he swung up onto Lady.

"I can promise dinner will be good," Brant responded. "The rest is a gamble, and you know it."

Kurt shot him a dirty look as he wheeled the horse around to head back out onto the ranch. But he didn't end up minding the extra work, because he spent the time daydreaming about finally having the chance to touch Jane.

What if Talulah's involvement really could make a difference?

LaVeryle gave Averil permission to move in early. Just knowing she was getting out on her own again had given her a far more positive mindset. She received a call from Jordan as she was packing her car and was able to ignore it, which signaled an emotional shift. She'd been so lonely and desperate over the past year she'd continued seeing him even after she realized Ellen was right. Even though he was a dentist and supposedly respectable, he was a total narcissist, no one she should ever get serious about.

At least he'd given her someone to go out with on occasion—not that their last evening together had turned out well. They'd gone to dinner in Libby, where he lived, and ended up having a big argument at his place afterward about how he'd treated their server.

Trying to shake off the irritation and frustration he caused, she got out and hauled a box out of her back seat.

Jane must've heard her come through the back door because she climbed the stairs right after Averil let herself into the apartment.

"Hey, you're moving in already?"

Averil set down the box she was carrying—filled with dishes, as she'd decided to start with the kitchen stuff she had stored in her parents' garage—and dusted off her hands. "LaVeryle said I might as well. It was just sitting here empty."

"So she gave you the key early—before your lease even starts?"

"Yep. Said I could have the next three weeks to get settled."

"She's such a nice person."

Averil wandered through the empty rooms—and saw freedom. The only downside of moving into the apartment was having Jane so close. Initially, she'd counted that as a benefit, had hoped it might restore their friendship and help her patch the rift between her and Talulah. But after learning of Talulah's pregnancy, she knew being so close to her two friends—former friends, for the most part—

would just evoke more jealousy. And she was already grappling with enough of that. "She really is."

"Do you have more boxes to bring up? I can help."

"There're more in the car. But can you leave the store unattended?"

"The store's not open today. I'm only here because I had to go to the grocery store and had a few things to drop off that've been shifting around in my trunk, getting on my nerves."

"More merchandise?"

"Yeah. Some of the wooden signs Peter Hankel engraves."

"He sells his stuff in the boot shop down the street, right? Isn't it too Western for you?"

"It is, but I asked him to scale back a bit on some of those elements. His wife's in rehab again and facing liver failure, and I felt so sorry for him I thought I might be able to help him make more money if I showed people how his signs can fit in with more modern decor."

"That's really nice of you."

"It's the least I can do. Poor guy's in such a mess."

They tromped back and forth to the car until they'd unloaded everything and carried it up. Then they stood in the apartment and looked at the pile they'd created.

"How much more do you have to bring over?" Jane asked.

"Several loads. But there's no hurry. I feel better just knowing I'll be here soon."

"How'd your mother take the news that you're moving out?"

"She's not too happy about it. She loves having Mitch there, didn't expect me to find my own place so soon. But I think she understands."

"I'm happy you're able to do it," Jane said. "It'll be good for you."

Was Jane being sincere? That was the other thing that plagued Averil of late. Insecurity. Feeling as though her friends no longer wanted to be around her because of the way she'd behaved. She still cringed whenever she remembered Ellen overhearing her talking about Talulah at the grocery store and making a scene...

She pulled her car keys from her pocket. She had to pick up her son from school. "Thanks for the help."

When Jane smiled, it gave Averil hope once again that she might be able to repair their friendship. She'd lost so much, been her own worst enemy. And yet she couldn't figure out how to overcome her own anger and resentment—and the anger and resentment she'd evoked in others—which had kept her so isolated. "Do you think I'll *ever* get over Brant?" she asked.

Jane seemed surprised she'd been so open and transparent. "I'm sure you will. They say time heals all wounds..."

Averil frowned. "How much time does it take? That's the question. Because nothing seems to change. I never got the man I wanted—and I lost you and Talulah along the way."

Jane pulled her in for an embrace. "Don't say that, Av. You haven't lost us. Friendship is more resilient than that. We'll get beyond what's happened eventually."

Averil wanted to believe her, but the reality of the past year was working against her.

Jane could already feel the pressure. She was going to have Averil living above the store, feeling hurt and left out, still angry and jealous over Brant, while Talulah was working down the street, expecting the relationship they'd reestablished over the past year to continue without change or challenge. How would she juggle a relationship with both?

She wasn't convinced it was possible to do that without one emotional flare-up after another interrupting her peaceful routine, and she didn't need any more emotional flare-ups in her life.

She stood at the counter, making crust for a pecan pie, wishing she could finally move to San Francisco. She used her grandmother's recipes whenever she could—to bring Papa comfort through the food he'd always loved. When she arrived home, he'd been sitting on the porch with Otis at his feet, looking lost. But fortunately, he'd perked up the instant he saw her and insisted on helping her carry in the groceries.

Normally, she took him shopping with her to get him out of the house. He'd lived in Coyote Canyon for more than fifty years and liked seeing the old friends and acquaintances he'd run into when they were in town. Once every six weeks, she'd take him to Sally's to have his hair cut before heading home. The barbershop was closed on Mondays, but Sally worked out of her house, so she was willing to do it when Jane was off work.

Jane had been hoping to get his hair trimmed today, but he'd been particularly confused this morning and refused to go anywhere, saying that he didn't want to miss Nana when she came back.

Since Jane couldn't convince him that he wouldn't miss Nana, she'd let him stay home rather than trying to force him to get in the car. She could take him to get his hair cut another time. Sally insisted that would be fine, that she was flexible. Jane would see if he'd at least be willing to go on a drive with her tonight. She felt he needed to get out of the house every once in a while, and he rarely refused a trip to the mountains. But the notion that his wife of fifty-three years might be returning had shackled him to the property.

Now he was trying to put away the groceries. She was pretending to let him handle it, but since he wasn't putting most items in their proper place, she had to keep a close eye on him. Otherwise, she wouldn't know where to find what she'd purchased. When he put a frozen chicken pot pie in the pantry, for instance, she had to secretly slip in after he turned away and stuff it in the freezer, where it belonged.

"What is it you're making again?" he asked as he folded up the paper sacks.

"Pecan pie," she told him, even though there was a large bag of pecans on the table that should've reminded him. "Isn't it your favorite?"

"I love all kinds of pie," he said. "Hard to pick a favorite."

"No one made better pies than Nana." She brought up her grandmother often, because Ruby deserved to be remembered and because it gave Papa a chance to feel as though his wife was still close.

"She taught *you* well," he said proudly, and Jane smiled.

Using a pastry blender, she began to cut the butter into the flour. "Have I told you that Averil is moving into my old apartment?"

"Above the store?"

She'd lived there for ten years, so Jane was grateful he remembered. It gave her hope that his mind wasn't getting as bad as she thought. "Yep."

He looked perplexed. "Does she want you to move in with her?"

"No. She has her son, Mitch."

"I don't know Mitch," he said.

"You haven't seen much of him." *She* hadn't seen much of Mitch, either—not since Talulah moved back and the tension between Averil and Talulah intensified. "He's a cute kid."

Otis put a paw on her leg. A brown labradoodle Papa had adopted five years ago from a neighbor who was moving to the city, he was the perfect companion for an elderly man—devoted and gentle. She stopped what she was doing long enough to give him a scratch under the collar, since he was obviously looking for some attention.

"Is she married?" Papa asked as she washed her hands so she could get back to the pie.

"Averil? She's divorced." She almost added, *Remember?* But she'd promised herself she'd quit reminding him of all the things he was forgetting. It had to add stress to his life to know his mind was slipping, and she didn't want to be demeaning.

"Oh, that's right," he said. "And your other friend— Talulah—is having a baby."

She looked up. Did he remember she'd told him *she* wanted to have a baby? "Yes."

Her phone went off. She hesitated because she'd just washed her hands and didn't want to have to do it again before finishing the crust, but it was Talulah, who was also off on Mondays, and she wanted to invite her and Brant over for the dinner she was making. People, laughter, stimulating conversation—she felt all those things were good for Papa. And Lord knew *she* needed the social interaction herself.

Grabbing her phone before the call could transfer to voice mail, she hit the talk button. "Hello?"

"What are you up to today?"

"Making a pecan pie. Would you and Brant like to join me and Papa for dinner tonight?"

"I'm afraid we already have plans," Talulah said. "But it's funny you should ask me that, because I was calling to invite *you* to dinner—next Monday."

The dessert diner was closed on Mondays and Tuesdays, but they both had Mondays off, so that was the best day to get together—beyond the impromptu visits they shared when they appeared at each other's businesses. "Sure," Jane said. "What can I bring?"

"Nothing," Talulah replied. "I've got it. But I should probably prepare you—it's a double date."

Jane tucked a loose strand of hair behind her ear to get it out of her face. "You're setting me up?"

"I am."

"No one's tried to do that in a long time. Where's he from?"

"You'll see."

"You're not going to tell me?"

"Nope."

"That's a little alarming, to be honest," she said jokingly. "Why can't I know more?"

"Because I want you to be totally surprised."

"You think I'll like this guy?"

"I do."

Talulah had good taste, which was reassuring, at least. "Is he local?"

"You'll see."

She guessed he didn't live in Coyote Canyon, that he

was someone Brant had met buying or selling cattle, feed or ranch equipment. "Is he your friend—or Brant's?"

"We both like him."

"Interesting. Where'd you meet him?"

"I've said enough. Just…trust me. I would never lead you astray."

Jane believed that to be true, which caused her spirits to rise. She'd assumed she'd have a very difficult year ahead. She had no clear direction on whether she should have a baby on her own. Averil had leased the apartment she used to live in, effectively cutting off her retreat, should she need one. And Papa had refused to go with her to get his hair cut today because he was waiting for a woman who'd died ten years ago to come home.

Sometimes the best things in life happen when you least expect them, her Nana used to say.

Maybe, in this case, that would prove to be true.

"Okay," she said. "I'll be patient and look for something to wear."

Eight

The text Kurt received from Jane on Tuesday night, asking if he was interested in getting a drink after work, was unexpected. He was afraid Talulah or Brant had told her *he* was the one who'd be joining them for dinner the following Monday, and that Jane was going to try to let him down easy before backing out.

But after he arrived at Hank's, she told him Brant and Talulah were setting her up with someone—and sounded excited about it. That was when he realized she had no clue it was him.

"What do you think I should wear?" she asked.

He wasn't sure how to answer that question. Revealing the truth could potentially ruin what Talulah was trying to do for him. But answering without telling her *he* was her date seemed deceptive.

He lifted his beer and took a long pull so he wouldn't have to maintain eye contact. "I don't think it really matters," he said. "You always look great."

"Blind dates are the worst," she complained.

The beer in his mouth went down with a hard swallow. "It's just one night," he said. "If you don't like the dude, you don't have to go out with him again."

She grimaced. "It's just awkward, you know?"

He set his beer on the table and began peeling off the label. "When's the last time you were in a relationship?"

"A serious relationship? I've had a few steady boyfriends through the years, but I couldn't classify any of them as serious, especially those in the last ten years." She looked thoughtful as she added, "The span of my romantic relationships seems to be getting shorter and shorter as I grow older. What's up with that?"

"The older you get, the busier you get, I guess. Your friends start marrying off. You go out less and less." He shrugged. "The pool of possibilities shrinks."

"And here I was hoping you were going to cheer me up," she said wryly.

"What about sex?" He'd never brought up this subject with her before, but he thought of it constantly, of course—had wanted her in that way for so long.

"What about it?"

"How long's it been for you?"

"Three years." She sighed. "Feels like an eternity..."

His body immediately reacted to her response. He was more than willing to bring that eternity to an end, but he knew she didn't look at him as a potential sex partner. "Don't you miss it?" he asked, peeling more of the label.

"Of course I miss it. But what can I do? We live in a small town, which doesn't afford us a lot of opportunities. You didn't include that on your list of reasons we're both on our own, but it's definitely a factor."

"Is that why you're so set on moving?"

"I'm set on moving so that I don't live and die in the

same small town without ever experiencing the bigger world."

"Won't experiencing the bigger world be hard to do with a child?"

"It won't be as easy as doing it by myself, but other people have children and make the most of life. Besides, I want to share what I find with someone. I can make it work."

He took another drink of his beer. "You've never considered marrying any of the guys you dated?"

"Nope. That magic has never been there." She frowned. "Maybe there's something wrong with me, and not them. What about you? Have you ever been close to proposing?"

He shook his head.

"It's so hard to meet the right person," she complained. "How do you know if they'll love you even when times get hard? How do you know you'll be satisfied with them *for life*? How do you know you won't outgrow them or vice versa?" She lowered her voice, giving her next words a greater dramatic impact. "How do you know they won't turn out to be John Wayne Gacy?"

"John Wayne Gacy?" he repeated. "I've never met him. Is that someone who lives around here?"

"No. He was a serial killer who murdered more than thirty young men and hid them under his house *while he was married*."

"His wife had no clue?"

"Apparently not. He owned a business, too."

Kurt winced. "That's an extreme example."

She lifted her glass. "I'm just saying…you never know what you're getting."

"Brant and Talulah seem happy."

"My grandma and grandpa were happy, too," she conceded. "But couples like that are extremely rare. Then Nana died, and Papa's been miserable ever since. It's been *ten years*, and he's still waiting for her to come back." She sipped from her glass of wine. "I'm not sure I want to sign up for that."

"Children can bring grief, too," he pointed out.

She opened her mouth as though she'd refute his statement but closed it again.

"Life is risk, Jane. I mean, what are you really afraid of? You can't seriously think you're going to marry a serial killer."

"I guess I'm afraid I'll get someone like my father— a smooth talker, someone who's handsome and seems wonderful on the surface but is really a parasite." She took another sip of her drink. "Besides, a serial killer *is* a possibility. Anything's a possibility."

He chuckled. "I don't think I've ever known anyone more afraid of love."

"I'm not afraid of love, I'm just—"

"Afraid of love," he finished for her.

She rolled her eyes. "I'm afraid of making a mistake."

"Is that why you want a child?"

"What do you mean?"

"You crave love, but only the love of a child feels safe?"

She made a show of looking under the table. "Damn. Did you come up with that all on your own?"

He rolled his eyes right back at her. "You're not that hard to figure out."

"I just never pegged you as someone who was into psychoanalysis," she said with a laugh.

"Maybe you don't know me that well." He wanted to

add that maybe he could surprise her in a good way, but he was afraid that would reveal too much.

"Without You" came on. It was an old song. Kurt couldn't remember the name of the artist, but his parents had listened to it over and over while he was growing up, so it was familiar to him. It was also the first slow song he'd heard since they arrived.

Spontaneously, because he felt talking was only getting him into trouble—he knew he'd have to answer for all the things he *wasn't* saying on Monday—he got up and held out his hand. "Let's dance."

She blinked at him. During the past several months, they'd played pool and darts and enjoyed plenty of food and drink at Hank's, but he'd never asked her to dance. He typically avoided that type of thing. He wasn't good at it. But the place was almost empty, and anyone could handle a slow song.

"Okay," she said and took his hand.

He'd let himself enjoy holding her in his arms this one time, he told himself. Then he'd break the disappointing news that *he* was her date for Monday and walk away and leave her alone.

But as the song came to a close, he couldn't bring the words to his lips.

"Kurt?" Jane said.

His gaze had shifted to her lips. When he heard his name, he lifted it to her eyes. "What?"

The lines that appeared on her forehead showed confusion. "The song's over."

"Oh, right." He let go of her. "Sorry, I was…I was thinking about something else."

"What?" she asked, sounding perplexed.

He'd been imagining what it might be like to kiss her.

He'd wanted to do it for so long, and the desire only grew stronger the more time they spent together. "Just…work stuff," he mumbled and led the way back to the table.

It felt like Jane had barely fallen asleep when she heard someone at the front door.

She lifted her head to check the time on her alarm clock and saw that it was nearly two in the morning. Afraid Papa had gotten up and was going outside, she threw off the covers and hurried from her room, only to discover her sister coming down the dark hallway.

"What are you doing?" she asked with a startled gasp when they nearly collided.

Kate tried to answer but burst into tears instead.

As usual, Otis was shut in the room with Papa. He whined, aware that something was going on, but fortunately he didn't bark. Hoping they wouldn't wake their grandfather since it would mean he might not be able to go back to sleep, Jane took her sister's arm and propelled her back into the living room before whispering, "What's wrong?"

"It's Will," Kate managed to say.

A wave of concern and adrenaline passed through Jane. "He hasn't been hurt, has he?"

Kate's chest jerked as if she'd been crying for some time. "I just caught him cheating on me."

Jane was as stunned as Kate must've been. "*Will?* He would never cheat on you!"

"That's what I thought. But—" she gasped for breath "—when I got up to go to the bathroom tonight, I saw that he'd left his computer—" another breath "—on the table. I was just going to…to close it for him when I saw a message on the screen from…from another woman," she finished before dissolving completely into tears and throwing herself into Jane's arms.

Jane held her and patted her back while trying to absorb the news. Kate and Will had been so happy. They'd been planning to get married! How long had this been going on? "Did you confront him about it?" she asked.

Kate pulled away and used the back of her hand to wipe her nose. "Of course. I was…I was furious. And he…he couldn't deny it. It was all right there."

"*What* was right there?" Jane asked. "What did the woman say?"

"She said she couldn't…couldn't wait to…to see him again. And that—" she sniffed "—she'd never forget the feel of his hands on her body."

Jane led her sister farther into the living room, where they both sank onto the old, comfortable sofa. "Who is she? Where did he meet her?"

"She's a client. He shod her horse."

"Is that what he said?"

"I got that much out of him. But he wouldn't elaborate—just flew into a rage when he realized he'd been caught and couldn't lie his way out of it. Said I had no right to be snooping on his computer. I told him I hadn't been snooping, but…I don't know…it turned into the biggest—" she paused to wipe the fresh tears streaming down her cheeks "—biggest fight we've ever had."

"I'm *so* sorry," Jane said. "It's hard to believe… I mean, the way Will comes across, I would never have suspected him of anything like that."

"There was one other time when I caught him sending flirty texts to his ex-girlfriend," she admitted. "But I forgave him for that. She was someone he once cared about, after all, and it can be hard to let go. I never dreamed he was…he was having sex with a client."

"Are you sure it went that far?" Jane asked.

She nodded. "Once I saw that message come up on the screen, I put in his password—he uses the same one for everything—and read the whole exchange."

Jane grimaced. "Oh God…"

"Exactly. It was explicit and—" she put a hand on her stomach "—sickening. I actually vomited. That was what woke him up. He could hear me retching."

Jane felt like throwing up herself. "So…do you think he'll get with the woman? Is that where it was leading?"

"I don't think so," Kate said.

"Why not?"

"She's married."

Jane jumped to her feet. "You're kidding me!"

"Unfortunately, I'm not. Her husband owns an equestrian center in Livingston. That's partly what made Will so mad. I said—" more tears filled her eyes "—I was going to tell her husband."

"Oh, wow…" Jane was suddenly filled with so much energy and anger, she began to pace. "So…what are you going to do?"

"I was hoping you and Papa would let me move in with you. I don't have anywhere else to go."

She'd given up the house she'd been renting with two girlfriends five months ago when she'd decided to live with Will. So Papa's house was all they both had now. "Of course you can move in here. But…are you sure you want to go that far? You don't want to try to work things out with—" she almost said *the bastard* but quickly curbed her tongue "—Will?"

"How?" she asked. "I'd never be able to trust him again."

Jane knew she probably felt strongly about that now. But the situation could easily change. People cheated all the time—and many were forgiven for it. What was important in this moment was for Kate to feel she had an emotionally safe place to stay for as long as she wanted—and plenty of love to help her get through this crisis. "You're always welcome here. You know that."

The fourth bedroom was used for storage, mostly Nana's clothes and other personal belongings, which Jane had gathered and put there for safekeeping, but the guest bedroom was available. "Did you bring a suitcase or a bag or anything? Do you need me to get it from the car?"

Additional tears rolled down her face as she shook her head. "I didn't take the time to gather anything. I don't even have my makeup. I couldn't think straight. What I'd seen hurt too bad. I just…walked out."

"I can go back with you tomorrow and help you pack."

"If he'll even let me get my stuff."

"He'd better," Jane said and meant it. Nothing would make her angrier. "He was the one who cheated, not you."

"I *hate* him," Kate cried.

This was yet another example of a man appearing to be one way and turning out to be the exact opposite, Jane thought but didn't point that out.

Since her sister was obviously too upset to sleep, she turned on the TV, with the volume on low, and got a blanket from the linen closet to cover them both. Then she put her arm around Kate and sat with her as the minutes ticked away and she continued to cry until she couldn't cry any longer.

Jane was just thinking about how badly love sucked when Kate finally fell asleep and she was able to slip away to once again find her own bed.

* * *

"What's Kate doing on the couch?" Papa bellowed.

It was so early the sun hadn't even begun to creep around the blinds in the room. Jane's eyelids felt like sandpaper when she opened them to see him looming large in her doorway, with Otis sitting dutifully at his feet, wagging his tail. "Shh…" She raised a finger to her lips. "Kate, um…" She cleared her throat to be able to speak more clearly. "She and Will broke up last night."

Jane was reluctant to say why. Even if Kate could forgive Will for what he'd done, he'd hurt her badly enough that their grandfather never would, and Jane didn't want Papa to make an already bad situation worse. Kate deserved some time to assess the damage, see if Will was remorseful and decide how she was going to proceed before dealing with pressure from anyone else.

"Why?" he demanded. "Didn't you tell me they were going to have a baby?"

That was *her*. *She* wanted the baby. But in case Kate could hear what they were saying, she didn't clarify. "They were talking about getting married, Papa."

"Well? What's stopping them?"

"You'll have to ask Kate," she said. "But, please, wait until she wakes up. It was really late when she got here last night. We're both exhausted."

"Oh. Sorry," he mumbled, finally speaking more softly. "I was just surprised to see her."

He was also probably eager for some early-morning company since Nana used to get up with him, but this was one day Jane couldn't roll out of bed any earlier than her alarm dictated. She'd have to handle work at the store on very little sleep as it was. "I'm also going to try to grab another couple of hours, okay? Then I'll get up and make you some coffee and breakfast."

"I'll go out to the workshop and let the two of you rest," he said, but Jane heard Kate's voice as soon as Papa reached the living room.

"Sorry to surprise you, Papa," Kate said. "You don't mind having me here, do you?"

"Are you kidding?" he said. "I love having you here. You can come whenever you're willing and able. But what's going on with you and your young man?"

Jane held her breath while trying to hear what Kate said next.

"Will and I are just…going through a rough patch," she replied. "And I need a place to stay for a while."

"Stay as long as you'd like," he said. Then Jane must've drifted off to sleep, because the next thing she knew, her alarm was bleating.

Averil was carrying a box up the stairs to her new apartment when Jane poked her head out of Vintage by Jane to ask if she needed any help.

"Can you leave the store unattended?" she asked in surprise.

"I don't open for another thirty minutes."

It wasn't even noon? Averil hadn't realized that. But still… "You must have things to do, or you wouldn't have come in early."

"It'll be okay. I'm mostly ready, just have to dust and clean a few fixtures. I clean one section each day before I open so the work doesn't get overwhelming and I don't have to hire a service. But I can make a few trips for you. Today I can probably clean *after* I open. Sundays are usually busy, but since it's raining, I doubt that'll be the case."

Dark clouds had rolled in overnight, but it hadn't started sprinkling until Averil was on her way over. She'd considered turning around—it was no fun moving in the rain—but since she had the time and had already committed herself to the trip, she'd decided to go ahead and get it done while Mitch was with her parents at church. It was always fun to see the apartment. "Okay. My car's unlocked if you don't mind grabbing a box."

Jane propped the back door open before ducking out into the weather. She was obviously a seasoned veteran when it came to bringing things in through the back. Averil hadn't even thought to use the doorstop.

Averil continued up the stairs and propped the box on her leg while jostling for her keys so she could unlock the apartment.

As she walked in, she felt the most amazing feeling— the same sense of freedom and independence she'd experienced when she rented the place and when she'd made her first trip with the dishes and other kitchen items. She was really going through with it! She was getting out on her own again, making progress in her life for the first time in four years—ever since she'd returned home with her tail between her legs, so hurt she could barely function, and yet she'd had to function for the sake of her child.

"Life…" she muttered as she wrangled the box inside and put it down near the ones she'd brought in before. She couldn't wait to unpack and get some furniture. That would be the fun part. But she couldn't start today. She planned to spend some quality time with Mitch before he had to go back to school tomorrow.

Footsteps sounded behind her, and she stepped aside to make more room for Jane. "Jeez. What'd you put in this thing?" her friend complained, straining beneath the weight of the load she was carrying. "Feels like it's full of rocks," she added, nearly dropping the box while lowering it to the floor.

"Sorry. I definitely overpacked that one. It's filled with books for the shelves I plan on putting here in the living room." She loved the exposed brick of one whole wall and had already ordered the bookshelves she wanted to put there from an online site.

"No wonder. Are the rest of the boxes filled with books, too, or did I just happen to grab the heaviest one?"

"You grabbed the heaviest one," Averil confirmed with a laugh.

"Just my luck." Jane sighed dramatically—teasing— as she rested her hands on her hips and looked around. "God, I miss this place."

"I bet." A flicker of guilt put a slight damper on Averil's enthusiasm. She'd been so caught up in her own situation that she hadn't given enough thought to Jane's. It couldn't be any easier to live with a grandfather battling dementia than to live with strong-willed and opinionated parents after having already left home. At least Dinah and Bill were fully functional; they helped her instead of it being the other way around.

Someone else was coming up the stairs. Surprised to have a visitor, Averil looked at Jane, who shrugged, and they both turned. Averil expected to see the landlady or someone looking for the proprietor of Vintage by Jane, since Jane wasn't in the store, but it was Charlie, her brother, who stepped through the door they'd left standing open.

"So this is it, huh? These are your new digs?" he said.

He was dressed up and wearing a tie since he'd gone to church with their parents. He was also wet from the rain. But Averil didn't care. She rushed over to throw her arms around him. She generally wasn't so demonstrative. They saw each other too often for a hug at every meeting. But she was excited he'd taken the time to stop by and see what she had going on.

"Whoa! I'm glad to see you, too," he said jokingly when she let him go.

"Isn't this great?" She spread out her arms and twirled in a circle. "I'm going to live here, in this cool apartment, and I'm going to have dinner parties, for which I'll make charcuterie boards and waffles with all kinds of toppings and guacamole toast. I'll string lights out on the balcony and sit outside with a glass of wine while looking down on Lincoln Street. And I'll create a room for Mitch that'll be much better than making do with your old bunk beds at Mom's."

"In other words, you're going to start living again—whether it's practical or not," he said.

"I am." She drew in a deep, cleansing breath. "Forget Chase. Forget Brant. Forget all men, for the time being." She'd been hoping something would finally happen to get her out of the situation she was in—that she'd fall in love and find a good father for Mitch—but she'd had the power to change her life all along. It meant she had to pick herself up, dust herself off and charge forward. And possibly fight much harder than she'd ever fought before. But she could do that. Andra Day's song "Rise Up" came to mind. She'd been playing it in the car on the way over because it made her feel empowered.

"I'm excited for you." He turned to greet Jane. "Hey, what's been going on with you, Janey?"

She'd hung out at their house so much growing up that he'd given her a nickname. Sometimes, when he really wanted to get under her skin, he'd call her "Plain Jane." With long blond hair and green eyes that slanted up slightly, she was far too attractive to be called plain. But that was exactly why he could get away with it—it was so obviously untrue.

"Not much," she replied. "I've just been running the store and taking care of my grandpa."

What she was doing for her grandfather proved she was just as pretty on the inside, which made Averil jealous, too. Holding the moral high ground seemed to be so easy for her.

"I hear your little sister will be getting married soon," Charlie said.

A pained expression crossed Jane's face.

He blinked at her. "What? Did I say something wrong?"

Jane's reaction made Averil wonder the same.

"Not wrong, no," she said. "I'm just…not sure there'll be a wedding. At least not in the near future."

Charlie frowned. "What do you mean?"

"Kate and Will aren't getting along. At the moment, she's staying with me and Papa."

Averil stepped closer. "Since when?"

"Since last night," Jane replied with a wince.

"Oh, wow." Charlie flipped his damp bangs out of his eyes. "I'm sorry to hear that."

"Maybe she'll get with Kurt," Averil said.

Jane looked startled, as if the mere suggestion was shocking or repugnant or both. "Why would you say that?"

"Because they've been together on and off over the years, right? And I always felt like maybe they were meant to be together."

"I've never gotten that impression."

Averil was sure she hadn't misremembered their on-again, off-again flings. "Really? Because they definitely liked each other at various times. I remember talking to her about it."

"I guess," Jane said, but she seemed reluctant to admit even that much.

Averil had seen Jane with Kurt on various occasions in the last six months, but she'd always assumed they were just friends. They acted like friends—maintained a single status on social media, were never seen touching or holding hands, often included others so it was a group and not only the two of them. But was there something more going on behind the scenes? She wanted to ask—but not in front of Charlie.

"She'll probably get back with Will," Charlie said. "A lot of couples fight. Doesn't mean it's over—not in every case, anyway."

"We'll see," Jane said, but she didn't sound particularly convinced things would go that way for her sister.

Averil wanted to ask for more details about Kate and Will's split but held off on that, too. She knew Jane wouldn't talk as freely if Charlie was around.

He gestured at the apartment. "You used to live here, didn't you?"

"I did. And I really miss it," she said, then obviously tried to be a good sport by adding, "but at least it's in good hands."

Averil linked her arm through her former best friend's.

"You're welcome here anytime. If you need a break or a meal or just a listening ear, come on up."

Jane smiled, but it seemed a bit wobbly. "Thank you."

"Is it true that Talulah's expecting a baby?" Charlie asked.

Averil had called him the morning after she'd learned herself, because she knew her brother would want to know. She felt so bad for him. He couldn't get over Talulah. It didn't matter how long it'd been since they were together. She was his first love and no one had been able to match her. She sort of understood what that was like. Brant hadn't been her first love, but she considered him the one who got away and couldn't seem to get over him.

"That's the latest," Jane confirmed.

He scratched the back of his neck. "Damn."

"Right?" Averil said.

"I guess…things change and there's no stopping it," Jane murmured.

She didn't say it as though she saw that as a good thing. She was probably thinking of what was happening to Papa—and her, too, thanks to the disruption of *his* life. But change was something they all had to face— and Averil was learning it was smarter to do it bravely.

Nine

Jane was exhausted by the time she got home. Sundays were her short day at work, but after being up so much the night before—and being so angry with Will for what he'd done to her little sister—she just wanted to put on her pajamas, start a fire in the fireplace and dive into a good book.

But Kate was waiting for her when she got home. "Can we go get my stuff now?"

Jane didn't want Kate to go alone. She didn't want to give Will the chance to continue the fight that'd erupted last night—or plead with Kate to forgive him. Her sister needed to take a much longer break from the relationship and give her mind a chance to clear, so she could look beyond the heartbreak and make a good decision. Because of that, she didn't reveal how tired she was. She smiled and said, "Of course. Just let me change into a pair of yoga pants and a sweatshirt."

If she was going over to help Kate move out, she at least wanted to be comfortable.

Her sister waited patiently. Then they drove Kate's SUV over to the small two bedroom, one bath Will had bought with a little help from his aunt, who'd taken him in when he ran away in high school. It wasn't an expensive home, but he took good care of it.

He had that going for him, Jane supposed.

It was getting dark but was no longer drizzling when they parked in the drive.

"You ready?" Kate asked as she turned off the engine.

"*I'm* ready," Jane said. "What about you?"

Tears welled up in Kate's eyes, but she blinked them back. "I don't have a choice. I don't even have my electric toothbrush or any clothes."

Jane opened her door. "He'd better not be too hard to deal with. You don't think he will be, do you?" She'd never seen Will angry—and she really didn't want to.

"I don't know," Kate said. "He's been trying to call me all day, and I've ignored him. I have no idea how he'll behave."

Jane eyed the house—and saw movement at the window. Will must've heard them drive up, because he obviously knew they were there. "Let's get this over with."

With a final sniff, her sister nodded and climbed out.

Jane waited for Kate to join her before they walked to the front stoop together.

The door opened before they could knock, and Will peered out at them. "What's going on? Why'd you bring your sister?" he asked Kate.

"Why do you think?" Kate said. "She's here to help me get my things."

His eyes darted Jane's way before he turned his attention back to Kate. "You're really moving out?"

"Of course I'm moving out!"

"Why?" he said. "We've been happy together. You're

making too big a deal out of this. I'm telling you…what you saw…it doesn't mean anything."

"It means something to me," she said. "Will you please let us in?"

"You don't want to talk about this?"

"I'm too hurt right now, Will. I just… I need to get my stuff."

"You don't need to be hurt! That's the thing. You're the one I love." He threw up his hands. "None of this would be happening if you hadn't been messing with my computer."

"Don't you dare try to make *me* the bad guy, just because I caught you. What I did last night was innocent enough. I wasn't checking up on you. *You're* the one who's at fault here."

Jane wanted to say something to back up Kate's side of the argument. He was so obviously out of line. But she knew if they ever got back together, what she said today would define her future relationship with this man, and if he was going to become her brother-in-law in spite of what he'd done, she had to protect that.

"Please, just…just come in so we can talk." He turned to Jane. "Can you give us a few minutes? This is so unnecessary."

Jane felt her jaw clench. "I'm here to help her," she said. "I'll only give you a few minutes if that's what *she* wants."

"I don't want it," Kate said. "I still can't believe some of the things I read. It's been going through my head like a ticker tape ever since, making me so nauseous I haven't even been able to eat. I just want to get my things and… and try to forget and move on."

"This is bullshit!" he said and slammed the door so

hard against the inside wall it bounced back and nearly hit him.

It was Jane who put up a hand to stop it. "I suggest you go in the other room until we're gone," she said softly.

He pointed at her. "*This* is none of your business."

"It is now," Kate said. "I've made it her business."

He didn't move. He just glared at them both for several seconds.

"Do we need to call the police?" Jane asked.

When he didn't answer, she got out her phone, and he finally stepped back. "Get your shit," he snapped. "I don't care."

Kate wept the whole time they were in the house, but she worked quickly, too. They threw everything they could get their hands on—all her clothes, makeup, shoes, perfume, jewelry, papers and books—into the suitcases they'd brought over from Papa's and put the rest in black garbage bags. Kate said she didn't care how they made the transfer; she just wanted to get it over with as soon as possible.

"What about your pictures?" Jane asked, indicating the ten frames that covered the dresser.

Kate lifted each one and stared down at it. They were all of her and Will. Most were with horses. "Leave 'em," she said, and they dragged her stuff out through the house because some of the bags were too heavy to carry the whole way.

"Are you okay?" Jane murmured once they'd hefted it all into the back of the SUV and were climbing into their seats.

"No," she said. "And I don't know if I'll ever be okay again."

Will came out on the porch to watch them, but Jane

ignored him. She could see Kate glancing his way every few minutes, but she was proud that her sister didn't crumble beneath the pain and confusion and give in.

"Wow," Jane said when they were backing down the drive. "I thought he'd be more apologetic."

"He can't ever be in the wrong," Kate said.

Jane reached over to squeeze her sister's shoulder. "You're better off without him, Katie. I know it's hard right now, but after witnessing the way he behaved, it might be lucky you saw this side of him before you married him."

Kate nodded, but Jane knew mere words couldn't do much to make her feel better.

It was Monday. Jane had dinner at Talulah's to look forward to. She was trying to figure out what to wear when Kate knocked on her door.

"How late do you think you'll be out tonight?" her sister asked.

"I'm not sure. It's a blind date, so I might be home early," she said with a laugh. She hated that Kate was miserable and wished Will hadn't cheated, but it was nice to have her sister around. Going out was much easier. She always felt guilty leaving the house if Papa was going to be home alone. "Why?"

"Will's been bugging me. He wants me to come over so we can talk."

Jane draped the thin taupe, black and cream sweater she'd decided to wear on the bed. After what Will had done, she didn't believe her sister should be eager to race over to him. It'd only been a day. But she had to be careful not to become too bossy. She certainly didn't want to steer her sister wrong; whatever happened should be up to Kate. "And you want to go? Tonight?"

"Of course I *want* to go," she said. "I feel like I'm dying without him."

Jane had never experienced that kind of love. She was afraid she never would. She knew Talulah was still holding out hope it would happen for her, or she wouldn't have set up this double date. But Jane wasn't overly optimistic. "Have you ever thought there might be someone else out there who'd be better for you?"

"Who?" Kate demanded.

Jane thought of what Averil had said about Kurt but purposely didn't mention it. She didn't want Kate turning her attention his way. She liked hanging out with him, and if he got back together with Kate she'd be on her own again. "I don't know. But you're gorgeous and sweet and would make a fantastic partner for anyone."

Kate leaned against the doorjamb, looking dejected. "That's tough to believe at this point."

"I get it." Jane had the same reaction when people tried to encourage her. "Still, you never know what's right around the corner."

"Are you listening to yourself? You're suddenly becoming optimistic about love."

"Not optimistic for me—optimistic for *you*," she said. After all, love seemed to work for most others. Until this had happened with Will, Kate was one of her many examples.

"So…what should I say to Will?"

"If you really want to see him—and think now is the best time—you could go over there. Papa is used to being here alone when I'm gone, and we've both been around all day, so he's had company." This week he'd actually been willing to go grocery shopping with her and get his hair cut, although he'd told the clerk at the grocery store to "get a fucking move on" when she kept chatting with the customer ahead of them, which had embarrassed Jane.

"Maybe I'll just watch a movie with Papa. I'm not sure I feel strong enough for a conversation with Will."

"Waiting until you know you won't break down and do something that wouldn't be smart in the long run might be the wisest choice."

Her shoulders slumped as she nodded. "Why do I still love him, Jane?"

Jane gave her an empathetic smile. "Love has to be durable. Otherwise, where would the world be?"

"But how do I stop? I can't go back to him, and yet that's all I want to do. I wish I could feel his arms around me just one more time."

"If you let that happen, it'll be even harder to make the right choice."

"I know."

"I'm sorry, Katie. I wish there was a way I could fix things for you." She wished she could help Charlie and Averil, too. "Love seems to bring the highest highs but also the lowest lows."

So maybe having a baby on her own wasn't a bad idea. Maybe it was the safer path…

"I'm going to tell him I'm not ready."

He didn't deserve to hear from Kate at all, but Jane didn't say that.

"I hope you have fun tonight," Kate told her.

"I enjoy Brant and Talulah, so regardless of who my mystery date is, it'll be fine."

As soon as she was ready, she walked into the living room, hugged her sister, kissed Papa on the cheek and hurried out the door. But when she pulled up to Talulah and Brant's, she sat in her Mustang, staring at a truck that was already parked in front of their place. She recognized it instantly—it belonged to Kurt.

She turned down her radio. *He* couldn't be her date, could he?

No. Talulah and Brant would never set her up with Brant's younger brother. Kurt wasn't even the Elway closest to them in age. That would be Miles.

But Miles had a girlfriend he'd met online and was constantly visiting her in Billings…

Jane had just decided Kurt must've stopped by to drop something off and her real date hadn't yet arrived when she climbed out and went to the door. She was curious about what the night would hold—if she'd have the time of her life, merely a pleasant evening or be uncomfortable and impatient to leave. Depending on who Talulah had set her up with, it could go in any direction.

But when Brant came to the door, she caught sight of Kurt standing behind him and noticed that he was all dressed up and had his hair slicked back. That wasn't how he usually wore it. She didn't even like it that way. And then Talulah came out of the kitchen, wearing a coy smile and said, "You know Kurt, right?"

That was when the realization hit her: he *was* her date!

Kurt felt out of place. Maybe this had been a bad idea. He'd had fun hanging out with Jane once or twice a week, but this would probably put an end to that. The casual dynamic between them had already shifted to something strained and uncomfortable. By agreeing to this date, he'd let her know he was interested in more than what she'd offered him in the past and was afraid that would make her avoid him in the future.

Why'd I have to make it weird? he asked himself as Jane talked to Talulah and Brant while they started to eat. Although she'd been polite, Jane had focused much more on the others. But if she was going to ask him for a baby and he was going to give it to her—which he was tempted to do despite his earlier refusal—he at least wanted to explore the possibilities to see if they could have more than just an "arrangement."

"What do you think, Kurt?"

Talulah had asked him a question, but his mind had been so far away, he didn't know how to answer. "Sorry. I was thinking about...something else," he said. "What'd you say?"

"I said we're planning to name the baby after Brant, if it's a boy, with Lucas, your father's middle name, as his middle name."

"Sounds good to me. What will you call him? Junior?"

"No, he'll probably go by Lucas."

He swallowed the bite he'd just taken. "I like that. It differentiates him from his grandfather and father, and yet it honors both men. Of course, you could always name him Kurt. That would be even better," he teased.

Talulah smiled at him. "I'd be happy if he turns out like you."

He felt like hugging her. Her response was generous, considering she knew he wanted to impress her friend.

"When do you see the doctor?" Jane asked Talulah.

"This Thursday."

Jane twirled the garlic tomato fettuccine Talulah had made onto her fork. "It'll soon be official."

"Nine months is a long time to wait, but at least the clock has started ticking," Brant said. "I thought it never would." He lifted his glass. "Let's have a toast. To entering an entirely new phase of life and learning exactly what our parents went through raising us."

They chuckled as they clinked glasses—Talulah with her sparkling cider—and Talulah once again tried to draw Kurt into the conversation. He could tell she was making an effort. "Brant tells me you've been talking about getting a new truck."

He lowered the piece of garlic bread he'd been about to eat. "It's that time—where I have to decide whether to pay repair bills on an older vehicle or spring for a new one."

"What kind will you get?"

He told her about the trucks he'd been looking at. Then they talked about the diner and Jane's business, and eventually the conversation moved on to Averil and the fact that she was renting the apartment above Jane's store.

"When did that happen?" Talulah asked.

Jane cast her a rueful glance. "Last week. You were so excited about the baby I didn't want to mention it."

"But...that's *your* apartment. I mean...I know you don't have a lease on it anymore. But you lived there for so long. Must be hard to see it go to someone else, especially Averil."

Jane admitted it was. "My life has changed so much since Papa got dementia. I never dreamed something like this would happen, especially to him. He deserves better."

"Sadly, dementia can hit anyone," Brant said.

"It's a horrible way to spend the end of your life," Jane said. "Half the time he's waiting for Nana to come home. Or swearing at the waitress who's serving us at a restaurant or someone else who's only trying to help."

"And you have a front row seat to it all," Talulah said.

"Most people wouldn't stick around and take care of him the way you are."

"Sure, they would," she argued.

"I don't think so," Brant said. "They'd put him in a facility and do what they wanted—in your case it would mean moving to San Francisco, right?"

An affectionate smile curved Talulah's lips. "That you're putting him first proves how special you are."

"Not really. A lot of people have to deal with the same issue," she said, and something about the way she shrugged off the praise hit Kurt hard. She *was* a good person. He sincerely admired her. She was beautiful besides and had been through enough with her parents' divorce, her deadbeat dad and having to shoulder the entire responsibility of caring for her grandfather—for an indefinite period—right when she'd planned to move away and discover the world.

He knew in that moment he was going to give her the baby she wanted. He just couldn't imagine handing over a vial of semen. To him, that wasn't how babies were made. It would be too...he didn't know what—foreign, clinical, transactional.

If she wasn't opposed to it, he preferred to get her pregnant the usual way. Then, even if she wasn't interested in him long-term, at least he'd have had the opportunity to make love to her.

He'd begun to dream about that...

And if he lived to regret his decision?

He'd have the memories.

Jane couldn't help stealing a glance at Kurt. He didn't feel comfortable. That was apparent. Neither did she. She couldn't believe he'd known this was going to be a date—that Talulah was setting them up—and had come in spite of that. When she and Talulah were in the kitchen getting the pasta into a serving bowl and taking the garlic bread out of the oven while the brothers were looking at the garden Brant had just put in the backyard, Talulah had told her he wanted to date her.

"He has a thing for you," she'd said. "And he's had it for a long time."

"Really?" Jane had responded. He'd done a good job of couching it in friendship. He'd never even tried to touch her in a romantic way. Neither had he asked her to go out with him. There was that brief moment on the dance floor the other night when she'd caught him staring at her mouth, but she'd shrugged that off. Although it had made her believe he *might* want to kiss her, it was so subtle she'd decided she'd misread the cues.

Maybe she hadn't. *Obviously* she hadn't. She'd told him repeatedly there was no one in Coyote Canyon she was interested in. No doubt that was why he hadn't asked her out. She'd shut him down before he could say anything. It made sense he'd act like they were just friends.

"What are you thinking?" Talulah whispered while they puttered around the kitchen, putting the leftovers away. The guys had tried to help, but Talulah had shooed them into the living room, where they were watching a March Madness basketball game.

Jane was wondering if Kurt's desire to date her was the reason he'd been somewhat amenable to helping her conceive when she'd first mentioned her desire for a baby. She'd been surprised he'd even consider it. Most guys who were just friends wouldn't—unless it was an especially deep friendship.

The baby aspect added a whole new dimension to how

she and Kurt felt about each other, but she wasn't going to bring Talulah in on that. Not now, anyway. It was all too fresh and up in the air. "I like Kurt," she said simply. "I always have."

"But…"

How *did* she feel? Sort of mortified, she decided. He was one of Kate's old boyfriends. For all she knew, Kate would want him back—if her relationship with Will had truly come to an end. Why wouldn't Kate want that? Kurt was hardworking, honest, virile, attractive, strong, kind and good-natured. Jane could go on… There was so much about him to like. Maybe this time he and Kate would get together in a serious way, and he would prove to be the man Will wasn't. "But…Kate," she said simply.

Talulah shot her a look that said she shouldn't be worried about her sister. "She's with Will. She won't really care, will she? I mean, it might seem odd to her at first, but as long as you're happy, what does the age gap or anything else matter?"

Jane put the leftover pasta in the fridge. Did she want to get stuck in Coyote Canyon indefinitely—with a man five years her junior who'd slept with her sister now and then? "I've never thought of him in that way," she said.

It wasn't because he wasn't attractive. She'd just refused to let herself go down that road. Whenever she started to consider him anything other than a friend, she'd shove him out of her mind and turn her attention to her business or her dreams for the future or what she had to do for Papa instead. She didn't want to feel as though she couldn't get a man her own age so she was swooping in on a younger guy, a guy Kate had left behind.

But was that fair to Kurt? He was a long way from sloppy leftovers. To her mind, he was more handsome than Will. And after what Will had done, she was willing to bet he was a better person.

Which was exactly why her sister might circle around to him again now that she was determined not to go back to the man who'd just broken her heart...

Jane lowered her voice so Kurt and Brant wouldn't be able to hear her. "I didn't want to say anything at dinner, but Kate moved in with Papa and me yesterday."

Talulah looked stunned. "She did? *Why?*"

"This is just between you and me, but...she caught Will cheating on her."

"No!" Talulah cried, clapping a hand over her mouth.

"Yes, I'm afraid so."

"That's terrible!" Talulah said.

Jane shook her head. "I feel so bad for her. She's heartbroken."

"How could he do that to her?"

"He doesn't seem to think he did anything wrong. Told her it didn't really matter that he was messing around with other women, since they weren't married yet."

Talulah's mouth fell open. "His response is more alarming than the fact that he was cheating."

"I agree. He's turned into someone she feels she barely knows. When I went to help get her stuff, he wouldn't even speak to me, except to show his contempt for my support of her."

"I'm shocked. I never saw that coming."

"Me, neither. It's been rough."

"So...you feel you have to stand back until Kate finds someone else to truly know you won't be infringing if you start going out with Kurt?"

"I plan on leaving Coyote Canyon, Lu. I'm not sure I should *ever* start going out with Kurt."

Talulah sighed. "Well, it was worth a dinner. He's such a good guy. He's probably my favorite of Brant's brothers."

Jane liked him, too. But he was Kate's age. Because of that and everything else, including where she hoped to be in the future, she just couldn't imagine him as anything more than a friend.

Ten

"So what do you think?" Kurt asked Talulah. It was only ten thirty but Jane had already left for the night, and he was about to leave, too. They all had to work in the morning, except Talulah, whose diner was also closed on Tuesdays.

Talulah didn't look over, which wasn't an encouraging sign. She was lying beside Brant on the couch, and there was a sports recap show on TV—something Brant had flipped to once the movie they'd watched with Jane was over. "I personally think you two would be wonderful together. I don't care about the age difference, especially because it'll matter even less as we get older."

"But the stigma is still there?" he guessed.

"While that might make her uncomfortable at first, I don't think that's what would ultimately hold her back."

Knowing he had to get going—6:00 a.m. came awfully early when he stayed out too late—he scooted forward in his chair. "Then...what would?"

"Kate's no longer with Will."

He got to his feet. "Are you serious? From what I heard they were going to get married."

"Apparently, that's off."

Brant pulled his attention away from the TV long enough to join the conversation. "Since when?"

"They broke up this past weekend," she replied.

"What happened?" Kurt asked.

Talulah sent him an apologetic glance. "I can't say. It's up to Kate whether she wants to tell people or not."

"But you know the answer…"

Talulah didn't confirm or deny it.

"What are the chances they'll get back together?" Kurt needed that to happen, or he'd never have a chance with Jane.

"I wouldn't say they're high," she admitted ruefully.

That meant the breakup had been bad—or there was a good reason behind it. "Shit," he said as he rubbed his temples. "I had enough going against me."

"I know," Talulah said. "I'm sorry."

"Terrible luck, bro," Brant said.

Did that mean Jane would give up on her idea to have a baby? Put it off?

Maybe he should've said yes while it was still an option…

"Thanks for doing what you could," he said. "I'd better go. Brant's about to fall asleep."

Talulah got up, and his brother followed her lead, although he moved more slowly, indicating he was, indeed, exhausted.

"Thanks for coming tonight," she said. "I hope you enjoyed yourself in spite of…in spite of the bad news."

"Dinner was great," he said and gave his sister-in-law a hug. "I appreciate you making the effort."

He needed to move on, find someone else who interested him and leave Jane alone, he told himself after he said goodbye and strode to his truck.

After he climbed into his truck, he pulled his phone from his pocket to text her. He wanted to say he'd had a nice time tonight and tell her he was sorry if he'd made her uncomfortable by trying to change the relationship. For him, it was a completely natural progression, but he was afraid to admit that for fear it would only chase her further from him.

He put in the code that would unlock his screen, but when he navigated to his text messages, he saw that he had a message waiting for him from someone else— Kate.

Hey. I was wondering if you'd like to go out for a drink tonight. My grandfather's asleep, and I'm just sitting here alone, trying to distract myself from my thoughts.

That had come in at nine.
She'd texted again at ten after ten:

It's me, Kate, in case you don't have my number in your phone anymore. I guess I should've said that before. Are you around tonight? Will and I have broken up, and I'm dying to get out. We could head over to Hank's...

She was already reaching out to him?
Yikes! But he supposed he shouldn't be surprised. Considering their history, it would be natural for her to contact him. Besides, there weren't a lot of single people in town their age, so she didn't have that many options. "I can't believe this," he muttered as he stared down at her words.

Should he respond? If so, what should he say?

He decided it would be better to pretend he hadn't gotten her messages tonight. He could always answer her tomorrow, when meeting her was no longer a possibility because he was at work, and let the delay maintain the distance and space that'd cropped up between them in recent years.

The less contact he had with her the better.

A soft knock sounded on Jane's bedroom door before Kate's voice came through the panel. "You still awake?"

When Jane had come into the house, her sister had been asleep on the couch. Jane had shut off the TV, which had turned to news, and covered her sister with a blanket. But apparently, Kate had awakened in the twenty minutes since then.

Jane pressed the button on the side of her phone that would lock it and turned the screen face down on the nightstand so it couldn't light up if she got a reply to the message she'd just sent Kurt. She didn't want her sister to know she'd had dinner with him—or that she was attempting to communicate with him right now. "I'm up."

The door cracked open and Kate slipped into the room. "How was dinner tonight? Did you have fun?"

"I did," she said, and then she held her breath because she knew what the next question would be.

"Who'd Talulah and Brant set you up with?"

Jane got up from her desk and pulled back the covers on her bed. Did she tell her sister the truth?

She knew she should always tell the truth. But she couldn't bring herself to do it tonight. Knowing Kurt had been her date would upset Kate.

Jane could rely on Talulah and Brant not to say anything. She knew that. And she'd just texted Kurt to ask him to keep it to himself, too. She had no doubt he'd agree. "Some guy who knows Brant from the ranch," she said.

"You mean he buys beef from the Elways or something?"

"I guess so..."

"What was his name?"

Jane's heart began to pound as though she was running. "John," she said because it was the first name that popped into her brain.

"You didn't like him?"

Jane hated to keep lying. But there was no way she was going to discuss her relationship with one of Kate's old boyfriends—or almost boyfriends, or lovers, or whatever Kurt had been to her. "I liked him fine. But there was no...spark."

"Oh. That's a bummer," Kate said. "I'm sorry."

"It's okay." Jane stripped off her clothes as they talked and pulled on a tank top to sleep in. "I enjoyed myself, like I said."

"I'm glad."

"Any word from Will?" Jane asked, eager to change the subject.

"Of course. He texts me constantly. He goes from begging me to come back to him to telling me he doesn't care if I walk away if I'm going to be snooping around in his things and making something out of nothing."

Jane felt her spine stiffen. "Don't let him fool you. Cheating is *not* nothing."

"I know. But if I could be sure he wouldn't do it again—"

"You'd go back to him?"

"Probably," she admitted. "Isn't that pathetic?"

Jane didn't bother denying it. "Yes. But it's also what a lot of women would do. That's what's *really* pathetic."

"You should be glad you've never fallen in love."

"I am," she said. No one had control of her heart. No one could hurt her.

But was being lonely any better?

Kate sighed. "I'd better let you get to bed. I need some sleep, too—if I can get any. We both have to work tomorrow."

"Maybe you should give yourself the day off, call in sick."

"I can't. There's no one to replace me on such short notice. And when word gets around town about the breakup, I don't want Leon wondering if I was lying about calling in sick. I wouldn't put it past him to say something to the Vidlars."

"You think you can make it?"

"If I don't want to risk losing my job on top of everything else, I don't have any choice."

Jane wished her sister could have more time. "Okay. Can you turn off the light on your way out?" she said and waited for Kate to do that and close the door before checking her phone for a response from Kurt.

She'd been afraid she'd messaged him too late, that he'd be in bed. He typically got up two hours earlier than she did, so it was possible she'd hear from him in the morning instead. That was what she expected. But he had a message waiting for her.

I won't say a word.

Thank you.

Sorry if tonight was awkward. I should've been more up-
front from the beginning. I mean...I've been attracted
to you since I can remember.

Surprised he'd be so candid, she propped her pillows
behind her back while trying to decide how to respond.
Should she just leave the conversation as it was? Or
should she try to explain?

Because it took courage to reveal interest when that
interest might not be returned, she decided to write him
back.

I would be open to a relationship with you if the situation was different. I hope you know that.

Despite my age?

The age difference bothered her, but she was old
enough to realize how little it would really impact their
lives.

Despite your age.

She started to set her phone aside and scoot down in
bed but saw her screen light up again.

I've decided to give you what you want.

Her heart leaped into her throat as she sat up again.
He couldn't mean...

A baby?

Yes. If you want semen in a vial, I'll provide it. But honestly that would feel pretty weird. I'd much rather do it the old-fashioned way. And if that sounds self-serving, I guess it is. I definitely wouldn't mind making love to you.

Making love. She'd thought of that, of course. Allowed herself to imagine it a few times—just for the sake of a baby. After all, it would be the fastest and easiest way to go, and it would save her the cryobank fee *and* the insemination fee. It would also mean she wouldn't have to keep the semen from going bad until she could get it to the appropriate doctor for storage before implantation—or worry about it being switched out for some other man's sperm. And if she didn't get pregnant, Kurt might be amenable to trying until she did…

It was the perfect solution in so many ways.

But getting that close to him came with obvious drawbacks. One was how Kate would feel about it if she knew. Another would be how uncomfortable it would be to see him around town afterward. She was trading their friendship for a child.

He had to understand that, which made it especially nice of him.

Are you sure?

About wanting to make love to you? Positive!

A trickle of excitement ran through her as she chuckled. He was so cute… But was she really going to do this?

She had to, didn't she? Now was her chance—and she might not get another one.

She pictured Kate trying to go to sleep in the other

room. Would she be doing her sister a disservice? Would it hurt Kate in any way?

Jane couldn't see how it would, not if she and Kurt kept it a secret. Kate would never have to know she wasn't artificially inseminated from semen purchased at a cryobank. Neither would Talulah or Brant, even though their children would be related. That would be a little strange—but also appealing.

Maybe one day she would be able to tell them...

You're okay with the rest of it, too?

It took him a few seconds to respond. But she was glad he was taking some time to think it over again. She didn't want to get her hopes up only to have them dashed.

She was shivering—from excitement and trepidation—while burrowing beneath her covers when she received his answer.

I am. Just tell me how you want it to go.

Jane covered her mouth so she wouldn't squeal with excitement. "Oh, my gosh... Oh, my gosh," she kept muttering.

Can I think about the details and get back to you?

Of course.

She set her phone on the charger, but it must've been hours before her pulse slowed to its normal pace and she finally fell asleep because it felt like she'd barely closed her eyes when she had to get up.

* * *

Ellen was back in town. Jane saw her when she noticed Talulah's van parked in the alley behind the store and ducked into the diner to say hello. Although the diner was closed on Tuesdays, Talulah spent a lot of time there—cleaning, stocking and paying suppliers.

"How was your backpacking trip?" Jane asked Ellen.

"Incredible," she said.

Jane knew Talulah had heard them when she poked her head out of the pantry to wave.

"So much for your day off," Jane said to her.

Talulah shrugged. "Tuesdays are more of a prep day than a day off. I have to get ready for the week ahead."

"You helping out this morning?" Jane asked Ellen.

Ellen lifted her leg, which had been hidden by a stack of boxes, to show she had it wrapped in an elastic bandage. "I'm not much good to anyone right now. That's why I'm not at work myself."

Jane saw the crutches lying nearby, which she hadn't noticed before. "Oh, no! What happened?"

"I tripped and sprained my ankle coming down into a gulch. Can you believe that? Fortunately, it was on the second-to-last day of the trip, so it didn't ruin the whole thing."

"It's not broken…"

"Just sprained," she confirmed. "But it hurts like hell."

Jane grimaced. "What a bummer!"

Talulah had gone back to whatever she'd been doing in the pantry, but her voice floated out to them. "Ellen, show her your new ring!"

Ellen had tattoos and piercings and used to color her hair pink or purple. Jane was under the impression she'd done those things to defy the status quo in the conservative town where she'd been born and raised and in Coyote Canyon, because these days—now that she was satisfied and happy—she seemed to be calming down and moving toward conforming. For the past year, she'd simply bleached her hair blond. But she still maintained the short, jagged cut that looked so good on her.

"You remember Hendrix used his mother's ring to propose…" Ellen said.

Jane nodded. "I do. Since he lost his mother when he was so young, I thought that was a beautiful way to pay tribute to her."

"That ring holds so much sentimental value to both of us. I told him I was totally happy with it. But it's still an eighties ring, you know what I mean?"

"Not the best style?" Jane guessed with a laugh.

"Exactly. If it was something from the fifties or sixties, I might feel differently. But… Anyway, he insisted I should have a wedding ring that fits *my* taste, so he bought me this gorgeous lab diamond." She stuck out her hand for Jane to see a yellow gold ring with a simple yet large, emerald-cut diamond.

"Wow! It's gorgeous!"

"I love it, and now I wear his mother's ring on this other hand."

"He spoils you," Jane said with a grin.

Ellen's face turned red. She was tough—had started her own well-drilling business when she first came to Coyote Canyon and competed against her fiancé, who was in the same line of work. Not many women did that job, but she'd been successful at it. He often joked that she was stealing too much business from him, so he decided to join forces with her instead. "If you can't beat 'em, join 'em. That's what I always say," he'd joke. Ellen wasn't comfortable with praise. She'd never trusted that sort of thing—never trusted people in general—so it'd been remarkable to see her flourish in the sunshine of Hendrix's love. Everyone who was familiar with them knew how much he adored her.

"We're talking about having the wedding in August," she said.

"And I'm doing the wedding cake!" Talulah called out.

"Then I know it'll be beautiful." Jane checked her watch. She had to get over to the store, or she'd be behind before she even opened. "I'm sure you've heard about the baby," she said to Ellen.

"I walked over to tell her as soon as they got home last night," Talulah said, still in the pantry. "I didn't want her to hear it from someone else, and it wasn't something I was prepared to text her about."

"I'm so excited," Ellen said. "She's going to be a great mother."

Jane smiled. "I'm excited for her, too," she said, and she was, but at the same time she couldn't help thinking about the last text exchange she'd had with Kurt. He'd agreed to help get her pregnant. So maybe she'd be shopping for cribs and other nursery items right along with Talulah. "We'll have to throw her a shower."

Ellen perked up. "That's what I was just telling her!"

"I'll bake the cake for that, too," Talulah called back, jokingly.

"We can bake a cake," Jane said.

"It might not be as pretty as one of yours, but…it'll taste almost as good—I hope!" Ellen added.

Jane decided that even if she got pregnant, she wouldn't tell anyone for as long as she could hide it. She didn't want to steal any of the limelight from Talulah.

Besides, people were more prone to take something in stride if it had happened in the distant past rather than the recent past. Why make Kurt suffer through nine months of gossip and conjecture when she could cut that down to three or four months simply by waiting until later?

Instead of being a year she'd simply have to endure, this was shaping up to be the best year of her life, she decided. She couldn't believe she'd be planning a baby shower for her best friend—while expecting a baby herself.

Eleven

Kurt was still suprised he'd made the commitment to get Jane pregnant. To create a child. To know there was another person in the world to whom he'd passed on his genetic material. And to also know he might not—depending on what he chose—be included in that person's life.

The potential for regret that raised was the most frightening part. But ever since he'd told her he'd do it, he'd been so excited he felt almost intoxicated.

He hadn't surrendered all hope that Jane would finally give him a chance. If she slept with him—and getting pregnant could easily take more than one encounter, which was the best part of all—she'd *have* to see him in a different light. Maybe that would be enough to convince her the obstacles standing between them weren't anything they should worry about. A five-year age difference was nothing. And he wasn't going to get back with Kate even if Jane rejected him. It was sort of like the situation between Brant and Averil.

Of course, that *had* ruined Talulah's friendship with Averil, who'd just started to make up after Talulah had

jilted her brother at the altar. So as happy as Brant and
Talulah were together, there'd been a cost, and Kurt understood why Jane wouldn't be willing to pay that price
when it came to her sister.

He brought his truck to a stop at the first traffic light
on Lincoln Street. The two situations were as different as
they were alike, he reminded himself. Kate loved Will,
not him. She was only circling back because she was on
the rebound. She needed someone to distract her from
the pain of losing a relationship she thought would be for
life—or convince her she was still desirable or whatever.
It wasn't as if he'd ever had her undying love…

Jane's store was located on the next block. After the
light turned green, it was hard not to slow down as he
passed by and try to glance inside. But the glint of the
sun against the glass storefront made that impossible.

Maybe he'd buy her a sandwich and take it to her. His
brothers had sent him to town to get a few salt licks and
pick up lunch for them. He'd suggested hamburgers from
Rocko's, but Miles had insisted on meatball sandwiches
from Vidlar's, so Kurt knew chances were good he'd run
into Kate. She might be busy while he was in the store,
which could save him from having to speak to her, but
he figured he was going to run into her eventually. He
might as well get it over with. He'd responded to her text
this morning to say he was sorry he'd missed her messages last night, that he'd been hanging out at home and
hadn't been checking his phone. She couldn't make too
much of that—one way or another.

With any luck, she'd get back together with Will soon.
That would be the best-case scenario for him. Then as he
tried to get Jane pregnant over the next several weeks or

months—whenever she wanted to do it—who could say what might happen?

A lot could change this spring...

He stopped at the feedstore first and saw Averil working the register. They spoke for a moment as he checked out, but he left as soon as he could. He knew she was no longer much of a friend to Talulah, and since Talulah was his sister-in-law, he felt protective of her.

He drove to Vidlar's next. He'd called in the food order, but the deli was so slammed—prices were better here than anywhere in town, and the sandwiches were legendary—he had to wait. While he stood around, he stayed close to the counter where they were preparing the food and kept his attention mostly on his phone with only a peek here and there to see what Kate was doing in the pharmacy.

Fortunately, she was busy, too. When he heard his name, he looked up and grabbed the sacks Denise Johns was handing him as quickly as possible. Then he turned to go. But Kate had left the pharmacy and was walking toward him.

"Hey, you," she said.

He forced a smile. "Hello."

"You weren't even going to come over and say hi to me?"

"I saw that you were busy," he replied lamely.

She shoved up the sleeves of her work smock. "Sorry we couldn't hook up last night."

He knew she meant *Sorry we couldn't meet at Hank's*, but because they *had* hooked up in the other sense over the years, he couldn't help thinking it was a poor choice of words. Or maybe he was just ultrasensitive to it because his attraction to her sister had grown beyond just his own little secret. "I was pretty tired. Not sure I would've been good company, anyway." He cleared his throat as he moved the sandwich sacks to his other hand to be able to dig his key fob from his pocket. "I'm sorry to hear things aren't working out with Will."

A sulky look descended on her face. "It's been terrible. Would you believe the douchebag cheated on me?"

"I can't." That response *was* sincere. He'd believed there was probably a good reason for the breakup, but he hadn't guessed it would be *this* good. "With who?"

"The wife of some guy who owns an equestrian center. I doubt you know them. They don't live in town."

An equestrian center didn't ring a bell, but the "married" part caught his attention. "Did you say it was with a married woman?"

"I did."

Kurt whistled softly under his breath. "He should be careful. Her husband might come after him."

"He deserves to have his ass kicked," she said.

"So is it over for good?" he asked.

"As far as I'm concerned it is."

That was disappointing. "That's too bad."

"I'll get over it eventually." She blew her bangs out of her eyes. "Might take a while."

"You were together a long time."

"Hey," Leon Johnson called from the pharmacy department. "You said you had to go to the bathroom. Can you hurry? We're getting behind over here."

"I'll be there in just a sec," she told him, then rolled her eyes when he was no longer looking. "It was hard to work with him before I broke up with Will," she said to Kurt. "Today, it's almost impossible."

"One day at a time," Kurt reminded her. "You'll get through this."

"It doesn't feel that way right now." Her chest lifted as she drew a deep breath. "What are your plans for tonight?"

He tried to think of a quick excuse for why he wouldn't be able to go out with her. But he was afraid if he gave her one, she'd just ask about tomorrow or contact him again on the weekend. He needed to put a stop to her thinking he was an option. "I've been doing a little online dating and plan to have a Zoom call with someone I met."

"Oh…"

"But maybe this weekend, we can get a group of people together to shoot some darts or pool."

"Yeah. I'll text you if I'm available."

"Sounds good," he said and made sure she went into the bathroom and wasn't watching him before he turned left after leaving the pharmacy and strode down to her sister's store with the extra sandwich he'd bought.

Jane was ringing up a set of candelabras for a customer when Kurt came into the store. As he opened the door, the buzzer went off, and once she caught sight of him, she couldn't quit smiling. Knowing what they were going to do—and how intimate they'd have to get in order to do it—made her feel daring and reckless and even a little giddy.

Would she be *this* excited if she were getting pregnant via a cryobank? she wondered. Or was Kurt part of the reason she was suddenly so breathless?

"Thanks for coming in," she said to Sean Jamison— the only attorney in town. "Tilly is going to love those."

"I know. She told me to make sure I got them for her," he said with a laugh.

Jane maintained a polite smile until her first customer of the day left. Then she felt her smile falter as Kurt moved closer. A secret liaison with her sister's former boyfriend probably wasn't the wisest move...

But when her eyes met his, she knew she wasn't going to back out. She was hooked—not only by the desire to have a baby, but by the way she was going to make it a reality. She suddenly had an excuse to look at Kurt in a brand-new way, was able to contemplate and imagine things she never would've allowed herself to imagine otherwise.

Her eyes dropped to his hands as he gave her a sack from Vidlar's. Big and slightly calloused from working outside, they looked capable and strong—and they would soon touch her body in the most intimate of places.

"Thought you might like a sandwich for lunch," he said.

She swallowed hard as she tried to dispel the images in her mind. "You brought me lunch?"

He shrugged as if to say it was no big deal. "I had to pick up some sandwiches for me and my brothers, anyway, and thought... Well, Vidlar's is just down the street, so I was already close."

She obviously knew where Vidlar's was located. Her store was only a block away. And her sister worked there. But she found his reaction—the slight embarrassment for doing her this kindness—endearing. "That's very nice of you."

He grinned as he tried to play it off. "What can I say? I'm a nice guy."

"Who came with food at the perfect time. I was just thinking about what to do for lunch."

"I wanted to be sure you weren't going hungry—or changing your mind about—" he lowered his voice even though there was no one else in the store "—our plans."

"I haven't changed my mind. Have you?"

"You don't have to worry. I'm in."

More images popped into her mind—images of Kurt as she'd seen him at the lake once, in just his swimming trunks, and the memory of him staring at her lips at Hank's the other night.

She cleared her throat again. "Good," she said. Then she tore her gaze away from him to peer into the sack. "A meatball sub?"

"I hope you like that kind of sandwich."

"I do. It's one of their best. Thanks for thinking of me."

"You bet." He started to back up. "I'd better get going. My brothers are blowing up my phone, wondering where the hell I am. I think they're getting *hangry*."

"Kurt?" she said, stopping him.

He looked back at her from near the door. "What?"

"Should we do it this weekend?"

His eyebrows shot up. "That soon?"

"I figure why wait?"

"Where?" he said.

"Bozeman is a nice place to visit." And they didn't know anyone there, so there'd be no one to recognize them when they walked into a motel room together.

"Saturday?"

She nodded.

His grin hitched up on one side, making him even more attractive than usual. "We can meet on the far side of the ranch, leave your car there. No need to drive separately, since no one, not even my brothers, will be likely to see it there. At least, that's how I'd like to do it…"

Hoping to quell the butterflies in her stomach, she drew a calming breath. "Me, too."

"Okay. I'll text you," he said. Then he left and the door swung shut.

It was plenty cool in the store—the temperature was only in the sixties—and yet Jane was sweating. "Oh, my God," she murmured. "I must be losing my mind."

Averil had often complained about her ex-husband not taking more of an interest in their son. But now that Chase had invited Mitch to California, and she'd had to drive him to the Bozeman Gallatin Field Airport, where Chase met them to take him back, she was feeling a little bereft. She could use the time to get settled in the new apartment and prepare his room for when he got back in a week, which was exciting. But she was going to miss him. Since she'd alienated her closest friends, it felt like he was all she had.

She'd just delivered another carload of stuff to the new apartment when she came out to find Jane's Mustang still parked in the alley, even though they'd said good-night when she came in and the store was closed. Ellen's truck was now there, too, along with Talulah's van, which she'd had wrapped with the logo of her dessert diner. The three of them were obviously together, hanging out at the diner after hours.

Telling herself she didn't care that she'd been left out, Averil pulled her keys from her pocket and opened the door to her car, which was so old it squeaked. She went as far as to get in and put the key in the ignition before stopping. The situation was never going to improve if she couldn't overcome her hurt and resentment. Did she want the next couple of years to be as lonely as the last one or two? If so, she might have her own apartment, but she'd have no one, other than her son, to enjoy it with.

Gathering her nerve, she took her keys and got back out, forcing herself to approach the diner even though she knew it was going to be awkward and uncomfortable. As she drew close, she could see through the small square window in the 1950s back door that the lights were on. She could hear laughter and voices, too, which made interrupting even more difficult.

She almost talked herself out of it and went back to her car. She knew none of the three of them would be happy to see her. She'd never been close with Ellen, who'd come on the scene not too long before Talulah's great-aunt died. Jane had chosen Ellen over her, which Averil had to admit she sort of deserved. And Talulah…

Well, Talulah had the most reason to dislike her.

Averil stood in the alley, deliberating whether she should take such an emotional risk. She was just starting to feel better, stronger, but she was still fragile in a way that was difficult to define. If they made it clear they didn't want her there, she didn't feel she could take the rejection.

But if she didn't make the attempt, nothing would change, and she'd continue to be an island indefinitely.

Was she ready to put her life back together again? Could she *really* set aside her jealousy and disappointment and be the kind of friend she wanted to be? Only then would any type of reconciliation work. Halfway measures had done nothing. She couldn't effect any real change—be genuine and trust that her friends were being

genuine—by trying to move forward without truly forgiving.

It'd been years since she and Talulah first became
estranged. If Charlie had moved on and married someone else, maybe it wouldn't be such a big deal. But he
hadn't. He still regretted losing Talulah. And yet... How
had the loss of her friendship with Talulah helped him
in any way?

She couldn't see that it had. It was just hurting her.

Taking a deep, bolstering breath, she raised a hand
to knock.

She didn't knock loudly. She was too intimidated for
that. She told herself if someone didn't hear her and come
to the door right away, she'd simply leave and try to forget the sound of their laughter.

That would probably be for the best, anyway, she
thought as she waited.

She turned toward her car and was about to walk away
when light spilled into the alleyway as the door opened,
and she was standing face-to-face with Ellen.

Ellen's eyes narrowed. "Hey," she said flatly.

Talulah and Jane typically tried to act pleased when
they bumped into her around town. At least, they were
both polite and managed to smile. Ellen didn't play that
charade. She'd once caught Averil making derogatory
comments about Talulah in the grocery store and had
called her out right then and there, creating a public spec-
tacle. Ellen was like that—she was bold and determined
and fiercely defensive of those she loved, and she didn't
care about causing a scene.

Averil resisted the urge to reveal her insecurities by
clasping her hands tightly in front of her. "Hey."

"Who is it?" Talulah asked.

Ellen didn't answer. She just stepped to the side and held the door open wider so Talulah could see for herself.

"Oh! Averil…" Talulah got up from the table where they'd apparently been sitting, crowded around a laptop. "Is everything okay? Are you moving into the apartment right now? Do you need help?"

Averil regretted interrupting. Talulah and Jane had once been like sisters to her, and yet she'd never felt more uncomfortable in her life. "No, I…I saw your cars and thought… I just decided to say a quick hello."

"I'm glad you did," Talulah said, but Averil wished she could slink away and forget she'd ever interrupted.

"Hi, Averil!" Jane waved from the table. Ellen had already sat back down and was sipping from a glass of wine as if she was patiently biding her time until Averil was gone. Averil got the impression Ellen couldn't believe Talulah was even bothering to be nice to her after what she'd done.

"We were just looking at…" Talulah started, then stopped. "Well, we were planning…"

Ellen spoke up. "We're putting on a baby shower for Talulah, so we're trying to figure out the invitations, decorations and food. But you don't have to come if you don't want to."

Stung, Averil stiffened. "Of course I'd like to come."

Jane quickly jumped in to smooth over Ellen's brusque statement. "We don't have to continue with this right now," she said. "There's still plenty of time. Would you like to come in and have a glass of wine?"

The fact that Jane, rather than Talulah, had extended the invitation spoke volumes. It said she was comfortable enough to do that, even though she didn't own the diner. It also said she was feeling the same tension Averil was, because she was trying so hard to smooth over it.

But there was no way Averil was going into that kitchen. With Ellen glaring at her, it felt like she'd be walking into a lion's den. "No, you three go ahead."

"We could walk down to Hank's," Jane offered.

"I don't want you to feel you have to stop what you're doing because of me. Mitch is in California with his dad, and I have a lot of stuff to get done while he's gone, so…really, when I saw the cars here, I just wanted to say hello."

"We're glad you did," Talulah said.

Ellen's lips formed a straight, colorless line. Averil saw that when she glanced over but pasted a smile on her own face to cover for the terrible numb, stinging sensation that'd come over her. "Thanks. Have a great night."

In case anyone was still watching—maybe through the window—she made sure to keep plenty of energy in her step until she reached the car and got inside. By then, no one could see her anyway, but she was imagining the three of them returning to that table to talk about how surprised they were that she'd had the nerve to knock.

So much for trying to extend an olive branch, she thought, and fought back tears as she started her car.

Usually, Kurt was so busy the days flew by. But this week, every hour seemed interminable. He couldn't wait for Saturday—and yet he was nervous about its arrival. A nagging voice in his head insisted he should back out of his agreement with Jane. And yet…he couldn't make himself do it. He was too excited about getting his hands on her. To think he'd be able to hold her against him and kiss her bare skin and neck and lips after he'd fantasized about doing that for so long made it difficult to breathe. It didn't help that he hoped their intimacy might be the catalyst he'd been searching for to get them into a serious relationship at last.

"Look at this stuff Talulah's been sending me," Brant said.

They'd just come into the house after a long day on the ranch. Brant usually headed straight home—or since it was Thursday and the diner was open, he would probably stop by there first—but their mother was over. She'd made her broccoli-cheddar soup, and there was no way he was going to miss having a bowl.

"It's all so damn cute," Brant said, grinning like a smitten little boy as he handed Kurt his phone.

Kurt swiped through pictures of various cribs, dressers, changing tables, wallpaper, animal prints—even stuffed animals. "You're doing the nursery already?"

"Why wait? The doctor confirmed the pregnancy this morning. Our official due date is November 10."

That meant if he got Jane pregnant right away, she'd be due around Christmas, less than two months later. What would that feel like—to know Jane was carrying his child?

It was nothing he'd expected to happen just a few weeks ago. But he liked it. It made him feel connected to the woman he'd wanted for a long time. He wanted to be part of the whole process—the pregnancy, delivery and beyond—so he was glad she seemed open to that. But it would be an emotional rollercoaster if he couldn't get her to change her mind about him. Even if he did get her to change her mind, and they became committed to each other, would she still want to move away once her grandfather passed? What would that do to *his* life?

His thoughts were sobering. But the dangers didn't change his mind, which was a little scary. Did taking what he wanted now mean he'd suffer later?

"I think we should go with the white crib," Brant commented, taking his phone back and looking through the pictures again.

"Brown would be a safer bet," Kurt advised. "I feel like regular wood could go either way—for a girl *or* a boy."

"We're having a girl," Brant informed him.

Kurt felt his eyes widen in surprise. "I thought it was too early to tell the sex of the child."

"It is. But after being the oldest of four boys, I want a sweet little girl."

"That's sexist," Kurt teased. "Girls can be difficult, too, you know. Regardless of the gender, I hope you get a hellion just like me."

"Fortunately, they broke the mold when you came along," Brant grumbled and handed his phone to Ranson, who'd overheard them from where he was in the kitchen and come out to take a look.

"It won't be easy to wait most of a year," Ranson said.

"You're telling me," Brant said. Then Miles came in from outside and had to see what they were talking about.

"What's going on?" their mother called from the kitchen. "Why is everyone in the living room? Are you coming to eat or not?"

"Yeah, we're coming," Brant hollered back and reclaimed his phone. "Want to see some of the stuff Talulah and I are thinking about buying for the nursery?" he asked her.

Ranson and Miles trailed after Brant as he went to show their mother what he'd shown them. But Kurt hung back. Would *he* soon be helping Jane search for baby furniture?

"It's about time you gave me a grandchild," he heard his mother chide Brant. Jeanie had been coming over, cooking and cleaning for them more than ever since she'd heard the news. The baby was all she could talk about. She wanted a girl, too, since she never had one of her own.

Again, Kurt's plans for Saturday loomed large in his mind. As usual, what he was doing wasn't nearly as conventional or safe as his older brother. He couldn't imagine his family would be too excited about *his* plans. Fortunately, Brant had been as good as his word and not told anyone, even Talulah. Kurt had that going for him, but if things went the way he and Jane hoped, it couldn't remain a secret forever.

Maybe his mother would forgive him if it meant she would soon have *two* grandchildren…

Twelve

Kate came into Jane's room as she was getting ready for work on Saturday. "What are your plans tonight?" she asked.

Jane had been afraid her sister would hit her up to go out. After spending a week watching TV with Papa after she got home from the pharmacy, and crying over Will, Kate was going stir-crazy. Because Jane was at the store until late in the evening on weekdays, she'd been exhausted when she got home last night and had begged off a trip to Hank's—also because she'd been eager to get ready for her date with Kurt. He'd texted her earlier in the week to say she should drive over to the far side of the ranch and park among the trees along Bell Road as soon as she closed the store, and to text him right before she left, so he could be waiting for her. That way, no one would see her car, because it would be well hidden, and no one would see them together, because they'd head straight out of town. She also wouldn't encounter Kate or Papa by coming home to change, which would necessitate a conversation and a possible delay.

Still, she'd had to get out of the house this morning

without raising suspicion or making Kate feel any worse, and that was proving to be more difficult than she'd expected. She couldn't tell her sister she was hanging out with Talulah and Ellen tonight, or Kate would expect to be included. They'd all gone out together before, several times. And she couldn't say she was having a drink with Kurt, because the same problem would occur— Kate would want to join them. She couldn't even say she'd be helping Averil move without the possibility of Kate volunteering to pitch in. Kate was *that* desperate to get out of the house.

So Jane was hard-pressed to come up with a believable excuse. "Actually, I…I have a date," she said.

Kate straightened in apparent surprise. "With whom?"

"A guy I met online."

"You're on an online dating site?" Kate asked skeptically. "I thought you were done with that."

"I am, but I've been talking to this dude for a while, and he invited me up to go to dinner with him in Bozeman before all of this happened with…with Will." She couldn't look her sister in the eye—she was such a terrible liar. She busied herself packing the bag she'd be taking with her instead.

"So you're going to Bozeman tonight? You're staying over?"

"In separate rooms."

"But…you've never even mentioned him." Kate sounded confused and with good reason. This was something Jane should've brought up before, but she'd been hoping to get out of the house without having to make up a story.

"I don't think it'll go anywhere," Jane said, downplaying it as much as possible. "I probably should've canceled."

"No, you shouldn't have cancelled. You never get out. Go and have a good time. Maybe this guy will turn out to be someone you were glad you met."

The generosity of her sister's response made her deception feel even worse. She had to remind herself that Kate had felt free to devote all her time to Will when she was with him, which had left Jane at loose ends on many occasions. She wasn't trying to get back at Kate—held no grudge—but she did want to take this opportunity to get what she most wanted in life without a guilt trip. "I'm sorry I'm leaving you on your own..."

"Don't be!" Kate insisted. "I'm a big girl. I'll be fine."

"But...I'm afraid you'll break down and see Will, and if you get back together with him and he doesn't treat you right, I'll feel like it's my fault."

"I'm not going to get back together with him."

Jane stopped shoving makeup into her bag. "You sound more convinced than ever before."

"I am." Kate's shoulders slumped. "This week, I accused him of seeing other women—"

"Besides the one who owns the equestrian center with her husband?" Jane broke in.

"Yes. I bluffed him into believing I found other texts and emails, even though I was so upset I didn't take the time to search his computer very thoroughly, and he finally admitted that there *have* been other women."

"Are you kidding me? What an asshole!"

"I would call him worse," Jane responded with a frown. "But what good does the anger do? The bottom line is that I can't pin my future happiness on a serial cheater."

Impulsively, Jane pulled her sister in for a brief hug. "I know you're going through hell but gutting it out is the only thing you can do—it's the *right* thing."

"I just never realized how empty my life would be if I suddenly lost Will," she said. "I was so caught up in the relationship, so happy to spend every second with him, that I neglected my other relationships, and now those people have moved on and filled the place I once held in their lives. So I'm paying the price."

"I'll go out with you tomorrow," Jane promised, letting go of her. "If you could just get through tonight, we'll have tomorrow night and Monday, when the store is closed, to hang out and talk and decide on the best path forward."

"Okay."

Kate remained in the room, watching as Jane finished gathering the items she wanted to take. "Are you not coming home before your date?"

She picked up her bag. "No, I'm going to get ready at the store."

"I hope you like this guy."

She wouldn't hope that if she knew who it was. "The chances of that aren't very high."

"You never know. You seem excited."

She was—although she'd rather not admit it, even to herself. She was also nervous. Fortunately, tonight had been on her mind for an entire week, so she'd had a chance to get prepared and had hidden the black strappy high-neck teddy she'd ordered online in the trunk of her Mustang. Otherwise, with Kate on her heels at every turn this morning, she wouldn't have been able to get it out of the house.

Jane couldn't imagine having sex with a man she

hadn't even dated. She'd never done anything like that before. The fact that she'd known Kurt for so long and he had a history with her sister might even make the encounter more uncomfortable. But she hoped if they had a few drinks beforehand, it wouldn't be *too* cringeworthy.

When she was ready, she said goodbye to Papa and her sister and rushed out of the house. She was just putting on her seat belt when she got a text from Kurt.

Are you as nervous as I am?

Yes. Maybe we should take a bottle of wine—or two or three. lol

I got you covered.

She couldn't help chuckling as she backed down the long drive. Kurt was sweet and funny. He knew how to put her at ease.

Everything would be okay, she told herself. She was going to be in good hands—in more ways than one.

Kurt waited back off the road in the trees where anyone who happened to pass by would be unlikely to see him. There wasn't much traffic out where he lived, especially in the evenings. Even if someone did drive by and notice him there, he owned the ranch, so it wouldn't be remarkable. And if it was one of his brothers, he could easily say he'd spotted a mountain lion or a bobcat and wanted to make sure the cattle weren't in any danger.

He'd have a harder time explaining why Jane's Mustang was on the property once she parked nearby, but he highly doubted any of his brothers would come out to the south forty in the next twelve to eighteen hours. Brant had no reason to be around—he was off today— Miles was at his girlfriend's house in Billings and Ranson was probably gone for the rest of the evening. It was Saturday, after all. If they weren't hunting, fishing, riding ATVs, snow-skiing if it was winter, or water-skiing if it was summer, they typically went to Hank's for a drink, over to a buddy's house to play poker or had a date. They worked so hard during the week they didn't waste their weekends. Someone had to be available in case there was a problem with the cattle—bloat or a broken water line or fence—but that responsibility rotated between the four of them and was more of an on-call or quick-check kind of situation that didn't require anywhere near the number of hours they worked during the week.

Fortunately, it was Ranson's turn to be in charge of the ranch this weekend. Kurt didn't have to worry about anything—except whether he was ruining his future, in any number of ways.

A car was coming down the road. There she was, he realized when he recognized the Mustang. Right on time.

He got out and directed Jane to pull deep into the trees. Then he grabbed her bag, deposited it in the back and opened the passenger door of his truck before coming around to the driver's side. They hadn't clarified whether they'd be staying the entire night in Bozeman or driving back after they'd done the deed. He didn't know what to expect, but he'd brought his shaving kit with his toothbrush and other toiletries and a change of clothes, just in case.

It felt weird that he hadn't needed to pack condoms. Until tonight, if he had sex, the goal was *not* to get the girl pregnant.

"How was work?" he asked once they were both inside the vehicle.

"Busy," she replied as she fastened her seat belt. "Spring is usually my best time—other than Christmas, of course."

He pulled onto the road heading toward Bozeman, where he had a reservation at the River Grove Motel, a place he'd vetted online that looked clean, private and comfortable. She'd insisted she'd pay for it, but it felt too odd for him to allow that, so he'd refused. "What will you do about the store if you move?"

"After my lease expires, I'll take what inventory I've got left and start over somewhere else."

"You still considering San Francisco?"

"Or Seattle. Talulah really liked living there."

When he allowed himself to look at her for more than a split second, he tightened his grip on the steering wheel. She looked good. He'd always thought she was beautiful. "Why not New York?"

"It's not out of the question."

Holy cow. What was he getting himself into? What if she took his child and moved clear across the country? "When does your lease on the store expire again?"

"In a year. I just...I just re-upped."

So she'd be in town for at least twelve months. Then... who could say what might happen? The good news was that if he got her pregnant right away, she'd be around for the entire pregnancy.

Maybe she'd even let him attend the birth...

That was partly up to him and whether he was willing to let other people, besides Brant, know he was the father, he realized. She'd said the choice was his. But... didn't she have a preference?

Part of him wanted to be transparent about his role

in her life. He wasn't used to hiding things. He figured he wouldn't enjoy having such a big secret. But if Jane preferred he not be involved in her life—or the baby's—he'd rather keep it to himself. Otherwise, he'd catch all kinds of grief from his family for, once again, being too reckless. And if Jane wasn't receptive to having Jeanie as a grandparent or moved too far away, no one would be angrier with him than his mother.

"Have you been having any second thoughts?" she asked.

He could tell she was nervous, which ironically made him calm down. It wasn't as if what they were about to do would be difficult. "I've had a lot of them."

She looked alarmed. "Then…why haven't you said something?"

He shot her a glance. "Because I'm still committed."

"What you're doing… I really appreciate it. It…it's very nice of you."

"I found a good place for dinner. Have you ever eaten at Huxley's?"

"No," she said. "What kind of food do they serve?"

"Pretty much everything—burgers, pasta, pizza. But we can go to a fancier place, if you prefer." He'd considered taking her to an upscale, expensive restaurant but ultimately decided it might make the evening feel too much like a prom date—or a meal for two people who were celebrating an engagement or other big milestone. He didn't want to make them even more uncomfortable, so he'd decided on a restaurant that would be nice enough but not over the top.

"Sounds good to me."

"Do you want to take more time to think about this?"

he asked. "We could just grab a bite to eat instead. It's not like we have to make a baby this weekend."

"I'd rather not put it off," she said. "But...can we go to the motel first? Once we get it over with, there'll be no reason to be nervous, and I'll be able to relax and eat. Then we could do it again later—just to increase the odds."

He caught his jaw before it could drop. He'd never had a woman approach sex this way before, but he'd never gone into it with the same goal. "Um, sure," he said, but that meant they were getting right down to it, and he had only the length of the drive to back out.

He kept telling himself he should apologize and change his mind—that there was still time—and yet he kept driving, found the motel, checked in and carried what little luggage they'd brought into the room.

Jane couldn't wait to get the next part over with. She knew touching Kurt intimately would be most uncomfortable the first time around. They didn't have to have sex more than once, but why not? They already had the motel. She figured they should have intercourse as many times as possible to stack the odds even higher in favor of a pregnancy.

"You sure you wouldn't rather have a vial?" he teased when she took a bolstering breath and began rubbing her sweaty palms on her jeans.

"No. That process would be much longer and more expensive, not to mention cumbersome." She stopped talking to see if he'd insist, but he didn't. "We haven't completely decided on what we'll tell other people, though," she continued. "We should probably do that."

"What would you like to tell them?"

"I'm thinking it might be easiest—and smartest—all

things considered, to say I used a vial, even if we admit you made the genetic contribution."

"To save your reputation?" he asked, obviously teasing.

"To preserve Kate's feelings."

He sighed. "It's too bad Will didn't treat her right—for a lot of reasons, including some selfish ones."

"The timing of the breakup…it definitely wasn't to our advantage," she concurred, but she knew, even as she spoke, they were using conversation as a means to procrastinate and decided it was time to just step up and make it happen.

"I guess… I bought something. I'll go put it on." She was reaching for her bag to get the black teddy she'd stuffed into it before leaving the store when she felt the warmth of Kurt's body close behind her.

"Jane?" he murmured.

She lifted her head but didn't turn until he put his hands on her shoulders and brought her around to face him. She was tall, but he was several inches taller, so she was staring at his chin. "What?"

"Relax," he said softly. "This isn't going to hurt."

She studied the shape of his mouth, the strength of his jaw and the brief flashes of teeth as he spoke. He was right—this wasn't going to hurt. She was jumpy and ill at ease not because she thought it would be terrible, but because she was beginning to worry about the opposite. What if it was really good?

Whatever happened, she couldn't allow her emotions to get involved… "I just…feel so guilty."

"For…"

"Sleeping with you in the first place. If Kate knew, she'd be so upset."

"Why would it matter to her? She isn't in love with me. She's in love with Will."

"You're her old boyfriend."

"We were never officially together," he corrected.

"You were together now and then. Enough to have a history and make her feel proprietary."

"Do we have to talk about Kate?" he asked. "Because you're all that matters to me right now."

Swallowing hard, she lifted her gaze until she could see the gold flecks in his green irises. "But this is all so unconventional. Other people wouldn't approve, which makes me feel as though we must be doing something wrong."

"Jane?" he said again.

"What?"

"We had plenty of time to deliberate on the drive here."

"What does that mean? You don't want to talk?"

"Not unless you've changed your mind. If that's the case, let me know. Otherwise…"

She could smell his cologne. She wasn't sure what brand it was, but she liked it. "I haven't changed my mind." She was, however, growing more and more anxious about the method they'd decided to use. She'd envisioned sex with Kurt being merely the most practical way to get a baby, but she was experiencing far more desire than she'd anticipated.

"I'm glad to hear it. Because—" he lowered his head as he brushed his lips gently across hers "—I can't wait to make love to you."

"I thought we were going to have a drink."

"I was planning on that, but I decided, for the first time at least, we should both know we are going into it with clear heads. That sort of…matters to me."

"Right. Makes sense."

Awareness prickled across her skin like static electricity, which wasn't something she could remember feeling with anyone else. The anticipation alone was intoxicating; she didn't need the wine.

"Are you okay with this?" he asked.

She wasn't even tempted to pull away. She suddenly craved the fulfillment promised by his first kiss, which had been as light as the brush of a butterfly's wings. "I think I'm going to like it," she whispered and stood on her tiptoes to be able to place her mouth directly on his.

She parted her lips, expecting his tongue, and he used it but as more of an invitation than an invasion. He seemed to be taking everything slow, waiting for her to relax and get involved, and that happened much more quickly than she thought it would. Within moments, she was driven by only one thought: get closer to him.

He cradled her face in his large hands as he gazed down at her. "You're gorgeous, Jane Tanner. You know that, right?"

It was a rhetorical question, but what he'd said only heightened the excitement building inside her. He made her feel attractive, emotionally and physically safe, and desired—all of which proved to be an incredible aphrodisiac.

"What's happening to me?" she whispered, suddenly worried about something she'd never considered a danger until now. "I can't fall in love with you," she clarified. She'd never get out of Coyote Canyon if she did. "And you can't fall in love with me."

"We'll see about that," he said and lifted her sweater over her head.

Thirteen

Jane didn't have a chance to worry about Kurt's response to her warning, didn't even have time to question it, because once he unlatched her bra, and she let it fall to the floor with her sweater, he wrapped her in his arms and kissed her even more deeply. Then, after a few kisses that grew deeper and deeper, everything started moving faster.

She'd planned to put on her teddy first thing, had imagined this evening going step by step—purposeful, if not downright mechanical. After all, she wouldn't have to carry so much guilt about it if she didn't feel anything when it happened. She was merely joining a sperm with an egg, no different than a doctor would do with artificial insemination. They were just saving a little money, trouble and time by doing it the old-fashioned way. If it ever came out that he was the father, she wanted to be able to claim—to herself and Kate and anyone else who asked—that the sex aspect, if they admitted to that, hadn't meant anything.

But what came next was nothing like what she'd scripted in her mind. It was too spontaneous and got messy very quickly as they hurried to get their clothes off. The next few minutes were also filled with far more urgency and intensity than she'd anticipated. The best part—or worst part, depending on her perspective—was that it felt so natural.

She remembered climbing onto the bed as Kurt removed his pants, feeling the crisp white sheets beneath her back and the soft pillow give way before Kurt climbed on top of her and his chest came into contact with her breasts.

She could scarcely breathe as she looked up at him, knew she'd never forget the pirate's smile he gave her. That expression, the victory and excitement it conveyed, as well as a measure of male pride, was oddly captivating. She told herself to close her eyes so she wouldn't see it or him as they continued. Allowing herself to be swept away like this was probably the worst thing she could do.

But she couldn't bring herself to break eye contact. She was mesmerized by the look on his face. She'd never seen him quite so focused, and that evoked a strong reaction because she could tell how much he wanted her.

He kissed her deeply again before running his lips over her jawline, up to her ear and then slowly down her throat, pulling her skin into his mouth and nipping at her as he went along. Her chest was rising and falling fast by the time he reached her breasts, and her nerves were so sensitive she jumped when he focused on her nipples. How she'd thought she could ever remain detached was a mystery.

She wanted more and more and more of him, but at the same time grew increasingly worried. When he pressed inside her, she nearly panicked and tried to push him off. What was she doing? Had she just opened Pandora's box?

Instead of remaining in tight control—instead of going about this in a measured, matter-of-fact, get-it-done sort of way—she was moaning and arching her back to encourage him, and the muscles of his arms and chest were bunching as he drove into her as if it was all he could do not to climax immediately.

"Jane, I don't think—"

"What?" she gasped when he stopped speaking.

"I can't hold off," he said, and she felt his body jerk as he ejaculated inside her.

"That wasn't how I imagined it going," he mumbled with a laugh as he supported most of his weight on his elbows and caught his breath. "In my dreams, you came at the same time."

"There's no need to apologize." Truth be told, she was relieved. The rushed, too-soon ending had reined in everything, made her feel as though she hadn't gone too far, after all.

I can handle this, she reassured herself, feeling as though she was gaining a small amount of control.

But once they cleaned up so they could go out to dinner, he told her not to get dressed quite yet. He guided her to the bed and pressed her back onto it, then pushed away the towel she was wrapped in and began kissing his way up her thighs.

This had nothing to do with having a baby. Her brain ordered her body to stop him, and she promised herself she would *in a second*, but that slight procrastination changed everything. Her willpower dissolved almost immediately, and she clenched her hands in his hair.

"Kurt?" She was breathing so heavily she barely had the breath to call out his name.

His response was a mere grunt. "Hmm?"

She was planning to make one more concerted effort to stop. She needed to get her mind on something else. But then every muscle in her body went taut, and the pleasure she'd been denied a few minutes earlier began to radiate from deep inside her, and her only answer was a satisfied groan.

As they walked into the restaurant, Jane told herself she'd forget about that last part. She'd simply been too aroused to refuse—that was all. It was years since she'd been with a man, and a young, healthy woman would naturally crave the kind of completion Kurt had brought her.

"You okay?" Kurt asked after the hostess seated them in a corner booth at the restaurant where he'd made reservations.

"I'm fine," she said. "Why?"

"Because you'll look anywhere but at me," he said. "Are you upset, freaked out, embarrassed?"

"All three," she admitted. "I didn't expect to…"

He leaned forward. "What?" he asked, sounding genuinely curious, maybe even slightly concerned.

"Get so carried away."

His teeth appeared in a quick smile. "I, for one, enjoyed that aspect."

"It was just unexpected that…that… Never mind," she said. "I guess I'm still trying to process everything."

The waitress approached with two waters.

"Now that it's over and we can't take it back, you don't regret what we've done, do you?" he asked, after they'd accepted their glasses and the waitress had left.

"No, of course not," she replied.

His Adam's apple moved as he swallowed. He was saying and doing all the right things, but something gave her the impression he might be a little overwhelmed himself. The possible consequences of what they were doing couldn't be overstated. "So what do you think?" he asked. "Are you possibly expecting?"

"It's not a high probability."

His eyebrows slid up. "That was the first time I've ever had unprotected sex. I guess when you're *that* careful, you feel one time is all it takes."

"It's more likely to happen if you don't want it to," she said jokingly. "Murphy's Law, right?"

He nodded.

"Maybe I should've explained better from the beginning, but according to the statistics I've seen online, only about thirty percent of women who start trying to get pregnant do so in the first month."

He managed to swallow the water in his mouth as he put down his glass, but she got the feeling he'd nearly spit it out. "Did you say *month*?"

"That surprises you?"

"Such a long time would have to take into account multiple attempts."

When she'd solicited his help, it'd seemed that gaining his participation would be all it took. Although she'd done the research, she hadn't been thinking beyond the first hurdle—getting him to say yes. But now she had to face the fact that accomplishing her goal might not be so easy. "That's how I interpret the data, too. And the statistics probably include all age groups—from teenage girls on up."

He seemed perplexed. "Meaning?"

"Since I'm on the, um, older side of the spectrum, it could take longer." She looked away as she said this because she was still sensitive to the age gap between them.

"From what I read, by thirty, fertility begins to decline, and the decline becomes more rapid as you reach your midthirties."

"That's just five years," he scoffed.

"But an important five years when it comes to fertility."

"You're saying it might take several tries…beyond this weekend?"

"It could. Would that be a problem?" she asked and held her breath as she awaited his response.

He shifted in the booth. "Um…"

"We could set a time limit, so this doesn't drag on forever," she volunteered.

He rubbed his chin as if this *was* something he hadn't fully considered. "I say we just…take it one day at a time."

"Okay." She picked up her menu and began skimming the selections, but it was more of an orchestrated effort to make what she had to say next sound casual. "If I *do* get pregnant, are you thinking you'd want to come forward as the father?"

He looked troubled as he considered his answer. "That depends."

"On?"

"A lot of factors," he said.

"You don't want to talk about it right now?"

"No. I just want to enjoy dinner and the rest of the evening. We'll cross that bridge when we come to it."

Jane would've liked an answer one way or the other. The next few weeks and months would be easier if she knew what she could count on where he was concerned—which way he wanted to go. But he was doing her a huge favor, so she figured she could have a little patience. "Okay. I'm open to…whatever you want."

It was only fair that she let him make the decision. Giving her a child was no small thing. But every time she imagined how Kate or Talulah or Brant—especially Brant and the rest of Kurt's family—would react to the news, she cringed.

If she could say she'd used a cryobank, the gossip and criticism would be bad but nothing like what she'd face if she had to admit that her baby would be related to the Elways.

Kurt had never flipped back and forth on a decision so many times in his life. He'd been convinced that sex would be the catalyst he needed to bring him and Jane together. But since they'd left the motel, her defenses had gone back up. He could tell that she was busy mentally walling him out even while they had dinner.

Maybe she wasn't attracted to him. It had certainly seemed like she was when they were making love. Being with her had been as good as he'd hoped. She hadn't been over-the-top wild or weird or anything like that—just excitable, fun, receptive and warm. The right amount of everything.

But she'd told him she hadn't had sex in three years. Maybe that was the reason she'd enjoyed herself so much. It would certainly explain why it was so easy for her to turn off that level of engagement and go back to the way she'd been before—treating him like a casual friend.

Or maybe she was so set on being able to leave Coyote Canyon she simply refused to open up to him or anyone else who might get in the way.

Whatever the reason, he was pretty sure he'd just

made a drastic mistake—another one, since he'd always had a habit of screwing up.

If he was lucky, what he'd done so far wouldn't result in a baby. She'd just stated that chances were greater the weekend would end in a nonpregnancy. After feeling as though the last few hours hadn't changed anything in their relationship, his heart would be a little worse for wear, but other than that—and a little wounded pride— he might be able to escape a very sticky situation if he didn't make love to her again.

Except…how could he refuse? He'd said he'd help her conceive. He didn't feel he could change his mind. He'd already reneged once.

With a sigh at his own hopeful stupidity, he read a text message Brant had just sent to their brothers' chat group while he waited for Jane to get out of the bathroom so they could leave the restaurant.

Hey, Talulah has several slices of different cakes that are now two days old. You know what that means.

It meant she could no longer sell them, but they still tasted good, and the Elway boys were free to come eat what they wanted.

Only he couldn't go to the diner, because he was almost two hours away, trying to get Talulah's best friend pregnant.

He cringed. What he was doing sounded ridiculous to him now.

"All set," Jane announced when he glanced up and saw her walking toward him.

He forced a smile. He supposed they were heading

back to the motel. He couldn't tell her he wanted to go home and eat cake. The job he'd agreed to do wasn't done.

But...*damn*. If he didn't even have a chance with her, what the hell was he doing?

He made love to Jane twice more, once when they got back to the motel and once in the morning before they packed up to head home. He enjoyed himself; he liked sex the way he liked her—*too much*. But having to do it for what he considered to be the wrong reason made those encounters far less than they could've been. What he really wanted was an emotional attachment, and he could already tell she wasn't open to giving him that.

"You're quiet," Jane commented as he drove back to Coyote Canyon.

"Just...tired," he lied. Actually, it wasn't a complete lie. He'd been awake most of the night, lying on his side of the bed, feeling a strange sort of panic—like he wanted to run for the hills.

She looked over at him. He could feel her gaze, but he kept his eyes on the road. "Are you sure?" she asked.

He reached for his coffee in the cup holder. He'd gotten himself in deep on this one. He shouldn't have agreed to help her in the first place. But even though he had agreed, he had the right to be honest, didn't he?

He was just thinking about how to frame his response when she spoke again.

"Kurt? Are you upset?"

He almost came right out and told her he was having second thoughts, that he wouldn't be able to continue. But he figured she was probably freaked out, too.

If he managed to escape this weekend without any consequences, he wouldn't take the risk again. But there

wasn't any need to upset her by saying that right now
when it was possible that she was already pregnant. Why
make her feel he resented his contribution?

Even if she wasn't pregnant, she was dealing with a
lot. He knew she'd deny it, but he felt she wouldn't be
trying to have a baby on her own if not for her grandfather. If she felt free to leave town, go out and live her life
and make the most of it, she wouldn't need to change it
up so drastically any way she could.

"I'm not upset," he reassured her.

"You seem remote."

"Like I said, I'm just tired."

"I'm afraid I got you into something you wish you
hadn't done."

"That's not true," he lied again. "Everything is fine."
He managed a smile for her sake, then turned up the radio
so he wouldn't have to continue to fend off allegations
that were all too accurate.

"If last night didn't work, I can go to a sperm bank in
the future," she said.

"Let's not make any decisions right now. Let's just
wait and see."

"Okay," she said. "But just to clarify—at the moment
we aren't saying anything about this to anyone, right?"

This time, he made eye contact, because he definitely
didn't want her to misunderstand his level of conviction
on this point. "That's absolutely correct. We aren't telling *anyone*."

"Even Brant?"

He'd already said more than he should to Brant. Kurt
didn't want him knowing any more. "Even Brant. Or
Talulah."

"Got it."

"Great," he said. Because, with any luck, he'd still be able to get himself out of the messy situation he'd just gotten himself into...

Averil sat in the middle of the kitchen floor—she'd been putting pans and lids in the drawer beneath the stove in the kitchen of her new place—and paused to read Jordan's latest text. She'd been having a great weekend looking for secondhand furniture in the immediate area to fill in for what she wasn't able to bum off her siblings and had found a cute coffee table and an orange ultra-modern couch that looked like something Jane would like. She was excited to show her friend and get it moved into the apartment, so she kept checking the time, but the store didn't open until noon on Sundays, and Jane wasn't there yet.

Because no one else was in the building, Averil could have the volume of her music much higher than usual, and she was taking advantage of that. It was so loud she'd been afraid she wouldn't hear her phone if it went off, and because she wanted to be available in case Chase or Mitch tried to reach her, she'd set it to vibrate before sliding it into the pocket of her most comfortable jeans.

Why aren't you responding to me? Are you mad? Jordan had written.

That wasn't the case at all. She was just *finally* feeling strong enough to stay away from someone she knew wasn't right for her. Jordan wasn't out to make her happy; he cared only about his own happiness. That meant he wouldn't be a good stepdad for Mitch. Although he'd met Mitch once, he never even mentioned her son, never asked about him or showed interest, never tried to include him. Averil knew they were only hanging out because they had no one else. But spending so much time together could be dangerous, especially since they'd started having sex several months ago. A lot of people in that situation wound up married for entirely the wrong reasons—and it often didn't end well.

I've been busy. Sorry.

Want to come to Libby tonight? Go out to dinner?

He usually convinced *her* to make the long drive so he wouldn't have to. He used the fact that he didn't want to come to Coyote Canyon and possibly run into Ellen as an excuse, and it was a testament to how lonely and bored Averil had gotten that she'd been willing to go along with that. Averil knew Jordan had said and done some things he shouldn't have, and Ellen didn't like him because of it. Averil pretended Ellen didn't have a good reason, but she knew that although Ellen could be prickly and defensive, she was inherently honest. And if Jordan hadn't constantly been chirping in Averil's ear, stirring up her own anger and jealousy, she probably wouldn't have acted as badly as she'd acted.

She had to take responsibility for her own mistakes, of course, had to acknowledge that she wasn't innocent. He wasn't the kind of man she wanted to be with. Even her parents told her to stay away from him. They didn't like him because he came across as arrogant and showed zero interest in them or Mitch.

Averil would snap back that Dinah was just angry Jordan wouldn't come to dinner and that he couldn't be available to entertain them because he was busy running a dental practice out of town. She insisted that was no reason to dislike him. But she knew in her heart that her mother was right. He'd make time if he really wanted to.

She probably should've ignored this text, too. But she was so relieved that she was starting to care less than she had in the past. It was a welcome change to have a little power in the relationship.

Sorry. I can't.

Why not?

I'm moving into my apartment.

You got your own apartment?

She smiled proudly.

Yep. I'm unpacking some things right now.

Sometimes she got the impression he thought he was better than she was, because he had an education and "Dr." before his name, and she hadn't finished even one full year of college.

That's awesome. Privacy at last. Want me to come see the new place?

She thought of the weekend she'd just spent. She'd enjoyed shopping for the apartment, which was the best thing to happen to her in a long while—but it was sad that she didn't have anyone to share her excitement with. On both Friday and Saturday nights, she'd gone home and been in bed before ten.

She felt so left out of the social scene in Coyote Canyon—like she was getting old before her time.

When I get settled, she wrote back.

Why not tonight?

He was willing to make the drive? That was a switch. He must be eager for another booty call, she thought wryly. She'd justified what had been going on because he usually took her out before they went back to his place. That was more than some guys did. But over time, their relationship had changed into something she didn't feel good about. She no longer had any hope that they'd fall in love. It felt more like Jordan was using her until he could find someone he considered "better," and that chipped away at her self-esteem and had ever since she'd met him.

Still, she could always stop seeing him *next* weekend. This weekend, Mitch was with his father, and she wanted to feel as though she had *something* going on in her social life.

She was also excited to be able to show off her new apartment. Maybe she'd finally get to feel good about herself, as though he wasn't the only one who had his life together.

Fourteen

When Ellen invited her to come over for homemade ice cream and trivia on Sunday night, Jane asked if she could bring Kate. She'd told Kate she'd hang out with her, and since Talulah and Brant would be there, as well as Hendrix, Ellen's fiancé, it made sense from a practical standpoint, too. Then the teams would be even. She couldn't imagine Ellen would mind, especially since she seemed to like Kate, and Jane was relieved when Ellen wrote back to say it wouldn't be a problem, to go ahead and invite her.

After spending each night for the past week sitting around with Papa, Kate was eager for anything that might get her mind off Will, and Jane was also looking for a distraction. She couldn't quit thinking about Kurt. She hadn't heard from him since he dropped her off at her car around eleven that morning and she quickly drove off— not only to get to the store in time to open it but also so they wouldn't be seen together. She kept telling herself it hadn't even been one day. She shouldn't expect him to contact her again so soon. She was being too insecure.

Except his response to her definitely seemed cooler

than normal. Had she ruined their friendship? She'd known she'd be taking that risk when she asked him to help her have a baby. She'd chosen to look forward to becoming a mother instead of continuing to go out for drinks with Brant's little brother.

But the fact that he seemed to be pulling away from her stung more than she'd expected it to. And while she worked, she couldn't stop dwelling on the time they'd spent in that Bozeman motel—what his kisses were like, what his body felt like, the way he'd smiled down at her that first time...

"What are you doing?"

Her sister had come into the kitchen. "What do you mean?" Jane asked. "I just finished the dishes so we can go."

"You were fanning yourself. Are you hot? Because I think it's freezing in here." She rubbed her arms even though she was wearing a long-sleeved flannel shirt over a thermal.

It wasn't hot. Jane had just been thinking about the wrong things. Again. But her preoccupation with Kurt and what they'd done was understandable. Sex had a way of distorting feelings. She'd known that going in and thought she'd prepared herself for it.

She told herself she'd forget the intimate details of Saturday night as soon as she knew if she was pregnant. It was far too early to tell whether that had occurred, and yet she paused every now and then to see if she felt any different. "I was wearing a heavy sweater." She'd taken it off so she wouldn't have to keep pushing up the sleeves while doing the dishes, but she didn't add that. She'd been fine until she'd started remembering every detail of last night...

"You ready to go?" Kate asked. "Do you need a jacket?"

"Yeah. You might want one, too. It's starting to rain." Jane had watched big fat drops slide down the window while standing at the kitchen sink.

"I'll grab one." Kate glanced back over her shoulder, where Papa was sitting in the living room, brushing Otis, and the TV was on full blast. "Will Papa be okay on his own?"

Kate had been with him enough recently to realize how diminished he'd become. Jane was relieved to have her around. It felt so much better knowing someone was with him when she was gone. But he'd had more company and support this week than ever before, and he'd already eaten the meatloaf she'd made for dinner. All he had to do now was get into bed as soon as he finished watching TV. And he could handle that. He hadn't started wandering around the neighborhood or anything like that. Worst-case scenario, they'd find him in his recliner when they got home, but at least that wouldn't hurt him. "I'll ask Mr. Hensley to come over, let Otis out one last time and help Papa get to bed."

Kate nodded and left—presumably to grab her jacket— and met Jane at the front door, after which they walked to the Mustang. "It's a relief to get out," she said as she slid into the passenger seat. "Thanks for including me."

"No problem," Jane said. "It's been a hell of a week for you."

A click sounded as Kate snapped on her seat belt. "Have you been hearing much from Kurt Elway?"

Jane froze as she was about to put the key in the ignition. "No. Why?"

"Because I've texted him several times this week, and he never really responds to me."

"He ignores your messages?"

"He doesn't ignore them, exactly. He'll text back. But never right away and only with a few words that are non-committal or too general. It's weird."

"Give me an example," Jane said as she started the car.

"I'll ask if he wants to go get a drink, and he won't answer until the next morning. Then he'll say he didn't have his phone with him. Or I'll ask what he's doing after work, and he'll say he's visiting a friend out of town."

Jane twisted around to be able to see through the back window while reversing down the drive. "What's wrong with that?"

"He never initiates the contact, never follows up to see if I want to do something. It's sort of hurting my feelings, you know?"

"Maybe he already has a woman in his life."

"Has he mentioned that he's seeing someone?"

"No, but that doesn't mean he's not. He wouldn't necessarily tell me. We're not that close."

"I suppose he *could* have a girlfriend of sorts," Kate mused. "But it seems like he always has time for you."

Jane gripped the steering wheel that much tighter, waiting for a break in traffic before pulling out onto the highway. "It might seem as though we've spent a lot of time together, but it hasn't been that much. You were with Will for over a year. You weren't really paying attention." She felt it was smart to distance herself from Kurt as much as possible, especially now that her sister seemed to have renewed interest in him.

Kate pulled the twisty from her hair and combed it into a better ponytail with her fingers while obviously stewing about the situation. "After we go to Ellen's, can we stop by the ranch to see him?"

Jane cleared her throat. She wanted to say no, absolutely not. After what she'd done with Kurt last night, she had no idea how he felt about her and was willing to bet he wouldn't welcome the intrusion. But how could she say no?

"I feel like it might help break the ice if you're with me," Kate added.

With some effort, Jane pasted a smile on her face. "I don't see why not," she replied but left herself an out she hoped she'd be able to take advantage of by adding, "as long as it doesn't get too late. Tomorrow's Monday—my day off. But he has to be up early during the workweek."

Kate checked her phone. "Ellen and Hendrix own well-drilling businesses. They get up early, too. I can't imagine this evening will go on for too long."

Jane tensed. She'd be on pins and needles all night, trying to draw out their stay at Ellen's. And she might not be successful. She knew how tenacious her sister could be. If Kate was set on seeing Kurt, and on having Jane act as a connection, bringing them back together, there'd be no getting out of driving over there.

Shit, she thought. But she said, "We'll see…"

Kurt had dozed off on the couch while watching a movie with Ranson. It was an action flick he'd seen before—one of the many superhero movies that'd been out in the last five years—so he wasn't all that interested. And he was exhausted after being up so much of last night and stewing about what he'd done ever since. Worry wasn't something he generally had to contend with. That was Brant's department. But he'd just taken one of the biggest risks ever, because he was crazy about one particular woman.

Idiot. That was the thought he'd drifted off with, and since what he'd done wasn't anything he'd be able to forget until he knew he was in the clear, it was the first thought that ran through his head when he was jolted awake by a knock at the door.

His brother glanced over at him. "You expecting someone?"

There was a clock on the wall that'd been there since their parents owned the house. They hadn't bothered to change anything their parents had left behind, because they were comfortable as they were. It showed nine o'clock, but that wasn't outrageously late, even on a Sunday night, especially for their friends. Any of the guys they hung out with could be at the door. Because there were three single men living under the same roof, and some of Brant's friends had started to hang out with them since he'd gotten married and wasn't available as often, there were a lot of possibilities. "No," Kurt said as he covered a yawn. "You?"

Ranson didn't bother answering. He shoved out of the recliner he'd nabbed before Kurt could get it—it was the best seat in the house—and answered the door.

"Hey, how are you, Ran? It's been a while."

Kurt's fatigue fell away the second he recognized Kate's voice. She'd come to his house?

"No kidding," Ranson responded. "You've been so caught up with that boyfriend of yours, you've neglected all your old friends. How're things going? I hear you're planning to get married."

That was old news—and no longer accurate—but Kurt was glad he hadn't mentioned the latest to his brothers. It would've made him look like he was keeping tabs on Jane and Kate, something he hoped to avoid, because if Jane wound up pregnant, he might be outed as the father whether he wanted to be or not.

Of course, it also meant his brother had just said something he was going to wish he hadn't, but as far as Kurt was concerned, that was the lesser of two evils.

"They broke up last week," another female voice said.

Jane was at the door, too? What was going on? Why would they come over without even texting him?

"I'm sorry," Ranson said. "I…I hadn't heard."

"That's okay," Kate said. "Is Kurt around?"

Kurt had already jumped to his feet and started toward the door. They just couldn't see him yet. Once he stepped into view, Kate smiled widely. "Oh, I didn't realize you were in the room."

He couldn't help glancing at Jane, who looked as miserable as he felt, before responding. "I was sacked out. Took me a minute to come around." He yawned again—this one feigned—to highlight his fatigue. "What's going on?"

"We were out and about and just thought we'd come over and say hi." Kate nudged her sister, probably because Jane hadn't even said hello yet.

"We were just on our way home from Ellen's," Jane murmured.

They'd driven out of their way. But the ranch was far enough from town that almost anyone who visited had to go out of the way. "Oh." He stepped back. "I'm glad you did. Come on in."

Kate walked through the door first, giving Jane the opportunity to shoot him a quick *I'm sorry* look. If, for a second, he'd thought this visit might've been her idea, he now knew it wasn't.

"It's been a long time since I've seen you, too, Ran," Kate said to his brother.

Ranson grabbed the remote and paused the movie. "I'm devoted to our cattle—don't get off the ranch much," he joked.

"None of us do. Spring is busy around here," Kurt volunteered before she could also accuse him of being too scarce. Whenever she'd contacted him the past week, he'd followed up but only with the bare minimum required to remain polite and friendly. He hadn't wanted to encourage her. He knew that was the quickest way to get Jane to turn away from him. But he didn't want Kate to call him out on that, either. Especially in front of her sister. He hadn't mentioned to Jane that Kate had made several attempts to get hold of him. "Have a seat."

Kate sat on the couch; Jane moved into the room but remained standing, as if she was trying to signal that she didn't plan on staying very long.

He hoped that was true. Having them both in the same room made him feel self-conscious. Besides, after crashing on the couch, he was pretty sure his hair was standing up. "Can I get you a beer or something?"

"I'll take a beer," Kate said.

Jane declined.

Despite beating himself up all day for agreeing to father a baby with a woman who wasn't romantically interested in him, it was hard for Kurt not to let his gaze gravitate—again and again—to the woman he wanted. He'd never had such a terrible crush on anyone else. Last night might've made him want to avoid getting caught up in her baby pursuits, but it'd done little to kill his interest in her overall. Now that he'd been with her— intimately—he only wanted to get back in her bed.

As Kurt returned from the kitchen with her beer, Ranson got back into the recliner. "You were living with Will, weren't you, Kate?"

She grimaced. "Unfortunately."

"Where are you staying now?"

"I've moved in with Papa and Jane, but I hope to get my own place eventually."

"You don't think you'll go back to Will?" Ranson asked.

"No way," she said emphatically. "I won't have anything to do with him. It's been a living hell," she admitted. "The messages and pictures I found on his computer made me physically ill."

"He was cheating on you?" Ranson guessed.

"It went beyond a simple affair." She gave them a flirty grin. "But the good news is…I'm available again."

Kurt caught his breath. He knew that statement was aimed more his way, but, fortunately, Ranson spoke up. "That's great. Just let us know when you want to go out. We'll meet you for a drink or something."

"I've been trying to get this dude to hang out with me all week," she said, hitching her thumb in Kurt's direction. "But he's never available."

Ranson looked mildly surprised. Fortunately, he didn't argue. He turned his response into a joke instead. "Yeah, well, he's always been the most popular in the family."

Kate turned to Kurt. "Speaking of which, where were you last night?"

His mind quickly shuffled through possible responses. He couldn't say he was in town, or it would seem rude he hadn't offered to get together with her. "I…I had to drive to Bozeman," he said, figuring it would be smart to stick as close to the truth as possible.

His brother gave him a funny look. "You went to Bozeman last night?"

"Yeah."

"Why didn't you tell me?" he said. "I would've gone with you."

"I had a date." What else could he say? Ranson would know he didn't have business in Bozeman.

"How weird!" Kate exclaimed. "Jane was there last night, too. Did you know that?"

Kurt hoped the color hadn't just drained out of his face. "No. You were?" he said, blinking innocently at Jane. "That's crazy."

"I had a date, too," she responded. "Some guy I met online."

"How'd it go?" Kurt knew he was pressing his luck but found this part sort of funny.

"Um—" she cleared her throat "—better than I expected."

"Are you planning to see the dude again?" Ranson asked.

She stared at her feet. "I'm not sure. I guess…I guess that depends on him."

"Look at you!" Kate said to her sister. "She's definitely downplaying it," she added for their sake. "She had so much fun—told me she got laid for the first time in years and loved every second of it."

Jane's head snapped up as her jaw dropped. "Kate! I didn't say that."

"You said you enjoyed it, so don't be such a prude." Kate started laughing so hard she rocked back into the couch. "You think *these* guys are celibate?"

"It doesn't matter. That was personal information!"

Jane said, her eyes round, her face flushed with embarrassment.

Kurt certainly didn't mind what Kate had shared. That was exactly the type of thing he wanted to hear. Giving Jane a slow, knowing smile, he said, "I'm glad you had a good time."

"How was *your* date?" Kate asked, drawing the attention back to him.

He could no longer maintain eye contact with Jane. Looking down, he scratched his neck, remembering. "I had a good time, too."

"Oh, my God!" Jane railed as she marched to the car well ahead of her sister, who'd had one beer too many before Jane could drag her out of the house. "What were you thinking, saying what you did to Kurt and Ranson about my date last night?"

"What do you mean?" Kate asked, playing stupid.

"I know you're tipsy, but certainly you remember spouting off that I slept with my date last night."

"Oh, that." Kate played it off as though it was nothing as she continued to stumble along. "Don't be mad. I mean, I could see you getting angry if Ranson and Kurt were *your* friends. But they're five and six years younger than you—*my* friends. What do they care if you slept with some guy on a date?"

Jane had to be careful not to go too far. She didn't want to plant any suspicion in her sister's mind. "When I tell you stuff like that, it's private. If I want other people to know, I'll tell them myself."

"You're overreacting," she insisted.

"It was none of their business. I'm sorry I ever told you."

"Oh, stop."

Jane jerked away when Kate tried to catch her arm.

"Wow. You're really mad."

"Of course I'm mad. You embarrassed me."

Kate slid into the passenger seat as Jane got behind the wheel. "All right, all right. I'm sorry. I thought it was funny, and I'm sure they did, too, but I'll respect your privacy from now on."

Grateful for the cover darkness provided, Jane started the car. If Kate ever found out that it was Kurt she'd seen in Bozeman, her sister would never forgive her. But she wasn't going to find out. Unless…

Jane's hand automatically went to her stomach as she drove around the horseshoe-shaped driveway to get back on the main road. Chances were, she wasn't pregnant. Even if she was, they might still keep it a total secret.

"You can be so uptight," her sister grumbled.

Jane figured she needed to cut Kate a break. Her sister had just gone through a harrowing week. And she was right about Kurt being *her* school friend and, sometimes, quasi-boyfriend. The guilt Jane felt for getting involved with him in spite of that took the fire out of her umbrage. "Maybe I just haven't had as much to drink," she muttered. She actually hadn't had any, just in case she was pregnant, and Kate immediately called her on it.

"I don't remember you having *one*, but maybe you should have," her sister countered. "Then you might've had some fun like the rest of us."

Kurt hadn't drunk much, either, but Jane didn't point that out. She didn't want to reveal how closely she'd been watching him. She'd been able to feel the heat of his body when he moved past her, even though they never touched, had felt the weight of his gaze on more than one occasion and looked up to see him watching her.

"At least I won at beer pong," Jane pointed out. Fortunately, they'd put water in the cups, or maybe she'd be as drunk as Kate. At first, when they were playing against Kurt and Ranson, they'd lost almost every game.

"I'm glad we went over," Kate said with a sigh, sounding happier than she'd been since the breakup. "I needed that."

Worried that she might've started something that would be difficult to get out of, Jane curled her fingernails into her palms. "I'm glad you had a good time," she said softly.

"Isn't Kurt hot?" her sister asked. "I mean…did you see the way he looked in those jeans? I should've gone for him in the first place. Will didn't deserve me."

Alarm caused Jane to tense. "You're not interested in Kurt again…"

"Of course I'm interested in Kurt. I've always been interested in him. We just haven't been able to get on the same page. But…maybe now things will be different."

Jane swallowed a groan. Her sister was going to hate her. What was she going to do?

Fifteen

When Averil woke up on Monday and saw the beautiful pattern of white rectangles on the floor next to her—from the sun streaming through the windows of her new apartment—her first thought was that it was wonderful to have such peace and quiet. What a relief that she didn't have to worry about her mother barging in to scold her for being out too late or parking too far over in the driveway. Or to tell her she had to get up right away and do something she was already planning to do for Mitch. Having a taskmaster watching every move she made and constantly harping and correcting her—as if she wasn't a full-grown adult—had been irritating and made her hate Chase even more for contributing to her current situation. She'd tried to be a good wife. *He* was the one who'd disappear for several days at a time with no warning. When he got back, he'd insist it was all innocent, that he'd been surfing or camping or hiking, but she needed a partner she could rely on to help earn a living and raise Mitch, and he simply wouldn't stand up and be responsible.

As she yawned and stretched, her leg brushed against

Jordan's, which startled her. She'd expected him to be gone by now. He always said how much he hated Coyote Canyon, that the people who lived in her hometown were just a bunch of rednecks. She'd assumed he would get up bright and early and head home the way she always did.

Fortunately, Jane was closed on Monday. That meant no one would have to know she'd been with him for the entire night.

A second later, however, she heard the door downstairs and knew it had to be Jane. Who else would have keys to the building? And that meant Jane would already have seen Jordan's Audi in the alley.

"Shoot," she muttered.

"What is it?" Jordan sounded groggy with his head partway beneath his pillow. They'd made a place to sleep on the floor using bedding she'd already carted over from her parents' and watched a movie on her laptop before making love.

Not only had he not gotten up and left, but he didn't seem to be in a hurry to go even now. Was he planning to spend the day with her? It wasn't as if either one of them had to work. The wife of the man who owned the feedstore handled the register on Mondays, and Jordan's practice was closed. He chose to work Saturdays instead, to accommodate patients who had less flexibility in their own work schedules, which would've been nice of him, except he was only doing it because he'd lost so many patients since he'd purchased the practice right out of dental school. Saturday hours were his attempt to slow or stop the attrition. But after coming to know him, Averil believed it was his bedside manner patients had a problem with, not the lack of weekend availability.

She couldn't tell him that, though. The slightest criticism set him off, and she didn't want to get into another argument like the last one.

"Jane's here," she said as she used her fingers to comb through the worst snarls in her hair.

"Where?" When he sat up, his dark hair was matted to the sides of his head and the imprint of the blanket scored one cheek. She wished she could say he looked sexy, but he didn't. That he was still in her bed, naked, brought regret and shame, not excitement or admiration.

"Downstairs," she clarified. "She owns Vintage by Jane."

"Oh." He dropped back onto the pillow. "I knew that. What's she doing here? Last night you told me it was closed on Mondays."

"It is. But sometimes she stops by to drop something off or whatever."

"What time is it?" he asked.

How would she know? Did he expect her to get up and check for him?

Why not? she decided. Maybe if it was later than he anticipated, he'd leave.

Dragging herself out from the warmth of the covers, she collected her phone from where she'd left it charging on the counter. "Nearly ten," she told him before going into the bathroom.

When she came out, it looked as though he'd dozed off again. "What's going on?" she asked.

He lifted his head and squinted against the sunlight. "What do you mean?"

"What are your plans for today?"

"I don't really have any. What about you?"

"I need to get some more stuff from my mother's

house. I'm hoping to be moved by the time Mitch gets back."

"You're going to your folks' house right now?"

"Yeah. Why not? It'll be easier to shower there and get ready, since all my moisturizers and soaps and razor are in that bathroom." She pulled on her panties and bra. "Want to help me move today? My parents have been asking when they might meet you."

"I can't," he said immediately. "I should probably head back."

He'd just said he didn't have any plans today. Why did she continue to hope he'd act more interested in her than he was?

For the sake of her ego, she supposed. And because she hadn't been able to find anyone else. "Fine," she said. "But if you want to use the bathroom before you go, you'd better get up."

"Wow," he said. "What's the rush? Are you mad?"

She wasn't mad; she was disappointed. It was always the same story with him. She didn't know why she didn't put an end to the relationship.

Have some self-respect, she told herself. But the divorce and the humbling experience of raising her son in her parents' home had damaged her self-esteem to the point that she was beginning to think she couldn't do any better.

Not only that, but she was tired of being alone. "No, I just have a lot to get done."

"You don't have time for breakfast? Can't we eat, at least, before I go?"

Breakfast sounded good to her, too. But he'd only offered because *he* was hungry, and it wasn't any fun to eat alone. Couldn't he ever do something simply because *she'd* like it?

That question made her think of Brant. Why weren't there more men in the world like him?

"Well?" Jordan prompted when she didn't answer right away.

"As long as we go over to the next town," she agreed.

"Why do we have to eat somewhere else?"

Because she didn't want her parents to know Jordan had spent the night. They wouldn't approve. "I'd rather not start any gossip."

He rolled his eyes. "Give me a break. You're in your thirties. You should be able to do whatever the hell you want."

"It doesn't work that way around here." Not without some serious blowback, anyway. Ellen seemed determined to live her best life no matter what anyone else thought, but Averil needed her family too badly to risk losing their support.

"Fine, we'll go to the next town," he grumbled. "Are you sure you don't want to wear a disguise, too?"

She gave him a dirty look for the sarcasm. "Thanks for being so understanding."

"I'd be understanding if it wasn't ridiculous to begin with," he said, but she let it go so that it wouldn't escalate and combed her hair with the brush she carried in her purse while he got dressed.

After piling her hair on top of her head with a twisty she'd been wearing around her wrist, she grabbed her phone and purse and told him to be quiet as they descended the stairs. She was hoping to slip out before Jane could see them. But the stairs were old and creaky—there was no way to avoid making noise.

Jane poked her head out of the store before they could reach the landing. "Hey, I'm off today if you'd like some help mov—" She fell silent once she saw Jordan coming down the stairs, too. "Oh, sorry. I forgot you had company."

"Jordan's not company exactly," Averil said. "I mean… we're just going out to breakfast. Then he's heading back to Libby."

"I see. Well, if you need help after he goes, let me know. I'm going to spend the rest of the morning with Kate, but when she has to go to work, I'll be free."

"It's really nice of you to offer," Averil said and meant it. With everything Jane had to do—maintain the store on her own, care for her grandfather and try to be there for Kate—she'd offered time on her only day off to help when the man Averil had just slept with wasn't willing to lift a finger.

Averil knew she had to get her life under control. Moving into the apartment was supposed to be part of that, so why had she taken a step back and let Jordan come to town and spend the night with her? "I can't tell you how much I appreciate it," she said.

Jane looked surprised by the sincerity in Averil's voice. "I don't mind. That's what friends are for, right?"

Averil smiled. "Yeah, that's what friends are for."

"What's this I hear about you having a date last weekend?"

It was Wednesday at lunchtime, and Ellen had stopped by the store. Since she owned a well-drilling business and operated heavy machinery, she was wearing steel-toed boots, a long-sleeved flannel shirt and worn jeans. Although she was only about five-two, maybe one hundred pounds, she was a force to be reckoned with and didn't play the usual game of being polite simply for the sake of being polite. She was outspoken and frank and always genuinely herself, regardless of how she might be perceived, which could be a little off-putting at first. That was why it'd taken Jane longer to embrace her than it'd taken Talulah. But now that she'd gotten to know Ellen, Jane *loved* her. Ellen wasn't only tough; she was fiercely independent and loyal—definitely someone you'd want on your side if you had to fight for anything—not to mention completely honest and reliable.

"What are you talking about?" Jane's mind raced as she tried to decide how to handle this situation. When she'd told Kate she was going out with a guy she'd met online, she hadn't expected her sister to blab about it to their friends. What was so remarkable about one date?

The fact that she hadn't told any of them about it, she thought, answering her own question. They would find that odd because she told them almost everything.

"I saw Kate at the diner a few minutes ago. I stopped to get Hendrix a slice of apple pie," Ellen explained. "When she mentioned that you're seeing someone, Talulah and I were both shocked."

"I'm not really *seeing* someone," Jane said. "I had a date. *One* date. That's all."

"With who?"

So she'd have an excuse to look away, Jane straightened the display of refrigerator magnets with pithy sayings by the register. "Just some guy I met online."

"What site are you using these days? Last I heard, the online stuff wasn't really working for you."

Jane hated lying, especially to someone she trusted as much as Ellen. In some ways, she trusted Ellen even

more than Talulah. Ellen generally held a wider view of
the world than anyone else she knew. "It *wasn't* working for me. It's still not. I mean…I'm not active anymore.
That date was…"

Ellen raised her eyebrows as Jane let her words trail
off.

With a sigh, Jane glanced through the front window
to be sure no one else was about to walk into the store.
She also poked her head out the back door to make sure
Averil's car wasn't in the alley. She didn't expect to find
it—she could usually hear Averil when she came and
went—but she wasn't going to say anything until she
felt safe.

Fortunately, the alley was empty, as she'd expected.

"Why are you acting so secretive?" Ellen asked, obviously confused.

Jane had promised Kurt she wouldn't tell anyone he'd
been involved in her plan to get pregnant, but she was
torn enough about what was going on in her own life
that she wanted to share as much as she could without
crossing that line. Ellen could cut right to the heart of
any matter and always spoke the truth—and the truth
was what Jane most needed to hear. "I wasn't on a date
exactly. I was…"

"What?" Ellen prompted. "Just say it. You're starting
to freak me out."

"I was trying to get pregnant," Jane blurted.

Ellen looked astonished. "Excuse me?"

"You heard me. I want to have a baby."

"Eventually, yes. But—"

"This year!" Jane broke in. "Why wait any longer?"

"Because—unless there's something going on that I

don't know about—you'll be entirely on your own. You don't have anyone to help support and raise a child."

"I'm getting this from *you*?" Jane said with a scowl. "Come on. I thought you were more progressive than that. I can do it myself, you know."

Ellen raked her fingers through her short, choppy haircut. "I guess I can't argue with that. You *could* do it on your own. The question is—why would you want to? Raising a child is hard enough with a partner."

Ellen had been raised by a single mother who hadn't been very reliable. Jane could see why she might not believe taking on so much responsibility would be the best way to go. But Jane would be a far better mother than Ellen's was. "Because I don't have a significant other, and I'm in my midthirties. I'm afraid if I wait any longer it'll be too late."

This information was met with a low whistle. "I didn't see this coming. You've never even mentioned wanting a baby. Or…did I miss it?"

Jane had confided in Talulah, but so far, Talulah was the only person who knew how serious she was about having a child. "It's never been something I was willing to talk about. I couldn't see it happening. But now I'm taking control and making sure it does."

"To be totally honest, I could see *myself* doing something like this. I can't see *you* doing it."

"Because I've always played by the rules! That's why I'm stuck here in Coyote Canyon without any romantic prospects well into my thirties."

Ellen nibbled on her bottom lip for a few seconds. "Your love for your grandfather has a lot to do with that."

"I won't leave him when he needs me most."

"I wouldn't, either."

"I know." Ellen's strength and tenacity—and her conviction when it came to standing by her loved ones—had inspired Jane on many occasions, which was sort of ironic, given the number of people who'd thought the worst of Ellen simply because she had a lot of tattoos and piercings and occasionally made very bold choices when it came to her hair color and style.

"So…who'd you get to father your child?"

"I can't tell you that."

"Why not?"

"Because I'm respecting his privacy."

Lines of consternation appeared on Ellen's forehead. "That means he must not be a stranger."

Shit. Jane didn't even want her to know that much, but she was so worried and wound up she was making some stupid mistakes. "He's just a guy I met online."

"If that's true, you would've said so."

"I did say so. That's what I told Kate."

"Not exactly. You said you were going on a date."

"I just left out the last part—about the baby."

Ellen studied her more closely. "Why? Why can't Kate know?"

"Because I don't want her to."

"She's going to find out when you wind up pregnant. What will you tell her then?"

"I'll say I went to a sperm bank. That's what I'll tell everyone."

"What's the difference between some guy she doesn't know and a sperm bank? Wouldn't both be the same to her?"

Jane wished she could go back in time and not get into this conversation in the first place. Ellen knew her too well, and she was so quick-witted.

"This is unlike you," Ellen commented. "What aren't you telling me?"

"Nothing!" Jane insisted. "At this point, you know more than anyone else."

Ellen sank into a leather chair Jane had for sale near the register.

"What are you doing?" Jane knew Hendrix had to be waiting for her. They still ran separate businesses, but they worked together most days—he helped her with her wells, and she helped him with his. When they got married, the businesses would eventually merge.

"I'm thinking."

There was some real danger in that. Ellen could figure out anything if she put her mind to it. "Please don't."

Ellen's phone went off; she ignored it.

"You're not going to answer that?" Jane asked. "It's probably Hendrix. He's got to be wondering where you are. You stopped to get him that piece of apple pie for lunch, right?"

She seemed deep in thought. "I'll call him back in a minute."

Jane came around the cash register. "Ellen, I'm sorry I said anything. Please…just forget this whole conversation."

"But it's so inexplicable and unexpected. So unlike you. The only man I've seen you with lately is…" She jumped to her feet. "Oh, my God!"

Dread filled Jane's body, rooting her to the spot as she said, "What?"

"You're sleeping with Kurt Elway! *That's* why you haven't told Talulah about Bozeman. And that's why you told Kate you were going out with someone you met on the internet."

* * *

It was nearly ten. Jane needed to be in bed. She was exhausted from working—and stewing all day on top of working. But her friends had called an emergency meeting at the diner. Jane could easily guess why they'd asked her to meet them there. They wanted to talk to her without Brant overhearing.

"Is it true?" Talulah demanded as soon as Jane walked through the back door.

Jane hitched her purse higher and frowned at Ellen, who was leaning against the sink, holding a cup of what smelled like chamomile tea. "You told her?"

"It wasn't a secret I agreed to keep," Ellen clarified. "If I thought doing that would help you in some way, I might've made a different decision. But knowing she cares about you as much as I do, I decided to bring her in on it and see if it worried her as much as it did me."

"What are you worried about?" Jane demanded. "It's *my* life. I can do what I want."

"No one's more friendly to that concept than I am," Ellen said. "I've been fighting the same battle for years, which is how I know that sometimes people can be their own worst enemy. We're not judging you, Jane. We're just concerned where the path you're taking might lead you."

"Exactly," Talulah chimed in. "We want you to think a few things through—that's all."

Ellen set her cup on the counter and came over to the table. "And since this affects Talulah's brother-in-law, it affects her and Brant, too. You could be carrying their niece or nephew."

"Brant's very defensive of his brothers," Talulah said. "I don't want him to get mad about this. What if it creates a situation where I'm forced to choose between you and Kurt? Even if that doesn't happen, it could get to where you don't want to be in the same room, which will be hard enough. You're both such important parts of my life!"

All the consequences of Jane's actions were beginning to crystallize in her mind. What had seemed easy on the one hand was actually very complicated on the other.

Bottom line, she should've gone through a sperm bank. She'd been a fool not to. "It doesn't *have* to affect Kurt or Brant or anyone else," she said. "I might not even be pregnant."

"Which is why I spoke up," Ellen volunteered. "There might still be time for you to think twice about this."

"You don't want Kurt to be the father of my baby?" Jane asked. "Why not? If I don't expect anything other than the necessary DNA, why would it matter?"

"It could create a lot of regret and—" Talulah started to say, but Ellen spoke at the same time.

"It's not that we *don't* want him to be the father of your baby. We're worried that you're doing something that could become painful, for you and a lot of other people, including Brant's family."

"Kurt agreed to do it," Jane insisted. "It should be up to the two of us."

"It *is* up to the two of you," Ellen said. "We just want you to consider a few things."

"That I haven't already considered?" Jane challenged. "Like what?"

"Like lying about the identity of your baby's father," Talulah replied. "I know you think you can say you used a sperm bank, and no one will be the wiser. But secrets have a way of getting out—and they can make big waves when they do. I'm willing to bet Brant's family would gladly be part of your baby's life. I *know* Brant would. Do you really want to cut them out—without even asking them?"

Jane threw up her hands. "Fine. If I'm not pregnant, I *will* use a cryobank, okay? That'll solve everything."

"Jane—" Ellen said, but Jane was too frustrated and upset to listen. She wheeled around and walked out, letting the door slam behind her despite their efforts to call her back into the room.

She told herself they should be more understanding. They were both lucky enough to have found the man of their dreams. They had good businesses with a lot of forward momentum and nothing holding them back. They had no idea what it felt like to be left behind, stuck and unable to move forward.

And yet, deep down, Jane knew what really made her mad was...they were right. Involving Kurt risked hurting too many people. She shouldn't have done it.

Sixteen

Kurt hadn't contacted Jane all week. He was afraid to learn if she was pregnant. If she was, there'd be no backing out. And if she wasn't, she might ask him to try again. To make matters worse, he had Kate pressing him every few days to get together and had finally agreed to have a drink with her.

Fortunately, he'd coerced Miles into going with him. Miles hadn't wanted to, but when Kurt wouldn't take no for an answer Miles had finally caved in and agreed. But he didn't understand why Kurt needed a wingman tonight, and Kurt couldn't explain that he didn't want anyone to see him with Kate and assume they were dating. Although he was trying to give up on Jane, to convince himself she wasn't interested despite the conflicting signals he'd gotten the first time they'd made love, he was hopelessly stuck on her. And just in case he was wrong, and she did feel some small amount of interest that could grow into more, he didn't want to turn her off by making her think he was interested in Kate again.

"I'm tired tonight, bro," Miles complained as they walked into Hank's. "I don't know what I'm doing here."

"You're hanging out with me for an hour or so," he said. "That's what you're doing."

"But *why*? You don't need me. You've known Kate for years. You two have even been a couple here and there."

Eager to downplay that connection, he shook his head. "No, we haven't. We've almost gotten together once or twice—but that's it."

"You slept with her," Miles insisted, as if that made him right.

Kurt swallowed a sigh. Why did everyone have to keep pointing that out? That was the trouble of living with his brothers. They knew everything! He hadn't known he might have a chance with Jane back then. "It was strictly casual," he said, then nudged his brother because he'd just spotted Kate waiting for him in a booth near the stage, which was empty since live bands played only on the weekend.

"Hi," she said as she got up and gave him a hug. "I didn't realize you'd be bringing Miles. I could've brought a friend or…or someone with me."

That someone would most likely have been Jane, which was exactly why he hadn't told her. "When he saw me getting ready to go, he said he'd like to come along."

Kurt could feel his brother's surprise, but fortunately, Miles knew better than to contradict what he'd said. That wasn't the role of a wingman.

"Hope you don't mind," Miles said instead.

"Of course I don't mind." She gave him a hug next, but Kurt could tell she wasn't pleased that they wouldn't be alone and guessed Miles could tell, too.

"I'm afraid we only have an hour or so," Kurt said. "My mother wants us to pick up some food and other stuff while we're in town, and she goes to bed early."

"Oh, okay," Kate said.

That comment was met with more disappointment, but Kurt purposely ignored her reaction. She already had a drink, so he flagged down the waitress, and he and Miles ordered beer.

"How've things been going?" he asked. "You hearing much from Will these days?"

"Too much." She grimaced. "He sends me hateful texts every day."

"Why? *He* was the one who cheated."

"He insists he didn't do anything wrong. Says I'm making a big deal out of nothing."

"You're lucky you found out what he's really like before you got married."

She nodded.

The manager spotted Miles and came over to ask if he'd like to sing a few songs. He had a good voice and performed at Hank's or other dive bars occasionally. But he hadn't brought his guitar with him tonight. Kurt was glad of that, or Miles would've ended up on stage instead of sitting at the booth where Kurt wanted him to be.

"Sorry, not tonight, man," Miles said.

Then the owner sauntered over and booked Miles for one Sunday a month over the next three months, which took a few minutes. Then Kate suggested they play some darts. After three games, Kurt was just about to say they had to go—he'd been keeping one eye on the clock—when Kate asked him to dance.

He didn't want to get on the dance floor with her, but he also didn't feel he could refuse. "Sure. We'll be right back," he told his brother.

"This feels like old times," Kate murmured as she slipped into his arms.

Kurt tried to hold her at an appropriate distance, but she kept pushing her body up against his. It would've been too obvious that he didn't want to come into contact with her if he did anything except shift slightly, so he eventually gave up the battle, thinking he just needed to get through the song and leave.

He'd almost accomplished that. The song was just coming to a close when he looked up and saw Miles talking to Talulah and Brant—and right there with them was Jane.

Jane had spent most of the time since she'd recruited Kurt to help her get pregnant worrying about what Kate would think if she found out, especially now that Talulah and Ellen were aware of what was going on. Kate was already going through a terrible time. Jane didn't want to add to her sister's disappointment and heartbreak. She didn't want her to think she was horning in on something that Kate felt should belong to her, either. But when she'd told Kurt what she wanted to do that fateful night right here at Hank's, she'd never expected Kate and Will to break up. She'd never really considered what it would be like if Kurt and Kate got back together—or together for the first time since nothing in the past had ever been official.

Her hand automatically went to her stomach. She was nauseous just watching them dance. She might've thought she had morning sickness, but she'd read online that morning sickness didn't typically set in until two weeks after conception, and it hadn't even been a full week since Bozeman. Whether she wanted to admit it or not, that terrible feeling in her gut had to be jealousy.

No. It was regret, she decided. It *couldn't* be jealousy.

"Jane?" Talulah said. "Did you hear me?"

Jane pulled her attention back to the conversation. She'd been so deep in the well of her own thoughts she'd missed what had just been said. "I'm sorry. What was that?"

"Would you like some cranberry juice or something?"

"Cranberry juice!" Miles made a face, obviously taken aback by the suggestion. "I can see why *you* might want juice," he said to Talulah, "but why would anyone else? We're at a bar, for crying out loud. Can I get you a beer or a glass of wine?" he asked Jane. "Maybe a mixed drink?"

"No, I…"

"*I'm* having a cranberry juice," Talulah said to her.

Jane understood why she was suggesting it, but she didn't want to be associated with the nonalcoholic beverage Talulah had to drink, didn't want any parallels drawn between them. After all, she might not be pregnant. If she could get out of the mess she'd gotten herself into and go to a sperm bank, that would be the best course.

"Nothing for me, thanks," she said. "I'm…good right now."

"Okay." Since the only waitress they'd seen since coming in was busy with a large party in the corner, Miles walked over to the bar.

"What's wrong?" Talulah murmured while he was gone and some guys who knew Brant had pulled him aside to say hello.

"Nothing," Jane insisted, but Talulah obviously didn't believe her.

"You're not still mad about the other night…"

"Of course not. I know you meant well." Both Ellen and Talulah had called to apologize and tell her they were only looking out for her best interests, and since she knew that was true, she'd let it go. It wasn't that. It was walking into Hank's to find Kate in Kurt's arms, slow-dancing as *she'd* slow-danced with him while they were planning whether he'd help her get pregnant. But it wasn't fair, wasn't even reasonable, that she'd feel so possessive of him. He'd made her no promises.

Actually, it went even further than that. *She* was the one who'd insisted there'd be no commitments or obligations on either side.

Talulah lowered her voice since Kurt and Kate were coming off the dance floor. "Is it Kurt? Are you upset he's with Kate?"

"No, of course not," she lied.

Fortunately, she didn't have to continue to protest because Kate and Kurt were now close enough that they could overhear.

"Hey," Kate said. "When you told me you were hanging out with Talulah and Brant tonight, I didn't know you'd be here."

Jane pasted a smile on her face. "We didn't have anything planned. This was sort of…last minute." She forced herself to turn and acknowledge Kurt, even though it was uncomfortable and all she could think about was the first time they'd taken off their clothes.

His eyes searched hers. "Hello. How are you feeling— I mean…doing?"

She cleared her throat. "Good. You?"

"Great," he said.

Jane knew he had to be wondering if she was pregnant. Would he be happier if she wasn't?

She imagined he'd have to be. What she'd asked of him seemed so huge now she was embarrassed she'd ever gone in that direction. Why would he want to help her with something like that? Was he interested in her sister? Because if he was, and she was pregnant…

Jane didn't even want to think about that. The chances of conception weren't high, she told herself. They'd had unprotected sex three times, and she'd made sure it was at the ideal time in her cycle. But still. There were those statistics. They indicated the chances of *not* conceiving were greater…

"We're going to need a bigger booth," Kate said and grabbed Kurt's arm. "Let's go get one."

Kurt could tell Talulah knew something. The way she watched him, the things she said. Had Jane told her best friend he was helping her get pregnant? And, if so, would Talulah tell Brant?

He bet she would. Talulah told Brant everything. Then Brant would know he'd actually gone through with it. But as they all sat and talked in the bigger booth he and Kate had secured, he watched his older brother for signs of disapproval and couldn't detect any change in him. Maybe, for Jane, Talulah would keep the secret.

Or was it just a matter of time before she spoke up?

After only a few minutes, Jane went to the bathroom. Then she went to the bar to get some ginger ale. Then she crossed the room to speak to an older woman—one of her store customers, he assumed—who seemed startled enough that she'd made the effort. Kurt decided it was more of an excuse to get away from their group than anything else. She had to be as uncomfortable as he was— possibly more so. She refused to meet his gaze, barely sipped her ginger ale, once she finally got it, and hardly said a word to anyone.

Fortunately, Kate and Talulah carried the conversation, with a few comments thrown in by Miles and Brant. No one seemed to notice that Jane wasn't herself, except him. But he was probably more closely attuned to her every expression, every word, every movement. She drew his attention like a high-powered magnet drew a piece of steel. Seeing her made him regret not calling her since Bozeman. He'd been trying to navigate this tricky situation in the best possible way—to capitalize on any chance he had to explore a possible relationship with her without destroying his own life in the process. But maybe last weekend *would've* changed something between them if only he'd followed up.

Her coming to Hank's and finding him with Kate certainly couldn't be helping his case.

Kate turned to him. "Do you want another drink?" she asked before flagging down the server.

Before he could answer, Jane jumped up again and mumbled something about the bathroom, which would be her second trip in an hour. He watched her go as he said, "No, I've had enough. I need to head over to my mother's soon. But I think I'll go to the bathroom first."

He didn't wait for a response. He got up, dodged the waitress, who was approaching the table, and strode purposefully to the hallway where the bathrooms were located. He'd already missed catching Jane, so he stood near the entrance to the women's side and waited for her to come back out.

Through the door, he heard the sink go on and off and the hand dryer start up. When she finally appeared, she stepped back. "Kurt…"

Taking her elbow, he pulled her a step forward so the door, which was closing, wouldn't hit her. "I just… I wanted to see if you're okay," he said.

She lifted her chin. "I'm fine."

He studied her for several seconds. "Any news?"

"Not yet."

"When will you know?"

"Not for a while. According to the internet, I shouldn't even bother testing until I miss my period. And it's not supposed to start for another week. Actually, what I read said you should wait a week beyond that," she added.

"You don't feel any different?"

"I feel a lot different. But that could all be in my head."

"What do you mean?"

"It's not indicative of a pregnancy. I'm just…torn. I want to have a baby. But I feel terrible that I may have put you in a bad position, and I certainly don't want to hurt Kate."

Conscious of the fact that they didn't have much time, he glanced down the hall to make sure no one was coming. "Have you told Talulah about…Bozeman?"

Jane seemed startled. "Did she say something to you?"

"No. It's just the way she keeps looking at us. Something's different."

"I didn't tell her. I didn't tell anyone. Not on purpose. But I did mention something I shouldn't have to Ellen, something that made her suspicious enough to guess. I'm sorry. I should've been more careful. I never dreamed…" She shook her head. "Nothing gets past her."

"She must've told Talulah."

"She did. They cornered me about it the other night— wanted to caution me against what we're doing."

Shit. If Brant found out, everyone else in his family would, too, because Brant would raise hell that he'd gone through with what Jane wanted. "I don't get the impression my brother knows."

"Talulah said she wouldn't tell him. I made her promise she'd at least wait to see if there's a baby."

He bit back another curse. A lot was hanging on the next two weeks. He could only hope Jane wasn't pregnant. That was the only way he could get out of the situation now.

"I'm sorry," Jane said and she looked so miserable he believed her.

"It's okay." He hadn't truly believed it was a secret they'd be able to keep for long, anyway.

"I'd better get back." She started to leave, but he caught her arm.

"Come over tonight," he said.

Her eyes widened. "But…everything we just talked about."

It'd been an impulsive request, one that made no logical sense—not if he wanted to get out of the situation. But if he was capable of being logical about her, he never would've agreed to help her in the first place. "I know, but I can't quit thinking of Bozeman. I want to touch you again, be with you."

"Tonight?" she said.

"Why not?"

He expected her to refuse. He wasn't sure why he'd been impetuous enough to suggest another encounter in the first place.

But she said, "Where? When?"

His heart seemed to skip a beat. "Ten thirty at the ranch."

"But your brothers—"

"Won't know a thing," he said. "They won't even see you. It's a weeknight. They go to bed early."

Brant suddenly appeared in the hallway. Fortunately, Kurt spotted him right away and fell silent.

"Hey," his brother said, looking slightly puzzled when he saw them speaking so earnestly by the bathrooms instead of just talking at the table.

"Hey," Jane responded and got out of there immediately, without another word.

"What's going on?" Brant asked Kurt as they both looked after her. "You getting anywhere with her?"

"No," Kurt replied. After all, she hadn't agreed to see him. He didn't want to raise expectations, didn't want his brother taking note of every interaction he had with Jane and asking him about it later.

"Is that why you've gone back to Kate?"

"I haven't gone back to Kate."

"Did Jane think you have?"

"No. I was just… I told her I'm looking for a new desk for my bedroom. That's all."

"What's wrong with the one you have?" Brant asked.

"Are you kidding? I did my homework on it when I was a kid and engraved superhero emblems in the wood. It's time for a new one, and she thinks she can find one I might like."

"Oh." Brant seemed to believe him, because he shrugged as if it made no difference to him and ducked into the bathroom.

Kurt waited a few seconds to give Jane time to reach the table. Then he returned himself.

He shouldn't have gone out on a limb, Kurt told himself as he paced in the living room thirty minutes or so after his brothers had gone to bed. He wasn't sure why he'd asked Jane to come over. He'd claimed Miles and Ranson would be none the wiser, but they were in the house, and something could happen that would give Jane's presence away. So there was that. And he knew it might be difficult for Jane to get out of her own house with Kate living there. She wouldn't want to risk getting caught.

But he hadn't been thinking of any of that when he was standing in that alcove by the bathrooms. The only thing that'd mattered then was the desire he felt to kiss her again, hold her against him, to feel her beneath him. If she wasn't already pregnant, he'd only raise the odds of conception by making love to her again. That was why he hadn't contacted her since they got back from Bozeman. He'd been trying to keep his life on a safe track and stay away. But he couldn't stop wanting her, and in that moment at Hank's, the words had simply tumbled out of his mouth.

He hadn't heard from her, and it was after ten thirty, so chances were good she wasn't coming. He needed to accept that she wasn't interested and move on. How many times did she have to make that clear?

He was about to turn off the porch light and go to his room when he saw headlights in the driveway. The vehicle didn't pull all the way down to the house. It just sat there. And then his phone buzzed with a text.

Is it safe?

It was Jane. She'd come after all. He didn't know whether to be excited or mad at himself for being unable to walk away while he might still have the chance.

It's safe but pull around where you parked before—
when we went to Bozeman. I'll come grab you.

A thumbs-up appeared on his text, and she swung
back out onto the road. If Miles had seen her headlights,
he'd just think someone was turning around in the drive,
and Miles was the only one who had a window facing
in that direction. Ranson's room was at the back of the
house, like his.

He hurried to his room, grabbed his truck fob and
slipped out the front door. He didn't think his brothers
would react to the noise—not unless they heard a female
voice or something out of the ordinary. They all moved
around the house at various times, and no one kept close
tabs on what anyone else was doing.

It only took a few minutes to reach the far side of the
ranch and the copse of trees where they'd left Jane's car
when they went to Bozeman last Saturday. She was just
shutting off her engine when he pulled in behind her.

As soon as she got out and came toward him, he
leaned over the console to open the door.

She was wearing a pair of yoga pants, fur-lined boots
since it was cold out tonight, a thin sweater and a beanie,
with her hair poking out the bottom in pigtails, and she
seemed slightly breathless when she climbed in.

"You were able to get out of the house okay?" he
asked.

"Yeah. I live such a boring life no one would suspect
me of sneaking out, so I had that going for me," she said
with a laugh. "Besides, I'm thirty-five. I don't know if
you can call it sneaking out when you get to be that age."

He laughed as he threw the truck into Reverse and
drove back to the house.

"Are you sure your brothers are asleep?" she asked as he parked in the drive.

"They should be. But my room has a slider leading onto the deck, so we can go around. That way, you won't have to worry about walking through the house. I also have a bathroom off my bedroom. My parents built it that way in case they needed to take in one of their parents. But then they retired and turned the ranch over to us and moved to town, next to my mom's parents, so no one ever had to move in with us."

When she nodded but didn't say anything, he couldn't help wondering if she was having second thoughts. What had made her come? Was it only the hope of making a baby?

He wanted to believe otherwise—that he held some appeal for her, too—but she'd clearly stated her desires, so he knew better than to get his hopes up too high.

Whatever was going on, he refused to worry about it tonight. He'd had too much on his mind in Bozeman, too much holding him back. He wouldn't let that happen again. Tonight he was going to allow himself to enjoy the hours ahead of him and worry about everything else later.

Seventeen

Something had changed since Bozeman, Jane decided. There was an added, intangible element between them that made her time with Kurt even better. Maybe it was just that they were more familiar with each other. After being together before, they'd built up some trust and could let go of any self-consciousness or embarrassment.

While they were making love, Jane allowed her body to move as it wanted to move without trying to hold back or overthink what she was doing. Bozeman had been purposeful—all about getting pregnant. But since she hadn't planned on being with Kurt again, this time was different. She didn't have the same excuse for being with him, but she also didn't have the same constraint.

They shed their clothes almost as soon as she walked into his bedroom and he closed the door. Then they were hungrily kissing and touching each other, and only minutes later, he was moving inside her. Their lovemaking wasn't frantic, but it was focused and thorough and exquisitely satisfying, and she could smell his warm, masculine scent all around her on his body and the sheets.

When it was over, she lay next to him, physically

spent. It had been a long day, and this had been a wonderful release. But in coming to the ranch, she'd definitely
crossed another boundary she shouldn't have crossed.
She'd just decided to move forward with a cryobank, if
necessary. Why had she decided to sleep with him again?

She couldn't come up with a good excuse. She'd simply craved his hands on her body so much she hadn't
been able to refuse. There was something about him that
was beginning to appeal to her more than any other man
ever had—not only the way he smelled but the way he
moved and kissed and handled her body. He had a certain reverence for her when they were making love that
made her feel special, as though she mattered to him beyond the here and now.

"Wow," he said, still trying to catch his breath when
they were through. "*That* was good."

She could tell he thought it was way better than Bozeman, and he was right. It'd been *so* good, the guilt she'd
been pushing away all evening began to jab her like a
cattle prod. To escape the discomfort of that, she rolled
away from him, got up and started putting on her clothes.

He leaned up on one elbow. "Are you leaving? Already?"

The fear of being discovered kept her moving. "It's
late. And we both have work tomorrow."

"Okay. Um, that was quick. Will you come back
again? Tomorrow or later in the week?"

She opened her mouth to say no but couldn't force
the word through her lips. "Maybe," she said instead,
and he got up and dressed so he could drive her back to
her Mustang.

Mitch was back home, but Averil had just dropped him
off at school. He'd been out of class for so long, doing his

schoolwork with his father, that he didn't want to go back, but she'd encouraged him by reminding him that it was Friday, only one day before the weekend, and they could stay in their new apartment for the first time tonight.

She hated that the place now reminded her of her last night with Jordan. She shouldn't have allowed him to become part of this new phase of her life. The apartment was all about starting over and getting beyond the mistakes of the past.

At least since then she'd called and told him she didn't want to see him anymore. He'd been shocked and angry, as she'd expected. He thought he was too good for her, so it was a blow that *she'd* broken off the relationship, but she was relieved. From now on, she was going to have the mental fortitude to do what was best for her and her son. And this apartment was a symbol of that. She'd slipped up once—because Mitch had been gone and she'd gotten too lonely—but she wouldn't allow it to happen again.

As soon as she let herself in, she put down the basket of clean laundry she'd hauled from her parents' house and up the stairs and propped her hands on her hips while catching her breath. Moving had been no small feat. She was exhausted after all the packing and loading and carrying she'd done, but the place was looking good. Her brother and two nephews had brought over some furniture they no longer needed, so she had beds, dressers and the orange couch and coffee table she'd bought, and her father had given her an old TV out of the garage she hadn't even known he'd been storing. She'd also hung some pictures on the walls and purchased a few houseplants to make the apartment feel homier. Today all she had to do was make their beds, fill their drawers and drag over the last of Mitch's toys and her toiletries.

Then the move would be complete and her transformation into someone more independent and respectable, like Talulah and Jane, would occur. She was tired of feeling "less than."

She turned on some music and had just finished making Mitch's bed when she heard movement downstairs. Jane had arrived at the store. She was earlier than usual, Averil realized, checking her watch. She planned to leave her friend to get ready to open the store as usual, but remembering the hours they'd spent together Monday night, while Jane had helped her move, made Averil put on a pot of coffee instead.

Want to come up for coffee and a piece of avocado toast? The way I make it with pesto on the bottom and balsamic vinegar on top is to die for...

She assumed Jane would turn her down. She'd probably eaten before she left and had to get some stuff done or she wouldn't have shown up so early. It was only eight thirty, and Jane had been leery enough of her lately that Averil knew they could get only so close, which made the quick, positive response she received a bit of a surprise.

On my way.

Averil opened the door leading to the stairs for Jane while she put two slices of thickly sliced sourdough bread in the toaster and two plates on her kitchen table.

Jane appeared in the doorway only a few seconds later.

"Come on in," Averil said.

Her friend's smile seemed a bit wan, and the rings under her eyes suggested she hadn't had much sleep.

Averil quit worrying about the food she was trying to prepare and straightened. "What's going on?"

"Nothing," Jane replied, but it was hardly believable.

"What are you doing here so early?"

"I couldn't sleep last night, and Kate was around to feed Papa breakfast, so I said I had to take care of some things."

"Said? You didn't?"

"Not really," she admitted.

"Why couldn't you sleep?"

"I was…thinking."

"About…?"

"Things."

"That's vague." She gestured toward a chair. The table had seen better days. Someone had left it on the side of the road with a sign that read Free, and she'd picked it up because she needed a table and was out of money. It had four chairs with it, but two were so broken she'd had to leave them behind.

"There's too much to go into," Jane mumbled. "But it's nice to be here and have someone serve me coffee and breakfast. Thank you."

"What's wrong, Jane?"

"Nothing," she replied.

"I've known you too long to buy that," Averil said and slid Jane's plate toward her.

"I think I'm screwing up my life," she admitted.

Averil poured the coffee. Her mugs weren't anything fancy, either. Her mother had let her take a few, and they were the oldest ones, all of them chipped. But at least she had cups. She'd decided she wasn't going to dwell on the negative. She'd spent far too much time doing that the past few years. "Well, I seem to be somewhat of an expert at screwing up my own life, so tell me what's going on, and I'll tell you if you're in any danger."

This comment brought a genuine smile to Jane's lips. "You're too hard on yourself. You know that?"

"Not really. I've been an idiot. But I feel ready for a fresh start, so…thanks for acting as though you didn't mind if I moved in here."

"I don't mind. I'm jealous it's not me, but since I can't do it, I'm happy for you," she said and seemed to mean it, which made Averil feel even better.

"Jane, tell me, what's going on."

When Jane still hesitated, Averil cocked her head. "You can trust me, you know," she said softly. "I won't let you down. I promise."

Jane must've believed her, must've remembered that she'd been solid before marrying and divorcing Chase, because tears welled up in her eyes. "I'm so glad to have you back," she said.

Averil reached across the table, and Jane accepted her hand. "I'm happy to be back. Now tell me what's wrong, and let's see if we can fix it."

"Something's different with you."

Startled by this unexpected comment, Jane looked up to see her grandfather watching her closely. They'd just had dinner, and he was sitting in his recliner watching TV, which meant the volume was so loud she could scarcely think. She'd assumed he was engrossed in the World War II documentary she'd put on for him, so she'd let her mind wander and had no idea what kind of expressions had flitted across her face as she relived her latest rendezvous with Kurt. "What do you mean?" she asked.

Papa had once been so perceptive. Occasionally, he

seemed to be his old self—as shrewd as ever. The clarity in his eyes at this moment suggested now was one of those times. "You're quieter these days, preoccupied."

"I hadn't realized anything had changed," she said, hoping he'd let it go at that.

He twisted around, presumably to see if Kate was in the room. She wasn't. She was in her bedroom talking on the phone to Will. From the occasional snatches of conversation Jane could make out—when the narrator on TV paused for a few seconds to show video clips or pictures—it sounded as though she'd lost a necklace their mother had given her and thought he must have it because it hadn't made the move when they picked up her stuff.

He brought his chair into more of a sitting position. "Why don't you tell me what's going on?"

She wished she could confide in him. She could use someone to talk to. She couldn't share the latest with Talulah or Ellen, didn't want them to know she'd seen Kurt after they'd expressed their concern about the risks she was taking. Since visiting the ranch nine days ago, she'd told Averil what she was doing and how she was doing it—everything except how Kurt made her feel on a personal level. She'd made their relationship sound perfunctory—merely a means to an end—because that was all she felt safe acknowledging to herself. That she enjoyed him as much as she did was just a bonus. It didn't change anything. But the "friend time" she had with Averil in the mornings after Averil took Mitch to school had helped. She was coming to trust and enjoy Averil again.

Still, there were moments when she doubted involving her old friend had been a wise decision. Given the division between Averil and Talulah, it might not end well. There were definitely moments when she worried about that.

"Nothing's changed," she insisted.

"Don't you like having Kate live here?"

"I don't mind it," she said and, for the most part, that was true. She loved her little sister, was glad Kate hadn't married Will. Jane hated hearing her talk about Kurt all the time, though. That added guilt and stress to her own life, especially because she should've started her period today. Was it going to come? Was she just late? Or...did it mean she'd conceived? "This is your house," she told Papa. "What matters is whether *you're* okay with having her here."

"I'm fine with it. I love having both of you around."

She smiled. "I'm glad you're not home alone so much these days."

"Oh, I'm okay when I'm here alone," he said. "I've got Otis, don't I, boy?"

Hearing his name, Otis got up and wagged his tail before padding over to give her hand a lick. She scratched behind his ears before he returned, as he always did, to Papa's feet.

"We love being here with you," she said.

"I wish Ruby would come home," he said. "I sure do miss her."

And with that, Jane knew she'd lost him again. That was the hardest thing about dementia, she decided. There were times when she was able to once again connect and really grab hold of the grandfather she'd always loved and respected, only to have him slip away moments later. For her, dementia meant a constant state of mourning. "I miss her, too," Jane murmured.

Kate came out of her bedroom. "Can you believe it?"

she said. "He claims he doesn't have my diamond necklace, but it was on the dresser before I moved out."

"Are you sure?" Jane asked. "Because I feel like we would've seen it."

"I was so upset I wasn't thinking straight. I just grabbed whatever I could."

"But what would he want with it?"

"Are you kidding me? He wants to punish me for leaving him! He thinks I should forgive him and come back."

"What are you going to do?"

"I'm going over there."

"Right now?"

She scooped up her keys from the bowl on the coffee table. "Yes. I'm not going to let him keep my necklace. Mom gave that to me for high school graduation."

"Do you think pounding on his door after that big argument's a good idea?" Jane asked at the same time Papa said, "What's going on?"

"It's okay," Jane said, scooting forward to put a reassuring hand on his knee.

Kate was so upset she didn't even acknowledge their grandfather's question. "I don't care if it's a good idea," she said, keeping her focus on Jane. "I can't *not* go. I have to get my necklace!"

Jane jumped to her feet. "I'll go with you."

"Are you sure?" she said. "Because he's not going to treat us very well."

"Who's not going to treat you well?" Papa asked, clearly bewildered. "What's wrong?"

"Nothing's wrong," Jane told him. "We just have to pick up something. We won't be gone long."

He managed to get out of his recliner, but he still held the remote in his hand. "Wait. Where are you going?"

"To Will's house," Kate said while she grabbed her jacket.

"Who's Will?" he asked.

By then, they were walking out the door. "Don't worry. Just watch your show," Jane called back, "and we'll be home soon."

Will had been drinking. Jane could smell the alcohol on his breath as soon as he answered their knock. It was almost as if he'd been sitting in the living room, waiting for them because he'd popped out of the house like a jack-in-the-box. "I don't have your damn necklace," he insisted before Kate could even say anything. "What would I want with it?"

"It's got to be here somewhere," Kate said. "Just let me look myself."

"No! You don't live here anymore," he said. "You can't just barge in anytime you like and start going through my shit. Your snooping is what caused all our problems in the first place."

"My *snooping*?" Kate cried. "It was your cheating, you son of a bitch! How dare you try to blame everything on me!"

"Oh, you're brave enough to call me names now that your big sister's with you? Is that it? What's she going to do? Huh?" He gave Jane an unexpected push, which made her stumble back, and that set Kate off like a match to dynamite.

"Don't you dare touch my sister," she screamed, shoving him, and as soon as he caught his balance, his face filled with even more rage.

"You're such a stupid bitch!" he yelled and slapped Kate so hard Jane saw her head snap back.

"Oh, my God! What are you doing?" Jane tried to get between them, to stop what was happening, but Will shoved her again. This time, it was just to get her out of the way, but he'd used so much force she fell and hit her mouth on the concrete. Stunned by the blow and the eruption of sudden violence, she lay on the ground for several seconds before she had the mental wherewithal and the physical strength to get back on her feet. By then, Will had grabbed Kate by the hair and dragged her inside, and Kate was yelling for Jane to call the police.

"Do you see your fucking necklace?" he was yelling. "Huh? Do you see it? Maybe you want to look in here." Their voices grew fainter as he dragged her down the hall. "Or here."

The adrenaline that shot through Jane made her knees weak. Her mouth was bleeding—she thought she might've loosened a tooth—and her hands were shaking so badly she dropped her phone. Once she recovered it, she couldn't seem to hit the right numbers. The next thing she knew, there was a voice on the phone, but it wasn't an emergency operator. It was the last person who'd called her. Kurt had tried to reach her last night to see if she could come over again, but Kate had been in the living room until almost midnight, so she hadn't been able to get out of the house.

"K-Kurt," she stammered as soon as she heard his voice. "Can you...can you call the police? Will's beating up Kate!"

"What?" he cried. "Where are you?"

"At his house." Only belatedly did her befuddled mind register that he might not even know where Will lived. In case he didn't, she added, "N-never mind. I'll call the police."

"I'll do it," he said. "And I'm on my way. Just get out of there."

Then he was gone.

Eighteen

Kurt drove as fast as he could. Will was quite a bit taller than Kate and Jane, and he had them both by a hundred pounds. He might even have a gun he'd be willing to use. A lot of people in Montana owned firearms, especially single men who lived out in the country. Kurt could easily see Jane trying to step in to save her sister, and…

He forced his mind away from the gruesome picture his thoughts were painting. That there was even the potential for that kind of violence enraged him.

By the time he reached Will's house, which he'd been to once, years ago, for a poker party, there was so much adrenaline pouring through him he didn't even turn off his engine. He shoved the gearshift into Park, jumped out and left his truck running with the keys inside.

He'd called the cops before leaving the ranch, but he lived fairly close to Will, while the police station was in town. No one in law enforcement had reached the scene.

The door of Will's house stood open. As Kurt ran across the driveway, he could see a rectangle of light falling onto the porch.

He took the four steps to the landing two at a time.

But then he stopped. He wouldn't be able to help Jane or Kate if he barged in like an idiot and got shot.

Pressing himself to the outside of the house, he leaned around the doorway so he could retain some cover while peering in.

There didn't seem to be anyone in the living room—certainly no one he could see. He could hear Will swearing and calling Kate or Jane terrible names, and he could hear Kate's voice, higher in pitch than usual, screaming back at him.

"You started this!"

"You're the one who came over here, thinking you could do whatever you want in *my* house!"

"Stop. Everyone please...just stop!"

That last comment came from Jane. He recognized her voice and was instantly relieved. God willing, he'd arrived before the situation had gotten too bad.

"Jane?" he called. "Kate?"

"We're back here," Jane yelled, and he followed the sound of her voice to the main bedroom.

He wasn't sure what he'd been expecting, but it certainly wasn't what he saw. Jane had blood on her face, but it was Will who was lying on the floor, acting like he couldn't get up. Kate was kneeling next to him, her cheeks streaked with tears, and Jane was standing over them both, wielding a frying pan.

"Are you okay?" he asked. Because he was most concerned about Jane, his eyes locked with hers first.

Dropping the pan onto the floor, she burst into tears and ran into his arms. "I hit him," she said. "We need to call an ambulance."

"I don't need an ambulance," Will said, but he winced as he spoke and seemed too unsteady to get up.

"I was scared," Jane explained. "He had a hold of Kate's hair and was dragging her around. I...I thought he might hurt her—he *was* hurting her."

"You didn't have to hit him!" Kate said. "He was just mad."

Kurt blinked in surprise. "You're taking *his* side?" he said to Kate. "After what he's done to you?"

"No," she said but seemed to realize a second later that she had been sticking up for him. "She could've killed him. She hit him with that thing." She gestured at the frying pan. "You don't hit someone with that!"

"You do if you're trying to defend yourself," he said before Jane could respond. "You do whatever's necessary."

"But he wasn't doing anything to *her*!" Kate argued. "It was *me* he had a hold of."

"She was trying to protect you!" he yelled.

Will managed to lift himself up onto his elbows. "I feel woozy."

Jane winced. "I want to go home. I might be sick."

"I'll take you," Kurt told her, but they heard a siren outside, coming closer, and by the time they reached the porch, a squad car was parking behind Kurt's truck, blocking him in.

Ross Smith, someone Kurt had known in school, hopped out. "What's going on?"

Kurt led Jane down the steps to meet him. "Domestic disturbance."

"I think I'm going to need a little more information than that."

Kurt hated to say too much. He didn't want to get Jane in trouble. None of this was her fault. But if Kate minimized what her ex-boyfriend had done, it could be that Jane's actions would seem unwarranted. "Will got physical with Kate. Jane was afraid he was going to hurt her, so she hit him over the head with a frying pan to get him to let go of her. That's the gist of it."

"You hit him over the head with a *frying pan*?" Ross echoed, addressing Jane.

She wiped the tears from her cheeks. "That was all I could think of at the time. I panicked, didn't know how to stop what was happening any other way. He wouldn't listen to me. He was shouting too loudly. Besides, he pushed me first."

Ross lowered his voice. "Pushed you?"

"Yes. I fell and hit my mouth on the concrete," she told him, showing him her cut lip.

"Are you okay?"

She nodded.

Ross winced as he scratched his neck. "Is he?"

"I think so," Kurt said.

"I wasn't trying to hurt him," Jane assured him. "I just…had to get him off my sister."

"Someone should take him to the emergency room and have him checked out—in case he has a concussion," Kurt said.

"I'll definitely keep that in mind." Ross pointed back at them as he moved into the house. "Don't go anywhere."

Kurt wanted to take Jane to the ranch, where he could comfort her and reassure himself that she was okay. He'd always known, especially lately, that he liked her. But the level of panic he'd felt when he thought she might be in harm's way surprised him. "It's getting late, and we both work tomorrow. Why can't we leave?"

"Because I may want to talk to you again," Ross replied.

Kurt frowned. "You know where to find us. It's not like we're going to skip town."

"Like I said, you're not going anywhere," he reiterated and went inside.

It was chilly out as they stood on the porch, but Kurt could easily guess it was more than the temperature that was making Jane shiver. She was reacting to the violence. He lifted her chin to get a better look at her mouth and wiped away a trickle of blood. "Looks like you still have all your teeth."

"Thank God. When I fell, I thought I'd at least chipped one."

Kurt felt himself tense. Will was lucky he was already subdued. Otherwise, Kurt would've been tempted to do a lot more than Jane had. "Doesn't look that way. Are any loose?"

"No. Physically, I'm fine. Just rattled. That fight erupted so fast..."

"I'm glad you called me." He pulled her against him, rubbing her arms to help keep her warm. He thought she might resist getting that close to him for fear Kate would come out and see them, or another police officer they knew would pull onto the scene. But she didn't. She closed her eyes and rested her head on his shoulder as if she was infinitely relieved to see him.

"I've got you," he whispered, kissing her forehead. "Everything's going to be okay."

Kurt was solid and warm and caring. Jane considered it fortunate she'd accidentally dialed his number because the police were not nearly as sympathetic to her. After asking them to come back inside the house, Ross had them take a seat in the living room with Kate and a wobbly Will, who'd used the walls to help him stay on his feet. Ross asked each of them to explain what'd happened.

"They showed up at my house, accusing me of stealing her necklace, and I don't have it," Will said. "I tried to tell them that, but they got pushy."

"Pushy!" Jane exclaimed. "You're the one who shoved me. How do you think I cut my mouth?"

"That was an accident," he responded sullenly. "I wasn't trying to hurt you, and you know it."

"Well, you *did* hurt me. Then you started in on Kate. Tell Officer Smith about that, Kate."

Kate covered her face and hung her head.

Jane felt a flicker of panic. "You're not going to say anything?"

"I don't know what to say," her sister mumbled.

"You had no right to hit me," Will said, then glared at Kurt. "She's lucky I didn't deck her."

"So are you," Kurt said. "Because you'd be hurting a lot worse right now if you had."

"What's that supposed to mean?" Will tried to get up but groaned and fell back onto the couch instead.

"I'm sure you can figure it out," Kurt snapped.

Ross lifted one hand in the classic stop position. "That's enough. There's been too much trouble already."

"I should never have come over here," Kate said as though she was speaking to herself.

Jane caught her jaw before it could hit her lap. "What about your necklace? The one Mom gave you? I thought you were sure it was here, that he was keeping it from you. Did you find it?"

Will piped up before she could answer. "No. I don't have it, like I tried to tell both of you before you caused this mess."

Jane regretted going here with Kate. She'd come to offer support and had broken up an ugly scene, and yet her sister seemed almost as angry with her as Will did. What did they expect her to do? Let the fight continue? She'd had no idea what he might do! "Then where is it?"

"I don't know," Kate admitted.

"Not here," Will reiterated.

Kate began to rub her forehead. "Maybe I lost it in the move."

Jane gaped at her sister. *Now* she showed some doubt?

"How are you feeling?" Officer Smith asked Will. "Why don't I drive you over to the hospital? The rest of you can go home and get some rest. We'll see how everyone feels in the morning."

"I already know how I'll feel," Will said. "She hit me over the head with a frying pan. I'll feel like shit, and I want to press charges."

"You assaulted me first!" Jane cried.

"This was all so stupid," Kate said.

Jane gave her a dirty look. "He was dragging you around by your hair!"

"I wasn't hurting her," Will insisted.

She'd been screaming, and it hadn't looked good. Whether he was actually hurting her or not was beside the point. He didn't have the right to lay hands on her. Jane expected Kate to speak up and say as much, but she didn't. "Thanks for standing beside me," she grumbled.

Kate stiffened. "I never asked you to hit him!"

"I did it because he was hurting you!"

"That's enough," Ross repeated, putting up both hands this time. "Will, let's go."

Instead of getting up, Will scooted lower and covered his eyes with one hand as if the light was hurting them.

"I'm not going to the hospital. Why spend the money that'll cost when there's nothing they can do for a concussion?"

"To be safe," Ross said.

"I'm fine."

Ross rested his hands on his utility belt. "How do you know?"

"It's just a bump on the head."

"Go to the hospital," Kate muttered.

His eyebrows drew together as he glanced over at her. "No way. I'm not going—unless Jane's paying the bill."

Feeling defeated, Jane sighed. "Fine. I'll pay for it." After all, he could be truly injured. She couldn't risk having him refuse to seek medical help.

"No, you won't," Kurt argued. "It's his own fault he's hurt, not yours."

"I'll stay over tonight to watch him," Kate said. "If he starts to throw up or act weird, I'll take him to the hospital."

That seemed like the perfect solution, except that Jane didn't want Kate around Will. She was afraid they'd get back together, and she no longer believed Will to be a good guy. If he could cheat on Kate like he did, and then drag her around the house by her hair…

But she was so upset by how Kate was reacting, she didn't argue. She didn't think it would do her any good, anyway.

"Sounds good to me," Kurt said, getting up.

It was only then that Kate seemed to register the fact that someone was at the house who didn't really belong. "What are *you* doing here?" she asked Kurt, sounding confused.

Jane hurried to answer before Kurt could. "It was an

accident, I...I was trying to call for help, but I was so panicked I was hitting the wrong buttons, and somehow Kurt answered the phone."

Kate's eyes slid from her to him and back again. "And he came? Right away?"

"Of course," he said. "I didn't want anyone to get hurt."

"There's something odd about this. I mean, that you, of all people, would show up to save the day?"

"She reached me by accident," he clarified. "But I live close, so I hurried over to see if I could help."

"That's not all of it," Kate said. "The way you've been looking at her—like you'll go after anyone who threatens her... What you said to Will when he said he should've decked her." She peered closely at them. "You're not seeing each other or anything like that, are you?"

Jane caught her breath. They'd been sleeping together. Jane assumed that qualified for a category called "anything like that."

"I just came to help," he said, avoiding the question altogether and moving to the door. "Come on, Jane. I'll give you a ride so Kate will have a car."

Jane let her breath seep out before she agreed. "Okay."

Officer Smith seemed to be waiting for them to leave first, just to be sure there'd be no more trouble tonight. And Kate didn't try to stop them. But now that she suspected there was more going on between them than she'd realized, Jane knew there'd be more questions to answer later.

And what if she was pregnant?

"You okay with going to the ranch with me?" Kurt asked after they'd waited for Officer Smith to follow them out and move his car so they could back out of

Will's drive. He knew Kate wouldn't be going home, since she was staying with Will, but that would leave their grandfather alone.

Jane surprised him by nodding.

"Your grandfather will be safe?"

She pulled her phone out of her purse, seemed to think twice about whatever she was going to do and looked over at him. "Can we just swing by to check on him? Make sure he made it to bed and we can take Otis out one last time?"

"Of course." It wasn't on the way, but Kurt was so pleased Jane was willing to go home with him he certainly didn't mind driving over there. When they got to the house, she even let him come inside.

"Hey, Papa," she said as she held the door for Kurt to follow her.

"There you are," her grandfather said. "I've been worried about you." The old guy ignored Kurt; he was too worried about the injury Jane had sustained. "What happened to your lip?"

She reached up to touch where her lip was cut and swelling. "Oh, I...bumped into a door."

He started to get up. "Let me get you some ice."

She waved off his concern. "No, it's fine."

"Where's Kate?" he asked, falling back into his seat as if it was too much effort to get up unless she would allow him to get the ice.

"Kate is going to stay somewhere else tonight," Jane said. "And I'm going to go have a drink with Kurt—"

"Isn't it a little late for that?" he broke in.

She glanced at the clock on the wall over the fireplace. "It's only eleven. But that's past your bedtime, so let me help you to your room."

The TV was still on, but Jane's grandfather seemed disoriented enough that Kurt guessed he'd fallen asleep before they got there, and they'd awakened him when they came in. He bent to pet the dog, which had to be Otis, who'd come over to sniff him and say hello.

"I could wait up for you, watch another show," he offered.

"No," she said. "I wouldn't be able to have any fun if I was worried about you sitting here for too long. Besides, you need your rest."

He allowed her to take the remote from his hand. "Who's your friend?" he asked when he finally noticed Kurt crouching down with Otis.

"This is Kurt Elway. He's going to take Otis out while I get you to bed. You know his parents, Derrick and Jeanie," Jane said, trying to help orient him. "You used to buy beef from them."

"Oh, yeah. This is one of their kids?"

"I'm the second youngest of the four boys," Kurt volunteered as he straightened and stepped forward to shake hands.

Her grandfather still had a strong grip. "What are you doing with my Jane?" he asked.

"I'm just..." Kurt cleared his throat. "I'm just going to take her out for a drink."

The old man gave him a stern look. "Make sure you bring her back safely."

Kurt tried not to smile too widely. "I will, sir."

Jane chuckled when he addressed her grandfather as "sir," and he grinned back. Then he took the dog out while the two of them disappeared down the hall.

"You don't need any help, do you?" he called out when he brought the dog inside.

"No, we're okay," she yelled back.

He could hear voices even though he couldn't make out the words. Then Jane came into the room with a small overnight bag. "You're staying the whole night?" he asked in surprise.

"Won't that be better than making you get up to drive me home? Will I be able to slip out in the morning without any of your brothers noticing?"

"They'll be on the ranch by the time you're ready to leave. I'll have to be there with them at first light, but I'll come drive you to the store whenever you text me."

"Okay," she said and let him take her hand as they walked to his truck.

Jane couldn't sleep. After what'd happened, she was too wound up, too angry at Kate for being more sympathetic to the man who'd cheated on her and dragged her around his house by the hair than the sister who'd been trying to protect her. But the warmth of Kurt's body in the bed beside her felt comforting. She liked listening to the steady metronome of his breathing, too. They'd made love before he dropped off—a sweet but intense coupling that'd been far more satisfying that it should've been, given the distance she was trying to maintain between them. She was beginning to crave his body, she realized. She was also starting to crave his presence and the sound of his voice and the sight of his smile—and all of that was making her think. Could there be more between them? Was she rejecting the idea that they could become a couple for all the wrong reasons?

She hadn't wanted to hurt Kate. She still didn't. But she was feeling less inclined to sacrifice a relationship that could be fulfilling for her after how Kate had just behaved. That incident with Will proved how much she still cared about her ex. She couldn't have dibs on Kurt, hold him in reserve, indefinitely. That wasn't fair. Kate wouldn't be happy to see them get together, and Jane had no idea how she'd react or just how mad she'd get, but she was beginning to worry more about what it might mean for her own future. If she could get over the stigma of his age and dating one of her younger sister's previous love interests, could she also get over her desire to leave Coyote Canyon? Could she be happy here indefinitely if she were to get married and have a kid? Was Kurt even ready for something like that?

"You okay?" he muttered when she shifted.

"Yeah."

He didn't speak again, just pulled her into the cradle of his body and drifted back to sleep.

Jane heard someone else in the house. A door closed and a toilet flushed. But she wasn't alarmed. That she was in Kurt's bed would surprise his brothers as well as almost everyone else in town. But it felt as though she was right where she belonged.

Nineteen

"What's gotten into *you*?"

At the sound of Miles's voice, Kurt turned to see his brother watching him with a quizzical expression. "What do you mean?"

"Whatever you're thinking about, it must be good, because you've been wearing that silly smile all morning."

They'd just repaired a fence on the far paddock, but Kurt hadn't realized his brother had been watching him that closely. "I don't know what you're talking about."

His brother lowered his voice. "Are you hooking up with Kate?"

"No!"

"Ross Smith texted me this morning. Said there was a disturbance at Will's house last night, and you raced over to make sure everything was okay."

Eager to get out of this conversation—he didn't want anyone to say or do anything that might scare Jane away—he pulled his horse closer so he could swing up into the saddle. "I didn't want the situation to get out of hand."

Miles held his own horse's reins but didn't get in the saddle. "She's on the rebound, you know. Making a play for her—at least right now—probably wouldn't be a wise move."

"I'm not making a play for her."

"You went to Hank's to meet her."

"Exactly. But I had you go with me, remember? What does that tell you?"

Miles looked perplexed, but before he could press, his phone went off.

Kurt turned his horse away. They had a lot to get done today—they had a lot to get done every day—and he was still waiting for Jane's text, letting him know she was ready to be taken to the store. He knew he'd soon be disappearing for about half an hour and wanted to get some stuff done so the fact that he'd gone missing wouldn't be annoying to his brothers.

But then he heard Miles say into the phone, "Wait! *What?*" and couldn't help turning Poseidon around to see what was going on.

"What is it?" he murmured as he drew closer to Miles. "Who's calling?"

Miles pulled his phone from his ear and pointed at it. "Ranson."

"So?" Kurt said.

"He forgot his coffee thermos when we left the house this morning, so once he had a few seconds, he went back to grab it."

Kurt's heart sank. He could guess what was coming, but he asked anyway. "And…"

"He just scared the hell out of Jane, who was in the kitchen getting a drink of water."

"Damn it," he said with a wince.

Miles started laughing. "She was wearing your T-shirt and not much else."

"What'd he say to her?"

"What could he say? He asked her if she wanted a cup of coffee."

"Of all days for him to forget his thermos…"

Miles was still laughing. "Shooting high, aren't you, little brother? Jane's like…what…five years older than you? She's older than me, which is why I've never had the nerve to ask her out."

"Stay away from her," he muttered and wheeled his horse around to head for the house.

The secret was out. Ranson would tell his brothers that he'd found her in their kitchen wearing Kurt's T-shirt, and Brant would tell Talulah. Then Talulah and Ellen would think she'd continued with her plan to use Kurt—with his permission—to get pregnant, despite their warnings and concern.

And they'd be right. This was still all about getting pregnant, wasn't it?

It had to be. She couldn't get into a romantic relationship with Kurt. She already had her grandfather handcuffing her to this place; she'd be a fool to add any other emotional tethers. If she did, maybe she'd never leave. Maybe she'd spend her whole life right here, in this small town, and never experience the rest of the world. The ranch was everything to Kurt and his brothers—all he'd ever known and all he ever wanted to know. If he was remotely open to leaving, if he had any interest in it at all, he would've mentioned it by now, especially considering how often she'd talked about moving away.

Forcing herself to get up off his bed, which she'd sunk onto after the embarrassing encounter in the kitchen with Ranson, she pulled on the dress she'd planned to wear to work today and went into the bathroom to apply some lip gloss. Her lip was still cut, of course, but the swelling was already down. So that was good. And she was ready otherwise. Why she'd risked grabbing a glass of water before getting dressed, she didn't know. The house had been quiet for so long she'd felt safe and confident that she wouldn't see anyone until she texted Kurt to come get her. He'd made it sound as though she'd be in the clear once everyone left for work.

But even if she'd been in her dress, Ranson would've realized she'd stayed the night, so it was no use kicking herself. It was half an hour ago that he'd surprised her—only eight thirty—and her car wasn't on the property. Surely, he would've put two and two together...

"I shouldn't have come here in the first place," she muttered.

After she put her lip gloss on, which felt nice on her hurt lip, she took a final glance at herself in the mirror and walked out of the bathroom to get her phone. She was going to text Kurt to let him know she was ready to go, but the door opened before she could—and there he was.

"Sorry to startle you," he said when she jumped. "I just...thought it was getting time that I should come see if you were ready for a ride."

It *was* getting time. As a matter of fact, she'd arrive at the store later than usual even if they left right away. It'd been hard to get up after such a rough night. "I'm ready," she said. "Did Ranson tell you what just happened?"

A certain wariness settled in his eyes. "He did. Are you upset that he knows you stayed over?"

"Sort of," she admitted as she gathered her purse. "He'll definitely tell Brant."

He shoved his hands in his pockets. "Do we have to be a secret, Jane? And, if so, *why*?"

The "we" in that statement revealed that he was starting to believe their relationship was more than what she'd initially set it up to be. She couldn't blame him for making that assumption. Recently, she'd been acting more like a girlfriend than a friend receiving a sperm donation. But she couldn't say whether she felt she could fully embrace the change.

"Kate already knows," he said, anticipating her objection before she could even voice it. "Or she'll soon figure it out. I think it's time we told her either way."

Told her what, exactly? That Jane wanted to have a baby and Kurt was being kind enough to make it possible? Or that they were seeing each other?

Jane didn't think Kate would be happy to hear either of those things. Then there was the question of whether it would be wise to confront her *right now*. Last night had already driven a wedge between them; it would be hell if this created a serious division. Maybe the risk of that wouldn't be so great if Kate was in a better situation. But she wasn't. She was hurt and miserable and would view this as a betrayal.

Jane glanced at her phone before slipping it in her purse. "Can we talk about this later? If I don't get going soon, I won't be able to open the shop on time. At this point, I'll be lucky to make it by ten."

He seemed disappointed by her response, but he nodded. "Of course."

Saturday was her biggest day, but Jane was running late—so late that she was fidgeting nervously by the time Kurt dropped her off. She was only going to have ten minutes to open the store. If she missed it by a few minutes, it probably wouldn't be a big deal. She tried to adhere as much as possible to her posted hours, but there were always shoppers who wanted to get in right at ten.

"How will you get home?" Kurt asked when she stepped down from his truck.

"I don't know," she replied. "I'm going to call Kate once I get the store open to see what happened last night. Maybe she'll come get me."

He held the steering wheel loosely, comfortably—the way he handled most things. A memory welled up from last night, but she pushed it away. Remembering those more tender moments wouldn't do her any good if she was trying to retain some objectivity. "If she won't, I will," he said.

She could tell he felt uncertain of her after what she'd said—or *hadn't* said—when he'd tried to talk to her this morning, so it was kind of him to offer. He had to be somewhat disappointed, worried about whether she was pregnant and unsure of how to continue. "Thank you."

She wanted to reassure him by telling him that her feelings for him *had* started to change. It was true. But she was afraid that would only lock her into a relationship she'd ultimately regret, one that would trap her in Coyote Canyon. She didn't want to break anyone's heart—

especially his. And she was afraid if she let what was happening get out of control, that was exactly what she'd wind up doing. Then she'd have Talulah and Brant to answer to, as well...

Averil must've heard her come in, because footsteps pounded down the stairs almost as soon as she turned on the lights. She knew her friend was worried. She'd received several texts from Averil that she hadn't been able to answer.

Hey, where are you? You're normally here by now.

Aren't we having a cup of coffee this morning? I have news.

Jane hadn't even had a second to respond. She'd figured she'd just have to explain when she saw her friend in person.

"There you are!" Averil exclaimed as she poked her head inside the back entrance of the store.

After such a long, tumultuous night—on so many fronts—Jane was exhausted. She wondered how she was going to hold up over the next eight hours. "Hey." She tried to put some energy into her voice, but Averil's expression showed that she hadn't managed to cover her roiling emotions.

"What's going on? Is something wrong? Did you have a problem with your grandfather last night?"

"No. Papa's fine." She'd just talked to Herbert Hensley, their neighbor. Contacting him on the drive over had provided an excuse for not having a conversation with Kurt. Her grandfather had gotten himself up this morning, as always, and because she'd texted Herbert earlier, he'd made sure Papa had something to eat. It was just a bowl of cold cereal, but she made him a hot meal almost every day, so she didn't think that mattered too much. "I'm hoping to go home over lunch and eat with him."

Averil pulled the big, bulky, cardigan-style sweater she was wearing with a T-shirt, leggings and a pair of slippers around her. It was cold; Jane hadn't yet turned on the heat. "I can watch the store for you while you're gone," she volunteered.

"Since it takes so much longer to go home than grab a bite from around here, I typically don't do it. I hate leaving the store unattended for too long in the middle of the day, so…I'd really appreciate the help," she said in relief. "You don't work today?"

"Not until two."

"I'll make sure I'm back before then. Is there any chance I could take your car when I go?"

"Of course." Averil got the duster from the back room and started part of Jane's opening routine. "Where's your Mustang? Don't tell me it broke down."

"No." Jane was dying to talk to someone, and Averil felt like the best candidate to confide in. She'd been the one listening to Jane every morning lately, while Ellen and Talulah had been living their happy lives with the men they loved. But Jane felt as though her whole life was unraveling. She wanted to catch the spool, stop it from unrolling more thread that would just get tangled with all the rest, which meant she needed to keep her mouth shut. "You tell me your news first. What's going on?"

Averil stopped dusting. "Oh, no, you don't. I won't be distracted. I'll tell you my news when you tell me how you got that cut on your top lip and why you don't have a car today."

Jane's tongue sought the injury Averil had mentioned. "There was an incident at Will's last night," she confessed.

Averil cocked her head. "Kate's Will? The bastard who cheated on her? *That* Will?"

"That Will," Jane confirmed.

Her eyes narrowed. "What kind of incident?"

Jane thought she could explain without saying too much, but the deeper she got into her story, the more questions Averil asked, the more Jane ended up saying. Pretty soon, she'd revealed the whole thing, including that she'd spent the night with Kurt and what he'd said to her this morning about keeping their relationship a secret.

"Wow," Averil said when she'd finished and forgot about dusting as she returned to the register. "So…you're in a mess."

"Yes."

"What are you going to say to Kurt?"

"What *can* I say to Kurt?"

"Do you care about him?"

"Of course I care about him. I'm just not sure I want to give up all the future opportunities I planned to take advantage of and stay here for the rest of my life."

"You're trying to make that decision now?"

"The paths I'm considering lead to very different places, Av," she pointed out.

"But a lot could happen between now and when you'll be able to leave."

"What do you mean?"

"I mean you can't look too far ahead. There are *so* many variables."

"You're saying I should just run with what I'm feeling for Kurt?" Jane asked in surprise. "What if I hurt him?"

After thinking that over for a few seconds, Averil shrugged. "I don't know. To my mind, he's not the type of guy a woman passes up, but I could be judging that according to my own wants and desires. On second thought, maybe you shouldn't take advice from someone who's already screwed up her own life. Who am I to tell anybody else what to do?"

"You haven't screwed up your life," Jane said.

Averil made a face. "The decisions I've made have not been good ones."

"You married the wrong guy. You're certainly not the first woman to do that. Anyone could be fooled. And maybe without the decisions you've made so far you wouldn't end up where you're ultimately meant to go. If you hadn't married Chase, you wouldn't have Mitch."

"True... And I wouldn't trade my boy for anything. I'm going to quit with all the regrets and simply try to chart a better course from here on."

"Good."

Averil started to dust again. "What are you going to do about Kate?"

Jane shoved the pen she'd left on the counter back in the mug where she kept all her pens. "What *can* I do except call her to see if Will's okay?"

"Don't you think you would've heard from her if he wasn't?"

"That depends on how mad she is. She could be at the hospital with him, stewing as they run tests or whatever, blaming me."

"She has no right to be mad."

"I hit someone she loves over the head with a frying pan."

"For good reason!"

"I don't know about that," Jane said with a sigh. "It all happened so fast. Maybe I overreacted. Or should've waited longer to see what would unfold."

"Then you might've missed the opportunity to stop something that could easily have gone from bad to worse."

"That's what I was thinking at the time. That I had to do something before it was too late."

"She should understand."

"Normally, she would," Jane said. "But right now she's hurt and emotional and not thinking straight."

"Trust me, just because you're going through hell doesn't mean you don't have to be reasonable. No one gave me a pass when I was swimming in despair and disappointment over losing my marriage."

Jane finally felt the compassion she probably should've felt long before. She'd been Averil's friend, but had she been as supportive as she should've been? "I'm sorry," she said. "I don't think I was in a position to truly understand how much you were hurting." Neither she nor Talulah could comprehend how devastating a divorce, especially one that involved a child, could be. Averil had been so young when her marriage fell apart, and of course, Jane and Talulah had been just as young—too young to be there for her in the way she needed.

Tears sprang to Averil's eyes. "I appreciate that," she said. "I know I could've behaved better—"

"Stop." Jane waved her words away. "What's in the past is in the past."

Averil smiled through her tears, and Jane realized that

whatever she'd been holding against her friend for behaving badly the past few years was completely forgiven.

"When will you know if you're pregnant?" Averil asked.

Jane had wanted a baby for so long, but she'd started to think that now would probably not be a good time for it to happen. Maybe in a month or two, once Kate's situation was more settled and she had a clearer understanding of what asking someone like Kurt would mean in reality, she could revisit that desire. But as complicated as things were at the moment, she didn't need to make it all worse. "I'm supposed to start my period any day."

Averil looked worried. "We'll see if it comes..."

"I'm sure it will," Jane said. "We've only been together a handful of times. At my age, chances aren't very good I'll get pregnant that easily."

"A handful of times *without protection*?" Averil raised her eyebrows. "You never know. You might be more fertile than you realize."

Twenty

Kurt was trying to relax and enjoy the evening at his folks' house. He was tired of worrying about Jane, had promised himself he wouldn't even think of her. That wasn't working out exactly as he'd planned it—she crept into his thoughts even when he was trying to keep her out of them—but it was his father's birthday, so his grandparents were there, as well as an aunt, an uncle and several cousins.

His mother had fried some chicken and made mashed potatoes and gravy, and they'd just finished eating and were looking forward to the German-chocolate cake she'd made from scratch when she asked him to get the extra tub of ice cream from the freezer in the garage and bring it into the kitchen.

He often helped her serve the food or clean up the kitchen. It made him mad that more often than not his brothers didn't bother to even think about the work she put into what she did for them. But tonight, he decided he wasn't worrying about that, either. He assumed his mother had asked him because he was usually the one who stepped up—until she had him in the room alone. Then he knew she'd chosen him for another reason.

"Ranson tells me you're seeing someone," she said as she dug through the utensil drawer and handed him the ice cream scoop.

He tensed as he took it from her. "No, I'm not."

"He said he thought it might be serious."

What? *Why?* Telling his mother there might be a committed relationship on the horizon would be like waving a red cape in front of a bull. "I can't imagine why he'd tell you that," Kurt said, which was true; Ranson knew better.

"I don't understand why it's taking your generation so long to settle down," she complained as she cut the cake. "I have four sons. The youngest is nearly thirty, and I am finally going to be a grandmother for the first time. That's not how things are supposed to go."

He watched as she lifted the first piece onto a plate. "Maybe that isn't the way things worked back in the day but it's the way things work now."

She looked exasperated. "Don't you want a family?"

That was just it. He *did* want a family. He was looking forward to coming home to the same woman every night. He'd never seen Brant happier and wished he could have the same thing. But Jane was the only one he'd ever wanted to build a future with, and she preferred to go out and discover the world. If he couldn't compete with the appeal of her wanderlust, there wasn't anything he could do. He'd been a fool to get as involved as he had because now he couldn't imagine having a child in New York City or, God forbid, somewhere in Europe that would be even harder for him to reach. "When the time is right," he said in an attempt to get his mother to back off.

She held out another plate. "How much longer is it going to take?"

"Are you looking for a date?" he asked as he added a big scoop of ice cream.

"It would be nice," she said and gestured for him to set the plates they'd made on the counter while they prepared several more.

"Don't you think I should find the right person first?" he asked.

"What about Jane Tanner?"

He nearly dropped the plate she'd just handed him. "What about her?"

"Ranson said she stayed with you last night."

What the hell was wrong with Ranson? He'd *never* broken the bro code like this before. "He did? What else did he tell you?"

"Said he bumped into her in the kitchen this morning, and she wasn't wearing much of anything other than *your* shirt."

Kurt's face grew hot. He couldn't wait to get hold of his brother...

"Isn't she quite a few years older than you?" Jeanie asked, gesturing for him to add the ice cream, since he was just standing there, frozen.

He forced himself to keep scooping. "Five years. She's only *five* years older. That's nothing."

Even *he* heard the defensiveness in his voice but, fortunately, his mother didn't pick up on that. At least, she didn't comment on it. "It's nothing to me. I was just thinking she's getting up there—if you're considering having kids."

"We're not considering having kids," he said and immediately wished he could take back those words. Jane could already be pregnant! What would he say then?

Ranson appeared in the doorway. "Good lord, what could be taking so long? Are we ever going to get cake?"

Kurt sent him a dirty look. "Really? You told Mom about Jane?"

He started to laugh. "Of course. I would've done anything to get her to leave *me* alone."

"Excuse me?" Jeanie said, gaping at him.

"I'm not getting married anytime soon, Mom," Ranson said. "I know this is sacrilege to you, but I might *never* get married. This is your man right there." He pointed at Kurt, then left immediately.

"Hey, come get some of these plates and carry them out!" she yelled, but Ranson didn't come back. For the moment, he was out of the line of fire—from both of them—and it appeared he was going to stay that way.

Biting back a curse, Kurt finished dishing up the ice cream. Then he helped his mother carry the plates to the living room himself. He smiled and laughed so he wouldn't ruin his father's birthday. But he had no doubt his mother would tell her many friends that he was seeing Jane—which meant the whole town would soon know.

Ranson thought their mother would just start pressuring *him* to get married and give her grandchildren, but there was far more to it than his brother realized. Because of what he'd done, if Jane *did* wind up pregnant, it would no longer be an option for Kurt to pretend he wasn't involved.

Jane hadn't seen or heard from Kate. She'd tried calling and texting her sister several times but there'd been no response. And Kate hadn't been at Vidlar's when she'd walked down there in the middle of the afternoon, while Averil was still watching the store, to check. Leon said she'd called in sick, and although Jane waited up for her after Averil brought her home and she made Papa dinner and helped him to bed, it was getting late and didn't look as though she was coming home.

Jane hated to do it—she was afraid it would cause another fight—but she was getting worried enough that she grabbed her keys and headed over to Will's.

Kate could've at least returned one of her texts, she thought, disgruntled that she was still having to deal with this issue. She'd asked how Will was doing. It wasn't as if she'd meant to injure him—only to stop him.

She knew Kurt wouldn't like the idea of her showing up there on her own. Not after what'd happened. But the fact that he'd come last night was at least part of the reason Kate wasn't getting back to her. Or was she assuming too much?

Taking a deep breath, she turned off the engine and got out. Whatever was happening, she couldn't imagine it was good.

After she knocked, she waited several seconds. She was about to walk around to the back and bang on the other door and the windows, if necessary, to get a response, when the porch light snapped on, and Will finally cracked open the door.

"What do *you* want?" he asked, his eyes narrowing when he saw her.

She could've asked if he was okay—and she would have if he'd been less hostile. But he didn't look happy to see her. She got the impression she'd gotten him out of bed. "I want to talk to Kate. She hasn't answered my calls or my texts today, and I need to know that she's okay."

"She's fine," he said. "What'd you think? That I've done something to her?"

At this point, she wouldn't put it past him. But she didn't see anything to be gained by saying so. "I just want to be sure she's okay," she reiterated. "Can you get her? Please?"

"She's asleep."

"Then you'll have to wake her up, because I'm not leaving until I know my sister's safe."

"Oh, for God's sake," he said. "You're making me out to be some sort of asshole."

As far as she was concerned, he was an asshole. But, she stayed calm. "I'll wait here," she said.

"Who is it?"

Jane felt a wave of relief when she heard Kate's voice in the background.

"It's your sister. She's demanding to talk to you. She thinks I might've done something to harm you," he said as if that was the most ridiculous thing he could imagine.

Kate appeared, wearing only her shirt and panties. And her hair was mussed like Will's. They'd obviously been in bed, most assuredly together.

"What do you want?" Kate asked.

Hurt by her sharp tone, Jane stiffened. "Why haven't you returned any of my calls or texts? Surely, you could've let me know you're okay."

"We've been busy."

"Did you have to go to the hospital?"

Kate raked her fingers through her hair. "No, but I was up until dawn, making sure Will wasn't going to throw up or pass out or talk gibberish. We've been in bed most of the day, trying to catch up on our sleep."

"Surely you're not holding what I did to Will against me…"

"*I* am," Will said.

Jane shot him a dirty look. "I don't care about you."

"Because you're too busy moving in on Kurt Elway," Kate said, her voice sullen.

"Because Will's proven he's no one you should trust," Jane corrected. "Don't you remember why we came here yesterday? To get the necklace you forgot when you left. And why'd you leave? Because he cheated on you, and you moved out after seeing all that sickening crap on his computer and he got physical with you. So now…what? Are you just going to forgive him? Assume nothing like that will ever happen again?"

"It *won't* happen again," Will said.

Jane rolled her eyes. "Sure, it won't. That isn't a bet I'd take."

"You don't know it will," Kate argued, but she sounded far less certain.

"The best indicator of future behavior is past behavior," Jane said. "And by the way, unless you want to lose your job on top of everything that's been going on, I wouldn't call in sick again tomorrow."

Jane started to walk away, but Kate called after her. "Wait! Why? Did Leon say something to you?"

Jane pivoted in the yard. "He told me you called in sick, but he didn't seem to believe it, and you know he'd love nothing more than to get back at you for going to the Vidlars about him. I may be able to take a frying pan to him—" she pointed at Will "—but I can't protect you from yourself."

She probably shouldn't have said that last part. She was worried and disappointed, and she knew if she was pregnant with Kurt's baby, it'd drive her and her sister even further apart.

"Is that what you've been doing with Kurt? Protecting me?" Kate yelled and slammed the door.

Jane stomped to her car, got in and fired up the engine. Then she heard her phone ding. She hoped it was a text from Kate, that her sister was calling her back to the door so she could apologize and put the past twenty-four hours behind them.

But the text was from Kurt.

Any word from your sister?

She's been with Will since we left last night.

So he's okay?

Looked that way.

You've seen him?

I just went over there.

Are they back together then?

Fairly certain they are. When I knocked, I got them out of bed.

I'm sorry. I know you feel it would be a mistake for her to go back to him.

Didn't *he*? Didn't everyone think someone who'd cheated so egregiously, and was then unrepentant about it, was a bad person? What about the way Will had gotten physical with Kate last night?

The way she's acting, I'm afraid she's going to lose her job on top of everything else.

She'll pull it together.

Jane wasn't so sure. She'd seen what'd happened to Averil when she went through her divorce. This wasn't the same, but Jane didn't feel Will was good for Kate in any way.

On a different topic…

Jane felt a sense of dread when she read those four words.

Yes?

Are you pregnant?

I don't know yet.

When do you expect your period?

I thought I might start yesterday.

And you didn't?

No. Not yet.

Will you do me a favor and take the test?

With a groan, she dropped her head in her hand—until she heard a noise and looked up to see Will poking his head out of the house to see why she hadn't left. Then she sent Kurt a quick text that said Tomorrow, and drove off.

Jane didn't go home. She went to Averil's apartment.

"Hey, what's going on?" Averil said when she opened the door. She was practically whispering; Jane guessed Mitch was in bed.

Jane gazed back down the stairs. Had she made a mistake coming here? She shouldn't continue to involve Averil in what was going on. She should handle it herself. But she needed to talk to someone, and she didn't feel she could go to Talulah or Ellen.

She certainly couldn't go to Kate.

She lifted the sack in her hand.

Averil took it and peered inside. "Oh, my gosh. A pregnancy test. Are you planning to find out right now?"

"I told Kurt I'd test tomorrow, but I want some time to process the results, especially if…if…"

"If you are," Averil finished and pushed the door open wider to admit her. "Come on in."

Once Jane was inside, Averil gestured toward the hallway. "You know where the bathroom is."

Jane hesitated. "I'm not quite ready."

"Well, I'd offer you a drink to settle your nerves, but I don't think you want to have any alcohol until you know you're not pregnant, right?"

"Right."

"I'll be waiting with a bottle of wine, just in case…"

The moment had arrived, and it seemed overwhelming. "Maybe just…give me a minute."

"No problem," Averil said. "You want to sit down and talk?"

"That sounds good." Jane sank onto the couch and let her head fall back on the cushion so that she was staring up at the ceiling—her old ceiling, which she missed. She'd lived here when life was so much less complicated.

"For someone who wants a baby, you don't seem very excited," Averil said as she sat on the arm of the worn recliner nearby.

"I'm worried, that's what I am."

"Why? What's changed?"

"Everything! I should've gone to a sperm bank, kept it simple. Instead, I thought it would be better to know my baby's father—a concept that is still appealing to me. It was hard to think about having a child without so much as a man's face in my mind. But now…now I see why sperm banks exist."

"What does that mean? Things are going badly with Kurt?"

"No, they're going well. So well it's confusing. I can't decide if the only thing I'm after is still a baby."

"Because he wants more?"

"That's part of it."

"But you're concerned about Kate and what she'll think if you get with him."

"That's also part of it. She's mad at me for seeing Kurt. But I don't feel I'm doing anything wrong. She's in love with Will. I'm pretty sure they're back together. So why would she care if I get together with Kurt?"

"Wait, she knows you're seeing Kurt? That's new."

Jane groaned and explained how she'd accidentally—or maybe it was a Freudian thing—called Kurt before the police because he'd called her last and his number came up when she was fumbling with her phone at Will's place.

"Aw… He came over to protect you?" Averil sounded envious.

"To protect both of us."

"Maybe you're right, but the way you told the story, Kate noticed how protective he was of you."

"That's what tipped her off, I guess."

"How long do you think she'll stay mad?"

"I have no clue."

Averil checked the time on her phone. "You'd better go take that test. I have to get Mitch to school on time tomorrow or my mother will insist she takes better care of him than I do. She's really missing him and looking for any excuse to step in and take over, so I have to get to bed."

Jane had procrastinated for as long as she could. Drawing a deep breath, she took hold of the sack as though she was gripping something that might bite her and went into the bathroom.

Twenty-One

Kurt kept checking his phone. He'd been on pins and needles all day. Jane had said she'd test and get back to him, and now it was nearly eight in the evening, and he was at Hank's with his two unmarried brothers, along with Hendrix, Ellen and Jimmy Deluca, a friend of Miles's, who'd joined their party once they arrived. He'd been trying to distract himself by playing pool and darts and watching some golf on one of the many TV screens hanging above the bar. But he was starting to go mad. How long was she going to make him wait?

He didn't want to have to contact her again—didn't want to seem pushy, overly worried or impatient.

And what did it mean that it was taking so long? They'd purchased the test when they were out of town so they wouldn't spark any suspicion. She should have what she needed to find out. Was she disappointed that she wasn't pregnant? Or did she not know how to break it to him that she was?

"Hey, you talking to me yet?" Ranson asked, handing him a cold beer.

Kurt shoved his phone back in his pocket and refused to take the drink.

"Whoa, you must be really pissed," Ranson said. "Come on. Get over it."

"You told Mom that I've been sleeping with Jane!"

"I let her know you *slept* with her. As in…once. I didn't know it was ongoing."

"So will I have to worry you're going to spread that around, too?"

Ranson's eyebrows slammed together. "Hey, hey. You weren't trying to make Mom believe you're still a virgin, right? So who cares? She'll forget about it eventually."

He tried to hand Kurt the beer again, and Kurt still wouldn't take it. His stomach had soured after his first beer. He was too wound up to drink more. "No, she won't. And it wasn't something I wanted her to know. I didn't want *anyone* to know."

"It's just Mom!"

"No, it's not. Mom knows everyone. She'll be so excited to tell her friends I'm seeing a local girl that the whole town will be talking about it—all because I can't trust my own brother to keep his mouth shut."

This response was caustic enough that Ranson finally took him seriously, lost the cocky smile he'd been wearing and set the extra beer he'd purchased on the closest table. "I didn't think it'd be that big a deal! I'm sorry. She was hounding me about when I was going to settle down, and I remembered seeing Jane in our kitchen that morning, and—"

"And had a sudden lapse in judgment," Kurt broke in.

"I guess I did," Ranson responded. "I never dreamed you'd get *this* mad."

Because he didn't know it wasn't as simple as starting

to see someone. Kurt checked his phone again. Maybe it *could* be that simple. Maybe Jane wasn't pregnant, and he could somehow stop himself from seeing her in the future, meaning he wouldn't sleep with her again, and nothing would come of the past several weeks. The rumors would fizzle, and no harm would be done.

"Who are you texting?" Ranson asked. "Jane?"

"Why do *you* want to know?" Kurt asked. "So you can report it to Mom?"

Ranson winced. "Damn. I said I was sorry." He started to stalk off, but Kurt grabbed his arm.

"Wait. You don't understand everything that's going on in my life right now. What you did… Never mind. I'll get through it."

"What's going on with you?" Ranson looked concerned. "If you'd told me, I would've known better than to do what I did."

"I assumed you already knew better than to do what you did," he grumbled.

"So are you going to tell me now?"

A text came in. Kurt glanced down as soon as he heard the sound. It was from Jane.

Can you meet me where I parked my car on the ranch when we went to Bozeman?

She had the results. Otherwise, she wouldn't be requesting this private meeting. What was she going to say?

His chest grew so tight he thought he might have a panic attack.

"Kurt?" Ranson sounded worried. "What the hell's wrong with you?"

Kurt handed him his pool stick. "Nothing. I—" he had to pause for breath "—I just don't feel that great and want to go home. Can you catch a ride with Miles or Hendrix or someone else?"

"Sure."

Kurt was on his way out and pulling his keys from his pocket when Ranson caught up with him at the door. "Do you want me to drive you home?"

That was the last thing he wanted. He needed to be able to meet with Jane without anyone noticing. "No. The others are back from the bar with their drinks and waiting for another game." He indicated Ellen, Hendrix and Miles, who were looking over at them in confusion.

Ranson seemed torn.

"Really," Kurt insisted. "I'm not *that* sick."

"Okay," his brother said, reluctantly, "but if I've screwed up something that really matters to you, I'm sorry. I mean it."

Kurt mustered his best approximation of a smile. "I've just been messing with you. I'm fine."

Ranson didn't seem convinced, but he said, "See you at home."

With a nod, Kurt pushed open the door and stepped out into the cool April night. Then he closed his eyes and drew in as much breath as the tension restricting his chest would allow. Was he about to find out he was going to be a father?

Kurt spotted Jane's Mustang right away. His brothers didn't have any reason to come to the far side of the ranch after dark, but he pulled deep into the cover of the trees anyway.

She was still waiting in her car when he cut his engine. The Mustang was more visible to anyone who might pass by, but she didn't have four-wheel drive, so she was smart to stay closer to the road.

She got out when he did.

"Hey," he said, his heart beating about a thousand beats per minute.

She offered him a nervous smile. "Hey."

"Is Kate back home yet?" He figured starting out with some casual conversation might help them ease into the discussion they needed to have.

"Not yet. When I got home from work today, Papa told me she came and got some of her stuff, but she didn't take everything, so I don't know what's going on. And I don't plan on calling to ask."

"Better to let emotions die down a bit."

"Exactly."

He cleared his throat as he searched for other things to say. "Now that she knows Will lied to her in the past, it'll be hard to trust him again."

"I bet it won't work out. I just hope she doesn't marry him before she leaves him the next time." Jane tucked her hands into the pockets of her jeans. She was wearing a lightweight sweater, could probably use a warmer coat, so he gestured at his truck.

"I've got a jacket if you'd like."

"No. I…I'm fine."

"Let me get it," he insisted and grabbed it out of the back seat of his crew cab.

He handed it to her, and she put it on.

"So…" he said. "How are you feeling?"

"Anxious," she admitted. "I took the pregnancy test we bought in Bozeman."

He caught his breath. This was the moment. "And…?"

"I'm pregnant, Kurt."

His knees went weak. Despite what the research suggested, she'd conceived. They were going to have a child.

"Are you disappointed?" she asked when he said nothing.

He was still trying to absorb the news, hadn't been able to formulate a sentence. "No." He wasn't sure that was true, but he'd signed up for this so it wouldn't be fair to make her feel terrible now.

She gave him a sheepish look. "What *are* you feeling?"

"Shock. Disbelief. Uncertainty." He tried to steady his breathing. "How long have you known?"

"Since last night."

He'd been agonizing over this all day. And she knew all along? "Why didn't you tell me sooner?"

"I was putting it off because…because I was afraid you were hoping for the opposite."

He said nothing.

"After all, I told you it was unlikely to happen this soon," she rambled on. "I set up your expectations for a negative response."

He nodded. That was true. He'd started to view the unlikelihood of a pregnancy as a possible escape.

"Are you upset?" she asked with a wince.

"No," he said again, but it was all he felt he could say, and she seemed to recognize that.

"I'm sorry I dragged you into this," she said.

"You didn't drag me." She'd been all he could think about. He was fairly sure he was in love with her. He'd gotten himself into this, and now it seemed as though the whole thing had just blown up in his face.

"Do you want to talk about…about whether or not you'd like people to know you're the father?" she asked.

He could no longer avoid it. His parents would find out—and be furious that he hadn't been smarter than to avoid this situation. His brothers would find out—and think he was an idiot. Everyone in town would find out. "Since Ranson discovered you in the kitchen, I think it'll be obvious who the father is."

She pressed her lips tightly shut for several seconds. Then she said, "You're probably right. Does that mean you'd like to be involved in the child's life?"

Yes! He wanted to be involved in *her* life, too, but in the traditional way. He wanted to be with her—possibly even marry her although they weren't quite at that point in their relationship—and have a family. But trying to win her over, he'd left himself completely vulnerable to forever being on the outside, paying child support and merely having visitation rights.

"Kurt?" she prompted.

He was so leveled he couldn't formulate coherent thoughts, let alone express them. "Can I...can I have some time to come to terms with this?"

She blinked quickly, as though she was fighting tears as she removed his coat. "Of course," she said softly and handed it to him.

He stood rooted to the ground as she got in her car and drove off. He told himself to stop her. To say something more reassuring. But he couldn't even move. A baby was a lifelong commitment. What the hell had he been thinking?

Jane wasn't sure why she felt weepy. It was the impending life change that a baby would signify, she told herself. It had nothing to do with Kurt.

But she hadn't felt quite this bad before she'd told him

about the pregnancy. His reaction had telegraphed his stunned disappointment, and she couldn't help taking it personally. He obviously regretted helping her, which made her regret getting him involved, which definitely took away from any excitement she would've felt over the fact that she was going to become a mother.

She wanted to call Averil and tell her how the meeting had gone. It was Averil who'd psyched her up for it; she hadn't yet brought Talulah or Ellen in on the latest. But she didn't have Bluetooth in her old Mustang. Now that she was at home, she could talk but it was getting late, and because of Mitch, Averil had to be up early again.

Tempted to call in spite of that, Jane picked up her phone twice but set it back down each time. So she was relieved when Averil called her.

"Did you tell him?" Averil asked as soon as she answered.

The sound of her friend's voice made Jane choke up again—so much that she couldn't answer.

"Oh, no," Averil said. "It went that badly? Want to come over and talk about it?"

Jane finally managed to speak around the lump in her throat. "You're already in bed, aren't you?"

"I am, but I'm willing to get up. Come on over."

Jane cracked open her bedroom door and peered out. Papa was asleep, and she didn't hear movement or anything in the rest of the house to indicate Kate was home. "I can talk from here," she said, closing her door again.

"So?" Averil said. "How'd it go?"

She wiped the tears from her cheeks. "It wasn't bad. I don't know why I'm crying. He was…polite."

"But not excited."

"Definitely not excited. Stunned would be a better word."

"That's to be expected," Averil pointed out. "Having a child is no small thing."

"I shouldn't have asked him. I feel I've taken advantage of our friendship, and he's going to end up hating me."

"He had his choice all along, Jane. He could've bailed out."

"What if he didn't because he likes me?"

"He's a big boy. He could've said something."

That was true. Averil's feedback was helping. "I'm not looking forward to having Talulah and Ellen find out."

"They'll be torn between supporting you and supporting Kurt, especially Talulah."

"Why *can't* Kurt have a child?" Jane asked. "How does that hurt anyone?"

"It doesn't. It's just that doing it this way is dangerous—fraught with emotional pitfalls—so his friends and family will be protective of him. For them, so much depends on how fair you'll be."

"They'll treat me like I stole something from him."

"No, they won't. They might be mad at first, but they'll get used to the idea and calm down when they see that you'll be as generous and kind with this as everything else."

But this mattered more than anything else. Could she stand to be as kind and generous as they might like? What if she disagreed with something Kurt did with the baby? What if she felt she was losing control over her own child's life? What if their son or daughter someday asked to live with Kurt?

Jane dropped onto her bed. "I have no idea what made me think this was a good idea," she said.

"You probably should've gone with a sperm bank," Averil agreed.

At this point, Jane wasn't even convinced using a sperm bank would've been the right thing. Her pregnancy felt unnatural, out of order and far too progressive for her background and where she currently lived. Bottom line, she'd taken a giant leap into a completely foreign world, and there would be no going back. "It's too late now," she said.

"You just need some time to adjust to the idea of having a child. It'll be okay."

"I hope so," she said. After all, Averil had a child. She should know about the rewards of motherhood. She was also single and making it work. That was encouraging.

But if Kurt wanted to be part of their baby's life, and he and their child grew close—and everyone in his family also grew close to the baby—no one would be happy when she wanted to leave.

The feedstore had been slow this morning, and the owner's daughter had come home for a visit and was willing to help out, so Averil had been sent home, which turned out to be fortunate. She'd arrived only a few minutes after Jane had received a call that her grandfather had fallen. The neighbor insisted he was okay, but Jane had been worried enough that she wanted to go see for herself, so Averil had agreed to come down and watch the store.

She probably wouldn't have been quite so amenable if she'd realized Talulah and Ellen would be coming in. It was hard enough when she bumped into just one of them around town. Confronting them when they were together was even more intimidating than when they were alone, and she knew they wouldn't like seeing her behind the register of Jane's store. She was an outcast, and because they believed she deserved it, Averil doubted they'd be friendly to her anytime soon—at least in any kind of authentic way. Talulah was always polite. She couldn't complain about that. Ellen, on the other hand, usually tried to ignore her entirely.

"Where's Jane?" Ellen asked as the jingle that had gone off over the door fell silent.

"Her grandfather had a fall," Averil replied.

Talulah clapped a hand over her mouth. "Oh, no! Is he okay?"

Averil eyed Mrs. Bybee, who bought feed for her horses, as the older woman browsed Jane's store. If a client were to approach the register to check out, it could cut Talulah and Ellen's visit short, which was an appealing thought. But the woman hadn't even picked up anything yet.

"I think so," Averil said. "Herbert Hensley, the neighbor, said he's fine—just tripped while tinkering in his workshop and couldn't get up. Fortunately, Herbert was outside at the time and heard Papa call for help, so he wasn't on the ground long, and he doesn't seem to be injured. Herbert helped him back into the house. Jane went home just to double-check that he doesn't need to see a doctor."

"I hope he hasn't broken a hip or something like that," Talulah said.

Averil glanced at Mrs. Bybee again. She was smelling the handmade soaps before putting them back. But she still didn't look serious about buying anything. "We don't think that's the case."

"So how do you like living above the store?" Ellen asked.

"I love it." Averil would've invited them over for a housewarming party—if she'd thought they might like to come. She was planning a brunch for her family when she had the money to dress the place up a bit more.

"It's a cool apartment," Talulah said.

They'd seen it when Jane lived there. "It is."

Talulah hitched her purse higher. "Ellen's really good at decorating. I can watch the store if you want to take her up and show her around. I bet she could give you some good tips."

This was a more generous offer than Averil had expected. But she was afraid to accept it. She didn't want to get her hopes up that they'd let the past go. It was enough, for now, that she had her own place, she'd gotten away from Jordan and Jane was back in her life in an honest, caring way. That was a start. She figured she should accept what she could get and not set herself up for any more disappointment. She needed to remain stable, didn't want to relapse and start seeing Jordan again. "That's okay. There's no need to put her out. I don't have a lot of money to spend on that sort of thing at the moment."

"That's just it," Talulah said. "She can make any place look good for a fraction of what it would usually cost."

Averil didn't know how to say no again without being rude. But Ellen frightened her more than Talulah. Ellen was the newcomer who'd taken her spot in the trio she'd once belonged to, and the way Averil saw it, Ellen had nothing to gain by including her. It wasn't as if they'd cared about each other before, like it was with Talulah.

"She's probably tired of doing that sort of thing," she said, shrugging off the comment.

"I'm not tired of it," Ellen said. "I'd be happy to take a look."

Averil hesitated. "Do you know how to ring people up on Jane's system?" Averil asked Talulah.

Talulah looked over at Mrs. Bybee. "I can probably figure it out. It can't be too different from what I use at the diner. And if I have a question, I'll come get you."

With that, Averil felt she had no choice except to lead her former best friend's new best friend up to her apartment. "I've just moved in, so I haven't had time to do much," she said apologetically as she opened the door.

Ellen walked past her and took a turn around each room. "Looks like you've gotten a good start."

Coming from Ellen, those were kind words indeed. "Thanks." She wanted to say that Jane would help her when she had the time, but she was afraid that would be interpreted as a snub, so she kept her mouth shut.

"You know, I have an old chair in my garage that we could reupholster. It would look great in your living room."

Averil didn't know how to respond. Did Ellen mean the two of them? "I don't know much about that sort of—" she started to say, but Ellen cut her off.

"I can show you. Why don't you come over on Saturday?"

Averil felt her jaw drop. "To *your* place?"

"Yeah. Where we have room to work in the garage."

"I have to be at the feedstore on Saturday. It's our busiest day." And she needed the money, since she was paid hourly, and they'd asked her to go home today.

"What about Sunday?" Ellen pressed.

Averil had thought saying she had to work would dampen Ellen's enthusiasm. Ellen had been kind enough to extend the invitation, so she'd get credit for that even if it never happened. She'd chosen not to take the out Averil had just given her, which came as a shock. "Um, yeah. That would work. I'm off that day."

"Great. You can bring Mitch if you'd like. Hendrix can help keep an eye on him while we work, maybe pitch him a few balls."

"Are you sure you want *me* there?" She hadn't meant to sound quite that surprised, but she knew she hadn't done a very good job of concealing her true reaction by the way Ellen smiled.

"I'm sure," she said.

Twenty-Two

Jane felt like she was holding a ticking time bomb—one she couldn't let go of even if she wanted to. She could hide the pregnancy for a short while, but soon it would become obvious, and after nine months her whole life would change.

She wished she felt more excited about it. She'd wanted a baby for so long, had anticipated an entirely different reaction to the news when she first set out on this journey. But right now, she was too worried and anxious to be happy about what she'd done.

She wondered if by the time the baby was born, she'd have everything resolved in her heart and mind and would be able to enjoy the process. She also wondered if Kate would be talking to her by then. Jane didn't expect people to be excited for her the way they were for Talulah—talking about baby showers and nursery colors and all the other things having a baby usually included. But it would be nice if her sister wasn't still holding a grudge—and Kurt's family wasn't too terribly upset.

Would he ask to be in the room when she had the baby? Jane had always assumed Kurt probably wouldn't want a large role in their child's life. He was single, after all. He'd never expressed any interest—to her—about starting a family. But wanting to be a mother wasn't something she'd talked much about, either—until she'd finally revealed it to him. And now that everyone would know he was the father, he'd feel as though he *had* to step up even if he wasn't eager to do so.

That opened a whole new host of questions and dilemmas.

She glanced over at Papa, who seemed to be absorbed in the news on TV, before picking up her phone to check her missed calls and messages.

She didn't have any. But she was bored and restless, so she checked again only five minutes later. There was so much turbulence inside her, the night seemed oddly uneventful by contrast.

With a frown, she finally dialed her sister.

Kate didn't pick up. Jane guessed she was more embarrassed to have gone back to Will than anything else. Or that she was using Jane's relationship with Kurt as an excuse to stay away and live in her own little bubble, where she could pretend forgiving Will was a decision that would end well. Either way, she didn't respond.

"Who are you calling?" Papa asked.

Jane set her phone back on the coffee table. "I was trying to get hold of Kate."

Otis lifted his head at the sound of their voices, and Papa scratched behind his ears as he always did. "Where is she? I thought she was living with us."

"She went back to Will."

"Who's Will?"

"Will's her boyfriend, Papa."

"Why'd she leave him in the first place?"

"Because he's not a good person."

"Then why'd she go back?"

Jane swallowed a sigh. "Because she's in love with him, and she doesn't want to face the truth."

"Maybe I should have a talk with her," he said.

Before Jane could respond, she got a call. But it wasn't from Kate; it was from her mother. Karen had tried to reach her earlier, while she was at work, but instead of answering, Jane had turned off her ringer and set her phone aside. Since she'd barely learned she was pregnant, she figured she deserved twenty-four hours to get accustomed to the idea—and come to terms with the possible consequences—before trying to fake a cheerfulness she was too worried to feel.

It'd been long enough now that she had to answer, however. Otherwise, her mother would start contacting others in town, asking them to check on her.

"Hi, Mom."

"There you are. I called earlier and left a voice mail…"

"Sorry," she said. "It's been a busy day."

"How are things at the store?"

"Business is growing."

"Good. What are you doing right now?"

"Watching TV with Papa. I made him chicken-fried steak and sweet potatoes for dinner, and now we're relaxing before bed."

"You're so kind to him."

It'd been easier to take care of him when Kate was around. Having someone else who could be there when she wasn't—at least some of the time—had offered a great deal of reassurance. But thanks to Will, that hadn't lasted.

For the first time, Jane began to wonder if she was

going to be able to handle Papa, a new baby *and* the store. When she guessed at her conception date using a pregnancy due date calculator, it said she was due on December 21, which was the busiest time of the year.

What she'd done suddenly seemed so reckless. She'd definitely overreacted to the claustrophobia she'd been feeling because she couldn't move away from Coyote Canyon…

"I try," she said.

"I just spoke with Kate…"

The change in her mother's tone alerted Jane that this wasn't just a catch-up call. "Then you know she's back with Will."

"She's not certain about that."

"She's been with him for five straight days."

"She said *you're* seeing Kurt Elway. Is that true?"

Since she was going to have to tell her mother she was pregnant at some point, Jane figured she'd better say yes. That they'd had a fling would be easier for Karen and everyone else to accept than the truth. Her mother would never understand her *trying* to get pregnant, not without marriage—or at least a relationship. She guessed Kurt's mother wouldn't understand it, either. "We've only been seeing each other for a few weeks."

"And you didn't tell me? Why?"

"It's too new. It probably doesn't mean anything."

"Well, if it does end up going somewhere, the Elways are a wonderful family."

"They are. But like I said, I doubt it'll get serious." She touched her stomach. Could it get any more serious than a baby?

"I'm excited by the possibility that you've found some-one, honey."

Assuming Kate had already told their mother how Jane had moved in on someone in her circle, she said, "Kate's not happy about it."

"I know. But I don't understand why she'd have a problem with it."

"Especially because, like I said, it's not serious."

"Are you sure *he* feels that way?"

She wasn't sure of anything. But at this point, she felt she'd be lucky if Kurt didn't hate her. "We haven't talked about it."

"He must be telling someone, because Jeanie called me."

Jane gripped her phone that much tighter. Was he telling people? If so, what, exactly, was he saying? "Why would his mother call you?"

"Because we're friends."

"I don't remember that."

"You were in college when we were both in the PTA. We worked on the floats for Homecoming together two years in a row."

"When Kate and Kurt were in high school…"

"Yeah. We thought *they'd* eventually get together and used to joke around that we'd probably be family one day. We never dreamed it would be you and Kurt instead."

Jane dropped her head in her hand.

"What is it?" Papa said, concerned by her reaction, but she looked up again, waving him off with a manufactured smile.

"I wouldn't get your hopes up too high," she said to her mother. "I mean…it's so new."

"That may be true, but you'd be perfect for each other," her mother announced—and that was when Jane said she had to go. Everything just seemed to be going from bad to worse.

"Is something wrong, honey?" Papa asked after she said goodbye and hung up.

"No, everything's fine," she insisted and wished she could crawl into his lap like she used to do when she was a little girl and feel the same comfort and protection. He'd always been able to set her world right. But this time there was nothing he could do that would erase what she'd done—or mitigate the consequences.

Although the store had been everything to Jane since she started the business, it was difficult to focus on work today. She went through the motions of dusting and making sure there was enough cash in the till, but her heart wasn't in it. She just needed to get it done. If traffic was slow at any point during the day, she planned to go online and find a good ob-gyn—they didn't have one in Coyote Canyon—to make sure she and her baby received the care they'd need.

When she thought of seeing a doctor and making everything official, she felt a niggle of excitement. Why be so remorseful? She was getting what she wanted, she reminded herself.

But that small flame of positive feeling was snuffed out almost immediately by the appearance of her first customer of the day—who just happened to be Jeanie Elway.

Choking back a groan, she clasped her hands in front of her as the older woman came in. "Good morning."

When Jeanie smiled widely, Jane could easily guess what she was thinking: *This could be my future daughter-*

in-law. Maybe she can get my reckless son to settle down at last.

Except Jane was responsible for the most foolish risk Kurt had taken to date. Jane couldn't imagine Jeanie would be quite so pleased when she realized the true nature of the situation.

"Good morning." Jeanie gestured at the windows, where the sun was shining through. "The weather has been incredible lately, hasn't it?"

Jane had scarcely noticed. She'd been too embroiled in all the drama in her life. "It has," she agreed.

"How's your grandfather?"

"He's doing the best he can."

"I spoke to your mother last night. She's so proud of you for taking care of him."

Was that what the world had come to? Everyone was shocked and surprised that she was willing to sacrifice for a man she owed everything? "I love him," she said simply. "He's been good to me."

"But not everybody would do what you're doing."

The compliment made Jane squirm. Jeanie was giving her too much credit, considering how she'd screwed up in other areas of her life. "It's not that big a deal."

Jeanie adjusted her heavy-looking purse. "How's Kate these days? I haven't seen her in forever."

"She's still working at Vidlar's." That was the best Jane could offer as an update on Kate, so she left it there.

"I'll have to stop by and say hello."

"I'm sure she'll be glad to see you."

Jeanie looked around the store. "You've got some nice things in here."

"Thank you. Is there anything in particular you're looking for?"

"My sister has a birthday coming up. So does my sister-in-law. I thought I'd see if I could find them each a nice gift."

"No problem. Let me know if you have any questions."

Jeanie browsed for about ten minutes before bringing a number of items to the register—so many that Jane was fairly certain Jeanie was buying more than she needed just to support her. And that made the guilt she was feeling even worse. "Looks like you're buying for several people," she said.

"I figured I might as well stock up. You never know when you'll need a nice gift."

Jane was tempted to point out that it would be expensive, but she didn't want to sound as if she was questioning Jeanie's financial viability. She froze for a second, wondering how to discourage Kurt's mother from spending so much just because it was *her* store, but couldn't quickly come up with a good solution.

"Is everything okay?" Jeanie asked.

"Yes. Yes, of course," Jane replied and went ahead and rang her up.

She was just bagging everything when Will came into the store. Kate wasn't with him, so Jane had no idea what he could want. He'd never been in her store before, at least not without Kate.

He milled about the outer edges until she could say goodbye to Kurt's mother.

"When it rains, it pours," she muttered.

"What?" he said as the door closed behind Jeanie.

Jane squared her shoulders. "Nothing. What can I do for you?"

He shifted on his feet. "I wanted to swing by and…

apologize," he said, his voice getting softer as the sentence went on.

Jane felt her eyebrows shoot up. "To *me*?"

"Yeah." He rubbed his head where she'd hit him. "I realize I scared you the other night. That's why you got that frying pan."

"That's true," she agreed. "I was afraid of what you might do to Kate."

"I would never really hurt her."

"Doing what you did crossed the line!"

He hung his head. "I know. I was feeling so bad I didn't know how to react. And now that I have a second chance with her—or even just the chance of a second chance—I plan to change whatever I need to. I definitely don't want to lose her."

"Don't you think you should've thought about that before you cheated with someone else's wife?" she asked. "And what about the other women?"

"I don't know why I was doing what I did," he said. "Once I got caught up in it, it was like…a drug, I guess. A rush—a big ego boost. But this made me realize I don't care about any of those other women. It's Kate I love."

Jane guessed he'd been telling Kate the same thing, or she would've come home.

A penitent Will was harder to turn away. Jane could only imagine how torn Kate was feeling and finally had some empathy for her sister's current dilemma. When was it safe to forgive a partner for something like that? And did forgiveness include getting back into the relationship? Would he be true to Kate in the future, or would she only get burned again?

Jane knew the statistics for this type of thing weren't in her sister's favor. Serial cheaters tended to keep cheating. But certainly there were people who turned their lives around. It had to be *possible*. What if he was the exception to the rule? "Whether Kate comes back to you or not is up to her," she said.

"I just don't want you working against me. I have enough to overcome."

What could she say? She'd soon be apologizing to people herself, hoping to find some forgiveness. "I'm protective of her, so this is difficult for me. But I'll try to stay out of it."

"Okay." He flashed her a relieved smile. "I appreciate it."

Jane came out from behind the counter. "But if you ever hurt her again, I swear I'll never give you another chance—"

"I won't," he broke in, sounding adamant.

Hopeful that he was being honest—and would remain true—she nodded. She'd made so many mistakes lately. She could only pray this wasn't another one.

On the other hand, maybe she didn't have to feel *too* much responsibility. She didn't think she could stop Kate from going back to him even if she tried.

Kurt drove up and down Lincoln Street, wrestling with himself. He'd asked Jane if he could have a day to think about the baby, and she'd given him that and two more days so far. She hadn't texted, called or tried to get hold of him since.

He should've reached out to her by now. He couldn't point to just one reason he hadn't. He was still wrestling with the reality of becoming a father, especially in this way. He was afraid of the disappointment he'd feel if she reacted as she had before—as if it was *only* a baby she wanted from him. And he was trying to decide how he was going to approach the situation now that his future had changed. Did he tell her what he truly wanted was a chance with her? Or would that only make things that much weirder when they had the baby?

Of course he had to be the Elway brother who would do something like this. If Ranson had any clue about Kurt's true situation, he would never have told their mother that Jane had spent the night. And once he learned what was going on, he'd think Kurt was an absolute fool.

Miles might be more understanding. He was kinder and gentler than the others by nature.

For a moment, Kurt considered going to Miles for advice. It would be a better experience than admitting to Brant that he'd gone through with what Brant had told him *not* to do. But understanding wasn't what he really needed. He needed to talk to someone who would level with him even if it was rough—to see if his thoughts made sense and to decide how he was going to handle things as they stood now—and Brant and Talulah knew Jane best. So instead of making another pass in front of Jane's store, he parked near Talulah's Dessert Diner and went in to see what she and Brant were doing and whether there might be an opportunity to have a private conversation with them.

The breakfast buns Talulah made every Saturday were a big hit with the morning crowd. But once they sold out—and they always did by ten thirty or so—there was a lull in business until people started to come in to pick up dessert for dinner. He could tell he'd hit that quiet period perfectly when he found the diner empty except for Talulah, who was bringing fresh cakes out from the kitchen in back.

"Hey, little brother," she said, sliding the display case closed after putting in a fresh four-layer carrot cake.

He liked her, had always liked her and hoped her opinion of him wouldn't change after she found out about the baby. "Hey."

"What are you up to?"

"Just thought I'd stop in for a cup of coffee."

"Is that all you want? I saved a breakfast bun for Brant, but he's been too busy building the new deck at our house and hasn't been able to make it over. I could warm it up for you instead."

"No, take it home to him. Black coffee is all I need."

"You got it. What's going on?"

"Not a whole lot."

She brought his cup around the counter and placed it on the table instead of handing it over the display case. Then she sat across from him and studied him while he drank it as if she was waiting for him to say what was on his mind. "Are you going to tell me why you're here?" she asked at length.

He hesitated to say what was really on his mind. He'd mostly been hoping to find Brant. After all, Talulah was Jane's best friend. It didn't feel right to tell her before Jane could.

"Jane's pregnant," he said without preamble.

She said nothing for several long seconds. Then she leaned back and folded her arms. "I was afraid of this."

He took another swallow of coffee. "You knew it was a possibility?"

"I advised her against it."

"When was that?"

"Fairly recently."

He set his cup down. "It was probably too late by then."

"Probably." Talulah remained quiet for several seconds, before asking, "How do you feel about it?"

"Torn," he admitted.

"In what way?"

"I wouldn't mind having a baby. I'm thirty, not eighteen. I'm financially stable and live a decent life with lots of family support. It's just that I would rather things had gone a different way, and I feel as though I may have screwed up my life by reaching for something I can't get."

Talulah scratched under her hair. "You don't think Jane likes you as much as you like her."

"Do *you*?"

"She's in so much denial about this whole baby thing that it's hard to tell what's going on in her heart and head."

At least he wasn't the only one having trouble reading Jane...

"When are you going to tell Brant?" Talulah asked.

"As soon as he finds out she's pregnant he'll know the baby's mine. I told him she asked me to help her have a child."

"Wait—he knew it was a possibility?"

"I'm sure he thought he'd squelched it."

"So we both knew but didn't tell each other," she said with a chuckle. "That's proof that we'd be torn between the two of you if this goes wrong. How do you think your mother will react?"

"She'll do whatever she has to in order to be part of the child's life."

"What about *you*?"

He stared down into his inky black coffee. He'd put off making a decision about that, hoped the situation with Jane would change and that his place and his duty as the baby's father would be natural and expected. But that didn't seem to be happening. Although Jane had said he'd have his choice as to whether he wanted to be involved, she might be hoping he'd walk away. That meant she'd pay for the child, which would not be cheap, but it would also give her the most freedom, and freedom was what she craved.

"Kurt?" Talulah prompted, leaning in to catch his eye.

He looked up. "I plan to take responsibility and have full parental rights."

Twenty-Three

Jane paced in her store. She needed to update her displays, order more bath products and bring some merchandise from storage to fill in where certain items had sold. She also needed to catch up on the accounting and do some financial planning, so she could figure out how she would afford new inventory throughout the year. Owning a business wasn't easy. There was so much to do, and she usually stayed on top of it. But she was so distracted by what lay ahead of her on a personal level. She was going to have a baby. She'd known for several days and yet she couldn't get over the shock of it. She'd waited for years and had gone to such drastic measures to make it happen. In the end, it was like she'd been pulling hard on something that had suddenly come loose and smacked her in the face.

She was getting what she wanted—but at what cost?

She glanced nervously out at the street. Normally, she hoped anyone who passed by would come in and shop. Today, she didn't want to see a single customer, even though it was Saturday and her whole week depended on weekend sales. She wished she could just go into the storeroom and hide.

She told herself she'd feel better if she could gain some resolution on certain questions. But that resolution was hard in coming. Should she tell Kate about the baby right away? Or wait until the first trimester was over?

A lot of pregnant women put off making the announcement until after the first twelve weeks. But word of her pregnancy could get back to Kate before then. And if they made their peace and all was well between them when Kate found out, she'd feel duped.

But telling her sister now, with Kate off-center and already feeling cheated, would be like shouting it to the whole town. Kate certainly wouldn't keep it to herself. Was Jane ready for the backlash? The stares and whispers? The reaction of Kurt's family? How would he react to all of that?

Given what'd happened already, everyone would know that he was the father. There were no secrets in Coyote Canyon.

"Shoot." She picked up her phone. Averil was at work, but if business was slow at the feedstore, she was occasionally able to text back during her shift.

Help! Should I tell her?

Averil would know who "her" was. They'd just talked about the dilemma Jane faced before Averil left for work. But Jane also had to figure out when to tell Talulah and Ellen. She didn't want to lose her best friends by suddenly backing away and leaving them out of something this important. They'd feel as though she'd suddenly begun to side with Averil to the exclusion of their friendship.

With a groan, she hurried to the bathroom. She felt sick. It could be morning sickness—though she knew it was early for that—or it could simply be the anxiety of having to cope with the consequences of her actions.

She was still in the bathroom, crouched near the toilet just in case her breakfast came back up, when she heard the bell over the door.

Someone had entered the store.

She hadn't thrown up and wasn't positive she was going to, so she took a deep breath and gathered her strength. She was still feeling queasy after standing up and washing her hands, but she pasted a smile on her face as she returned.

Her smile wilted the moment she saw who it was. Kurt was waiting for her at the register wearing a solemn expression.

The nausea she'd been battling a moment before welled up again, but she ignored it and steeled herself for what was coming. They needed to talk. "Hey," she said.

"Hey," he responded.

"Good to see you." It *was* good to see him. Not only had she been struggling with the ramifications of her pregnancy, but also she'd been missing him, thinking about the nights they'd spent together and wondering what he was thinking and feeling. She knew he had to assume she wasn't interested in him after the way she'd reacted when they last spoke. But she could hardly reassure him that she wanted an ongoing relationship when she was still planning to leave Coyote Canyon as soon as she could, even if that didn't happen for several years.

"Good to see you, too," he said, but he wasn't quite the same man he'd been before. There was a resoluteness about him that was new, and the steely look he gave her made it feel as though he was almost a stranger.

"I just wanted to stop by and offer a bit of clarification before…before news of the pregnancy can travel too far," he said.

"Clarification?" she repeated.

"There's been some question as to my level of involvement if a pregnancy were to happen. I haven't stated my position because… Well, I didn't even know whether you'd get pregnant."

She knew she'd contributed to his uncertainty with all her talk about how difficult conception could be for someone her age. "Yes, I—we need to figure that out."

"I've figured it out," he said.

She could only brace for what it might be. "Already?"

"There was never really any question. I thought things might go a different way, and we would… Never mind. This is where we are now, and I'm glad you promised that I can be as involved as I'd like."

Her heart was nearly pounding out of her chest. "And that means?"

"I'm the baby's father, so I'll help financially, take visitation rights and do whatever else fathers do."

Jane felt as though the air had just been knocked out of her. When she'd first presented him with her request, she would've bet her business that he'd take little interest. But this sounded like he was prepared for full-on fatherhood. "Are you…are you sure?"

"Pretty sure. I was hoping you'd allow my family to have access to the baby, too. I know we never discussed extended family. This all happened so…quickly. But my mother is a force of nature. She'll be absolutely *destroyed* if she doesn't get to be involved as a grandparent."

His mother… It felt as though her knees were about to give way, but she willed them to lock and continue to hold her up. The last thing she wanted to do in front of Kurt was slide to the floor. "And your brothers?"

"My whole family. This baby will be a first cousin to Brant's children. He or she should be allowed to play with Talulah's baby."

"Of course." She'd always envisioned that, knew with Kate living here she'd be back for regular visits even if she did move away. She just hadn't planned on her personal life and situation becoming common knowledge. When she'd thought of using Kurt's sperm to get pregnant, it'd always been with an element of secrecy—or the thought that she'd soon be gone from this place and it wouldn't matter.

He nodded as if that was that, and for a moment, the way he looked at her made her long for his embrace. She missed his touch, his smell, the comfort of his body. But she'd be stupid to make what was happening any more difficult.

"Thanks," he said softly.

"No problem." Jane could barely wait until he left the store and was out of earshot before running to the bathroom, where she crumpled in front of the toilet and threw up into the bowl.

Can you come over to the diner for a cup of tea or have you already gone home for the day?

Talulah's text came in just as Jane was vacuuming the store. She wished she had a reason to get out of going to the diner. After the visit Kurt had paid her a couple of hours ago, she knew Talulah might have an ulterior motive for inviting her.

The possibility made her leery, but she couldn't lie

and say she was gone. It would be too easy for Talulah to check the alley where they both parked.

Jane supposed she could say Papa needed her to get home right away, but she had to face Talulah at some point. If her best friend didn't already know about the baby, Jane had to tell her. The same thing held true for her that held true for Kate. The longer she put it off, the more upset Talulah would be. No one liked being kept in the dark, especially when it was one of your friends who believed she should be one of the chosen few—an insider.

With a sigh, she texted back.

Will be over in ten.

Jane didn't think Averil had told anyone about the baby. Averil acted as though she was grateful to be on good terms again and wouldn't do anything to sabotage their relationship. So if Talulah knew, it had to be Kurt. Talulah was, after all, his sister-in-law, and he also had a stake in what was happening, so it was reasonable he'd feel as though he could break the news.

Jane took her time putting the vacuum away, but eventually she locked up and walked down to the diner.

She hoped Brant wouldn't be there. She told herself it was possible he'd be at home, but then she saw him and noticed that the diner was clean and ready for business tomorrow. They were done for the day, which meant they were both there just waiting for her.

Oh, God...

Jane hadn't felt well all day, but she did her best to walk into the diner as if nothing had changed.

"There you are," Talulah said.

Jane looked around. "Where's Ellen?" If they were

going to ambush her, she figured Ellen would probably be involved. Why wouldn't she be? She'd already made it clear she agreed with them when it came to Jane's involvement with Kurt.

Talulah must've heard the wry note in her voice because she said, "We didn't want it to seem like we were ganging up on you."

Jane glanced at Brant. If that had been the goal, why was he here? Admittedly, he was one of the best guys she knew, but he could be intimidating without even meaning to be. Never mind that he wasn't going to like what she had to say.

Talulah indicated a chair at the table where they'd been sitting. "You look pale. Are you feeling okay?"

"I haven't gotten much sleep." She didn't mention that she'd been throwing up most of the day. She didn't want anyone who was unhappy about the pregnancy to gloat over the fact that she was getting exactly what she deserved.

Talulah headed around the corner, presumably to get Jane the tea she'd promised in her text. "I can understand why."

"So...you know," Jane said.

Brant's chair squeaked as he shoved it back to be able to face her more directly. "We both do."

Jane felt her face heat. "And...you're upset."

His face creased in a frown. "I can't say that I'm happy."

Feeling stubbornly defensive, Jane lifted her chin. "I'm sorry. I should've used a sperm bank. Then no one could criticize me because having a baby would only affect me and my life."

"We're not here to criticize you," Talulah started to say but Brant spoke at the same time.

"We're just worried, Jane." He raked his fingers through

his thick dark hair, making it stand up in front. "This type of parenting won't be easy for either one of you, but especially my brother, right? What guarantee does he have that he'll have plenty of time with his child? That you won't move somewhere that'll make it hard for him to see his son or daughter?"

Guilt caused her stomach to cramp. "He doesn't even have to be involved with the baby. It was supposed to be a…a genetic donation."

"Babies don't work that way," he said.

"Maybe not around here. But I thought… I don't know what I was thinking—just that it would be nice to know my baby's father." She sank into her chair. "That's all."

Talulah came back with a glass of milk and a piece of red velvet cake she put in front of Jane, but there was no way Jane would be able to eat it. She couldn't keep anything down. "I'm not hungry, thanks," she said as she shoved it away.

"It's your favorite," Talulah said.

Closing her eyes, Jane gripped her forehead with one hand. "I'm not feeling well enough to deal with this conversation right now. I think I have to go."

Talulah caught her arm as she got back up. "Jane, please don't be mad—or hurt. We know you've been under a lot of pressure taking care of your grandfather and running the store on your own. We can see why you might long for a child—for the change and excitement that would create, as well as all the rest of it. We know you'll make a great mother. We just don't want this to negatively impact your life. Or Kurt's."

"Kurt and I are both adults," she said. "We'll work it out on our own."

She'd just opened the front door when Brant spoke

again. "You know he's in love with you, right? That's why he did it…"

She whipped around. "That's not true!"

He got up and came toward her. "You haven't been able to tell?"

She opened her mouth to deny it, but what she'd been refusing to see was suddenly so obvious she couldn't hide from the truth anymore. Kurt wasn't in love with her. Jane wouldn't go that far. But he certainly cared for her, or he wouldn't have done what he'd done—and that was why everyone was so upset. They thought he cared, and she didn't.

Kurt saddled his horse and headed out onto the ranch. It was Sunday evening and he didn't want to hang around the house any longer. He was afraid word of the baby was spreading so fast it'd reach his brothers or his mother at any time.

Letting his head fall forward, he stared at the ground, allowing Poseidon to amble at will. Should he not be involved with the baby? Let Jane have him or her?

It might be easier, in an emotional sense, not to engage at all. If he committed his heart, he could be hurt, frustrated or disappointed with how things turned out. He was an "all in or all out" kind of guy. But he knew he'd regret not getting to know his own child, which meant he didn't really have a choice. He didn't want to be that guy in twenty years who had an angry young person show up on his doorstep demanding to know why he or she hadn't meant more…

His phone went off. He assumed it would be the call he'd been expecting from Brant—or maybe Talulah, since she was the one he'd confided in—and wasn't going to answer. He didn't want to have an upsetting conversation with either one of them right now. But the call came from a number he didn't recognize.

He almost let it transfer to voice mail but, at the last second, on impulse, he hit the talk button.

"Hello?"

"Hello?" The voice on the other end was overly loud, and the guy didn't seem to have heard him answer.

"Hel-lo?" Kurt said again, almost shouting. "This is Kurt Elway. What can I do for you?"

"Kurt, did you say?"

"Yes. Who is this?" Did this person even know him? It had to be a crank call or a misdial, he decided, and was about to hang up, when the caller spoke again.

"It's Jane's grandfather. Are you the fellow I met here the other night?"

Kurt reined in his horse. "Yes. How'd you get my number?"

"My neighbor gave it to me. Said he buys beef from you. I used to buy beef from you, too. I think. Anyway, is Jane with you?"

The old guy had remembered his name? That was something. "I'm afraid not."

"Oh. I thought maybe she would be."

"Is something wrong?"

"Well…" His first word was audible, but then he proceeded to mutter something Kurt couldn't quite make out.

"What'd you say?" Kurt asked, but it sounded like Jane's grandfather had dropped the phone. At any rate, it went dead, and he'd sounded so flustered Kurt wasn't certain he'd call back or pick up if Kurt tried to reach him.

Uncertain of what that call might mean, he scowled at the blazing sunset. It was a beautiful sight, but he was too caught up in his thoughts to admire it. What had made the old guy go to the trouble of finding his number and calling him? Jane had told Kurt a little about how her grandfather could be lucid and sharp one minute and completely disoriented the next. This was obviously an example of that.

Kurt checked his watch. Jane closed at five on Sundays. She'd been off for two hours. Where had she gone?

In any case, her grandfather was probably fine, he told himself. After all, according to what he'd said, he'd spoken to the neighbor. Surely, the neighbor would've helped him out if he needed anything. And even if he *did* need something—say, he was hungry—he wouldn't starve in an hour or two. No doubt Jane would be home soon. She took excellent care of him.

Kurt wheeled his horse around to head back to the house. If his brothers were going to confront him, he figured he'd be better off to face it and quit stalling. Although he'd enjoyed the solitude of his ride, he couldn't hang out on the ranch forever.

But something about the call from Jane's grandfather troubled him. The old guy had never tried to reach him before.

Drawing Poseidon to a halt, he dialed the number that'd appeared on his screen a few minutes earlier.

"Jane?" The name nearly blasted through the phone.

"It's Kurt. What's going on over there? How can I help?"

"It's my dog. He won't get up."

"Where's your neighbor? The one who stops by each night?"

"Herbert? I talked to him on the phone, but he visits his daughter on Sundays."

"And Jane?"

"Can't find her," he replied, sounding bewildered.

"Can't reach Kate right now, either, and I'm afraid Otis won't make it."

"Has he been hurt?"

"Not that I know of."

Had the dog had fallen ill? If something happened to that animal, it would come as a major blow to Jane's grandfather. By all accounts, Otis and Papa meant a great deal to each other.

"I'll be right there," Kurt said and gave Poseidon a gentle kick to let him know he had to reach the house as soon as possible.

When Kurt arrived at Jane's, he didn't see her Mustang. He didn't see Kate's Bronco, either.

He climbed out of his truck and jogged to the stoop. The door was standing open—even though it'd chilled off since the sun went down—so that seemed odd.

"Mr. Tanner?" He poked his head inside. He knew that most everyone in town simply called Jane's grandfather by his last name. Jane had said he'd gone by Tanner since he'd played baseball in high school. But putting the "Mr." in front seemed the politest approach, since they didn't really know each other.

When he didn't get a response, he stepped inside the living room. "Hello? Anyone home?"

Finally, he heard a voice call back to him. "In the kitchen!"

Kurt weaved through the furniture to reach the other room and found Jane's grandfather down on his knees on the linoleum, looking distraught as he tried to coax his dog to eat.

Otis wasn't interested in the food. He looked at the kibble in his bowl, then up at his elderly owner as if he wanted to comply but couldn't. He didn't even get up to greet Kurt like most dogs would. After a moment, he just rested his muzzle on his paws and watched them both with sad eyes.

"Something's wrong," Tanner said. "Look at him. He won't eat. He'll hardly move. That's not like Otis."

Dogs could get sick, just like humans. This didn't have to be life-threatening. But Kurt wasn't taking any chances. Jane had enough going on in her life; she didn't need to lose another member of her family, especially when it would leave her grandfather so bereft.

Bending down, he lifted the animal into his arms. "Let's get him to the vet."

"Right now?" Tanner's gaze shifted to the window, where it was easy to see it was dark outside. "Is the vet even open?"

"The clinic might not be. But you know Jim Stubing. He'll see a sick animal at any hour, and his house is connected to his clinic, so as long as he's home, it won't be hard to find him."

Jane's grandfather had to use the counter to get to his feet. "I don't know Jim Stubing," he said, sounding confused, but Kurt suspected he would've at least recognized the name before he started losing his memory. Jim was almost as old as Tanner. He'd been around Coyote Canyon forever.

"He'll take good care of Otis," Kurt said. "Don't worry."

Tanner seemed so relieved, Kurt thought a trip to the vet would be worth the price if only for the peace of mind it could offer.

"Where's Jane?" Tanner asked as Kurt headed out with the dog.

"I don't know," Kurt called back. He'd tried to call her on the drive over, but she hadn't picked up.

"I'm not sure I should leave without talking to her," he said as he followed Kurt into the living room.

Kurt paused at the door. "Would you rather stay and wait for her to come home? I can take Otis to the vet myself. I know him well, have had him out to the ranch plenty of times over the years to attend to a sick horse or any number of cattle."

"No, I'll go with you," he decided, probably because he didn't want to be separated from Otis. "I'll drive. Where're my keys?"

No way was Kurt going to allow that to happen. "We'll take my vehicle. It's in the drive."

"Okay," he responded—thankfully accepting Kurt's response—and tried to leave the house without a coat.

"It's cold out. You should grab a jacket or something," Kurt told him, and he went back inside, presumably to get one, while Kurt loaded Otis into the back seat of his crew cab.

When the old guy came out again, he had on a red cardigan, but it was buttoned wrong.

"Let me straighten this," Kurt said and helped him fix the buttons.

"You're a good man," Tanner told him when he was done. "I'm glad Jane's got you."

Kurt knew dementia was crippling the old man's brain, but the comment took him off guard all the same. "I wish *she* was glad," he said jokingly.

"Don't you underestimate my Jane," Tanner said, surprising him again. "She knows a good thing when she finds one."

Kurt couldn't help but smile—despite the baby, despite the backlash that would soon come when news of it hit, despite his current lack of belief that Jane would ever see him as anything special. That comment made him feel like he had nothing to worry about.

Twenty-Four

Jane was getting the worst of it over with in one fell swoop. Considering something could still go wrong with her pregnancy, maybe it wasn't the smartest approach. But she wasn't assuming there'd be a tragedy, and showing up at Will's house would put what was currently tormenting her out in the open, so she could eventually get beyond it. After all, Kurt knew about the baby. Talulah and Brant knew about the baby. Averil also knew about the baby. And if Ellen hadn't already guessed, she soon would. Jane figured she should tell Kate before word could spread any further.

Fortunately, she'd been forgiving of Will when he came to her store. She was glad of that—and glad she'd decided to pay her sister a visit when Will was home, since he was the one who'd answered the door, let her in and was trying to keep Kate from getting too upset. Jane had never thought she'd find an ally in *him*, but it was sort of working out that way.

"So…you were sleeping with Kurt, and you didn't tell me?" Kate said after Jane had told her about the baby.

"Not quite like that, but…" What could she say? They

had continued to see each other, and were intimate, after Bozeman, so technically Kate was right.

"Kurt's my age!" Kate snapped.

"He's five years younger than I am," Jane said. "That's not a lot. You make it sound like I was robbing the cradle."

"Five years is a lot!" her sister insisted.

Will scooted to the edge of the sofa. "What difference does that make?"

"Kurt and I went to school together!" Kate said.

He scowled at her. "So?"

Exasperated, Kate turned back to Jane. "You let me make a fool of myself by going over to the ranch and..." She stopped talking and Jane could easily guess why. She couldn't finish without upsetting Will. He wouldn't like hearing she'd tried to get back with a previous love interest right after she broke up with him.

"I started seeing Kurt before what happened between you and Will," Jane explained. "I tried to back away once you moved in with me and Papa, but by then it was too late."

"You could've told me," Kate said sullenly.

Jane shifted in her seat. Although Will had offered her a glass of water, she hadn't accepted it. She needed food, hadn't been able to hold anything down all day. But she wanted to plow through this conversation first. Then she'd go home and see what she could do to make herself feel better. "I didn't know how. You were going through hell. I didn't want to make things worse."

"And it's okay for you to make things worse now?"

"I have no choice," Jane said.

Kate slouched deeper into the couch. "Wow. A baby. You're going to have a baby, Jane? *Kurt's* baby? Do you know how weird that's going to be for me?"

Jane swallowed hard, partially to quell the nausea

that plagued her. If she was battling morning sickness this early, she could be facing a rough pregnancy. "Yes. But I thought you and Will were going to get married when...when Kurt and I started to become, er, closer."

"Closer? You fucked him! We've both slept with the same man!"

Jane winced. The profanity didn't make her feel any better. "Not an ideal situation, I agree. But it just worked out that way. Sometimes life can throw you a curve ball."

"Wait," Will said. "If you love *me*, why does it matter who she slept with?"

When Kate glowered at both of them, Jane knew it was because her sister wasn't entirely committed to Will—not like she'd been before. If Jane removed Kurt from the realm of possible love interests, in Kate's mind there was one less viable option for her, and there weren't many men like Kurt around, so he wasn't easy to replace. The fact that Kate seemed to feel her choices had been limited was concerning. Jane didn't want her sister to marry Will if it wasn't the best thing for her. But a baby changed everything. It definitely established a connection between her and Kurt that hadn't existed before.

"I'm sorry," Jane said again.

"So...are you going to marry him?" Kate asked. "Are you together or...what does this mean?"

Given the news she'd had to deliver to Kate, Jane had felt uncomfortable since showing up at Will's but never more than now, when she was faced with this particular question. Still, she'd known it would be coming. "We're not officially together. We...we need to figure out what the future will look like. As I said, this pregnancy started out as a genetic donation, and now we're sort of...swimming in murky waters where we need to decide the role he'll play in the future."

"Wow," Will said. "I wonder what's going on in *his* mind."

So did Jane. He couldn't be happy. It felt like, if she wasn't careful, everyone in Coyote Canyon would wind up hating her. "He…he says he wants to be involved in the child's life. That's as far as we've gotten."

Kate shook her head as if she had no words.

"I knew this wouldn't be welcome news for you, but… I'm hoping you can eventually be happy for me," Jane said.

"She will be," Will said before Kate could respond. "She just needs time to get used to the idea. She doesn't care about Kurt Elway."

Will wanted to believe that, but was it true?

Jane let her breath seep out in a long sigh. "It'll be an adjustment for everyone."

Kate remained silent. Fortunately, having Will there limited what she could say—and maybe that was a good thing. At the moment, she had to hold back. Maybe with time her anger would dissipate, and it would never get as ugly as it could have.

Regardless, Jane had said all she could say, so she got up. "I'd better head home. Before I left for work, I made soup for Papa, but I haven't been home to eat dinner myself." She hoped her grandfather had eaten. She figured, with a pot on the stove, he'd be capable of helping himself. He still managed pretty well when it came to that type of thing.

Will got up to show her out. "Thanks for stopping by."

Jane gave him a sad smile. "You bet." She glanced at her sister, but Kate stayed on the couch, glaring to show her displeasure.

Jane was disappointed that Kate hadn't been more understanding. She'd tried to be a big support, especially when Kate found out what Will had been doing, but she told herself to give her sister some time. Maybe it would be okay. She felt better just telling the truth. Without such a big secret weighing her down, maybe she could feel as excited as she should about the baby.

After she got in her car, she pulled out her phone to tell Papa she'd be home soon—and realized that he'd been trying to reach her. He'd called eight times, which was unusual enough to make her heart leap into her throat. What was wrong? And why hadn't those calls come through?

She checked to find out and realized she'd accidentally had her phone on silent. "No!" she said and tried to call him back.

He didn't answer, but a text came in from Kurt.

Where are you? Otis is sick. I have your grandfather and his dog at the vet's.

Jane felt her jaw drop. *Kurt* had stepped in to solve this problem? How had that happened?

What's wrong with him? she wrote back.

We don't know yet. Just got here.

At Stubing's?

He sent her a thumbs-up. Don't panic. I think everything's going to be fine.

It had to be. She couldn't face losing Otis. She loved him, too, but also felt that he was all her grandfather had left.

I'm on my way.

Briefly, she considered alerting Kate that there might be a problem. Her sister cared about Otis and Papa, too. But she decided to wait and see what was wrong before sounding the alarm. It would be awkward, to say the least, if Kate and Will showed up at the vet while Kurt was there.

With a final glance at the house, she started her Mustang and pulled out of the drive.

Kurt was waiting in the lobby of the clinic, which Dr. Stubing had opened for them, when Jane arrived. She looked drawn and tired, and he wondered if she'd been able to sleep since learning of the pregnancy.

"Is everything okay?" she asked, obviously worried. "Where's Papa?"

"He's in the back with the vet and Otis. They didn't need me getting in the way, so I said I'd stay here."

"Do we know what's wrong?" Her voice was filled with dread.

"Not yet. They just went back."

"I'm sorry you had to deal with this for me. Papa tried to reach me, but my phone was on silent. I must've accidentally hit that button while I was doing something else. I missed your call, too."

"Were you at the store? I thought of going by there, but it was out of the way, and as upset as your grandfather was, I didn't dare take the time."

She adjusted the strap of her purse. "No. I was at Will's, meeting with Kate."

"Not about…"

When she didn't answer, he knew he'd guessed right. "You told her?"

"I hope that's okay. I had to get ahead of the rumors. She'd be far more hurt if she was the last to know."

He rubbed his jaw as he imagined what that meeting must have been like. "How'd she take the news?"

"Not as badly as I'd imagined she would. But Will was there. She couldn't act too mad at me for getting involved with you since she's supposed to be in love with him."

"She *is* in love with him," he said. "You don't go back to a guy who did what he did if you're not."

"True. Anyway, she didn't say much, so I don't really know what she's thinking, but at least I did what I felt I should and got it out without too many fireworks."

His stomach sank. "The rest of the town will soon know."

"Since you want to be involved in the baby's life, I assume that's okay?"

"I expected as much." At least for the past few days he had. "Does Kate usually hold a grudge?"

"Not really. But we've never faced anything quite like this. She's usually the one who has to apologize to me— for ruining a blouse she borrowed without asking, little stuff like that. There's enough of an age difference between us that we never competed for…for men or friends or anything that might cause bigger trouble."

Until now. Apparently, the age thing was turning out to be a bigger deal than he'd thought.

"Jane?" Dr. Stubing called out. "Is that you?"

"Yeah, I just got here," she replied.

"Come on back."

She sent Kurt a look that said *Here goes* and started for the hallway that led to the examination room. But then she turned back. "I have my car and can get Papa and Otis home. There's no need to make you wait, especially when you have to get up so early tomorrow."

He stood. It was odd to see her now, knowing she was carrying his child. He could never have guessed how he'd react to that, but he felt sort of possessive, which was foolish since she didn't feel anything for him.

"I'll head home, then. Call me if…if you need anything," he said. "I hope Otis will be okay."

Her pinched expression once again revealed her worry. "Me, too."

Jane had never been more grateful for a day off. It'd come right when she needed it most—after another late, stressful night. Fortunately, the vet had assured Papa that Otis would be okay. He had the dog flu, which was hardly ever fatal. Dr. Stubing said if they looked after him and were careful not to let him get dehydrated, he should recover within a week or so.

On the way home last night, Papa had lamented letting Otis play with Mr. Hensley's golden retriever. He said Hensley took Plato everywhere, and he was probably the source of the virus, since Otis had to have picked it up from somewhere. But Jane told him not to worry about that. Mr. Hensley took great care of his dog, and playtime was good for Otis. He needed the exercise. She didn't want Papa to refuse to take his dog out. Papa needed to see the sun and walk as much as the dog did.

She heard some rustling in the living room. True to form, Papa was up before her. She wished the poor guy could sleep in for a change.

With a yawn, she rolled over to check the time and was surprised to find it was much later than she'd expected—nearly ten. Maybe Papa *had* slept in because she hadn't heard anything until now.

Leaning up on one elbow, she reached for her phone on the nightstand beside her. She wanted to text Kurt to thank him once again for his help. They were both so anxious right now. Neither of them knew what to expect.

She planned to make sure he knew she wouldn't go back on anything she'd promised. As kind as he'd been, that would be patently unfair.

I really appreciate what you did last night. Thank you.

No problem. How's Otis?

He's going to be fine. Has a touch of the flu—that's all.

Happy to hear it's nothing serious.

She almost set her phone down and let it go at that, but she hadn't been able to get Kurt out of her mind since she'd learned she was pregnant. She believed they might both feel better if they had a chance to talk through how they would treat each other during the pregnancy, if he planned on being present at the birth and how often he hoped to have visitation with their child.

Were they going to set up these parameters? Or would they need to get lawyers involved?

She hoped that wouldn't be necessary and felt if they were both fair and kind, they could work out something on their own.

I'm off work today. Any chance I could bring you lunch?

He didn't respond immediately. But she imagined he was busy. He worked hard.

She'd gotten up, gone to the bathroom and dressed by the time she heard from him again.

Sure.

What time?

11:30 is when we normally eat.

That was earlier than she'd anticipated, but they started work at six, so it made sense.

Once again, she checked the time on her phone. She'd have to make breakfast for Papa and get ready quickly, but she could do it if she started right away.

See you soon.

More often than not, Kurt and his brothers ate lunch together back at the house. If one of them was going to town, he picked up an order for all four of them and they gathered to eat when he got back. That way, they could use the bathroom, wash their hands, relax for a few minutes and refill their thermoses. Occasionally, if they were going to be working on the far side of the property, they'd pack a lunch.

He'd briefly considered putting Jane off until tomorrow, when he could make it clear to his brothers that he wouldn't be back for lunch, but since Monday was her only day off, he'd decided to let her come. He was too agitated to wait longer than necessary to establish how they'd proceed now that the baby was a reality.

They had a lot of ground to cover...

The only problem was that his brothers would probably see Jane and take her visit to mean too much, especially after Ranson had made such a big deal of discovering her in their kitchen when she stayed over. Brant hadn't yet told Ranson or Miles about the baby. He seemed to understand that Kurt could use the reprieve—however short it turned out to be. But now that Jane was coming over, Ranson and Miles would most likely find out despite Brant's discretion, and Kurt wasn't looking forward to admitting he'd gotten her pregnant *on purpose*, without any kind of relationship or commitment.

Still hoping to put that off a little longer, he left them foraging in the kitchen and walked outside and down the drive the second she let him know she was on her way. There was a slim chance they could drive somewhere else for forty minutes or so without his brothers paying any attention. For all Brant, Ranson and Miles knew, he could be in his room. There wasn't really a set time they went back to work—just a general consensus once they were done eating—so there was no guarantee one of them wouldn't come looking for him.

Fairly confident he'd managed to leave without being noticed, he glanced back at the house but didn't see anyone at the window.

She pulled to a stop in front of him and reached over to roll down the window. A vintage Mustang was a cool car, but it didn't have any of the more modern conveniences people were used to today.

"Should we go to our spot on the other side of the ranch, where we can have a few minutes alone?" he asked as he got in.

"Sure."

While she turned around in the semicircular driveway, he tensed, hoping no one would hear her vehicle—and breathed a great deal easier once they were back on the road and driving to the more remote part of the property.

A bag from the burger joint in town sat between them. He hadn't realized how hungry he was until he smelled the food.

"Go ahead and eat while it's hot," she said, and he pulled the bag into his lap.

She'd brought him a bacon burger, sweet potato fries and a shake. "Thanks for this."

"No problem."

He was already halfway through his burger when she pulled into the copse of trees they'd used to hide her car before.

"How have you been feeling?" she asked after turning off her engine.

"A bit shell-shocked," he admitted. "There's a lot I'd never really thought about before, especially having a baby this way."

"I know. I realize that…I was too cavalier about a lot of things. It seemed like it would be no big deal, but it's been sobering to think through all the consequences."

"You're a little freaked out, too?"

She nodded.

"What concerns you the most?"

"Now that Kate knows, I guess it's when I should tell Papa, and whether he'll truly understand."

Kurt stuck a couple of french fries in his mouth. "He thinks we're together."

"I know. Last night, he talked about you the whole way home." She flashed him a smile despite the tension in the car. "Said I chose well."

Most women acted so much more interested in him than she ever had. Maybe that was the attraction, he told himself. Maybe he merely wanted what he couldn't have. That would be like him—to make what could be easy hard. "And you didn't tell him about the baby?"

"No, I don't want to do it while Otis is sick. Why give him something else to worry about?"

She didn't seem to have bought herself any food, so he offered her a bite of his burger. "Tanner's a cool old dude. And he thinks the world of you."

"The feeling is mutual," she said but waved away the food. "I can't eat."

"What do you mean?"

"I don't know if it's morning sickness or general anxiety, but it's been tough to keep anything down."

"That can't be good for you or the baby," he said with a frown.

"A lot of pregnant women go through it."

But as she'd already pointed out, she was having a baby later in life, which would make any difficulty harder. "You should probably get to your doctor, just to be safe."

"I'll make an appointment."

Finished eating, he put the wrapper from his burger in the sack with the empty container for the fries and balled them up together.

"What about you?" she asked. "What are you most worried about…moving forward?"

There were so many things to worry about, he didn't know where to start. "Access, I guess."

"I won't make it difficult."

"Not on purpose," he allowed. "I don't doubt that. But what if your situation changes and you move away?"

"I can agree not to go too far. I mean…not until the child is older. Seattle would be nice. Or Portland. Or San Francisco."

Those places were closer than Boston or New York City, but Kurt had never even left Montana. He had no desire to. Everything he wanted was right here. "So… I'd be expected to go there?"

"We could trade off. I could bring the baby back here one weekend a month. Even when something happens to Papa, my sister will still be here. Talulah and Brant and Ellen and Averil—all my friends are here, too. So—

provided Kate will eventually forgive me—I'll have a place to stay and other reasons to return besides letting you see our child."

Our child. Those words were so foreign to his ear. "Okay." That was something, and it didn't sound entirely horrible. At some point, the child would be old enough to come on his or her own, so there was that, too. "It won't take long for the news that you're pregnant to start getting around," he said. "Are you okay with that—with facing the various responses you might get?"

"I have to be. I don't have any choice now."

"You don't think it'll affect your business, do you? To be pregnant and single, without even a boyfriend?"

"I certainly hope not. But…around here? Who knows?" She toyed with her keychain. "What about you? Are you worried about how people will react?"

"I don't see myself as being quite so vulnerable to public backlash. My brothers and I own a business, but—"

"Traditionally, people go easier on the guy who gets a girl pregnant than on the girl."

He considered that for a moment. He probably didn't feel the same fear a woman would under the same set of circumstances. "I guess that's part of it."

"Do your brothers know, other than Brant? How do you think they'll react?"

They'd think he lost his mind. They'd point out all the difficulties he could face. But he didn't want to make her feel bad, so he merely shrugged. "They're not who I'm worried about."

"You're more worried about your parents."

"My mother in particular."

"Not your dad?"

"He's gotten soft with age." He felt nothing but fondness when he thought of his father, who was tough on the outside but an absolute marshmallow on the inside. "He'll just sigh and roll his eyes. I think he's given up trying to keep me out of trouble. It's my mom who'll raise hell. She's the one who can be relentless."

"She's had to keep you four boys in line for a long time," she said and started to chuckle.

What Jane had said was true, but he couldn't imagine why that would be funny. "What?"

She shook her head, still laughing. "It's just… What have we done?"

He gazed at her. *He'd* fallen in love. That was what'd gotten him into this. He wouldn't have made such a stupid mistake otherwise. As he sat in that car, looking at the woman he found more beautiful than any other, he knew it. And that made it possible to forgive himself just a little. Love made people do crazy things. "We'll make the most of it," he promised, and she surprised him by reaching over to take his hand.

Twenty-Five

Jordan had texted Averil almost every day for the past week. His persistence shocked her. Ever since they'd started dating, he'd led her to believe he didn't care much about her, that if she ever did anything he didn't like he'd simply move on without batting an eye. So why was he still contacting her? Still trying to talk to her? She'd made it clear she was finished with the relationship.

She was staring down at her phone, trying to decide whether to reply, when a man cleared his throat, and she realized she had a customer. Brant Elway. His flatbed cart was loaded with a bag of protein cakes for cattle, a lick barrel and some poultry feed.

That was the problem with living in a small town, she told herself. There was no way to escape ex-boyfriends and old flames. And now that she worked at Miller's Tackle & Feed, she saw Brant and his brothers quite often, even though they probably had a couple of tons of protein cakes—or range cakes as they were called—regularly delivered to the ranch. They only used the feed-store to fill in here and there, but they ran such a big ranch that even that was significant.

Putting down her phone, she grabbed her scanning gun. "Good morning," she said politely, as if he was a total stranger, and began scanning his items.

"Morning." He stepped back so she could walk around to get the UPC on the lick barrel.

She wasn't going to say anything else. If she could help it, she never engaged with him. She knew how Talulah felt about her, and how defensive he was of his wife. Averil was Enemy Number One, even though all she'd ever done was want him—and, sadly, that hadn't been something she could control. Instead, she was going to minimize the pain of her rejection, and the embarrassment and shame of its being so public, by minding her own business and staying away from them both whenever possible.

So it took her off guard when, unlike the times he'd come through her line before, he attempted to speak to her.

"How's Mitch?"

She looked up in surprise. "He's...doing good," she said, the sentence involuntarily falling to a mumble after the first word.

"He's a great kid."

Brant's kindness made her even more uncomfortable, so she focused on finishing as quickly as possible. "Thank you."

She gave him the total for his purchases and waited, looking anywhere but at him, as he inserted his card. The transaction went through, and she ripped off his receipt. "Thank you for shopping at Miller's Tackle & Feed."

His hand brushed hers as he reached for the receipt, which caused her to let go and jerk back too soon—she didn't want him to think she was trying to touch him—and the paper fluttered to the concrete floor. "Sorry," she said, and they nearly cracked heads as they both bent over to grab it.

"I'm sorry," she said again when all she ended up doing was getting in the way.

He stood, the receipt safely in his hand, and she turned her attention to the space behind him, hoping she'd find another customer and that would be that. But there wasn't another customer. And he didn't take his items and leave.

Thinking he must need something else—a product he'd forgotten to get at the store, or a question he wanted to ask about when they might have a certain item he needed—she met his gaze expectantly. "I'm sorry. Did I... Was there something else?"

"You've now apologized to me three times," he said.

"I'm sorry," she responded automatically, then realized she'd just apologized *again*. "Oops! Sorry." She clapped a hand over her mouth. That word just kept coming out. She didn't know what else to say to him. She *was* sorry—sorry she'd ever fallen in love with him, sorry she'd ever seen him as the perfect father for her son, sorry she'd believed he would be everything her first husband wasn't. And sorry she'd reacted so badly when he got with Talulah instead.

"I hope we can get past any...hurt feelings or misunderstandings from the past," he said.

She blinked at him. *"Why?"* She didn't matter to him. He had everything he could ever want, especially now that he and Talulah were expecting a baby. She had no idea why he'd even make such a statement.

"Because I never meant to hurt you. And I know Talulah didn't, either. We'd both like to see you happy."

She couldn't tell if he was being sincere or simply trying to smooth things over for his wife. Or did Averil seem pathetic enough to evoke the kind of pity that would instigate such an exchange? "I'm doing great," she insisted with a stubborn smile. "Thank you. I'm sorry if—" She stopped talking, catching herself when she saw his eyebrows slide up.

"You don't owe me another apology," he said.

"Right. Understood. I was just saying… I'm doing fine," she repeated. "Thanks for asking."

He frowned. "I can tell you don't believe me, but I don't say something unless I mean it, Av," he said and pushed his flatbed away.

When he was gone, Averil let her breath go. She hadn't even realized she'd been holding it. He made her *so* self-conscious. And he'd called her "Av." Since when had he ever addressed her the way Talulah and Jane did?

She wished she didn't have to be reminded, every time she saw him, of the friendships and other relationships she'd lost. It'd been easier when she didn't work at the feedstore. Then she didn't have to see him quite as often.

She was so tired of obsessing about Brant and Talulah that she immediately directed her attention back to her phone and the dentist from Libby she'd been dating. Jordan wasn't nearly the man Brant was, but what'd happened with Brant had taught her that she wasn't worthy of a man like him. Maybe Jordan was the best she could get. Maybe she was stupid to reject him. If she didn't settle with Jordan, with what she could get, she could spend the rest of her life feeling isolated and alone…

She started to text him back.

Sorry I've been acting so weird lately. It isn't you. I've

just been going through a lot. Why don't you come over for dinner this Fri—

"Averil?"

She looked up again and slowly lowered her phone. It was her boss. Mick Miller had never told her she had to stay off her phone at work. She was simply supposed to handle the register, and there was no one in line at the moment. Still, maybe he wanted her to be doing nothing while she waited for the next customer.

"Yes?" she said, already bracing for his rebuke and formulating her *next* apology—this one to him.

"Brant Elway just paid you a great compliment."

Her mouth opened and closed twice before she could switch gears. It didn't sound as though she was in trouble. "He did?"

"He said he likes it when you're at the register because you're always quick and efficient."

"He did?"

"Said I should try to hang on to you if I can. And I might just do that. It was what I was already thinking, but the Elways spend a lot of money in here. So thanks for doing such a good job and keeping them happy."

"You...you're welcome," she stammered.

He didn't seem to mind that she'd been on her phone but she checked out a few more customers and waited until her break before returning her attention to the text she'd been writing to Jordan. He wasn't what she was looking for, and if she wasn't going to love herself enough to pass him over, how could she expect anyone else to love her?

Erasing what she'd written, she typed a different message.

I really appreciate the friendship you've offered me and the fun times we've had. But I'm looking for something else in my life, Jordan, something I doubt I'll find if I keep hanging out with you.

She needed to clear the slate, start over and raise her standards again. Just because her self-esteem had fallen into the toilet didn't mean it had to stay there.

You're just going through a weird transition.

Was that how he'd categorized her behavior lately? In some ways, it didn't surprise her. He never took responsibility for anything.

We're not right for each other. But I wish you all the best in the future.

Fuck you! I don't really want you anyway—you fat, ugly bitch.

She winced as his words took another chunk out of her self-esteem. She wasn't even overweight.

She knew her situation would most likely get worse before it got better. But she needed to be okay with that, to face the sting of it bravely and endure. Otherwise, she might never get herself going in the right direction.

Got it. Okay. Goodbye.

Wait! I'm sorry. I didn't mean that. We should talk about this.

Her phone lit up as he tried calling her. But she declined the call and blocked him just in case she ever lost her conviction in the future. There wasn't any point in having a conversation with him because this time she was done with Jordan for good.

"Are you okay?"

Papa was sitting across from Jane, petting Otis, who was, thankfully, fully recovered, while taking his turn at Rummikub—a game Jane used to play with her grandparents when she was ten or eleven that she and Papa had recently started playing again. Caught up in her own thoughts, she stared at the wall behind him. She didn't think it was good for him to watch television all the time. His mind needed more stimulation than that. She hoped playing games and doing puzzles together would help him retain his mental faculties for as long as possible.

"What do you mean?" she asked, pulling her attention back to the game.

"You haven't been yourself lately."

Since it was her turn to move, she studied her tiles, pretending to give her strategy some thought. But she won almost every time they played, so she was *trying* to lose. That meant what she put down didn't really matter. She only wanted to make him feel good. "In what way?"

"You've been quiet. Distracted. And you're throwing up all the time."

He'd noticed? He was so unaware of most things these days that she hadn't been overly worried he'd take note, but she hadn't thrown up right in front of him, either.

He leaned toward her, his once-shrewd eyes studying her closely. "Is there something wrong with you, Janey? Are you sick?"

"No," she said immediately, grabbing his free hand to reassure him. "I'm fine."

"You'd tell me if that weren't the case, wouldn't you? I wouldn't…I wouldn't want the way I've changed to make you feel you couldn't come to me."

He knew what was happening. That wasn't a secret, even to him. Those moments of realization on his part were some of the saddest for Jane. She would hate, most of all, to lose what he was losing, so it always made her feel sad when he acknowledged that something was going wrong with his brain—and that it was getting worse all the time. "Of course I would still come to you," she assured him. "You've always taken care of everything."

"Then why haven't you talked to me about it—told me why you've been throwing up?"

She laid down a tile, but he didn't pay any attention to it. His eyes remained on her. "I was going to wait to break the news until…until I was further along," she said. "But there's no need to make you worry." Especially after the scare he'd had with his beloved dog.

"What is it?" he asked.

"I'm pregnant, Papa. I'm going to have a baby."

He rocked back. "Will you be getting married?"

"No."

"Are you happy about the baby?" he asked.

She thought about all the baby books she'd sneaked into her room and read after he went to bed—and her appointment with a good ob-gyn in Lancaster, the next little town over, which was coming up on Monday, her day off. "I am."

He nodded solemnly. "Who's the father?"

"Kurt Elway. He helped with your dog, remember?"

He didn't say if he remembered. She generally tried

not to use that prompt, but it was such a habit with people in general that she'd slipped up. "He doesn't want to marry you?"

The idea of that seemed to make him sad, so she smiled to let him know she wasn't hurt. "Kurt's a good man. That just wasn't part of our deal."

"I don't understand," he said, obviously bewildered.

"You don't have to." She gave his gnarled hand another squeeze. "All you need to know is that everything is going to be okay."

"You're not moving out to start a family of your own?"

"No. I'm staying right here with you." At least for the foreseeable future...

"But that's all I've ever wanted for you. You're not making this decision—to stay here—because of me, are you? Because if it's your choice, I *want* you to go. I've lived my life, Janey. What happens to me now doesn't really matter. It's you I'm worried about. I hope...I hope you'll change your mind."

She blinked, trying to rid her eyes of the tears that'd suddenly sprung up. Even with the mental capacity he'd lost, he knew he loved her. She was terrified he'd lose that, too—forget who she was. "What happens to you matters a great deal to *me*," she insisted.

"But don't you understand? In some ways, you're all I have left. If you're not happy, I've lost everything."

"I *am* happy."

His craggy eyebrows came together in apparent confusion. "Then you don't love him..."

She opened her mouth to say she didn't but couldn't make the words come out. She liked Kurt more than any other man she'd met. She admired him more than any other man, too—at least of her generation. And she'd spent the last week lying awake in bed, dying to see him again, to feel his hands on her body and his mouth on hers. But he hadn't called. And she'd been afraid to reach out to him for fear she'd get his hopes up that they could get into a serious relationship only to crush them. "What happened is unusual and hard to explain. I plan to do some traveling eventually. I want to see the world."

"With a child?"

"Of course. Why not? It'll be a good experience—a good education—for a child, too."

"But wouldn't it be that much more wonderful with a loving companion at your side? I'd give anything—*any* experience I've ever had, anything I've ever done—if I could just see your beautiful grandmother again. When you're young, so many things seem to be important. But when you get old like me, you realize that there's only one thing that matters in the end. And that's people. *People*, Janey," he emphasized. "Those you love and spend your life with. The rest is just window dressing."

Jane felt as though she'd swallowed a boulder and it was sitting right where the baby was supposed to be. "Even if Kurt and I feel we have different paths ahead of us?"

"Can't you work out a good compromise?"

That was the thing. She didn't think they could.

The next few weeks, Kurt threw himself into his work. Once he'd learned about the baby, he was always the first to leave the house and the last to come home because he couldn't stand being idle. That was when his mind began to wander and paint pictures of a future he'd rather not see. Jane eventually getting with another man. Having to take that man into consideration whenever he dealt with his own child. Having to allow that man to be the live-in father *he* wanted to be and make decisions regarding Kurt's child he might not always agree with. Having to accept that as much as he wanted to be everything Jane could ever want, he wasn't what she was looking for.

He knew he should tell Ranson, Miles and his parents about the situation. But it was easier to ignore what was coming. Since there'd been no noticeable changes in his life—not yet—it wasn't hard to pretend nothing *had* changed. Whenever he grew worried that he was making the wrong decision, he'd just tell himself to relax, he had time to adjust to the idea of having a child before he invited his mother's displeasure.

But since some people knew about the baby and others didn't, every day was a gamble. He began to avoid his family and friends, just because he didn't want to know if word was getting around or have them ask if something was wrong. As long as he put enough into his work, which had always been physical, he could go home at night, drop into bed so exhausted he didn't even dream and get up and do the same thing the next day. Denial might not be the best coping mechanism, but it was the easiest for him—until Brant knocked on his bedroom door after dinner one night.

"Kurt? It's me."

Talulah had planned a girls' night with her friends at their place, so he hadn't gone home like he normally did after they came in from the ranch. He'd stayed to eat the parmesan chicken, brussels sprouts, homemade rolls and ginger carrots their mother had made and planned to watch a movie with Ranson and Miles.

Kurt had assumed his brother would be too preoccupied with what was going on in the rest of the house to notice he wasn't part of it, so he was surprised by Brant's interruption.

He didn't answer. He thought if he pretended to be asleep, Brant might leave him alone.

But his brother just knocked louder. "Kurt? I'd like to talk to you."

"Shit," Kurt muttered. Since he hadn't felt like being around the others, he'd been surfing YouTube on his phone, watching daredevil sports to distract him from the noise coming from the living room.

"Kurt?" Brant said.

Setting his phone aside, Kurt got up and cracked open the door. "What is it?"

"Can I come in?"

"I'm already in bed."

Brant gave him a sardonic look. "You're obviously awake, and this won't take long."

With a sigh, Kurt stood back. "What is it?" he asked as Brant came in and closed the door behind him.

"I just wanted to check in to see what's going on with Jane."

"Nothing's going on." Kurt hadn't even talked to her. He'd been avoiding her just like he'd been avoiding the fact that they'd be having a baby together.

"She still pregnant?"

"I'm sure she would've called me if she wasn't."

"Have you told Mom and Dad?"

"Not yet."

"Ranson and Miles don't know, either?"

Kurt scowled. "There's no rush."

"Except there is," Brant insisted. "Word has a way of getting around this town, bro. What if Averil tells Charlie? And he tells his parents?"

Kurt swallowed a groan. "*Averil* knows?"

"I can't imagine she doesn't. She lives above Jane's store. Talulah told me they have coffee together almost every morning."

And a pregnancy wasn't something Jane would be likely to keep to herself if she felt it was safe to speak, as she would with an old friend. The fact that she was having a baby would be on her mind constantly. How could she avoid it? "I need to tell them soon," he acknowledged.

"You know Mom and Averil's mom have been close ever since Mom started helping with the Fourth of July parade, right?"

"Seriously?"

"Yep. Dinah's on the committee, too."

Kurt jammed his hand through his hair. In the beginning, he felt as though he'd been running away from something terrible, something he was escaping. But instead of getting away as he'd hoped, the choices he'd made had slowly funneled him into ever narrower alleyways, finally dumping him in a dead end.

If Averil knew, there was nowhere else to run. She had no reason to keep his secrets.

"I'll go over to their place for lunch tomorrow." It would be Saturday, after all. It wasn't as if he had to work.

"Good idea. I think sooner is better."

Twenty-Six

Averil had been invited to Talulah's for a girls' night. Her mother had agreed to babysit, but she'd almost used the excuse that she couldn't go because her mother wasn't available. Two months ago, she would've turned down the invitation for sure. The animosity she'd felt coming from Ellen in particular seemed to be changing. Ever since they'd reupholstered the chair together, Ellen had been sending her links to inexpensive furniture and decorating ideas for her new apartment, some of which she'd actually used or planned to use.

Although Averil was still afraid to rely on those overtures, she got the impression Ellen was giving her a second chance, which was surprising. Ellen was so close to Talulah these days it would be all too easy for her to sabotage any kind of reconciliation.

"There you are!" Talulah said when she answered the door. "We were getting worried you wouldn't be able to make it."

Were they really? Or were they *hoping* she wouldn't be able to make it?

She grimaced at her own skepticism as she handed

Talulah a bottle of sparkling apple cider and the bottle of wine she'd just bought after spending more than twenty minutes in the grocery store trying to decide which kind to get. Since this was her first foray back into Talulah's social circle, it seemed important she bring the right thing. Nothing too pretentious; that would come off as trying too hard. Nothing too cheap, or they'd assume she hadn't contributed as much as she should. And nothing inconsiderate, hence the sparkling cider for those who were pregnant.

"Sorry if I'm a few minutes late. I had to drop off Mitch at my mom's."

"No problem. We've just been chatting. I don't know if I told you, but Linda Redmond is coming over at eight to give us facials. Won't that be fun?"

Linda was a stylist in town who had a large family and was currently going through a divorce. Averil guessed Talulah was trying to support her by giving her extra work. That was probably where the idea of a girls' night had originated in the first place.

"Sounds great."

Talulah stepped aside so Averil could come in. "She made it," she called out to the others.

Averil entered the kitchen to find Jane and Ellen sitting in the breakfast nook—Ellen with a margarita and Jane with a glass of water with a slice of lemon.

Talulah set the wine Averil had brought on the counter and offered her a margarita.

"I'd love one," Averil said.

After Talulah poured what was left in the blender into Averil's glass, she carried it to the table, along with her own water, and sat down.

They talked and laughed until Linda arrived. Then

they talked and laughed some more as they took turns getting exfoliated and hydrated. Although it took some time to grow comfortable, eventually Averil began to relax and enjoy herself. Talulah insisted the facials were on her—part of the party—so Averil was careful to tip well to show her appreciation and help Linda, too.

After Linda left, Averil assumed they'd break up and go their separate ways, but Talulah had a movie for them to watch—a chick flick she said Brant wouldn't care for. Then they sat around on Talulah's large, horseshoe-shaped couch, talking about Ellen's engagement to Hendrix and when they might be having the wedding—they still hadn't set a date and didn't seem to be in any hurry, since they were already living together.

"How are things going with Jordan?" Ellen asked, swinging the conversation around to Averil.

Averil always felt self-conscious when Ellen mentioned Jordan. "I'm not seeing him anymore."

Ellen didn't seem surprised. "Why not?"

Averil finished the last of the wine she'd poured for herself and Ellen before the movie started. "Because you were right about him."

Ellen drained her own glass, then made a face. "I was hoping he was different with you."

"No. I just… When you go through a divorce, the rejection is pretty tough to deal with. I mean, if the man who was supposed to love you more than anyone else doesn't want you anymore, you feel as though there must be something fundamentally wrong with you, and no one else will want you, either. At least, that's how *I* felt. Jordan seemed like the best I could get—better than nothing, anyway." Especially because she'd lost her closest friends, too. She'd felt as though she'd been tossed overboard in a vast, roiling and raging sea, and he was the only piece of driftwood she could find to cling to.

Ellen leaned forward. "You're selling yourself too short. You know that, don't you? You can get anyone you want. And you definitely don't want Jordan. If Hendrix hadn't been around the night Jordan followed me home, I don't know what would've happened."

Averil had heard he'd gotten physical with Ellen when their date hadn't gone as planned, and she'd believed Ellen from the start, even though she'd pretended not to. Jordan had never gotten that angry with her, but that had only reinforced the idea that she wasn't anyone he was all that interested in. She'd figured he must've wanted Ellen more. She was at such a low point in her life that every other woman she knew seemed more desirable. "That's scary. But I doubt I'll be hearing from him. I told him never to contact me again. Then I blocked him."

"I'm glad," Talulah said. "I hated to think he might be treating you the way he treated Ellen."

"No." Averil was sitting on the couch next to Jane, who reached over to squeeze her arm under the blanket they'd been sharing during the movie. Her smile was encouraging—it said she understood how difficult the past few years had been and that the transition she was making wasn't easy—and Averil was grateful for the support.

Ellen, on the other side of Jane, kicked off her blanket. "Well, I for one am happy to hear you're available because I have a friend I'd like to introduce you to."

"Me?" Averil pressed a hand to her chest.

"Yes, you," Ellen said. "I've had him in mind for a while. Thought I'd mention it if I ever got the opportunity. I used to work with him—before I moved to Coyote Canyon."

"So...he's a driller?" She liked the strong, rugged type. After dating Jordan, who was a dentist, and her ex, who was a salesman *when* he worked, she thought finding someone more like Hendrix—or Brant, although she didn't want to acknowledge that now that she was sitting in his home with Talulah—would be a welcome change.

Ellen yawned. "Yep. Stephen is the nephew of the guy who owns the drilling company I used to work for."

"Ross is the one who gave you your start, right?" Talulah said.

"The one and only."

"But where does Stephen live?" Jane asked. "Not in Anaconda?"

"Anaconda's not that far," Ellen replied. "It's a lot closer than Libby."

That was true, but Averil had never expected anything serious to happen between her and Jordan. He'd merely been a placeholder for her—just as she'd been a placeholder for him. "What makes you think we might be a good match?"

"Well...he's gorgeous, for one," Ellen said. "And super nice. He's also a hard worker, and he'll probably inherit Ross's business one day, so there's some stability there."

"Did *you* ever date him?" Averil asked.

Ellen grimaced. "*Ew*, no. He's like a little brother to me."

"*Little* brother?" Averil echoed. "How old is he?"

Ellen's gaze shifted to Jane. "He's Kurt's age."

"Five years younger than us?" That seemed like a lot to Averil, but she didn't want to sound as though it was *that* big a deal, not with Jane in her current situation.

"There's nothing wrong with dating a younger guy." Ellen nudged Jane. "Is there?"

Jane blushed. "Kurt and I were never really...*dating*. We were..."

"Just sleeping together?" Ellen said with a laugh.

"He agreed to help me," Jane finished lamely.

Talulah didn't seem to find teasing Jane as enjoyable as Ellen did, probably because they were talking about her brother-in-law, and it was a serious situation. Averil had noticed that it'd been a little tense between them tonight. They didn't interact as much as usual.

"But you enjoyed being with him," Talulah said, watching Jane closely.

"He's a great guy," Jane said, which certainly wasn't a denial.

"Have you two seen each other lately?" Talulah asked as she started to pick up the bags of chips and plates strewed about the coffee table.

When Jane shook her head, Averil saw Ellen exchange a glance with Talulah.

"Do you miss him?" Talulah prodded.

Jane began to rub her temples. "I don't know."

"*I* think you do," Ellen said.

"What makes you think that?" Jane sounded surly, defensive, which wasn't like her—but the pregnancy was changing a lot of things.

"You've been so quiet since you found out you're expecting," Ellen replied. "Just tonight, I'd look over at you while the rest of us were talking, and you'd be gazing off into space, your mind a million miles away."

Creases formed in Jane's forehead. "I've been thinking about my baby, and what might be best for him or her."

"You haven't been thinking of Kurt?" Ellen challenged.

"No," Jane insisted, but Averil was the one who heard what she had to say each morning when she wasn't watching her words quite so carefully. She could've jumped in and told Talulah and Ellen that Kurt was all Jane had been able to talk about lately. But she didn't want to betray Jane's confidence.

"Why would anyone turn away a man like Kurt?" Talulah asked.

"I'm not turning him away," Jane said. "He's not exactly banging down my door, okay? I haven't heard from him. And…I'm not sure I'm ready to settle down. I feel like I've been standing at the gate, waiting to bust out of this town for so long. It's hard to simply add another padlock."

"I get it," Averil said so that it wouldn't seem as though they were ganging up on her. After all, she felt most loyal to Jane, who'd forgiven her first.

"I get it, too," Talulah said. "I just don't understand how you'll find anything better than what you have right here."

Jane didn't say anything, but Averil knew she was worried about that, too.

Would she be missing out on something special? Would she regret not including her baby's father in *her* life, too?

Since she'd learned about the pregnancy, those questions swirled around in Jane's mind almost all the time. She'd never been more torn, worried and distracted. The decision she made could make a huge difference to her future. Was she being selfish by moving on with her original plan? Did she even want to? Because recalling what Brant had told her about Kurt's feelings made that even harder...

She didn't have a good answer—mostly because there were times when she wanted to see Kurt badly enough that nothing else seemed to matter. She was so tempted to give in to that desire, to tell herself it was okay to see him—for now. But she knew where that could possibly lead. Would she be locking herself in Coyote Canyon and throwing away the key?

She got a call as she was pulling into her driveway after leaving Talulah's and was surprised to see her sister's number, especially so late. Kate had watched Papa a few times while Jane was at the store, as usual, but she'd been careful to come after Jane left and leave before Jane could get home. This was the first time she'd called since Jane had told her about the baby.

"Hello?"

"I fed Papa spaghetti and meatballs tonight—in case he can't remember. Just wanted to let you know so you won't cook the same thing for him tomorrow."

"Got it. Thanks for coming over and being with him while I went out." Papa had mentioned she was coming by, so Jane had felt free to stay and enjoy herself, which was nice.

"He's *my* grandfather, too," she snapped.

"I understand that. I just..." Kate was obviously still angry with her. Jane didn't want to discuss what her responsibilities might be where Papa was concerned versus what constituted a favor. That was a minefield. When it was convenient to help, Kate acted like she was only fulfilling her responsibility. When it was inconvenient, she acted as though she was putting herself out for Jane. That grated on Jane, who had to carry the heavy end all the time. But she didn't want to create an even greater divide between her and Kate. Papa had done more for Jane, so Jane did more for him. She tried to leave it at that.

"No problem," Kate said. "He told me you're getting married, by the way. Is that true?"

Jane stiffened. Judging by the pique in Kate's voice, she wouldn't be happy if Jane got together with Kurt. She probably thought it was bad enough that they were having a baby together. But Jane had been watching Talulah closely tonight and couldn't miss how happy she was. The way Talulah's eyes lit up when she talked about her husband made their marriage seem pretty damn idyllic. But Talulah had had the chance to leave Coyote Canyon. She was gone for twenty years before she returned.

"No," Jane said. "He's confused. I told him I'm having a baby."

"They're almost one and the same to him. Back in the day, if you got pregnant, you got married."

Was that a leading statement to see if she was considering a relationship with Kurt? Jane wished she could allay her sister's fears, but there were moments when she *did* want to be with Kurt. She was just afraid to reach for what Talulah and Brant had for fear her wanderlust would eventually overcome her and she'd feel the need to back out. It would be much worse to leave him later than to never get with him in the first place.

"Papa doesn't understand that times have changed and that the last thing you want to do is get married," Kate added.

Jane turned off the engine but didn't leave her car. She thought of how it felt to make love with Kurt—those memories were never far from her mind—how easily he could make her laugh, what it would be like to have his warm body in bed with her on a regular basis. She'd feel safe, protected.

Would she be happy, too? "How are things with Will?" She couldn't reassure Kate, so she changed the subject, hoping for a reprieve.

"He's on his best behavior. He'd better be if he doesn't want me to leave him again."

Jane wondered how long his good behavior would last. Would he still be true after they were married? What about once Kate had a couple of kids or gained a few pounds? Kate had already proved that she'd put up with his cheating. Jane didn't think that had set a good precedent. "I'm happy to hear it."

"So…are you excited about the baby?"

"I am." But she was equally uncertain about so many things.

"Have you seen a doctor yet?"

"I have. I had to drive halfway to Anaconda, but I saw a woman named Dr. Hazar, and I love her."

"When are you due?"

"Around December 19."

"Wow. That's close to Christmas."

"Not ideal, considering that's my biggest selling season, but at least I should be able to get through most of it before I go into labor. If I'm late, I might even make it all the way."

"Have you told Mom and Dad about the baby yet?"

Jane was quickly coming to realize how many people her decision affected. She hadn't told her mother. She'd had several opportunities but had procrastinated, despite knowing Kate could say something before she did.

Maybe she was hoping Kate would do just that. It was starting the conversation that seemed hard. "Not yet."

"You'd better hurry. They still talk to people here in Coyote Canyon, so if word starts to get out…"

"I will."

Kate paused, as if she'd keep pushing but must've decided against it because her next question was about something else entirely. "How have you been feeling?"

"Nauseous most of the time."

"Really? Yet you've been working?"

"I have no choice. At least I work for myself so I can run to the bathroom and throw up if necessary. And the weekend's here. Tomorrow is a busy day but a bit shorter." Then Sunday was even shorter, and she had Monday off. She felt like she was going into the home stretch.

"Who watches the store when you're in the bathroom?"

"No one."

"You leave it unattended?"

"I'm not far away, and nothing's gone missing yet."

A few moments of silence ensued, then she said, "I'll try to help out more with Papa."

"I appreciate that," Jane said, but she knew her sister's support would wither if she changed her mind about Kurt.

That didn't matter, though, because she wasn't going to change her mind about Kurt—was she?

Averil had intended to go home at the same time Jane did, but Ellen wanted to show her something on her phone—a desk/dresser combo for Mitch's room that someone was selling secondhand—so she got held up, and once Jane was gone, they fell into another conversation, this one about Jane.

"She's making a mistake where Kurt's concerned," Talulah said. "He's such a great guy. She'll never find a better man."

"This is more about timing," Ellen said. "She wants to get out and see the world, not settle down in the same small town in which she was born and raised. Coyote Canyon isn't where she wants to spend her life."

Talulah frowned. "And I can't see Kurt going anywhere else. He works on his family's ranch—that's his inheritance. What would he do in a big city, anyway?"

"He could help her with her store, I guess," Ellen suggested.

"I can't imagine he'd be happy doing that," Talulah said.

Averil started to clean up, too. "Maybe they could go away for a while and then come back in a few years."

"It'd be weird for him to leave," Talulah insisted. "He couldn't just walk away and then expect to return and have everything remain equal between him and his brothers."

"You faced a similar choice about whether to stay," Ellen said. "Are you happy that you married Brant?"

"Of course. But I'd had the chance to see what was out there, in the bigger world. Jane's been handcuffed to Coyote Canyon since she was a child."

"She longs for freedom," Averil agreed.

"Then I guess she's already made her choice." Talulah sounded resigned.

"Actually, I don't believe that's the case." Averil wanted to be careful not to reveal too much of what Jane had shared with her. But she also agreed that Jane wouldn't find a better man than Kurt and knew, from being a single mother herself, how important a good companion could be, how easy it would be for her to regret walking away at this particular time.

Talulah, her hands filled with empty glasses, had been walking toward the kitchen but turned back. "What do you mean?"

"She cares more for Kurt than she wants to admit."

"She talks about him when you have coffee together?" Ellen asked.

Averil was hesitant to admit it. Would Jane get upset with her for sharing what she knew? She didn't want it to cost her the closeness she'd begun to feel with Jane. That was part of the reason she'd been so much happier of late and could cut Jordan out of her life. And yet... Jane's ultimate well-being was more important than anything. So she nodded. "All the time."

A contemplative expression came over Talulah's face.

"What?" Ellen said, noticing that look, too.

"Maybe...maybe even in this small town it's too easy for them to avoid each other."

"You've got an idea..." Averil said.

"I do." Her lips curved into the grin of the Cheshire cat. "I think it's time we went to the lake."

"The lake?" Averil echoed. She knew the Elways owned a boat and went water-skiing, and the weather was finally getting warm enough that they'd be able to do that soon. But how would one day of water-skiing help anything?

"A few months ago, Mick Miller, who owns the feed-store, offered to let Brant and I stay at his cabin at Canyon Ferry Lake for a week. We weren't sure we'd be able to go—it's hard for us to get away from our jobs—but we said we might go in May, for Brant's birthday. We just talked about it last night and said we should probably cancel. But instead of doing that, I think we need to find a way to make it work, and we need to make sure Jane and Kurt are both there with us, away from this small town and the pressures of their jobs, where they can unwind and simply enjoy each other."

"Maybe they'll discover they can't live without each other," Ellen said, catching on.

"But Jane has a business, too," Averil pointed out. "And her grandfather to take care of. I don't think she'd ever leave, not for a whole week."

"Maybe we can get Kate to agree to take care of Papa while she's gone."

"And I'm sure Hendrix would support me if I took a few days off so I could cover the store for her," Ellen said.

Averil had her own job working for the man who'd offered the cabin, but she could stand in for Ellen when she wasn't at the feedstore. "I can help with that," she volunteered, getting into the spirit of what they were planning. "I can cover evening hours and go in on my days off so you can have some time to work, too."

"You can work nights at Jane's store?" Ellen said. "What about Mitch?"

"He can be there with me, doing his homework and helping customers. He's old enough that he won't cause a problem. And we live above the store, so he could even watch TV upstairs or go to bed before I close."

Ellen used her fingers to spike the front of her hair, which, right now, was shorter than Hendrix's. "But will Kurt feel *he* can get away?"

"Brant could ask his father to help Ranson and Miles while we're gone," Talulah replied. "I doubt we'll run into a problem there, not if it's only for a week."

"Great," Averil said. "So it should be possible, if we

pull together and cover for them. But…how will you convince both of them to go? After hearing everything Jane's said, I think Kurt's afraid of getting hurt, and she's afraid of making the wrong decision, so they're avoiding each other. You heard her earlier tonight. She said Kurt hasn't even called."

Talulah nibbled at her bottom lip. "Getting them both all the way to Canyon Ferry without the other knowing might be tricky. Brant can probably devise something for Kurt, but—"

"Ranson and Miles won't cause a problem because they weren't invited?" Ellen broke in.

"They probably won't like it," Talulah allowed. "But it's understandable that we can't take all of them away from the ranch at the same time."

"True," Averil said. "I'm guessing Jane will be harder to convince than Kurt. She won't want to leave Papa even if we get Kate to help out."

"She seemed to enjoy coming over tonight," Ellen pointed out.

"Tonight was a girls' thing, and it didn't take her too far from him," Averil responded.

Talulah screwed up her face in thought, but before she could say anything else, Brant walked through the door, interrupting their conversation.

"Did I come back too early?" he asked when he saw that Averil and Ellen were still there.

Ellen threw away the dirty napkins she'd collected from the coffee table. "No, we were just leaving."

While Brant helped himself to some of the snacks they'd left, Averil and Ellen carried the rest of the dirty dishes into the kitchen. Then Talulah walked them both to the front door. "I'll think of something," she promised as they went out, and Averil knew—as did Jane, no doubt—that she was talking about Operation Canyon Ferry.

"Okay," they both said and waved.

After she'd said goodbye to Ellen, too, who was walking home since she lived right next door, Averil smiled to herself as she climbed behind the wheel of her car. Things really *were* looking up for her. Whatever had happened between her and her friends, it was over now—thank God—and, boy, did it feel good to be back.

Twenty-Seven

It was time to tell his mother he'd been an absolute idiot. As Kurt parked in front of his parents' house, he could see his father's truck in the drive and wished Derrick wasn't there. He'd rather tell Jeanie and let her tell his father after he left. But both parents were waiting for him to have lunch, probably assuming he had some good news to share—like he'd finally found the woman he wanted to marry.

Once he turned off his engine, he hesitated, mentally preparing himself for the emotional storm he was about to create. But he couldn't procrastinate for long. His mother must've been watching for him because he saw her face in the kitchen window.

"Here goes nothing," he said and climbed out, forcing one foot in front of the other until he'd reached the doorstep.

He put his hand on the doorknob, but it opened seemingly of its own accord, and there stood his father.

"Hello, son."

"Hey, Dad." So far, he'd downplayed in his mind what

he expected his father's response to be, but it certainly didn't seem as unworthy of concern at this point in time.

A smile spread across Derrick's face. "Your mother said you have something to tell us…"

"Don't you get him to tell you first!" his mother yelled from the kitchen. "Come on in here, Kurt! I've got chicken enchiladas ready."

Kurt's heart sank. She'd made his favorite meal. He should've tipped her off that this would not be a pleasant lunch. But then she would've worried and that didn't seem like a nice thing to do to her, either. "I'd better tell you both together," he mumbled, and the smile slipped from Derrick's face.

"What's going on?" his father asked.

"You won't like it," Kurt admitted.

Derrick's expression grew even more leery. "Will it upset your mother?"

That had always been a cardinal sin in the Elway family. Derrick felt it was his job to protect his wife from as much heartache as possible, so it made him angry when his sons' goals weren't in proper alignment.

His mother came to the entrance of the kitchen. "What are you two doing? Get in here, so we can eat while the food's hot."

His father shot him a warning glance, but Kurt had to do what he had to do. He couldn't change anything now.

Ducking his head, because he felt like such a shit, he trailed his father into the kitchen, where his mother slung orders at them both until they could get everything on the table.

After the blessing, in which his mother thanked God for her four healthy sons, Jeanie picked up her fork and looked at him expectantly. "So…what is it? You said you had something to tell us."

From the corner of his eye, Kurt could see his father cringe and brace for the worst, but his poor mother was wide open with positive expectation. She was about to be blindsided. "Jane's going to have a baby," he said.

Jeanie blinked. "*Your* baby?"

"*My* baby."

"Whew! For a minute there, you had me scared," she said with a laugh. "I mean…your father and I have been after you to give us grandkids for a few years now, but you didn't have to get her pregnant before you could even marry her!"

"*You've* been after him," his father clarified.

His mother ignored the interruption. "When's the wedding?"

"And don't you know what causes that?" his father growled at him.

His mother looked over. "Derrick, don't overreact. These days, kids often don't marry until later. Jane's a nice girl, a good person. We're happy with your choice, so don't worry, son," she said, turning back to him. "We can plan the wedding around the baby."

His mother smiled as if that was that. But there was more.

"Problem is…" Kurt shifted in his seat, searching for the best words he could use to mitigate her anger and disappointment. But the truth was the truth. "There won't be a wedding."

His mother put down her fork. "Why not? Don't you love her?"

"She doesn't love me," he clarified.

"But...how can that be?" She blinked several times. "What woman wouldn't love you?"

It was a testament to *her* love that she could say that with a straight face. She was completely convinced—which made it even harder to spell out the reality of his situation. "She doesn't want to settle here in Coyote Canyon, Mom. She wants to move away, live somewhere else, once she's in the clear with her grandfather."

His mother's chair scraped the hardwood floor as she scooted away from the table. "What does she think she's going to find that's any better than you?"

Derrick didn't say anything at this point. He just kept looking between the two of them, as if their dialogue was a Ping-Pong ball. To him, remaining calm was always of paramount importance; he didn't like histrionics. Poised to react to settle them down, as had always been his role, he seemed to be waiting to see which way things would go.

"She didn't say," Kurt said. "I only know she plans to have the baby on her own." Although he'd come prepared to tell the whole truth, at the last second, he decided to leave out that he'd agreed to a genetic donation and simply pray Jane and those who already knew never told anyone about that part. It was much better to let Jeanie believe he'd accidentally gotten Jane pregnant—and it seemed plausible, since she thought they'd been seeing each other.

Maybe he shouldn't have been so mad at Ranson for giving him away; what Ranson had done was helping now. He supposed they *had* been seeing each other. For a short while, the line had begun to blur. But she was now standing resolutely on one side of it—the side opposite to him—which made it feel as though it was impossible to reach her. He couldn't leave Coyote Canyon, even for her. His family, his future—everything was here.

He wished his child would be, too...

"She doesn't know what she's missing," his mother said.

Kurt cleared his throat. "I think her mind's made up, Mom."

"Oh, hogwash," she said, waving his words away. "Nice girl like Jane? She'll come around and do what's best for her baby."

"That's just it," he said. "I don't want Jane to stay out of guilt or obligation—make her feel she has yet *another* reason she can't live her life as she sees fit."

"But she'll be happiest if she stays," his mother argued. "Let me talk to her—"

"No," he insisted. "Leave her alone. What happens next is up to us."

His mother narrowed her eyes as she studied him.

"What?" he said.

"If she leaves, you'll both be sorry."

He knew that was true as far as he was concerned. But he wouldn't use their baby, the baby he'd tried to give Jane, to control her. He only wanted her to stay in Coyote Canyon if she'd be happy here. The baby mattered to him, but so did she. "*Don't* get involved," he reiterated.

His mother gave him another hard stare, but he stared right back to let her know he meant what he said.

"You finally give me a grandchild, and this is the way it goes?" she said.

"We'll do the best we can," he replied.

Jane was sitting on a stool she'd dragged in from the storage room because she didn't feel strong enough to continue standing when her phone lit up with another call from her mother. She groaned when she saw it because she knew she had to answer. Her mother had tried to reach her earlier today. Jane had ignored that call because she'd been helping a customer, so then her mother had sent a text message:

You've got to be kidding me.

That was it. No context. Nothing else. She didn't know exactly what her mother meant, but those words were ominous. Had Kate told her about the baby?

She'd been trying to work up the nerve to return Karen's call. But now her mother was calling back, so her time was up.

After taking a deep breath, Jane answered. "Hello?"

"Please tell me what I'm hearing isn't true," her mother said.

Jane had to swallow hard to keep from running to the bathroom again. The morning sickness she'd been having was bad enough when she wasn't upset. She didn't want to have an argument with her mother on top of it. Maybe when she was feeling better, she'd be able to cope with this conversation, but she was too diminished right now. As the days wore on, it was all she could do just to keep up with Papa's needs and her regular workload.

But she knew she'd better deal with this now, or her mother would only become more upset.

"What have you heard?" she asked.

"Are you pregnant? Because the last thing you said to me was that your relationship with Kurt wasn't serious."

"It's not," she insisted.

"Well, if you're expecting a child, it'd better get serious fast."

"I can't believe Kate told you," she muttered .

"It wasn't Kate," Karen said. "It was Jeanie. She told me that Kurt wants to marry you, but you're not interested."

Jane stiffened. "Kurt has never even mentioned marriage!"

"Doesn't matter. He doesn't want to lose you. That's the point. Jeanie said it's *you* who isn't interested in a long-term relationship. That you'd rather take your child and move away."

"You know I've wanted to leave Coyote Canyon for a long time," Jane said weakly, but even to her ears her decision sounded selfish.

"Right. But I always thought that was to find love. What else is out there?" her mother asked. "What more could you be looking for?"

An older couple came in, giving her an excuse to get off the phone. She told her mother she'd have to call back later and battled through the nausea welling up until Mr. and Mrs. Glover, who owned the gas station at one end of town, bought a reading journal and an antique opal ring for their granddaughter's birthday and left. Then she had to run for the bathroom again.

Throughout it all, she kept telling herself that it was fair to want what she wanted. She'd never misrepresented her intentions to Kurt or anyone else. But her mother had made a good point. If it wasn't love, what exactly was she looking for?

Averil had just left Talulah's house, where she, Ellen, Hendrix, Brant and Talulah had ordered pizza while making plans for the lake. They had Jane's store covered. Hendrix was going to look out for Ellen's drilling business, since he knew her jobs inside and out anyway, and Ellen was going to take over at Vintage by Jane whenever Averil had to work at the feedstore. Then, after hours and on her day off, Averil would relieve Ellen.

Brant had already called his father, who'd agreed to help Ranson and Miles with the ranch for a week, and Talulah's sister, Debbie, who lived in Billings, was coming to town to run the dessert diner. Talulah said if she did enough baking beforehand, and froze her most popular pies and cakes, Debbie should be able to get through the week. Handling the diner that way wasn't optimal; Talulah preferred everything to be fresh. But she deserved to take a vacation every once in a while, and they all thought this was important enough for Jane that they should do what they could.

The only thing left on their list was to contact Kate to see if she'd stay with Papa while Jane was gone, and Averil had volunteered for that assignment. She didn't tell the others why, but she felt she could probably best identify with the jealousy Kate would feel when Averil explained they were hoping to get Kurt and Jane together—or get them to at least open their hearts and minds to a committed relationship before deciding against it since it affected the future of Jane's unborn child and so many other people who loved them.

Averil checked the time on her phone while trying to decide whether she should swing by Will's house before heading back to get Mitch from her folks' or simply call Kate once she got back to her apartment. Talking to Kate over the phone would be easier. But she thought it might be more effective to speak to her in person, so she turned left where she would otherwise have turned right and drove over to Will's house. It wasn't hard to find his place. Over the years, Charlie had taken her with him to play poker there on numerous occasions.

Once she parked in front of the house, she leaned down so she could see out the passenger window. It could get weird if Will wasn't at work—her showing up to discuss a man Kate had shown a great deal of interest in recently—but she didn't see his truck. That was hopeful. A horse trainer could easily be working on a Saturday, she told herself, and assumed that was the case as she got out to approach the door.

She had to knock twice before Kate answered. When Jane's sister finally appeared, it was obvious she'd been in the shower. She was wearing a man's robe and had her hair up in a towel. "Averil. What are you doing here?" she asked.

Afraid Will would pull up any second, Averil glanced back at the drive. "I was hoping I could have a minute to talk to you."

Kate was understandably taken aback. "About what?"

"Your sister."

She grimaced. "What's wrong now?"

Averil glanced back again. "Where's Will?"

"Shoeing a horse. Why?"

"I was thinking this might be an easier conversation without him."

Obviously perplexed, Kate swung the door wider. "Come on in."

Averil stepped into the small living room/kitchen combo and closed the door behind her.

"What is it?" Kate asked.

"I was hoping I might get your blessing on something Talulah, Ellen and I are hoping to do for your sister."

A skeptical expression came over her face. "Why do you need *my* blessing?"

"Because it involves Kurt."

"I have no claim on Kurt."

That was exactly what Averil had been hoping to establish, and Kate had just acknowledged it. That was a good start. "So you wouldn't mind if he got together with your sister?"

She didn't answer for several seconds. "I don't know," she said at last and walked over to the couch.

Averil moved farther into the room, and sat across from her. "He's in love with Jane," she said. "Jane's pregnant with his baby."

"Jane doesn't want to stick around Coyote Canyon," Kate responded. "It'll never work."

Averil scooted forward. "Are you sure of that? Because if any two people deserve to be happy, I think they do."

Kate didn't say it, but Averil could guess she was thinking, *And what about me?*

"You deserve to be happy, too," Averil said. "But Kurt's already a lost cause where you're concerned. Even if Will wasn't in the picture, it's not as if he could ever change his mind now and start seeing you. He's having a baby with your sister."

"That doesn't mean they have to be together. She doesn't even want that."

"I'm not totally convinced of that," Averil said. "She could be holding back for other reasons. Maybe because he's younger and she's embarrassed about that? Or she's worried you'll resent it? It might even be that she's afraid of getting hurt."

"She's afraid of being stuck here. That's what she's afraid of," Kate said.

"So why not let *her* say so?"

"She's said it."

"I mean after truly considering what it might be like to have Kurt in her life as a romantic partner."

Kate adjusted the towel on her head. "I don't know what you're getting at."

Averil explained what they had in mind, and how they were going to execute what they had planned.

"You think a week away is going to fix everything?" Kate said when she was done.

"We don't know, but it'll give them time—time together—to figure this thing out. We hope whatever comes from it will be for the best."

"And you need my help to make it happen."

"Yes. You're her sister. Who could love her more than you?"

Kate sat deliberating for several seconds.

"You won't be losing anything—nothing you haven't already lost," Averil reiterated.

Finally, she sighed loudly. "I know. It's just…"

"I get it," Averil said when she didn't finish that statement. "If anyone understands, it's me."

Kate nodded. "I guess that's true."

"So, will you do it?" she asked. "Will you stay with Papa for a week so that Jane doesn't have that as an excuse to refuse Talulah's invitation to go to the lake?"

"Jane loves Talulah, but she won't want to take off just to sit around in a cabin with Talulah and Brant as a third wheel," Kate pointed out.

"She'd know something was up, for sure," Averil agreed. "Which is why Talulah will invite her to the cabin not only for some 'me' time but also for diet, exercise and prenatal wellness classes." This was something they'd come up with as they'd fine-tuned their plan, and Averil thought it was brilliant.

Kate looked intrigued. "That's a pretty good idea," she said, sounding surprised.

"Do you think it will work?"

"Giving her such a great place to escape to and a good reason to go at the same time, when she's been feeling so sick? Actually, I do."

Averil smiled in relief. "Does that mean you'll help?"

Kate unwrapped the towel and shook out her damp hair. "Of course," she said. "It's been hard to get used to the idea of Jane being with Kurt, but I want her to be happy as much as you do."

Twenty-Eight

Kate was being so nice. Jane couldn't understand what'd changed, but her sister started coming around often as the days passed, which was fortunate. If ever she'd needed Kate, it was now. She'd never dreamed being pregnant could make her so sick and tired, but, fortunately, her sister started helping with Papa more and more and would even stop by the store when she wasn't working herself and give Jane a break so she could go upstairs to Averil's apartment and lie down for an hour or two.

Jane had never been more grateful to Kate—and Averil, who was also trying to help whenever she could—for looking after her the way they were. So when they insisted they could cover for her while she went with Talulah and Brant to a cabin at Canyon Ferry Lake for some prenatal classes, she didn't put up much of a fight. She needed the chance to catch up on her sleep too badly. And the idea of having no pressure or responsibilities for almost seven days sounded too good to be true. If she wasn't so sick, she would've resisted leaning on them to such a degree. But she simply didn't have any fight left in her. She began counting the days until they were to go, and those days were so rough she'd lost ten pounds by the time the date finally arrived.

"You look tired and pale," Talulah said as Brant drove the three of them to the lake, which was about two hours away. "What's your doctor saying? Is everything okay?"

"So far." Jane leaned her head against the door in the back seat. The morning sickness was bad enough, but she was also beginning to experience some car sickness on top of it.

"When was your last appointment?"

"A week ago."

Talulah hadn't been sick at all. Jane's doctor said every pregnancy was unique, and Jane was glad her friend wasn't having as difficult a pregnancy as she was, but she couldn't help being envious. They were the same age, so it wasn't as if having a baby in her midthirties was the cause.

"And she wasn't worried?" Talulah asked.

"It's just morning sickness," Jane replied. "I should be getting toward the end of it. From what I've read, it stops around fourteen weeks." She didn't add that her doctor had said, for some, it lasted throughout the pregnancy. Surely, she couldn't be *that* unlucky.

Talulah twisted around to look at her. "I'm glad you're coming with us. You need this even more than I thought."

"Thanks so much for asking me," she said and let her eyes slide closed. If she didn't go to sleep, she was afraid she'd have to ask Brant to pull over so she could throw up.

"Go a little slower on the curves," she heard Talulah tell Brant. "I'm worried about her."

"Will do. I was hoping to—" he lowered his voice "—you know, get there first."

Get there first? What did that mean? Jane wondered, but she assumed it was to meet whoever was supposed to give them the key or let them in if it didn't have a lockbox. Regardless, she didn't have the energy to ask or even worry about it. All that mattered right now was surviving the drive—hanging on until she could get out of the vehicle and make it to a bed.

As he drove to Canyon Ferry Lake, Kurt couldn't help feeling anxious. He'd agreed to join Talulah, Brant and an unknowing Jane, but he knew what they were planning could easily be a mistake. He'd had little interaction with her of late. He'd texted her a few times over the past several weeks to check in and see how she was doing. According to Talulah, she'd been sick, so he'd been concerned. But her answers were as formal and polite as his queries. She always insisted she was "fine." End of story.

Bottom line, she'd walled him out. He could feel how cautious she was being to maintain her distance. Having him show up at the cabin could easily push her even further out of reach. But it didn't feel as though he had a lot to lose. They were sort of ambushing her, true, but he'd made it clear that he didn't want anyone to push *too* hard. As long as they were careful, he didn't feel she'd get mad enough to say he could no longer see the baby, and he wanted to be a full-time father, like his own father was, more and more as the days went by. Maybe he wouldn't have given this a try—he figured she should know if she wanted to be with him—but agreeing to come had been the only way he'd been able to talk his mother out of confronting her. That alone had made him decide to cooperate.

He turned down the volume on the stereo as a call came in, which he answered via Bluetooth. "Hello?"

"Where are you?"

Brant. "About an hour out. You?"

"We've been here since noon. I was afraid you'd beat us. What happened?"

Kurt could tell he was purposely keeping his voice low. "I had some things I had to get done at the ranch." And he'd been dragging his feet, but he didn't add that. "Have you told her I'm coming yet?"

"Of course not."

He could've guessed as much by the way his brother was talking, but he was also afraid of how she might react when she saw him and felt it might be smarter to give her a little advance notice. "I'm not sure I feel comfortable being a total surprise."

"I don't want her to come up with some excuse to go home," Brant said. "We've all worked hard to get her up here."

"Thanks a lot," he said with a grimace.

"Sorry. I didn't mean she'd leave if she saw you. I meant… Well…"

"Forget it. Anyway, how could she go anywhere? She rode with you."

"We're not that far from Coyote Canyon. She could ask Averil or Kate to pick her up."

Kurt's stomach tightened into knots. It hurt that she'd been avoiding him. He'd been avoiding her, too—so he wouldn't have to feel that pain. But everyone else insisted it was actually a good sign that she didn't want to see him—that if she didn't feel anything for him she wouldn't have a problem interacting with him.

He wanted to believe that, but even if it were true, she didn't plan to spend her life in Coyote Canyon, and he didn't know how he could overcome that. "Maybe this is futile…"

"Won't know until we try," Brant said. "Talulah thinks it's the right move, so…I'm trying to trust her."

His brother's admission of doubt only made him more uneasy. But he'd come this far.

Once again, Kurt told himself he was making the right move, that, at a minimum, he had nothing to lose. But when he finally arrived at the lake, pulled the duffel bag he'd packed from the bed of his truck and faced the cabin knowing he was about to surprise the hell out of Jane, it felt like he had *everything* to lose.

Jane could smell food, and for the first time in a long while, she felt hungry. She'd slept all afternoon. Maybe it had done her some good.

Part of the reason for coming to the lake was to focus on wellness, so she guessed whatever Talulah and Brant were making would be healthy. It would be good to get something in her stomach…

She allowed her eyes to slide closed again as she listened to them bustle about downstairs, enjoying the fact that the scent of food didn't make her want to run for the bathroom. She felt she should get up and help them, so she allowed herself only two or three more moments to enjoy feeling good. Then she forced herself to get up and brush her hair and pulled on a sweatshirt to go with her yoga pants, T-shirt and slippers.

In the morning, a prenatal coach would be coming to go over the course they'd be taking this week, which would include daily stretching, breathing and exercise sessions and classes on meditation, nutrition and parenting. Jane was grateful Talulah and Brant had found this opportunity and been willing to include her. Not only did she need a break from her regular life, so she'd have the chance to recover, but she was also eager to learn how to do what she could to make the rest of her pregnancy go more smoothly.

She noticed a duffel bag sitting in the living room as she came downstairs, but she didn't think anything of it until she walked into the kitchen—and saw Kurt sitting at the table. She was *so* surprised that it took a moment for his presence to fully register.

He stood up when he saw her. "Hey."

"Hi." She looked to Brant and Talulah for an explanation, but they wouldn't meet her gaze.

"I hope you don't mind if I join you this week," Kurt said.

She *did* mind. She was dealing with enough already. The thoughts and feelings he provoked were overwhelming, especially on top of everything else. She was torn between trying to hang on to her one chance to escape Coyote Canyon and missing even the little things she'd shared with him—like chatting for a couple of hours at Hank's after work. She could easily fall into that routine again, but if they grew close... "*You* want to go through the prenatal classes?"

"Not necessarily the stuff that deals strictly with pregnancy, but the parenting stuff might be valuable," he responded.

Brant and Talulah expressed no surprise, which told Jane she'd been set up. The three of them had planned this. And she'd ridden with Brant and Talulah, so she didn't have her own car.

"We thought you two should spend some time together, Jane—so you could decide how you want to proceed. We...we thought it would be best for everyone involved, including, ultimately, your child," Talulah said.

They thought they knew what was best for her? Jane

couldn't help but be offended. "Then why didn't you say so?" she asked. "Why did you lie to me to get me up here?"

A sheepish expression appeared on Talulah's face. "It wasn't a lie, exactly. It was…an opportunity for everyone to take a time out."

"You thought you knew, better than I did, what was best for me?" she said. "Or are you only worried about Kurt?"

Brant shifted as if this made him supremely uncomfortable, and the look he gave his wife said he probably shouldn't have gone along with the ruse. "We care about *both* of you," he insisted.

"I can leave," Kurt said.

"No!" Talulah cried. "Stay. What will it hurt to spend some time together?"

"I'm not going to force my presence on anyone," he said, and before Jane could even react, he walked past her, grabbed his duffel bag and went out, letting the door bang shut behind him.

Jane went from being angry at being manipulated to being shocked by Kurt's immediate reaction. He was part of the pregnancy, too. She was the one who'd dragged him into it.

She tried to go after him. She knew he saw her come out of the house. But he ignored her flailing arms, waving him back in, and drove off, leaving nothing but a cloud of dust in his wake.

Kurt wished he'd trusted his own instincts. He'd known surprising Jane in this way was not a good thing. So why'd he let Brant and Talulah—and his mother— talk him into it?

He was almost home when Brant called him. "Thanks

for that," he said as soon as he answered, without so much as a hello.

"Yeah. That was bad," Brant admitted. "I should've trusted my gut. I knew better. But…"

"I get it. Talulah and Mom."

"And Ellen and Averil. It wasn't just them. It seemed unanimous, besides me."

"And me!"

"But I could understand why *you'd* have some reservations."

"Regardless, it was a mistake," he insisted.

"Yeah. It was a mistake," Brant concurred. "But at least we tried. You know it's only because we care."

"I know," he admitted, but all he could think about was what the future might be like in its worst form. And the fact that he'd brought it on himself was infuriating.

"Sorry, bro," Brant said.

Kurt couldn't blame him. "No worries," he said. "I'm only getting what I deserve."

"I wouldn't say you *deserve* it, but…"

"It was certainly avoidable," he said, finishing his brother's statement. Then he disconnected the phone.

Jane felt absolutely terrible. She'd come to the lake at Talulah and Brant's invitation. They'd even insisted on paying for the cabin. Since it was their trip before it was hers, they could invite whomever they wanted to. It was just the shock of seeing Kurt when she wasn't expecting him—and the feeling that she'd been played—that'd gotten the best of her.

Instead of going back into the kitchen to face them, she'd gone up to her bedroom. Talulah had tried to coax her to come back down by saying dinner was ready. But she'd refused. She'd let them eat and waited until they went to bed, then she'd gone down and had a bowl of soup. But all she could think about was the hurt in Kurt's eyes and his set jaw when he stood up to leave.

He'd walked right past her without letting her stop him.

Taking out her phone, she sent him a text message.

I'm sorry.

He didn't respond.

She slept badly that night—tossed and turned until morning. She told herself it was because she'd slept too much the day before, but she knew, in her heart, that wasn't it. She had the nagging feeling she was ruining something important, and yet she didn't know how to stop being the wrecking ball she'd become.

After she showered and got dressed, she heard a knock at her door and assumed it would be Talulah, coming to get her for their first class. But when she called out that she'd be right down, it was Brant who answered.

"Is there any way you and I could talk for a few minutes?"

She hated the idea of facing Kurt's brother. She knew him to be inherently kind, fair and honest, but she also knew she'd involved his brother in something he wished she hadn't. She preferred to avoid talking to him, but she figured it was time to slow down and face reality—and clean up, as best she could, the mess she'd made.

Taking a deep breath, she walked over and opened the door. "Of course. Do you want to come in or—"

"If you don't mind, I'd rather Talulah not hear this. I know she'll think I'm overstepping to jump in on my own, but I can't help handling this the way I think is best."

"Okay." She stepped back, and as he walked in, she realized just how much he reminded her of Kurt. They were about the same height and weight, had the same thick hair, square jaw and kind eyes. His hands were large and showed evidence of his work, too, so that was another similarity.

"I'm sorry we tricked you," he said. "It wasn't meant as a trick, exactly. We thought we were doing something good, putting you both in the same place so you'd have to face each other and work out how you feel. But I can understand why you'd find that upsetting. In a way, it was none of our business."

"Except this baby affects you, too. I get it," she said with some resignation. "Besides, I'm your guest here. I shouldn't have said anything—"

"It's fine." He waved her words away. "We were in the wrong, and I admit it. But I would like to know how you feel about my brother."

"How do I feel?" she echoed weakly.

"Do you care about him? Or was your interaction all about getting the baby you wanted? Once we know that for sure we can adjust our thinking and do what's necessary to support both of you and make the most out of what's going to create a lot of drama around town and be a pretty emotional situation."

She opened her mouth to say she liked Kurt as a friend. She'd told herself and others that so many times it was automatic. But was it true? All through the night, she'd imagined him changing his mind about her and walking away—maybe starting to see another woman—and knew she'd be devastated if that happened.

If he was truly just a friend, she wouldn't mind if he ended up with someone else, would she? Had she been stupid enough to overlook what was right in front of her? Kurt was possibly the best thing to ever happen to her. She thought about all the hours she'd spent on dating sites, trying to meet a good guy. She had a good guy right here! He was five years younger, but so what? He was the father of her child.

Papa's words went through her mind: *"When you're young, so many things seem to be important. But when you get old like me, you realize that there's only one thing that matters in the end. And that's people...those you love and spend your life with."*

What meant more to her? Being able to escape Coyote Canyon, or having the love and support of a partner like Kurt?

"I'm scared," she admitted to Brant.

He looked confused by her comment. "Of what?"

"Of making a mistake. Of opening my heart to Kurt and then feeling as though I'm locked in forever and can't change my mind."

"But how will you know if you really want to leave Coyote Canyon if you won't even give him a chance? You won't know what you're leaving."

She'd never looked at it that way. "I'd feel terrible if I hurt him."

"I don't want to see him get hurt, either. And I don't want him to hurt you. But two people who fall in love take that risk every day, right?"

So maybe it wasn't Kurt she was afraid of. Maybe it was the risk involved. This was the first time she'd ever come so close to making a serious commitment, and it had scared her so badly she'd gone running in the opposite direction.

"I understand that you may not want to spend your

whole life in the small town we live in now. But circumstances could change. Maybe you should consider what would make you happiest right now and then take it day by day?"

That idea was so inviting—when she took out the fear of changing her mind.

"I've been single a long time, used to my freedom—"

"You don't have to marry him," he broke in. "He's not even asking. Not right now, anyway. Maybe if you could just quit pushing him away long enough to see what things could be like between you, you'll be glad you did."

A tear slid down her face. "You're right," she said. "I haven't even given him a chance." She wiped that tear away. "Do you think it's too late?"

"I don't know but—" he started laughing "—that'd be just our luck."

As soon as he was back in town, Kurt had called and told his parents, as well as Ranson and Miles, that nothing was going to change between him and Jane and not to mention her to him again—not until after the baby was born. He didn't even want to see her. He had several months during which he hoped to put the worst of the pain and disappointment behind him. Surely, time would help. That was what everyone said, anyway. So the last thing he expected was for Miles to call him out of his bedroom when it was almost midnight.

"What do you want?" he yelled instead of complying with his brother's request.

"Someone's here to see you."

Assuming it was his mother, with a cake or something to make him feel better—which didn't make a whole lot of sense because she was mad at him—he finally flung his door open so hard it hit the inside wall and stomped out to the living room. "What is it?" he growled.

Miles waved toward the front door, and he realized Jane was standing there.

"Can we talk?" she asked softly.

He almost said no, but then she said, "Please?" and, against his better judgment, he told her he'd grab his coat and they could go for a ride.

Jane didn't know how or where to start. She'd screwed up in so many ways. She'd be surprised if Kurt didn't hate her by now. He'd approached their relationship more openly and honestly than she had...

"If you're looking for an apology, I'm happy to give you one," he said, being the first to break the silence after she pulled out of his drive and onto the highway. "I'm sorry for surprising you at the cabin. If you've come to tell me how wrong that was, I get it. I shouldn't have done it. I got caught up listening to everyone who insisted it was a great idea."

"I think they meant well," she said.

His eyes widened as he looked over at her. "You're not mad at them? I mean...you must be mad. Either you had Brant and Talulah drive you all the way back from the lake so you could take it up with me, or you had Averil or Kate pick you up."

"Kate came to get me. I didn't want to ruin Brant and Talulah's plans."

He looked as though he wasn't sure how to respond. "That was nice of Kate, I guess, considering she hasn't been too excited about the baby."

"She actually had a few things to say on the way back that made a lot of sense."

"About what?" he asked with a scowl. "Because if it was about me…"

"It *was* about you, but it probably wasn't what you think."

He said nothing, just waited for her to explain.

Putting on her blinker, she turned onto a dirt side road and pulled over so she could focus entirely on what she'd come to say. "She said she thinks you'll make a great father. That any woman would be lucky to have you. And that I have her blessing if…if I want to pursue a relationship with you."

His eyes narrowed slightly, showing his skepticism. After how she'd behaved, he was reluctant to believe her—she could tell. "Did you need her blessing?"

"I guess I did," she admitted. "It helped me to feel better about what I've done and involving you in it."

"I agreed to help you. It's my own fault—"

"But you agreed because you care about me, right?" She bit her lip, searching for the courage to speak plainly despite what she might—deservedly—get back. "Is that still true?"

He hesitated. She'd put him on the spot.

She took a deep breath. "Because if it is, I'd like to see if we could have more than just a perfunctory relationship for the sake of the baby."

He looked stunned. "What are you saying?"

She couldn't blame him for wanting her to clarify. This was a complete reversal. "I'm saying that while I can't promise you I'll feel this way forever—life is too fluid, and I don't know what might come up—I'd like to officially date and…and see if we might be happiest as a couple."

"What about leaving town?" he asked. "Moving away as soon as you can?"

"I'd still like to see the world," she admitted. "That desire could reemerge at any time—I have to be honest. But I think it was more of a way to keep you at arm's length, so I didn't really have to risk my heart on someone I couldn't possibly believe was the man for me. I mean I've known you most of my life. To think I've overlooked you for that long…"

"Sometimes, it's all about timing."

"True. I also saw leaving as an escape and a chance to start over somewhere new. But like Kate told me in the car, Papa could last another ten years. I can't wait to start living. I need to live in the here and now and build the happiness I'm looking for."

"*Kate* said that?"

She nodded. She figured if the opportunity to move somewhere else—hopefully with Kurt—ever presented itself, great. And if it didn't? As long as they were happy, what would it really matter? No one got everything they wanted… "But I'll understand if after everything that's happened, and how I've behaved, you're no longer interested."

He stared down at his feet for a long time, long enough that she began to believe she *was* too late in realizing what she was about to lose.

"Kurt?" she said uncertainly and reached over to take his hand. "Are you not willing to take the risk?"

He watched her fingers curl through his before looking up, but then he grinned. "Fortunately, if I really want something, I don't mind a little risk," he said, and they both laughed before he leaned over to kiss her.

Epilogue

Christmas carols played soft and low throughout the corridors of the hospital. It was the season of joy—December 18 to be exact. They'd had a great holiday season, but Kurt couldn't remember another time when he'd felt more anxiety than in this moment. Jane had developed gestational diabetes as her pregnancy progressed—to the point she'd needed insulin shots during the last trimester—so she was considered high risk, meaning her doctor was going to deliver the baby via C-section. Jane preferred to at least try to deliver vaginally, and she'd expressed those wishes. But he'd managed to convince her to listen to Dr. Hazar. He'd said there were chances he was willing to take—and chances he wasn't. Losing her fell into the second category.

His only job was to hold her hand during the operation and provide comfort, but he wasn't sure what he'd do if something went wrong, how he'd be able to hold up. He'd never loved anyone or anything as much as he loved Jane, and considering their baby was on the line, too…

He tried to distract himself with his phone while they prepped her for the surgery and he couldn't be with her.

Because this was a scheduled event, his parents and her parents were in the waiting room. So were Kate, Ellen, Averil and Talulah with her new baby girl—Tabitha. His brothers were on the ranch, working, but they had each messaged him to wish them well and to say they were eager to learn the sex of the child, since he and Jane had decided not to find out early.

A new text appeared.

I'll be there with you in spirit.

That was from his mother. He knew she'd like to be included in more than spirit, which made him smile, but he loved her despite her tendency to hover. Everything will be okay, he wrote back, because that was what he needed to believe.

A nurse came to get him. He shoved his phone in his pocket, scrubbed up and put on the gown and hat they gave him. He could tell Jane was nervous, too, because she clung to his hand as soon as he could be by her side again.

"Don't worry," he told her.

"No matter what happens, I want you to know…" Tears sprang to her eyes, and he gave her hand a reassuring squeeze as she continued, "I want you to know that I'm so glad you surprised me at the cabin that day. Who knows how long I would've gone on like I was—maybe too long—and we wouldn't have what we have now."

He bent to kiss her forehead. "All's well that ends well, babe," he murmured. "Don't worry about that. This will end well, too."

"But if it doesn't… If something happens to me, I

know you'll take great care of our child. I've never met anyone like you."

"Don't talk like that," he said. "We'll raise this baby together."

The doctor walked in. "All set?"

"I can't feel anything below my waist, so I must be ready," Jane responded but looked up at Kurt at the last second. "In case I get caught up in everything or...or can't do it myself...don't forget to call Papa when this is over."

"I won't," he reassured her. The old guy would probably demand—again—that he marry her. Her grandfather got after him every chance he could, making Kurt explain over and over that they were waiting until after the baby was born and Jane felt like getting into a wedding dress. But Kurt didn't mind. He'd grown fond of her grandfather, too.

"And bring him over as soon as you can to meet the baby," she added.

Kate would be staying with him the next couple of nights, so he had the care he needed, but Kurt agreed to include him. Then the drapes went up and the doctor started the surgery, which she said should only last half an hour.

Kurt had done some reading. He knew the doctor would cut through six separate layers of abdominal wall and uterus and that once the baby was born, she'd close the uterus with a double layer of stitching in a smile line low on Jane's stomach. It all sounded difficult and risky, but he kept reassuring himself that women had babies by cesarean section all the time. Jane would be fine.

His back, neck and head ached from the tension he felt throughout the procedure, but he smiled and held Jane's hand and kissed her forehead—and after forty minutes, just when he was getting alarmed that it was taking longer than the doctor predicted, he was asked to cut the cord and a purplish newborn, barely wiped and quickly swaddled in a towel, was placed in his arms.

"Merry Christmas, Mr. Elway," the doctor said. "You have a strong, healthy son, who looks to be at least eight pounds."

Kurt started to laugh as the baby wailed his displeasure at emerging in a completely new environment. "We have a boy," he said to Jane, even though she had to have heard.

"Do you wish it was a girl?" she asked, wearing a fond smile.

He handed their son to her since she was already reaching for him. "No. I'm happy to have you as the only girl in my life for the time being," he said and helped hold the baby while he kissed her.

* * * * *